Blood Ecstasy

by Tessa Dawn

A Blood Curse Novel
Book Eight
In the Blood Curse Series

Published by Ghost Pines Publishing, LLC
http://www.ghostpinespublishing.com

Volume VIII of the Blood Curse Series by Tessa Dawn
First Edition Trade Paperback Published May 26, 2016
10 9 8 7 6 5 4 3 2 1

ISBN-13: 978-1-937223-19-9
Printed in the United States of America

Author may be contacted at: http://www.tessadawn.com

This is a work of fiction. All characters and events portrayed in this novel are either fictitious or are used fictitiously. Any resemblance to actual persons, living or dead, business establishments, events, or locales is entirely coincidental.

 Ghost Pines Publishing, LLC

Credits & Acknowledgments

Ghost Pines Publishing, LLC., *Publishing*
GreenHouse Design, Inc., *Cover Art*
Lidia Bircea, *Romanian Translations*
Machovi Creative, *Layout & Design*
Reba Hilbert, *Editing*

House of the Rising Sun – This song was recorded several times by various artists prior to the most-recognizable version by the Animals in 1964 (sung by lead singer, Eric Burdon). There is some controversy as to who wrote the lyrics, with one theory being Georgia Turner and Bert Martin. The song is in the public domain.

The Blood Curse

In 800 BC, Prince Jadon and Prince Jaegar Demir were banished from their Romanian homeland after being cursed by a ghostly apparition: *the reincarnated Blood of their numerous female victims*. The princes belonged to an ancient society that had sacrificed its females to the point of extinction, and the punishment was severe.

They were forced to roam the earth in darkness as creatures of the night. They were condemned to feed on the blood of the innocent and stripped of their ability to produce female offspring. They were damned to father twin sons by human hosts who would die wretchedly upon giving birth; and the firstborn of the first set would forever be required as a sacrifice of atonement for the sins of their forefathers.

Staggered by the enormity of *The Curse*, Prince Jadon, whose own hands had never shed blood, begged his accuser for leniency and received *four small mercies*—four exceptions to the curse that would apply to his house and his descendants, alone.

ψ   Though still creatures of the night, they would be allowed to walk in the sun.

ψ   Though still required to live on blood, they would not be forced to take the lives of the innocent.

ψ   While still incapable of producing female offspring, they would be given *one opportunity and thirty days* to obtain a mate—a human female chosen by the gods—following a sign that appeared in the heavens.

ψ   While they were still required to sacrifice a firstborn son, their twins would be born as one child of darkness and one child of light, allowing them to sacrifice the former while keeping the latter to carry on their race.

And so...forever banished from their homeland in the Transylvanian mountains of Eastern Europe, the descendants of

BLOOD POSSESSION

Jaegar and the descendants of Jadon became the Vampyr of legend: roaming the earth, ruling the elements, living on the blood of others...forever bound by an ancient curse. They were brothers of the same species, separated only by degrees of light and shadow.

Prologue

Julien Lacusta sank deep into the distressed-leather chair, letting the surrounding darkness envelop him, take him, soothe him.

Become him.

A soft knock sounded on the front door, and he slumped down further in his seat.

Come in.

He pushed the compulsion into Shelly's mind, knowing the door was unlocked, and then he waited to see her familiar face—would the gentle human servant be happy to see him, grateful to serve him, or scared out of her wits, like she often was these days?

No matter.

He tightened his fist around the crystal decanter, filled with 151-proof alcohol and liquid H, also called "liquid O," and waited for the untainted, fresh blood that Shelly Winters would provide. The short-lived cocktail would provide a much-needed escape, however temporary; and after all, that's all life really was: one endless series of short or long moments, always mundane, each following the other.

Shelly's footfalls were soft and timid as she crossed the threshold, left the door cracked open, and padded through the wide entry, putting her hand out in front of her to feel her way through the unlit space. She knew better than to turn on the lights, and she stopped abruptly when she saw Julien, sitting so quietly in the middle of an otherwise empty room. "Where's the rest of your furniture?"

He glanced around the cathedral-sized great room, thought

about the huge, exposed wooden beams above him, the towering moss-rock fireplace behind him, and shrugged. "Got rid of it."

She blanched. "Why?"

He slid down further in his chair, getting more comfortable. "Don't need it."

She blinked rapidly, appearing honestly concerned. "Are you okay?"

He didn't reply.

Julien didn't answer to humans.

Hell, Julien didn't answer to anybody, except maybe Napolean, sometimes, when the king asked an occasional question. Otherwise, he just did his job, and he did it so damn well that no one asked any questions. No one ever really noticed his true…absence.

"Do you want me to call Kagen?" Shelly whispered, referring to the house of Jadon's healer.

The corner of Julien's mouth quirked up in a sardonic smile. *That was sweet.* Shelly was sweet. He shook his head slowly and beckoned her forward with his hand. "I'm fine," he rasped. "Come here, baby." He patted his lap.

Shelly's tongue snaked out to lick her bottom lip, she fidgeted with the collar on her blouse, and then she glanced around the room nervously as if searching for an escape route. "Um, maybe I should go. Come back another time when you're feeling better."

For some reason, this made Julien more restless than angry.

Her voice was like a harsh, clanging symbol reverberating across the quiet room, the empty space, disturbing his fragile peace, when all he wanted to do was add some blood to his cocktail so he could zone out for a while. *Hell's minions*, the H wouldn't work without fresh human platelets, and it had to be now.

He needed it now.

Just five minutes of peace.

Just half an hour with nothing turning inside his head.

"Sh," he coaxed her softly, this time lacing his voice with a powerful compulsion. "Don't speak, Shelly. Just come forward and obey."

Her eyes glazed over, and her nervousness abated as the compulsion took hold. She kicked off her shoes, sauntered across the floor, and lowered her seat into his lap.

Damn. This shit is jacked up, he thought as he massaged the back of her neck.

He hated to treat her like this—see her like this—but once again, oblivion was calling his name, and he was all too eager to answer. Deciding that maybe *oblivion* was the best destination for Shelly, too, he wrapped one arm tightly around her waist, raised his decanter so he could tilt her head toward him, using the side of the glass, and locked his gaze with hers. "Sleep, angel," he whispered, catching her falling torso as she crumpled sideways against his arm.

It was too loud.

The situation.

The intensity of it all pierced the darkness.

He extended his forefinger, lifting it from the glass, and pointed at the stereo, which was nestled snugly atop a high, built-in ledge, turning the surround-sound on with an electric pulse from his fingertip.

Ah.

Yes…

Without preamble, he took a long, drugging pull from the decanter, testing the various properties of the alcohol and the H on his tongue, and then he sank his fangs deep into Shelly's throat, savoring each drop of her life-giving blood. As the cocktail began to course through his veins, rapidly slithering along the intersecting passageways like a gentle, erotic snake, just waiting to strike—precious poison appeasing his heart—his head lolled back on the edge of the chair, and his lids grew heavy and dense.

Shelly slid further down on his lap, drooping in his arms, and he tightened his grip *on the crystal glass*. Dark, sonorous music began to blast through the speakers, saturating the air all around him, and he nearly moaned from the vibrations as his body absorbed the lyrics:

"There is a house in New Orleans they call the Rising Sun...
And it's been the ruin of many a poor boy, and god I know I'm one.
My mother was a tailor, sewed my new blue jeans.
My father was a gamblin' man, down in New Orleans..."

Damn, the Animals could really sing that folk song— Burdon's voice was all grit, angst, and brutal melody. A sweet jolt of cocktail rocked him at his core, and he started to drift even further away...

"Now the only thing a gambler needs is a suitcase and a trunk,
And the only time he's satisfied is when he's on a drunk."

Something visceral seized Julien's attention, and he pulled himself away from the music, temporarily: *Shelly.*

Where was Shelly?

She was sliding down his lap, falling over his knees, slumping to the floor—*that wasn't right, was it?*

"Oh mother, tell your children not to do what I have done,
Spend your life in sin and misery in the house of the Rising Sun."

Julien thought he reached for the female, but rather, he tightened his grip on the glass even more, shattering the crystal into a dozen serrated pieces, each one immediately embedding in his flesh.

As crimson rivulets trickled down his wrist, soaked the pads of his fingers, and stained his nails, he fell back into the chair and dropped the remaining glass.

Nothing mattered in this moment.

Not the pain in his hand. Not the woman on the floor. Not the emptiness in his soul.

There was only darkness, ecstasy, and peace.

That, and the hauntingly beautiful melody pulsing through the dark.

Rebecca Johnston tucked several golden-brown wisps of hair

behind her ear, out of her tired eyes, as she checked her clipboard one more time. She crossed off the previous address, *619 Golden Antelope Way*, scribbling a messy note in the margin: *No one home.*

What kind of a town was this anyway?

Didn't anyone answer their door?

She sighed, glaring at the paltry numbers in front of her, the pitifully low donations, and then she checked her watch, feeling the weight of the day as well as the chill of the night.

Yes, it was late.

They had been at it since 9 AM, knocking on doors, practically begging residents to donate to VOSU (Victims of Stalkers United), and she should really give it a rest...but she just couldn't go home without a victory.

Just one victory.

VOSU was an extremely worthy cause, and to be honest, Rebecca was hardly objective about the struggling nonprofit organization. Not only had she spent the last five years of her life fleeing from one state to another, trying to escape a violent stalker of her own, but she had also taken a counseling position at a local Denver VOSU support group. At least once a week she donated her fund-raising time, as well as her valuable experience, trying to help victims of stalking.

She frowned, wishing desperately that her colleagues were still with her, still prodding her forward and providing encouragement, still knocking on potentially hopeful doors. As it stood, each one of them had bowed out the moment they had approached Dark Moon Vale. They had simply refused to go one step further than the Silverton Creek border.

It had been so, *so* strange...

Almost as if some invisible hand of doom had dipped down out of the sky and forced them back from their objective, as if it had physically stopped their progression. They hadn't been just hesitant to go on; they had been utterly and inexplicably terrified of crossing the municipal line and entering the secluded valley.

It had made no sense at all.

BLOOD ECSTASY

None.

Dark Moon Vale was a booming tourist town. Hordes of people came each winter and summer to enjoy the ski resort or the spa, the hiking, river-rafting, or horseback riding. Heck, the casino was a huge draw all by itself. And the wealth? Oh good heavens, there was more money tucked away in these wooded acres than in Beverly Hills, the Hamptons, and Wall Street combined. For all intents and purposes, Dark Moon Vale had the potential to be a fund-raising haven, a virtual gold mine of limitless potential; yet and still, her colleagues had utterly refused to step one single foot in the valley.

A sudden gust of January wind swirled around her, tossing light crystal snowflakes into her hair and eyes, and Rebecca grasped the collar of her stiff wool coat, drawing it tighter around her slender shoulders. She hunched forward to preserve warmth, tucked her clipboard beneath her arm, and stared at the large rustic house in front of her—at the long, winding driveway that led up to the distant front door.

Oh, hell, can't anybody live right next to someone else in this place?

As she made her way up the steep, snaking slope, the oddest thing began to happen: The sky grew ten shades darker, almost as if someone had just turned out the galactic lights, and the most brilliant configuration of stars began to twinkle in the deepening sky, like spotlights projecting cosmic beams at the earth.

And the moon...

What in the world?

The moon looked like it was *bleeding.*

It was fading from white to pale yellow; from pale yellow to rose; and finally, from rose to dark crimson-red.

Rebecca froze, suddenly wishing she had taken her coworkers' advice, that she had never stepped foot in Dark Moon Vale. She was about halfway up the driveway, ready to turn around, when the magic in the sky ironically pushed her forward:

Forget raising funds for charity!

She needed to get inside.

Whatever was happening with the sky—and she had no idea what it was—it certainly wasn't natural, and she was smart enough not to stand around and gawk. If comets were going to plummet from the heavens, leaving craters in the earth, she wasn't going to stand there and wave, completely vulnerable and out in the open, hoping they passed her by. Surely, someone in this town would give her sanctuary, just until she knew what was going on.

She hurried up the remaining segment of the driveway and hopped over a narrow bed of unkempt vegetation, perhaps some sort of xeriscape, landing on the large wide-planked front porch. She reached for the brass knocker on one of two thick wooden doors, and paused—

What the heck?

The door was partially open.

In fact, the panel was ajar, and there was a dark, brooding melody blasting through a set of crystal-clear speakers—*wasn't that "House of the Rising Sun"?*—yet all the lights in the residence were off. There wasn't a single flicker of illumination, not even the glow from a warm fire or the dim radiance of a pair of candles on a distant table. Yet the glitter from the dazzling stars above was so luminescent that it flashed inside the doorway like a pair of high-beams from an oncoming truck.

Rebecca crept slowly toward the threshold and then tapped the door lightly to force it further open. She leaned forward and peered inside...

Her breath caught in her throat.

Holy Mother of God.

There was a man sitting in the middle of the front room like an ancient slave from the time of the Roman Coliseum: He was built like a gladiator, at least six-foot-two, all hard, unforgiving muscle, with chiseled, granite-like features, and his crystalline, moonstone-gray eyes stared absently at the ceiling above him even as his head lolled back on a solitary chair. His right arm was hanging limply at his side, and his hand—*his hand was bleeding!*—

dripping steady droplets of dark red blood, like a leaky faucet, onto the coarse, wide-planked floors. There was no other furniture in the room, just the chair, the stereo, and—

Rebecca screamed, her throat instantly burning from the raw, sudden abuse of her windpipe.

She dropped the clipboard, clasped her hands over her mouth, and gagged, frantically trying to back away from the door. There was a beautiful blond woman lying on the floor at the gladiator's feet. She was clearly unconscious, and her neck was stained with dried, crusted blood. *Oh dear Lord, what had he done to her?*

Rebecca had to get help.

She had to call 911.

She had to get away!

Now.

Before she could turn and run, the man's head rocked forward; his smooth, constricted pupils met hers; and his lips turned up in a dark parody of a smile, as sardonic as it was savage. "Where are you going, *Rebecca?*"

one

The man knew her name.

Rebecca's heart seized in her chest as an abrupt surge of adrenaline flooded her veins, and for a moment, she actually believed her heart might stop, just simply quit beating, right then and there. She was going to drop dead from fear.

Embracing the sudden surge of cortisol instead, she gasped for air, sprang out the door, and leaped over the dried vegetation in a mad dash to scramble away.

And then she froze in midair.

What—the—hell?

"Get in the house!" A thick, gravelly voice reverberated all around her, rattled her bones, and caused her teeth to chatter. The male gladiator was looming in the doorway—*and just how had he moved so quickly?*—staring at her with those otherworldly, moonstone-gray eyes, and his thick, sculpted lips were plastered into a scowl, his wrists still stained with blood. She tried to kick her feet, to no avail, to force her body back down to the ground, but she couldn't.

She couldn't.

There was nothing she could do.

There was only him.

The terrifying man, his ungodly power over her desire to escape, and his otherworldly control.

For a moment, Rebecca couldn't help but wonder—was he the devil with flesh and blood, a reincarnated Viking from a time gone by? Somehow, she knew he was a thousand times more lethal than any stalker. His presence was so fierce, so intimidating, so all-pervasive and exacting.

Rebecca wished she could just disappear.

Or die.

A silent scream echoed in her mind, but it didn't pierce the air. Whatever he had done to her body, it had obviously included her throat, and she was utterly helpless to defy him. And then, as if of their own accord, her feet drifted softly to the ground, and her body began to slowly rotate, turning clockwise, toward the fearsome man. She felt like a puppet on a gifted master's strings, and something deep inside of her recoiled.

This wasn't right.

This wasn't natural.

This guy—was he even human?

Indifferent to the dark crimson stains on the pads of his fingers or the cuts still scoring his palms, the Viking tried to take a step forward and stumbled to the side, staggering in the doorway. *Was he drunk? High? Or just tanked up with malicious intent?* He braced a heavily muscled arm against the doorframe and ran his free hand through his strange mahogany hair, deepening the perfect, tapered layers with highlights, streaked in blood. He looked like he was struggling, trying to make sense of his surroundings, straining to regain his bearings. "Becca," he whispered, once again using her name. "Come to me, angel. I can't come to you."

Rebecca shuddered at the terrifying intimacy of his words, their audacious, affectionate nature.

Come to me, angel?

Was he insane?

She couldn't move!

And even if she could, hell would freeze over three times; pigs would fly as commonplace as birds; and Rebecca would have to lose her reasoning mind to ever consider such a demand.

No way.

No how.

And then her feet began to move...to swiftly shuffle forward...carrying her toward the man she feared more than death itself, taking her to his doorstep.

Rebecca whimpered helplessly as she quickly closed the distance between them. What the hell was happening! Why was this happening? Who was this guy—*what was this guy?*—and how was he moving her body with nothing more than his will?

Halting no fewer than twelve inches away from his towering frame, Rebecca peered into the stranger's haunted eyes and winced. Despite the fact that his pupils were constricted—he *was* clearly on something—his features were utterly arresting: perfect, harshly masculine, and set in a cold mask of granite. One look into those devilish eyes, and she knew he possessed an iron will, an indomitable spirit, and a complete lack of mercy toward anyone who opposed him, anyone who got in his way.

Stunned by the stark revelation, Rebecca began to sob.

She may as well have been locked somewhere with Trevor, her stalker, waiting to hear the explosion of a gun. "Oh God," she whispered beneath her breath, finally finding her voice, "I don't know who you are, and I don't know what you want, but please, *just please*…let me go."

He shook his head reflexively, like a dog stepping out of a bath, like he was trying to clear an entire attic littered with creepy cobwebs. "Sh," he droned in that powerful voice. "Too loud." He took a careful step back and gestured toward the foyer. "Come in."

Rebecca shook her head emphatically. "No way," she managed to squeak.

He blinked several times, extended his neck to rest his head against the doorframe—as if he was so very weary—and then he rubbed his eyes and sighed. "I'm not going to hurt you, Becca. But I can't…not now…get in the house."

She stiffened. "No."

He hung his head and growled.

Growled.

Like an animal.

"Get in the house," he repeated, and just like that, they were both standing in the foyer, and the huge thick-paneled door closed behind them.

Rebecca screamed like her *soul* was in danger, and the sound was her only lifeline.

She scrambled to the other side of the vestibule, pressed her back against a cool, slab-stone wall, and tried to make herself invisible. Her eyes darted this way and that, across the dark, empty space, as she scanned her surroundings out of desperation and habit: There were two gigantic log-pillars to her left, a potential place to hide. And high above her head, jutting from the ceiling, there were several more vertical log beams extending parallel from the ceiling. *And Blessed Mother, protect her.* The beams looked like perfect sacrificial anchors from which to tie her up, hang her like a lamb. All around her, and framing the door, were high granular walls made of thick, stacked stones, multicolored slabs of rock, and she couldn't help but muse that he could crush her skull against any one of them, and none would ever be the wiser. The polished slate tiles beneath her feet gave way to wide-planked wood floors, and the planks led back to his great room, to the unconscious victim he had left on the floor.

Rebecca shuddered violently. She felt like she had entered the lair of a dragon, and even if his home was a rustic architectural marvel, it only meant he had refined, creative taste. He would use his imagination with her. "Please," she pleaded again. "Please, just let me go."

He pressed his eyes closed, tightening his lids, like her voice was causing him pain, and then he slowly shook his head. "Not gonna happen." He pointed toward her small black purse, which was surprisingly still draped over her shoulder, and held out his hand. "Cell phone."

She gulped in despair, but since she didn't want to move toward him, she reached into the bag, slowly retrieved her smartphone, and tossed it into his palm.

He caught it without even looking, and then he tucked it into his back pocket and gestured toward the great room. "You can have my chair."

Rebecca sniffled. "I don't want it. Just please, let me—"

"Take a seat!" he bellowed, and she froze in place, terrified down to her very bones.

Holy Mother, the guy was unstable, maybe moments away from snapping. "I'm sorry," she whispered, trying to keep her voice both steady and calm. "Do you want to talk? Perhaps if I knew what you were thinking—what it is you need—I could help you."

He blew out a ragged breath and cringed. "*Shit.*"

Rebecca continued to tremble, and she hated every moment of her body's instinctive reaction. She may as well wave a red flag in front of a bull. She swallowed her terror—or at least she tried—and appealed to him again. "You know my name…" She spoke softly. "I have no idea how…but maybe you'd like to talk."

He didn't reply, and she took it as a sign to go on. *Hell, what did she have to lose?* "What's your name?" she coaxed, cautiously.

He chuckled, as if any of this was amusing. "Julien," he rasped, and there was a faint, timeless quality to his gruff, masculine tone.

Rebecca gulped and pressed forward. "Okay…Julien…it's nice to meet you."

"Baby," he whispered. "Stop. Just stop."

She froze.

What now?

"Now, you get in the chair," he said.

Rebecca shivered at the way he sensed her thoughts. *How in the world did he do that? Was he gifted? Clairvoyant?* She glanced over her shoulder at the great room and eyed the enormous lone chair sitting in the center of the cathedral-sized space, looming like a hangman's noose atop the gallows, and tried to think of an excuse—*any excuse*—to avoid going further into the house. "It's too dark; I can't see." And then, for the first time, she absently noticed that the house was silent. She could no longer hear "House of the Rising Sun" droning throughout the room.

He flicked his bloodstained wrist in an almost dismissive gesture, and two fireplaces suddenly sprang to life with soft, dancing flames: one, nearly ten feet into the entryway foyer, just beyond a magnificent set of iron-railed stairs; and another, at the back of the great room, just beyond the lone, ominous chair.

She blinked several times, trying to make sense of what had just happened, trying to locate the remote—the sensor—the technology that allowed him to start fires with his hands. "Thank you," she breathed nervously, still intent on appearing calm.

"Sit," he repeated, taking a languid step toward her.

She practically ran to the chair.

"I'm sitting," she said, curling up inside the massive space and wrapping her arms tightly around her body. *"I'm sitting."*

He nodded in approval, and headed toward the chair.

Rebecca glanced away, unnerved by his predatory approach. She couldn't watch him advance, and she couldn't stare at the floor. *The woman—the blonde—was still there.* Still unconscious. Still lying crumpled over, like a sleeping rag doll. And her throat was still caked with blood. The sight of her was simply too much to handle. Rebecca *had* to keep her wits.

She had to remain calm.

Choosing to glance, instead, around the fire-lit room, she tried to come up with a plan: On either side of the fireplace, just beyond the back of the chair, there were two large rounded windows, each set in a thick wooden frame, each high, rounded arc bordered in stone; and the centers were made of stained glass, not that hard to break. They had old-fashioned cranks for levers, and they didn't appear to be locked. Perhaps she could escape through one of the windows—if he ever fell asleep.

She turned her attention back to Julien and waited.

What would he do next?

He met her gaze for the briefest of moments and something indefinable flashed through his eyes...

Anger?

Domination?

Possession?

She couldn't say, but it gave her the chills.

The man looked at her like he owned her, like he wanted to

devour her soul.

He prowled in her direction—and just why the word *prowled* came to mind, she couldn't really say—but that was what he did. And then he stopped, just short of making physical contact with her legs, descended to the floor in a distinctly vulturine motion, and sprawled out in front of her, extending all six feet, *four* inches of his heavy muscular frame like a pagan feast in a macabre buffet.

Rebecca gulped.

"Just give me a minute," he murmured, resting the back of his hand against his forehead. "I need a minute to chill." Either he didn't notice or he didn't care about the woman lying no fewer than three feet away from him on the floor.

Perhaps she was already dead; thus, her presence didn't matter.

Her well-being was of no consequence.

And that's when it really hit Rebecca…

Hard.

Perhaps she was already dead, as well.

two

Julien Lacusta closed his eyes and tried to think.

Hell's inglorious minions, this shit could not be happening.

Not like this.

Not right now.

But it was—oh, was it ever.

He slowed his breathing to match the flow of the H and let the wicked concoction run its course. *He just needed fifteen, maybe twenty more minutes to come down*, and then he could deal with the situation.

And the female.

His *destiny*.

Holy hell.

The dark, languid arms of the liquid O were just about to embrace him, hold the outside word at bay, when he *felt* Rebecca stir in the chair. She was trying to be as quiet as a church-mouse, sliding out of the leather seat, tiptoeing around Shelly Winters—*oh, hell, Shelly Winters!*—and making her way…making her way…where?

Ah yes, to the painted glass windows.

Son of a jackal.

"Sit back down," he bit out through clenched, gritted teeth, not bothering to open his eyes. Yep, he heard her heartbeat stutter, caught the sudden inhale of breath, and listened as her footsteps receded back to the chair.

If this got any more messed up, Julien would gladly retrieve a dagger, hand it to the traumatized female, and help her behead him himself, perhaps remove his heart, just to mitigate the damage he had already caused. As it stood, he had no idea what he was going to do—what he wanted to do—with this Blood Moon. It wasn't like he had a golden history with the subject or a burning desire to meet some human female, create some bullshit fairy-tale love story, and provide the Curse with a prize.

That had never been his dream.

Yeah…so…what was he saying?

His legs felt like barbells, heavy rods of iron, yet his head felt feather-light, like insubstantial cotton…floating…drifting…twisting in the wind.

There was nothing.

Nothing.

Thank the celestial gods.

For one blessed moment, there was nothing in Julien's head—

Except…

That one thing…that…that girl…

The blonde or the brunette?

Something had bothered him…

A lot.

Ah, shit, Shelly Winters.

He moistened his lips with his tongue and tried once again to think.

Ramsey. He called out on a familiar telepathic bandwidth, the one used by the valley's sentinels, not needing cogent thought to find it. *Are you there?*

Ramsey Olaru answered right away. *What's up, J?*

Julien groaned. *Seen the moon?*

Ramsey grew ineffably quiet for a moment. *Of course. What do you need, brother?*

Ah, yeah, they weren't really brothers, but the sentinels shared a sort of brotherhood with the tracker, just the same, an indescribable bond…they were…they were…

Julien! Ramsey's deep, husky voice jolted him out of his distracted contemplation.

Yeah, I'm here.

What do you need, tracker? What's goin' on?

Shelly, Julien whispered with his psychic voice. *She's here, on the floor. Ah, hell…* He sighed. *I might've fed too much.*

Where is your destiny, *warrior?* Ramsey intoned, his psychic voice sounding all at once grave.

Chair, Julien grunted.

Ramsey didn't speak, but Julien felt a light tap on his temples, almost like a cerebral *knock-knock,* someone beating at the door of his memories. *Master Warrior,* Ramsey finally said, *permission to enter your head?*

It wasn't exactly the formal protocol, but Julien got the gist. *Shit,* he responded.

Is that a yes? Ramsey asked.

Yes, Julien grunted, wishing he could get a complete *do-over* for the day.

Not unlike the stalwart pit bull that he was often compared to, Ramsey Olaru ramrodded his way straight into Julien's gray matter, tunneled his way through his medial temporal lobe, and withdrew all the pictures, images, and short-term memories that he needed, greatly reducing Julien's high. *Ah, damn, brother,* Ramsey clipped, once he had finally finished. *Not gonna lie; I would hate to be you.* He took a moment, ostensibly to process the information—or something—and then he chimed back in, speaking in Julien's head. *Nachari Silivasi is only two miles west of your estate, and he has his Mustang with him. He can get there faster than any of us, and whoever comes, he's gonna need a car to transport Shelly.*

Julien nodded, as if Ramsey could see him.

Brother?

Yeah, yeah, *send him on.*

Will do, Ramsey said. *And once he gets there—what do you want him to do about Rebecca? Your* destiny?

A deep, feral growl rose in Julien's throat, and he practically hissed his psychic words: *He doesn't touch her,* he warned, feeling suddenly defensive. *Understood? That's not his business. That's not anyone's business. Tell the wizard to stay clear of my female.*

Ramsey spoke with even, deliberate words. *You're zoned out, J—*

BLOOD ECSTASY

I don't give a shit, warrior.

Ramsey took a calm, measured breath. *Understood.* He softened his tone, probably on purpose, and then he switched the focus of the conversation. *Hey, you okay? I mean…effed up circumstance aside…are you all right?*

Julien's head fell a bit more to the side and his lids twitched, just a microscopic flutter, over his eyes.

Julien?

I don't need this shit, Ramsey. Don't want it. Didn't ask for it. His throat felt suddenly raw, which really made no sense, considering the fact that he wasn't speaking with his voice. And *damnit* if that H wasn't messing with the neurons in his hippocampus because his heart was all kinds of heavy, and his eyes were suddenly moist.

Just in the corners.

But still…

What the hell am I gonna do with a destiny? he said almost absently. *We both know there's no room in my world for anyone but me.* He paused to remember his original train of thought. *Besides, I have half a mind to tell the Blood to go straight to hell and just let the Curse take me in the end.* He chuckled, yet the impression was absent of mirth. *Maybe take a trip to hell, visit dear ole dad. Finally have that conversation. You know the one—yo, pops, what the blazes was your problem?*

Ramsey immediately snarled, and his voice grew deathly grave. *That'd better be the H talkin', warrior. Don't even play like that. Let's not forget: The Blood can take you on a lifelong trip, an eternal, never-ending vacation. To hell.*

Julien exhaled slowly. *Yeah…I got it…believe me.*

Ramsey Olaru grew quiet for the space of several heartbeats, and then he gentled his psychic voice. *All right, brother, I'll call Nachari now.* He stopped talking, but he didn't disconnect.

Thank you, Julien murmured. *Be well.* He slurred his words.

Yeah, Ramsey chimed back in, *be well, warrior.* And then the sentinel closed the connection.

12

Ramsey Olaru kicked his feet up as he stretched out in the luxurious lawn chair, next to the fire pit on his tranquil wraparound deck, and reached out to Nachari Silivasi on a one-to-one telepathic bandwidth. He told the Master Wizard everything he needed to know, including the location of both human females in Julien's great room, the condition of the zoned-out tracker, and the need to use a whole lot of caution and a heavy dose of discretion, the moment he entered the chaotic home.

Not to misrepresent the situation, Julien Lacusta was not a heartless or sadistic male, at least not with his friends and females. He had just been dealt a terrible hand in life. Just the same, Ramsey warned the insightful wizard to keep a clear and generous distance between himself and the human *destiny*, letting Nachari know that Julien was channeling some raw, territorial instincts—whether he recognized them or not—and unless he wanted to fight the brutal son of a jackal, he had better proceed with caution. And then he broached a much more ominous and urgent subject.

Wizard. His voice had a no-nonsense, almost solemn tone to it—Ramsey fully intended to convey the full depth of his concern.

What is it, sentinel? Nachari asked, immediately registering the tone.

Before you go, before you leave Julien to his destiny, *there's something I need you to do...for me.*

Name it, Nachari said, *and consider it done.*

Ramsey did just that.

three

Ian Lacusta braced his forearms against the iron railing on the starboard deck of his sixty-meter yacht. He gazed out over the roiling ocean, noticing how the waves were really picking up, tossing, turning, practically churning now, and then he glanced up at the crystalline night sky.

He immediately drew back.

The moon was a stunning blood-red orb.

How odd, yet familiar.

The stark red globe was brutal with intensity; the entire sky was lit up like a bonfire; and the stars—*great sons of darkness, the stars*—they were meticulously aligned in a clear, deliberate pattern reflecting an unmistakable outline: the celestial constellation *Hercules*, kneeling with his foot on the head of Draco.

Drawn from someplace so primordial its origins were inscrutable, a feral snarl escaped Ian's throat. He immediately stood up straight, clenched his fists, and slowly backed away from the railing. Like a lion retreating from a maggot-infested meal, he turned up his nose and scented the air with disdain. The moon was beyond reprehensible; it was an abomination.

It was an omen, a sign, a scourge.

And it evoked a feeling—*a memory*—that Ian had long ago buried.

"Huh," he grunted, crossing his arms, leaning back against the balustrade, and forcing his emotions to heel. "Son of a bitch." He shook his head briskly to disrupt the thoughts, and then he snarled. "So Julien is still alive."

BLOOD ECSTASY

Certain that no one was home, Trevor Rainier clenched his gloved hand into a fist and slammed it straight through the back patio door of Rebecca's third-floor apartment. He reached around the broken glass, unlatched the lock, and quickly glanced over his shoulder to make sure no one was watching. And then he quietly slipped inside, emerging in the kitchen.

It had been five long years.

Five years of suffering, five years of rage, and five years of barren existence without Rebecca, while he had tracked, scoured, and hunted in a furious effort to find the *bitch* that belonged to him. And, honestly? He might not have ever found her if it hadn't been for that one stupid charity event: a multi-campaign fund-raiser held along the 16th Street Mall, where VOSU had hosted a booth.

A booth primarily manned by Rebecca Johnston.

Oh sure, she had worn a low baseball cap and a pair of ridiculously large sunglasses, but Trevor would've recognized those golden-brown, shoulder-length S-curls anywhere, that slender five-feet, six-inch frame…that long, elegant neck…especially when a local TV station picked up the story, and Trevor just happened to be watching from a Colorado hotel.

Rebecca had always preferred the western United States: The east was too cold; the south was too humid, and the Midwest was too unfamiliar for her comfort. Trevor had tracked her from Nevada to California, from California to Arizona, and finally, from Arizona to New Mexico, where he had eventually lost her trail. It didn't take a rocket scientist to figure out that she had moved on, or to connect the western dots. Rebecca was headed to Colorado next, and Trevor was right behind her, whether she knew it or not.

Despite her *holier than thou* attitude and her arrogant, misguided belief that she could outwit anyone, Rebecca had always been pathetically predictable. She had blown her *misunderstanding* with Trevor completely out of proportion, turned it into a full-fledged crisis—like he was some crazy, rabid animal and she was some distressed, helpless maiden—like the two of them weren't actually in love. Like she suddenly needed to fight for some greater cause: to save all women *everywhere* from the likes of Trevor Rainier.

He picked up a familiar coffee mug from the kitchen counter, one that had an adorable picture of Snoopy dancing on the side, one that Rebecca's mother had given her on her twenty-second birthday, and flung it across the room, shattering the stoneware into a dozen arbitrary pieces. And then he sauntered across the clean tile floor to the calendar and corkboard she always kept on the refrigerator, and he laughed.

Pathetically predictable.

As always.

He ran his forefinger over the calendar until he came to the correct date—Sunday, January 23rd—and then he smiled at the elegant, perfect print: D2D/DMV. Door-to-door…*fund-raising?* And DMV. So, what or where was DMV? *Department of Motor Vehicles?* And why the hell would she be fund-raising there? He laughed uproariously as an image of a bunch of middle-aged hags flashed through his mind. Maybe she was linking up with Mothers Against Drunk Drivers. They could all be MADD together, in every sense of the word.

And then he practically snarled.

Beneath the calendar, pinned to the corkboard, was a neatly written quote: *"You are NOT powerless."* And just below that one was another: *"It is okay to be angry. It is never okay to be cruel."* Yet another one, still: *"Don't ever stray away from yourself to get closer to someone else."*

What the hell was her issue?

Trevor ripped the quotes from the corkboard, crumpled them up in his hand, and tossed them in the same direction as the mug. That silly, stupid, *selfish* tramp. If she had just tried harder to listen, learned when to shut up and obey, made a greater effort to please him, she wouldn't be in this predicament: feeling powerless, all alone, and like she'd strayed from herself.

Strayed from Trevor and the life she had *promised* to share with him.

He could hardly contain his fury.

He stormed out the kitchen, stalked through the living room, and headed toward the long, narrow hall, throwing open every door that he passed in a wild frenzy, desperate to find her bedroom. At last, he came to the last door on the right, and the moment he flung it open, he recognized, smelled, and remembered...Rebecca.

Her stamp was all over the elegant, tasteful furniture; her gentle spirit was tucked into the soft, fringed pillows, placed neatly on the bed; her eye for color, contrast, and symmetry was in the paintings, the lighting, the modern but understated décor. Yes, this had Rebecca written all over it.

He inhaled deeply, taking in the faint hint of her scent, the vanilla-spiced perfume that still lingered gently in the air—it was probably sprayed on the pillows—and then he made his way to the bed, reclined atop the comforter, rolled around on the pillows, and buried his face in the thick, folded throw that was nestled at the foot of the mattress.

Rebecca.

His baby.

He could almost taste her.

He was so very close to finding her...at last.

The thought was erotic, and he moved his hand to the fly of his jeans, slowly releasing the buttons.

Ah yes, Rebecca: He would leave his beloved a gift.

four

Rebecca sat quietly, perfectly still, in the soft leather chair, her knees tucked to her chest, her arms embracing her knees, staring warily at the giant man on the floor.

He appeared to be sleeping, but she knew he was not.

Every time she rose to tiptoe away, he grunted, or snarled, or told her to sit back down. She was growing feverish with anxiety, paralyzed with fear, when the door to the rustic, secluded house creaked open.

Rebecca sat forward, her ears suddenly perking up. Instantly alert, she could have heard a pin drop from a half block away.

Was someone coming in?

Hope washed over her in a silent wave, and she squinted to see into the foyer.

Yes!

Yes.

There was someone entering the house: a tall, dark man with thick, wavy hair and a similar countenance to Julien's. *Sweet Mother of Mercy*, he moved like a panther, with absolute silence and grace. His shoulders were pulled back in a proud, almost arrogant bearing; his jaw was set in a determined line; and he prowled through the doorway more than he walked, scanning the entire room in the breadth of a second. As he headed toward her chair, Rebecca almost screamed—

For Julien.

She almost wanted the gladiator to help her.

She pressed her hand over her mouth to stifle the impulse.

No. No! *Don't be an idiot*, she told herself. The odds of two serial killers working together in collusion were slim at best. This was Rebecca's chance—a stranger—someone who could help her, even if he was scary as the day was long.

She gulped and gathered her courage, and then she raised her arm and waved her hand in a furious motion.

His eyes shot immediately to hers, and the breath rushed out of her body.

Holy Mother of God, he was the absolute personification of male perfection: strength, poise, and beauty that was nothing short of arresting. His eyes, those deep forest-green eyes, were so hypnotic that they drew her into him, clouded her mind, made her forget for a moment that she was desperate to escape and, likely, in mortal danger.

He shifted his glance to the woman on the floor, and reality came back with a vengeance: *Yes, do you see her?* Rebecca wondered. *Do you see me?* She could only hope and pray. *That man on the floor is crazy!*

Please, God, let him see…and understand.

Rebecca waved her hand again, and this time, the gorgeous man regaled her with his peripheral vision. "*Help me.*" She mouthed the words, too afraid to whisper.

Too afraid that Julien would stir.

The stranger turned away and continued padding across the floor, until, at last, he reached the woman's body and knelt down at her side. "*Oh, heaven give me strength*," Rebecca muttered. He was no more than three feet away from her chair. "Help me," she squeaked this time, perching forward to the edge of the seat. "*Help me!*"

He lowered his head—on purpose?

Was he ignoring her?

Rebecca's heart slammed into the back of her chest.

No!

"Please," she whispered louder, rocking so far forward she almost lost her balance, in an effort to demand his attention. "I'm not here of my own free will. He took me…that man…and I can't get away. Please, you have to help me."

The gorgeous man rocked back on his heels, twisted his body in her direction in an almost feline motion, and met her gaze head-on. And then he pressed his forefinger to his lips.

Rebecca nodded enthusiastically. Of course. *Of course!* She would be quiet. She gulped and pointed at Julien, trying to demonstrate her understanding, and then she gestured toward the door.

The stranger shook his head, *no.*

What?

Why not?

Rebecca glanced back and forth between the green-eyed man and Julien, and then she frowned as understanding dawned, even as the realization crushed her spirit: The stranger was afraid of Julien. He did not want to oppose the crazy man. And he wasn't going to take her out of there any time soon.

As bitter tears began to sting Rebecca's eyes, her mind raced a dozen miles a minute, and then she made a cradle with her hand, pressed her thumb to her ear, her pinky to her lips, and mouthed four words: *Call 911.* "Send the police," she whispered softly.

He bore his eyes into hers, and in a stunning, inexplicable moment, he seemed to be speaking inside of her mind. *I know you're afraid, but Julien will not hurt you. It's going to be okay.*

Rebecca jolted, falling backward in the chair.

For a moment, she couldn't make sense of anything: not the situation, not the stranger's words, not the fact that he had spoken in her mind...and certainly not the idea that Julien wouldn't hurt her, that she was in anything less than mortal danger.

That she would somehow be okay.

She shook her head in anger and frustration, feeling a sudden urge to pound the guy in the face. *Screw you!* she thought, growing more and more frantic by the moment. *This was her chance.* Perhaps her only chance.

There was someone else in the room, and he was lifting the other woman in his arms!

BLOOD ECSTASY

Why?
Why her?
Why not Rebecca?
And Julien was still on the floor…
To hell with it!

All Rebecca had to do was leap over the gladiator's massive body and scramble to the door. Surely, he wouldn't get up and chase her in front of the other man. And surely, the green-eyed stranger could not stop her while holding another full-grown woman in his arms.

Yes, this was her only chance!

Rebecca sprang from the distressed-leather chair like an Olympic sprinter coming out of the blocks. Her feet hit the floor with a surety she didn't know she possessed, and she vaulted over Julien's body with unexpected ease.

She didn't look back.

She just kept on running, sprinting for the door, or at least, that was how it had played out in her mind. Somehow, the reality was drastically different.

In the blink of an eye, Rebecca was back at Julien's side, and his massive, bloodstained hand was curled around her ankle like a vise, and he was tugging…jerking…pulling her to the ground.

"Nooo!" she cried in stunned alarm, even as her knees hit the floor and she toppled forward, landing on his massive chest.

She quickly scurried off him.

"Becca," he drawled groggily. "Do not."

She froze in terror, and her eyes darted around the room, searching for the other man, the one with the thick black hair. "Help me!" she screamed in a full-throated voice, uncaring if she shook the rafters. "Do something, damnit! Don't leave me here with him!" She leaped back up, once again darting to her feet, and tried to shuffle out of Julien's reach, but before she could get away, he shot upright.

And then he sprang to his feet in one lithe, fluid motion and literally towered over her, his eyes ablaze with something too powerful to name.

Fury?

Incredulity?

Ownership.

She recoiled and backed away.

And that's when the green-eyed man stepped forward, still carrying the sagging blonde in his arms, and the motion began to rouse her.

Rebecca's heart raced in her chest.

Maybe they could fight these guys together.

"Is she okay?" Julien spoke sensibly for the first time since Rebecca had met him, locking his gaze with the other man's.

"She appears to be fine," the guy answered in a dark, satiny voice. "No worse for the wear, but damn, J. *What the hell?*"

Julien narrowed his moonstone gaze and scowled. "Shit happens," he murmured gruffly.

The man lowered his head in a subtle, *respectful* nod. "Indeed. It sometimes does." And then he glanced right at Rebecca and slowly inclined his head in a graceful nod. "I am pleased to see she is here. Your *destiny*...at last."

Julien shrugged. "Bad day. Bad timing. Like I said, shit happens, but I guess we'll work it out."

Rebecca felt like Alice in Wonderland, absolutely certain she had just fallen down a rabbit hole! What the heck were they talking about? And why? *I am pleased to see she is here? Your destiny...at last? We'll work it out?*

Work what out!

She was too stunned to even think.

And that's when the blond woman stirred. "Julien?" She spoke in a faint, drowsy voice.

The gladiator took a generous step forward, flexing those muscular arms and legs, and placed his right hand on the woman's arm, even as the green-eyed man slowly lowered her to the floor, helping her to gain her footing. "Ah, baby," Julien rasped, "*prietena mea loiala,* I'm sorry." He bent to her neck, where the wounds were still raw, and did...something...Rebecca couldn't see, and when he pulled back, the flesh looked healed.

He wet the tip of his thumb with his tongue and tried to rub the bloodstains clean from her throat. "Forgive me."

The blonde winced and stepped back, and then she rubbed her neck in relief. "*Prietena mea loiala?*"

"My loyal friend," he said softly, and the words were almost touching.

The woman nodded. "Of course. I'm sorry if I wasn't able to...read the situation better. I should've called Kagen. I should've known—"

"I compelled you, sweetheart," Julien interrupted. "I...I was not in a good frame of mind. Again, my apologies."

The blonde looked deep into the gladiator's eyes, as if testing the truth of his words, and then she nodded. "I know. *I do.* I'm fine." She bent over to pick up her shoes, smoothed her blouse with one hand, and inadvertently turned her head to the side; and that's when she caught her first real glimpse of Rebecca, from the corner of her eye. She jerked in surprise and frowned, but before she could speak, Rebecca jumped in and tried to plead her own case.

"You have to help me!" she insisted. "Your friend—*Julien*—he took me from his front porch, and he's forcing me to stay here with him. I don't wanna be here! He's a complete freakin' stranger, and I'm scared half to death. *Please*; do something to help me!" Despite her desperation, she cut her eyes in anger, glaring at the other man.

The woman turned visibly pale, and the green-eyed man placed his hand on her shoulder. "While you were sleeping, Shelly, there was a Blood Moon. Julien's. This woman is his *destiny.*"

The blonde gulped, and her mouth fell open as she appraised Rebecca from head to toe in what appeared to be fascination, and then she turned toward Julien and sighed. "Oh...gods...this has been some kind of night, hasn't it?"

Rebecca threw her hands up in exasperation, utterly flabbergasted by the bizarre, unnatural conversation. She opened her mouth to protest—or to scream—but nothing came out.

She was beyond confusion.

"My Mustang's parked outside," the raven-haired stranger said with stunning indifference. "Go wait in the car, Shelly. I'll be there in a moment."

The woman paused, like she was thinking it over, and then she blinked her eyes several times, in quick succession, and started to walk away.

"Wait!" Rebecca cried frantically. "Wait! *Shelly*, wait!"

The woman paused in the doorway, just for a moment, but she didn't turn around.

"Go," Julien barked, returning to that deep, commanding voice, and the woman disappeared into the night.

Rebecca's bottom lip quivered like she was a three-year-old child, nothing more than a mere, frightened babe who had been chastised—and dismissed—by the grown-ups. "Why are you doing this?" She directed the question at the dark-haired man, knowing that Julien was unmovable.

Unreachable.

And that's when the gladiator snarled.

Just like a rabid dog.

His top lip twitched; his teeth flashed beneath his gums; and his throat virtually vibrated from the sound.

The dark-haired man took a cautious step back and averted his eyes, angling his body away from Rebecca's. He held one hand up in a gesture of surrender, reached into the pocket of his cargo pants, and withdrew what looked like a pale blue crystal. "I'm outta here," he said in a pacifying voice, "but before I go, Ramsey asked me to give this to you."

"What the hell is it?" Julien barked.

The man raised one shoulder and cocked both brows. "A diary of sorts." He wet his bottom lip and held up the crystal. "You can open it the same way you would unravel a holding cell, and then you can access the contents by channeling the same telepathic bandwidth, while focusing on the stone, that you would use to reach me on a private line." He extended his graceful hand and thrust the object at Julien. "It contains my memories, warrior. Not all of them, but enough. From my time in hell. You *need* to take a look. You need to understand."

Julien furrowed his brow and cocked his head to the side, glaring at the ominous offering. "You put your memories into that stone? *How?*"

The male smiled coyly, and when he did, his features were so luminous, they almost lit up the room. "I'm a wizard, my friend. Don't hate. Just view it."

Julien snorted, and Rebecca couldn't tell whether he was offended or impressed. Either way, he didn't join the playful banter. And why should he? He was a batshit-crazy serial killer; his friends were all his allies; and even the pitiful woman, the blond victim, who was probably his girlfriend, was quick to follow his orders. Hell, she didn't even care that he was holding another woman hostage.

The entire world had gone insane.

Julien reached out, took the crystal from the green-eyed man, and nodded. "Don't expect me to say thank you, Nachari. This is my life...my choice...my fate. I've served the house of Jadon for over nine hundred years, and I've served it well. It's not your place, or anyone else's, to tell me when I've had enough."

The wizard took a bold step forward, placed his right hand on Julien's shoulder, and regarded the gladiator with unconcealed concern...and affection. "And that's just it, what you still don't get, J. What you never seem to understand. Your life isn't just your own. Your choices don't exist in a vacuum. And your *fate* affects the entire house of Jadon. If you think for one moment that you can just step off the stage without completely screwing Ramsey, Santos, and Saxson—hell, even Saber Alexiares—then you've been sucking down that cocktail for way too long, and you have no idea how many sons of Jadon care for you. Believe in you. Honor you. *Revere you.* And I, for one, will tell you this much, now: You think it's impressive to embed memories in a stone? Oh, you don't know half of what I can do. Try skipping out on the Curse, skirting your way around this Blood Moon, offering yourself up like some suicidal sacrifice to the Blood at the end of these thirty days. Just try it, and see what happens." He tightened his grip on the gladiator's shoulder, and the grasp looked powerful…and painful. "*No one is going to let you die, brother*. And we don't give a *gods-damn* about what you want or whether or not you've had enough." He withdrew his hand from Julien's shoulder, took an angry step back, and then simply…

Disappeared.

He didn't storm out of the room or walk away.

He just…*vanished.*

And that's when Rebecca Johnston passed out.

five

Ian Lacusta had spent the past six hours pacing the deck of his ship, pondering, thinking, remembering…dredging up the past.

He had recalled his early childhood, those impossible, rage-filled years, when his mother had tried to teach him how to be a man, a vampire with honor, whatever the hell that had meant. He had remembered how she'd drilled the laws and the customs of the house of Jadon into his mind, and his brother's, as if Ian could have cared less. He'd remembered her endless nostalgia and her repetitive, fanciful tales, the stories she had told about Ian's father—*blah, blah, blah, blah*—the male had been a weakling, and he had died because of it, shortly after Ian and Julien's birth. Yet and still, Harietta Lacusta had spoken of him like he had been a god.

A legend.

A saint.

A hero.

Verily, Ian had hated them both.

He remembered the caustic feedings, being forced to latch onto her wrist, even as Julien had been allowed to hunt, to stalk his prey and feed at will, always faithful to discern the innocent from the evil, to only kill the latter. "But not you, Ian. 'Tis too much temptation for you to bear. I fear you will give in to your urges and kill at random; you must continue to feed from my vein."

Grrrrrh! Ian snarled as the memory enraged him. He didn't get it then, and he didn't get it now. What the hell had the stupid cow been talking about? Good people, innocent people, pure souls, and guilty? There was no such thing. There were no such concepts. His head had been ready to explode! *There are only two types of animals on this cursed planet!* he had wanted to shout into her head. *Predators and prey. Strong and weak. Lions and lambs. Those who obey their urges, and those who die at the lion's command.*

Devils, he had tried to tune her out!

And when that hadn't worked, he had tried to listen…and to obey. To mimic the utter nonsense that never stopped coming his way: *Watch your brother, Ian. Do as Julien does. See how he speaks, how he walks, how he smiles? Try that for me, son.*

Try harder.

Try again.

Try more often.

Try—*this!*

He had ripped her annoying throat out on his tenth birthday just to make her shut up.

Silence…at last.

And then he had tried to kill Julien, because he hated that bastard too, but that hadn't worked out so well. Julien wasn't a mere misguided female. He wasn't an endless nagging voice in a ruffled linen skirt. He was a growing, feeding, strapping young vampire, and he had fought for his life like a demon, virtually exploding with rage.

Ian had been lucky to escape the entire sordid event.

He scratched behind his ear, drawing blood with a pointed claw. He didn't want those early memories. He didn't want to revisit the past. He didn't want to revisit New Orleans. But then…where?

Where could his mind go that might bring solace?

Paris, France?

London, England?

Port Sudan?

The horn of Africa or Greece?

He had lived in them all.

There wasn't a city, a town, or a country that Ian Lacusta had not called home over the past 950 years. He had roamed the earth like a gypsy, living in hovels and caves, sneaking into palaces and mansions, slaughtering in brothels and dens.

He could mimic humans and live among them; he could round them up and force them to worship him; he could capture, torture, and dispose of them at will. The only thing Ian couldn't do was walk in the sun. That gods-forsaken orb had been his nemesis since the day he was born; that, and the fact that he had no clan, no people, no one to teach him...anything.

Ever.

He had learned to do everything on his own.

Ah, but he had learned well.

And now, he had slaughtered a sailor, pirated a yacht, and lived on the Mediterranean Sea for the past seven years, hunting, exploring, and bringing his prey back home, oftentimes from Greece. He glanced down at the sun-bleached deck beneath his feet and ran a moistened tongue along his thin, taut lips. How many bodies were buried in this ocean? How many worthless humans—men, women, and children—had Ian drained and tossed overboard, never to be seen again? How many females had he ravaged, just to feel the high of the erotic release, and then murdered before they could begin to swell with his children, sons he couldn't even imagine rearing? After all, what the hell would they be? Dark, light, a mixture of both? What manner of atrocity would the ancient Curse of his kind visit upon his offspring?

Ian didn't know, and he didn't care to find out.

As it stood, he remembered only what his mother had taught him about the Curse and the two archaic houses: the house of Jadon and the house of Jaegar.

He remembered that he didn't belong to either.

He stood eerily still and drew a deep breath, before his sanity began to wane. He couldn't afford to go into a memory-induced stupor, not tonight, at least not right now.

Daybreak was much too near.

Ian needed to think.

He needed to reason, to analyze his options, and to figure

out his next steps.

Julien's Blood Moon had brought so much turmoil to the surface that he hardly knew which way was up. There was a buzzing in his head, like in the days of the old transition radios, when one simply couldn't get any good reception—his dial was permanently stuck between two opposing channels: one, discordant, abrasive, and tinged with static; and another, distantly familiar but oddly faint.

Forbidden?

Somehow, Ian just knew that the channels in his head were links to those of his own kind, whatever that truly meant. He had spent a dozen lifetimes shutting them out, keeping the dial turned off. Only now, he was tempted to tune in briefly…just to try it out.

What if?

What if someone, who was like him, was actually there?

Ian grasped the railing before him, above the stern of the boat, and rolled his head back in a lazy, languid stretch, allowing his long, black-and-red mane to fall to his waist—normally, it fell to the middle of his back in wild, unkempt waves—and he luxuriated in the heavy feeling, all that thick, silken weight. He closed his eyes and reached for the static, the ever-present void, and tried to picture a radial dial in his mind.

Red. Black. Small.

Exact.

He could almost see miniature slashes along the edges of the knob, and he began to turn them back and forth, to the left, and then the right: listening, tuning, aligning his psychic energy.

And then, just like that, the dial clicked in place.

It hummed, then opened, and settled into space.

Ian gasped at the dark, errant energy that flooded his mind, swirled throughout his body, and settled in his heart. It was so deliciously evil and soothing to his mind.

He shivered.

And then he heard a shadowed, resonant purr, a deep, almost baritone voice. "Who the devil is this?"

Ian shot upright, but he was careful to hold the connection. He squinted, squeezing his eyelids together, even tighter, and strained to hear with his ears. But this wasn't an audible sound; it wasn't a tangible voice. It was a thin, chiming wave, pulsing in his head. "Ian." He tried out his cognitive voice.

"Ian who?" the baritone shot back.

Ian jolted from the pain in his temples and started to close the connection. He had been alone too long. He had been *safe*, in control, the master of his own domain—and the entire earth was Ian's domain—why risk that now?

"Wait!" The male must have sensed his hesitation. "Where the hell are you? I'm picking up a shit-ton of static, a crap-heap of...*water*?...and the first phase of the sun. You're in another time zone. What? Eight? No, nine hours ahead. Where the hell are you? *Who the hell are you?*"

"I am no one of concern," Ian snarled, feeling curiously irate.

The dark male chuckled, raspy, cruel, and deep in his throat. "Not my problem," he grunted, settling into the supernatural conversation. "But *you* reached out to *me*, not the other way around. Why, brother? What the hell do you need?"

Brother?

The male had called Ian *brother?*

Ian's ears perked up, and he leaned forward into the railing as if leaning into the curious exchange. "I...seek...others of my kind."

Now this got the male's attention. "Shit," he drawled. "What the hell are you on?"

Ian opened his eyes and glanced around. "A yacht," he said matter-of-factly. He wasn't much for innuendo.

The guy—*no, the vampire*—grunted with disdain. "And what *kind* would you be?"

"Vampyr." Ian drawled the word in a thick Romanian accent as if summoning an ancient memory. "Undead. Nosferatu. Sired of a curse."

The male grew gravely quiet for what felt like a day and one-half, and then he finally sighed, long and heavy, and murmured, "Brother, you need to tell me something I can make sense of, before you end up with a shitload of trouble on your...yacht. I've already got a bead on you—you're fourteen nautical miles off the coast of Greece, and about 6,012 miles, as the crow flies, from here. So I suggest you start talking."

"How?" Ian asked, more curious than afraid. "You have never taken my blood." Even without the benefit of training, Ian understood that an exchange of crimson *power* was necessary for that level of accuracy, for tracking another's precise whereabouts from such a great distance.

The male snorted again, this time with annoyance. "Are you lacking some basic cerebral functioning?" he mocked. "You opened a telepathic line. Your thoughts are my GPS, brother. All I have to do is follow them to—"

"What is your name?" Ian insisted, cutting the Dark One off. He had just about had enough of this condescending banter.

The male's voice grew five times harder, rougher, and far more cruel. "Achilles Zahora, the one they call *The Executioner*, a soldier in the Colony's formal guard."

Ian listened attentively, wondering about this colony, wondering about the guard. And then, making an instant decision, he chose to tell the truth. "I was born in Dark Moon Vale in 1044 AD, the twelfth day of April, beneath a Hercules Birth Moon. My father was Micah Lacusta; my mother was Harietta Noel; and my twin, the one who shared my mother's womb, was a vampire christened as Julien Zechariah. I know not where he is. I have lived as a wanderer, a male with no clan, for 957 years, and now...*and now*...I am speaking to you."

Achilles Zahora inhaled a harsh, deep breath, and then he either grunted or growled across the connection—Ian wasn't sure—before sending a powerful jolt of electricity through the bandwidth, rattling Ian's inner ear, and leaving a high-pitched hum in the air. "You were born to the house of *Jadon*?" he nearly gasped.

Ian snarled. "I was born to no house! I was born to no

family! *I am no one of concern.*" He repeated his initial assertion.

"Oh," Achilles echoed, "I beg to disagree. You were born to a male in the house of Jadon, conceived from the *four mercies* and a Light One's Blood Moon. But"—his voice grew thick with conviction—"you are not one of them. You're one of us. *Son-of-a-demon's-bitch!*" He pitched his voice an octave lower in an effort to convey a command. "Ian!"

Ian drew back in alarm.

"Ian!"

"What do you want, Soldier Zahora?"

"Do you...*esteem*...your father's memory?"

"I *abhor* my father's memory, Achilles."

"Did you...bond...with your mother?"

"I murdered my mother when I was ten years old. I *loathed* her."

"Do you *feed?*"

"I'm alive, am I not?"

Achilles chuckled. "Do you kill your prey?"

"Of course," Ian said.

"Do you torture, rape, or maim, just for the *pleasure* it gives you?"

This time, Ian snickered. "Do you have a point?"

Despite the psychic nature of the connection, Ian heard Achilles hock up a glob of phlegm and apparently spit it out on the floor. "Yeah, I've got a point."

"And that would be...*what?*"

"You are not a *lone wolf, Ian Lacusta.* You belong to the Dark Lord, Selucreh. You belong with the house of Jaegar." Achilles Zahora marshalled the full power of his baritone voice. "Come home."

Julien Lacusta shot upright in the burgundy chair beside his bed, stunned by the power of the dark energy that had just slammed into him. Panting in response to his racing pulse, he tried to regain his bearings. It was as if a dark, inky sludge was clouding his vision, and it was everywhere around him.

Above him.

Below him.

Within him.

He choked on the sheer malevolence of it, straining to separate fact from fiction, and then he immediately checked on Rebecca: He had given the human female a powerful compulsion to sleep, just moments after she had passed out, and then he had carried her to his bedroom and planted her in his bed, tucking her between the sheets. To his way of thinking, the female had been much too afraid, far too overwhelmed, and way too damned determined to escape to reason with at the time— maybe some sleep would do her some good, hit the reset button or something. Not to mention, Julien had been in no frame of mind to sit her down and explain the Curse; nor had he felt like restraining her, taking over her mind, or clarifying the incident with Shelly and Nachari, expounding upon the chaos she had walked in on while he was high on liquid O.

Truth be told, he had needed a moment to himself.

Now, as he prowled around the room, trying to calm his racing heart, he couldn't help but wonder if this Blood Moon wasn't an ill-fated and terrible omen.

If the timing wasn't beyond horrific.

If the Blood had not cursed him…twice.

Too unsettled to go back to the chair, he made his way to the bed, eased his heavy frame onto the mattress as quietly as he could, and settled atop the covers, careful not to awaken Rebecca. Sinking deep into the soft down pillow, he anchored both arms behind his head and returned his attention to the unsolicited dark energy. *Hell's minions, and may the gods have mercy.* It had been centuries since he had felt anything like that.

Yet and still, he would know that *darkness* anywhere.

That thick, psychic sludge.

That hatred.

That abomination.
And it could only mean one thing—
Ian was still alive.

six

Rebecca Johnston began to stir in the soft, queen-sized bed, around two or three in the morning, slowly opening her drowsy eyes. She had not slept that deeply in months, and her mind was still in a fog. She was just about to reach for her throw, tuck it around her shoulders, and amble to the bathroom, when she froze where she lay.

This was not a soft, queen-sized bed, flanked by a framed panel of ocher fabric squares. It was a huge iron-and-wood platform, probably custom made, situated in the center of a large rustic space, beneath a high-coffered ceiling framed in expensive panes of wood.

She gasped, sitting up abruptly.

There were two dome-shaped, stained-glass windows to her right, each propped open by a horizontal iron arm, an enormous ceiling fan circulating above her, and a thick tuft of carpet running along the wide-planked floor, which served as a narrow runner.

She turned her head to the right—

And screamed.

That man!

He was still there!

The one who knew her name.

The one who had forced her into his house and hurt the other woman. The one who had made the green-eyed guy vanish into thin air…and…and…and obviously placed her in his bed.

She peeked under the covers, instantly relieved to see that she was still wearing her clothes, but heaven help her, what had he done?

He sat up in a smooth, serpentine motion, like the Loch Ness monster rising from the sea, and turned to regard her with those dark moonstone eyes, and she almost came unglued. Snatching the covers and tucking them beneath her chin, she scrambled backward until her spine hit the heavy iron headboard, and then she gave way to her panic. "Get away from me!" she shouted.

He held up both hands, rolled off the bed, and took several languid steps away from Rebecca, backing into a large mission-style dresser, where he gently settled his weight. "This good?" he asked gruffly.

She sucked in air, afraid she might start hyperventilating. He was still wearing the same faded blue jeans and form-fitting, stainless-steel-gray tank he'd had on earlier—that had to be a good sign—and he had washed the blood off his hands and smoothed his mahogany hair. Yet he still looked like death in sensual clothing, a gladiator from another time.

He still looked like the scariest man she had ever seen.

"What are you doing?" she whispered tentatively, too intimidated to meet his eyes. "Why am I still here?" He stretched his shoulders, and the ensuing ripple of waves that cascaded along the muscles of his arms, and then his chest, forced a whimper from Rebecca's throat.

"You're here because of the celestial gods."

Rebecca drew back and cleared her throat. "Excuse me?"

The man—*Julien*—ran a strong, powerful hand through his gorgeous, tapered hair and sighed. "I've thought this through, several different ways, and there's just no gentle way to lay this out. No matter how I present it, it's gonna land like a ton of bricks, so to my way of thinking, I should just put it out there, let the shit hit the fan, and then deal with the aftermath later."

Rebecca gulped.

What was he talking about?

And what was he about to say?

Her stomach twisted into knots as she waited, half expecting to hear him confess that he planned to torture her, bit by bit, kill her slowly, and then bury her body in the woods. Was this guy really that self-aware—was he proud of being a sadist?—and blunt enough to just toss it out there like a leisurely morning chat?

Her teeth began to chatter.

Julien stiffened, but only a bit. "Rebecca Louise, you are not who you think you are, at least not entirely. You were born with a purpose beyond what you know, and so was I. My name is Julien Zechariah Lacusta; I'm a vampire, not a human; and you are my predestined mate. The moon that turned the color of blood last night was no anomaly or accident. It was an omen, a sign, a signal meant to tell me you were here. Look at your wrist."

She scrunched up her nose in a frown, still reeling from his bizarre, cryptic words, the fact that he knew her first and middle names, and the way he referred to her as *his*. Yet and still, she turned over her right arm and glanced—

"The other one," he instructed.

She jumped at the brusque sound of his voice and held up her other wrist. And then she gasped aloud. Why hadn't she seen that before? Why hadn't she felt it? Noticed it? *Dear lord*, it was as blatant as the day was long, as pronounced as a neon red sign: There were strange engravings and shadowy marks etched deep into her skin; raised symbols and mysterious images seamlessly woven into her flesh; and they looked like a familiar constellation, like Hercules in the northern sky.

"That's right, baby girl, Hercules, clad in a lion's pelt, my birth constellation. My ruling Blood Moon."

Rebecca had no idea what he was talking about, but things were *really* getting weird. There was simply no denying that something unnatural was going on, but this guy? He was truly psychotic. "I don't understand," she whispered, her voice as grave as she felt. "I...I...how can this be?"

Julien rocked forward, bracing his palms on the dresser behind him, and unwittingly flexed his arms. "I'm not human, sweetheart. As I said before, I'm a vampire, and I was born under a curse. To put it in terms you'd understand: You are my wife, my mate, the woman who is about to give me a son. Over the next twenty-nine days I will sire two children *with you*—twins, one dark and one light, one pure and one evil—and I will turn the evil twin over to…this curse…in order to spare my life. All of it is preordained. None of it is optional. And that is why you are here."

If a person could actually feel a surge of adrenaline, blood rushing to their muscles in the form of liquid heat, then Rebecca's veins instantly caught on fire, and the flames consumed her reason, singed away her fragile peace. She shot out of bed like a ball from a cannon, sprinted to the nearest window, and began to climb through the painted glass—two-story fall, be damned.

Julien was there in an instant, blocking her escape with a strategically placed arm. "Settle down, *iubito*. I'm not about to let you go. And I'm certainly not about to let you jump."

Rebecca struck out at him with an angry, clenched fist, nearly bruising her knuckles against his jaw. "Ouch!" she cried instinctively, and then she began to cry. "Please, just let me go. You don't understand. I can't be here. I don't care about any *curse*! I just wanna go home." And then something so primal, so irrational, so impulsive took her over that she could hardly contain her frenzy.

Fight or flight.

She had tried to flee, and it hadn't worked.

She smacked him across the face with an open palm, as hard as she could. "Screw you, you evil bastard. You're freaking insane!" She slapped him again, even harder this time. "And I will never, ever, *ever* let you touch me, so you'll have to kill me first." She was literally panting with rage. "Let me go!" *Smack.* "Back the hell up!" *Pop.* "I despise weak, broken, pathetic men like you who think they can just take what they want." She tried to knee him in the groin, but he blocked it. "Block this!" she shouted, and then she spat in his face. The gladiator took a startled step backward, and she came at him even harder, punching him in the throat. "What! What is it? Your mama didn't love you? Your daddy was a loser? Your uncle liked to play with you in the dark? Go to hell! Do you hear me? Go straight to hell!" She threw back her shoulders and side-stepped past him, hoping to take advantage of the element of surprise. "I'm leaving, and you're not going to stop me because you are a weak, pathetic little boy." She made her way past his broad, muscular shoulders, and her heart rate increased as she anxiously eyed the door. If she could just get through the threshold, she could run the rest of the way, while her psychotic, delusional captor continued to reel in confusion, hopefully reduced to his barest, broken form.

It was the only shot she had.

A gamble she had to take.

A deep, feral growl pierced the darkness, reverberating behind her, and her stomach lodged in her throat.

"I am so not cut out for this shit," her captive snarled. And then his voice dropped an octave deeper, into a savage, bestial purr. "Get on the bed."

Before she could respond or react, her body launched into the air and flew, of its own accord, halfway across the room, hitting the bed with a whoosh as her limbs spread out atop the mattress.

The male prowled toward the...*dresser?*...his eyes fixed on a heavy silver tray, where he opened a decanter of alcohol, poured a shot of some unknown spirit into a crystal glass, and then reached for an exquisite, ornate box to remove the black-and-gold lid. He retrieved a dark plastic pouch—it almost looked like a packet of soy sauce, the kind that came with a Chinese meal—and tore it open with his teeth. He dumped the contents into the glass and consumed it in a single gulp, and then he spun around to face Rebecca, and his mouth was edged with *fangs*.

Rebecca screamed like her life was ending, stunned by the impossible visage. It just couldn't be real...

None of it.

None of this.

Oh Blessed Saint Michael, what was he going to do next?

He pulled his tank over his shoulders and tossed it on the floor, taking a giant step toward the bed, his head lolling forward in ecstasy. "I don't care that you struck me," he growled. "And I don't care that you made a valiant effort to get away—kudos to you, Rebecca Johnston, at least you have some heart. But my mother? And my father?" He popped his neck several times, and the sound amplified throughout the room like bullets leaving the chamber of a gun. "That's just... *off limits.*" He opened the fly of his jeans with one swift rotation of his wrist and ran his tongue along those fangs. "Truth is: I don't want this shit any more than you do, but it is what it is. Now lie back, and we shall see what you will and will not do, what you will and will not want."

Much to her utter shock and horror, Rebecca's body obeyed, even as her mind protested, grievously. "Wait," she cried helplessly, holding up both hands. "Please...wait...*I'm sorry.*"

"Sh," he intoned, and just like before, her voice was trapped in her throat, no longer able to work. "Don't worry, baby, you're going to desire every moment of this." He waved his hand through the air, and a rush of erotic desire, so powerful that it shook her to the core, slammed into her body, tingled in her toes, and nestled in her womb.

She jackknifed off the bed, arching her back in need.

What the hell was happening?

Her body was virtually on fire, and she could hardly reason or think.

She wanted.

She needed.

She craved.

Him!

Like he was her last dying breath, and no one—and nothing—would satisfy the ache, the pain, the indescribable hunger, but his body, filling hers.

Rebecca gasped and moaned from the all-consuming sensation, reaching out to stroke his thigh, praying for *anything* he would give her, if only just a tease. When he didn't come to her fast enough, she panted to contain her arousal, like a woman in the throes of labor, trying to regulate her pain, just for another minute.

Just for another *second*.

This was crazy.

Unthinkable.

Beyond anything Rebecca had ever known or felt.

She needed him…

Now.

Twisting to remove her blouse, and then shimmying out of her jeans, Rebecca stretched an arched foot toward his hard-cut abs and tried to reach his arousal with her toes. He growled deep in his throat, and she felt instantly encouraged. "Please," she whimpered, barely recognizing her own sultry voice. "Oh, please, Julien…*please.*"

He descended like the darkness on a moonless night, blanketing her body with his own, and her stomach clenched in violent anticipation. "Tell me what you need, baby," he drawled, and her breath caught in her throat.

"You, I need you," she moaned.

"Indeed, you do," he rasped, and there was a faint hint of *something* unnamable in his voice—sarcasm, conquest, male satisfaction? He slid his glorious, powerful hands down the small of her waist, over her quivering hips, and hooked his thumbs inside the band of her lace bikinis.

And then he rocked forward, bit her in the throat, and began to drink her blood.

Nothing else mattered.

Nothing…

At all.

Rebecca had tumbled into an endless vortex of ecstasy, and she was luxuriating in the fall.

BLOOD ECSTASY

Julien Lacusta descended into the welcoming, velvet arms of the dragon—alcohol, blood, and liquid H—letting the heroin take him over completely.

Rebecca would never understand, nor would she ever forgive him.

But how could he explain?

And what other option did he have?

The last thing he wanted to do—the last thing he would *ever* want to do—is hurt his *destiny*, take away her reason, or remove her control, make her come to him through compulsion. But it was a helluva lot better than violence, harming her in *any* physical way, and she had pushed him so very close to that edge: He had almost lost his center of gravity, his hold on reality, if only for a moment, a split-second in time, when she had come at him with such rage and determination...

Her fist, her open hand, even spitting in his face; none of it had fazed him. She couldn't harm a flea. But her words, those hate-filled actions, that unfiltered rage; *that* had been eerily familiar, too reminiscent of his past. Rebecca Johnston had catapulted Julien into another place and time.

Harietta Lacusta sat down at the small barn-wood table and pressed her back against the coarse stone wall, staring at her beloved child, Ian. He had just turned ten years old that morning. "Obviously, you can't have a birthday cake, Ian," she teased, nervously brushing her hands along the folds of her skirt, "but I think you will really like what I brought you. I fed from a very pretty young lass last night." Despite her fervent attempt at gaiety, the mirth never reached her eyes. She held out her wrist, and Julien cringed, knowing exactly what Ian was thinking.

Ian hated feeding from his mother.

He hated it with a passion.

It was emasculating at best.

Yet Harietta was always so oblivious to Ian's burgeoning darkness, the hatred that consumed his blackened heart. "Come on, Ian; just try it. It's your birthday, after all. And I even have a gift for you...after you feed."

Julien sat up straighter on the rough, wooden bench, staring out the narrow twelve-inch window at the back of the shanty—he did not want to watch the scene play out. It was always the same: Ian came this close *to losing his control, and their mother pretended not to notice, like she could somehow will him into being something other than what he was.*

An aberrant scourge of nature, just waiting to implode.

Ian sat back and smiled, and even from the corner of his eye, Julien knew there was something wrong, something malicious and distinctly sinister in that false, wry smirk. At complete odds with his smile, the child rose from his seat, towered over Harietta, and slapped her so hard the echo ricocheted off the earthen walls. "To hell with you, you evil, maniacal wench. You're utterly insane!" He struck her at least nine or ten times, in lightning-quick succession, before Julien could move or intervene. "Go to hell! Do you hear me? Go straight to hell! I'm leaving this lords-forsaken hovel, and you're not going to stop me because you are a weak, pathetic little worm."

And then, Ian lunged at her throat.

Like a wild, feral cat—his claws fully extended, his fangs dripping with saliva, his eyes gleaming harsh, crimson red—he dove at their mother with pure, murderous intent.

*Julien tried to intercept him—*gods help him, how he tried—*but Ian was like a demon, possessed. He moved faster than Julien's eyes could follow. He struck so hard that Harietta's skeleton collapsed. He ravaged her jugular with such ferocity that her flesh, her cartilage, and her bones were in his jagged teeth before Julien could rise from his seat.*

Spurred on by some primal, instinctive hatred, Ian decimated the woman's throat with the ferocity of a beast. And just like that, in the blink of an eye, Julien's mother was dead.

The liquid O reclaimed the vampire's attention, and his eyes rolled back in his head as the memory drifted further and further away...

Thank the gods.

The blood seeping into his mouth; the soft, pliant body beneath him; Rebecca's soft, erotic pleas demanding the warrior's devotion were all he could feel, sense, or hear, and he whispered in her ear: "Tell me what you need, baby."

Her breath caught in her throat. "You, I need you," she moaned.

"Indeed, you do," he rasped, satisfied that the compulsion

had worked, that the madness had stopped, that he was at least feeling something he could control. He slid two strong, splayed hands down the small of her waist, over her quivering hip, and hooked his thumbs inside the band of her lace bikinis—

And then it hit him.

Like an oncoming train.

Dear celestial gods: He hadn't converted her yet.

And if he took her right now, released his seed, and gods forbid, had even a passing thought about pregnancy, he would kill her before he'd even claimed her, before he'd even had a chance to get to know her. He was one mindless, drug-induced mistake away from being no better than his evil brother.

Julien jolted backward, recoiling from Rebecca's touch, as he instantly released the compulsion. "Run, Becca!" he snarled. "Get away…and hide, but do not leave the house."

She blanched, turning a sickly shade of green, as awareness and control slammed into her. He didn't need to tell her twice. She scrambled from beneath him, rolled off the bed, and hit the ground running, scurrying out of the room.

She didn't even bother to get dressed.

Julien moved with the same sense of urgency, shimmying to the edge of the bed, opening the nightstand drawer, and retrieving a strange-looking remote, a device created by Santos Olaru, one of the valley's illustrious sentinels, who just happened to be a guru with technology, and Nachari Silivasi, a gifted Master Wizard in his own right: The device tripped both the alarms and the wards. The windows and doors would slide shut, secured by hidden, titanium bolts, and the magical wards, which kept people from crossing their barriers—in either direction—would also kick in.

With the push of a button, Julien's house shut down.

No one was getting in or out.

And that included Rebecca.

He reached for a second item—also given to him by Nachari Silivasi—the pale blue crystal containing the Master Wizard's memories from his time spent in the Abyss. Although Julien wasn't looking forward to the *viewing*, and gods knew he had other pressing matters to attend to, the H was gonna hang around for at least thirty minutes, and he needed the information. If there was any part of his heart that was actually considering using this Blood Moon to make an untimely exit from earth—*and there was*—then he owed it to himself and Rebecca to examine it more closely.

He needed to be absolutely sure of his next move.

Heavens knew; he had already screwed things up, six ways to Sunday.

Shifting onto his back, he folded one arm behind his head, crossed his legs at the ankle, and caressed the crystal resting in his palm. As the images in the stone began to come to life, playing like a DVD on his visual cortex, he sank deep into the mattress…and watched.

seven

Rebecca waited in the dark, huddled beneath a heavy trestle table in a long, narrow hallway, just above the twisting, iron-railed staircase that led to the second and third floors of the elaborate mountain home. She was somewhere on the third level, and she had already tried every hall, every possible nook and cranny, every doorway and window, on every successive floor, with zero success—nothing would open, and she wasn't about to go anywhere near the gladiator's bedroom to try to retrieve her cell phone.

It wasn't worth the risk.

She tightened her grip on the soft brown throw blanket wrapped around her shoulders, which she had snatched from the great room, and winced at her curious choice of words: *Gladiator*.

That wasn't exactly accurate, was it?

The male had claimed to be a *vampire*.

And, as bizarre and utterly psychotic as that might sound, Rebecca had begun to believe him. After all, he had known her name in an instant; he had moved her body through space, using nothing but his mind; and bless her for being crazy enough to believe it, but the male had flashed a wicked pair of *fangs*—fangs he had used to bite her, to siphon her blood, and to somehow seduce her like she was some sex-charged siren who couldn't get enough.

She shuddered at the memory, feeling curiously ashamed.

Dear angels and saints, she had wrapped her ankles around him, writhed like a harlot beneath him, and practically begged him to take her—to use her like he owned her—and she would have seen it through.

How had he done that to her?

And with nothing more than a mere suggestion: *You're going to desire every moment of this.* Rebecca Johnston didn't do one-night stands, and she certainly didn't go out of her way to seduce a brutal captor.

Yeah, Rebecca was pretty damn sure: Julien Lacusta was not a human male. He was a vampire, or at least an incredible magician, and if *any* part of what he'd told her was true, then the rest could be true, as well: the Curse, the twin sons, the terrifying Blood Moon, and maybe the fact that he was trying to...somehow...spare his own life.

She bit down on her tongue, trying to stifle a scream—it was all just way too much to process, and she felt like she was going insane. She brought her wrist to eye-level, a reality check of sorts, and stared at the very real emblems and symbols etched into her flesh.

The insignia of Hercules.

That's what he had said.

And he hadn't been high on morphine, or crack—or whatever it was that he took—at the time. Before she could consider the implications any further the fact that the vampire also ingested drugs, she heard a heavy set of footsteps meandering down a hall, on the first floor of the dwelling.

Oh shit, he was awake!

She backed further beneath the table, curled her body into a ball, and practically held her breath, trying to remain perfectly still...and quiet.

The footsteps continued through the great room, toward the foyer, and they were unerring in their progression—it was almost as if he knew *exactly* where she was. She tilted her head to the side, listening more intently, as he began to make his way up the staircase, his footfalls growing louder with every step.

No.

No!

No, no, no, no, no!

He paused on the second floor, but only for an instant, before he continued to climb the stairs to the third. And then, just like that, he took three long strides forward, advancing down the hall, and came to a sudden stop, about five feet away.

"Becca, come out from underneath the table, baby. We need to talk."

Julien knew that Rebecca was terrified, and of course, he knew where she was hiding: beneath the slender wooden trestle in the third-story hall. He was a seasoned, instinctive tracker, with incredible intuition and skills. Finding Rebecca in his own familiar home had been no more challenging than taking candy from a baby. Her scent, her blood, her heartbeat—everything gave her away—including his own familiar imprint on the throw blanket she had donned.

He closed his eyes and tried to chill, taking a moment to think.

Nachari Silivasi's memories, the time he had spent in the Abyss, had been sobering at the least; terrifying, without apology; and a major gut-check of the highest order. Julien didn't know what he was doing, and he didn't know what he wanted, going forward. But one thing was crystal clear: He didn't want to end up there, in the Valley of Death and Shadows, not if he didn't have to. Beyond that, he knew himself, at least peripherally: He knew why he took the H, he knew why he needed to be alone, and he knew that he could not function, or think, or reason when he was flying high. He was nothing but bare savage instincts, then—all his demons running loose—despite the fact that he was too zoned out to meet them.

But this?

Having his *destiny* here, hiding like a lost little lamb trying to avoid the slaughter, naked and afraid in his home? Running from the beast inside him?

Ah hell, this was beyond the pale.

Despite the fact that he was standing at a fork in the road—he could go left, he could go right, or he could just stand still—he needed to pull it together, if only for Rebecca, and show the female some warmth. Well, *warmth* was too strong of a word. He was still Julien Lacusta, after all. But he could at least show her some courtesy, let her know he wasn't always a beast—he wasn't always high—and offer her some basic consideration, perhaps a modicum of respect. More than that, he could at least try to get to know her, see what makes her tick. Maybe there was something she wanted, needed…desired…something he could give to her that she'd be willing to exchange for her required role in the Curse.

And didn't that just sound effed up, any way you turned it?

He sighed. *Ah hell, it was what it was.*

He opened his eyes and scrubbed his hand over his face—damn, was this really happening, *now?*

Yeah, it was.

It really, freakin' was.

And he needed to mend some fences.

Pronto.

He paused about five feet from his *destiny's* perch and tried mightily to gentle his voice: "Becca, come out from underneath the table, baby. We need to talk."

She jerked, inhaled a harsh, shallow breath, and then she grew inhumanly still.

He took a couple of steps forward and squatted down to place a soft white terrycloth robe on the floor, and then he added a bottle of Perrier water and a tray filled with cheese and crackers to the mix—*hell, it was the only food he kept in the house*—he didn't have that many human visitors. "Angel, I know you've got to be cold, and you haven't had anything to eat or drink since you got here—you're probably hungry." And didn't that just make him the *ass* of the year. He sighed in exasperation. "Look, I know exactly where you are, beneath the table, so there's no point in continuing to hide. Why don't you just come out, put on the robe, and have something to eat. At least have a drink of water, and I'll back up, have a seat at the top of the stairs. Nothing confrontational, baby. Just you and me...talking."

He backed away from the olive branch, such as it was, and waited.

When she still didn't come out, he made his way to the top of the staircase and sat down with his back flush against the wall, his legs sprawled out in front of him, and his feet crossed at the ankles. "C'mon, baby," he implored her again. "I am not going to hurt you, and I am not going to mess with your mind. I promise."

Rebecca looked like an adorable little turtle, slowly peeking her head out from beneath the heavy table, and for the first time, Julien became aware of just how beautiful she truly was: Her golden brown hair was filled with soft, silky S-curls that framed her gently rounded chin on the way to her slender shoulders. Her gorgeous, hooded eyes were nearly topaz in color, a rich smoky blue. And her naturally curved, arched brows were perfect in shape and fullness, accentuating her elegant features. She could have been a model if she chose, perhaps if she were a couple of inches taller, but either way, she had the kind of raw, organic beauty that turned heads in casual passing and probably stopped traffic on a daily basis.

And she didn't carry herself as if she knew it.

Always, a major plus.

"Do you think I'm a freakin' mouse?" she murmured, gesturing toward the tray full of cheese, as well as the water, as she crawled out from beneath the bench. "Or just too stupid to recognize a mouse-trap when I see one?"

Julien chuckled deep in his throat. *Touché*. "No, love, I do not. I think you are human, and you need to stay hydrated. I think you need something to eat."

She clutched the meager throw blanket as she reached out to snatch the robe. "If you give me back my phone, I'll order a pizza," she quipped. "Look away."

Julien turned his head to the side and laughed again. "I can order you a pizza. Is that what you want?" He waited, listening for the fall of the blanket and tuning in to the brush of the robe, the sound of the terrycloth sash twisting into place as she tied it.

"I want to go home," she said crossly. And just like that, the light-hearted banter had come to an end.

Julien met her serious gaze. "I know you do," he whispered, "and I completely understand. But that is not a wish I can grant." He inclined his head toward the tray. "Please, at least have something to drink."

"Like you did?" she replied curtly. Despite her courageous demeanor and her obvious irritation, the words were followed by a spike of fear. It was in her eyes. It was in her scent.

"Becca," Julien breathed, softly. "I'm...I'm sorry."

Her expression betrayed her surprise. "For what?" Her tone was increasingly caustic. "For biting me in the throat or making me act like a whore?"

A low, feral growl escaped Julien's throat. "In a thousand lifetimes, under a thousand compulsions, you would never be that, not to me. And that is not what happened in my room."

She drew back, and then, seeming suddenly self-conscious, she took a reluctant seat on the floor and folded her legs in crisscross fashion as she leaned over the tray. She took a small piece of cheese and plopped it in her mouth, chewing like she had to force the effort, and then she twisted the cap off the bottled water and took a long, generous drink.

Julien exhaled slowly, feeling surprisingly relieved. "About what happened in the bedroom," he began, knowing they needed to face it head-on, "you've gotta know, that's not who I am, a male who takes advantage of women...just because he can. That's not what happened, Rebecca."

She placed another slice of cheese on a cracker and slowly brought it to her lips, hesitating before she bit into it. "Then what did happen, Julien?" Her words were clipped, yet tentative.

He sighed. "When you came at me, by the window, you...you pushed a couple buttons...triggered some real ugly shit from my past. I wasn't thinking clearly, and I didn't want to hurt you—not that I would ever hurt a woman—but I just, I just wanted to change the scene. I made the wrong calculation. I made all the wrong moves."

She nodded, slowly. "And the opium doesn't help."

He narrowed his gaze and looked right at her, sweeping his hand through his hair. "Actually, it does—and it's not opium. But that's my thing, baby, not yours. And it isn't all the time."

She ate the cracker, stacked another one, and then took a second drag of water. "Why do you get high?"

He jolted, just a little, a bit taken aback by her bluntness, but he supposed the question was fair. He shrugged a weighty shoulder and sighed. "It's just…too loud, sometimes…the noise in my head. It gets dark…and heavy…and I just need a break." He pursed his lips together in contemplation. "I'm a soldier of sorts, a tracker for my kind, the Vampyr, and I have a lot of serious duties—so my head is usually straight. And when I'm not working, I spend a lot of time alone—it's just the way it is—and every now and again, I just need a break. A vacation from the noise." He paused, considering his next words carefully. "You've seen me high more times in the last two days than I've been in the last few months. It's just a thing, baby. I don't know what else to say."

She eyed him intensely, like she was trying to see his soul, and then she continued to work on the tray, saying nothing in reply.

He cleared his throat. "And what about you?"

She raised her eyebrows.

"When I glimpsed your mind, when I made contact with your thoughts, I saw all kinds of random images: a support group, a shit-load of locks on your apartment door, a recent request for a concealed-carry license. What's up with that, baby?"

Rebecca visibly paled. "You saw all that? You read my mind?"

"Didn't read it," he replied. "Just walked through the room."

She furrowed her brow in consternation, and then she sat

forward. "Well, as long as we're being candid: When I was twenty-one years old, I met the wrong guy. I spent one year falling in love with him and another year trying to get away from him. He followed me from Nevada to New Mexico and everywhere between. He told me he was going to kill me, and I believe that he will try. So maybe that's what you saw."

Something dark, primal, and unexpected rose in Julien's soul, and he clenched his hands into fists, trying to reroute the energy into his fingers. "What's the bastard's name?"

Rebecca frowned and shook her head. "What difference does that make?"

Julien licked his lips in a lazy glide of his tongue, and then they both drew back into a snarl. "Dead men should have something to put on their headstones."

She sputtered, spraying water from her mouth in surprise. "You're kidding, right?"

He chuckled, but there wasn't a humorous tone in the sound. "Let me make something exceedingly clear, baby girl. You might think you've wandered into the lion's den—and it just might be true—but the fact of the matter is this: You are safer now—*with me*—than you have ever been in your life. You may not know it. You may not feel it. But it's true, just the same. And while you don't yet understand all the intricacies of the Curse, all the complexities of my kind, there is one thing that has never changed: My species is extremely territorial. We are as possessive as we are loyal. And we don't adhere to human laws. We are not bound by human conventions. That man"—he reached inside her mind to retrieve the stalker's name—"*Trevor.* He was dead the day he met you. He was dead the day the gods chose you for me. And now? Now that I know what he has done to you...and your life...to your sense of safety, to your world? His death will not be swift or painless. Mark my words, sweet Rebecca; you no longer have a stalker."

Rebecca gaped at him like he had just arrived from another planet.

She opened her mouth to respond and stuttered something

incoherent, before instantly trying again. "And that somehow makes this okay? What you've done? What you're doing...*to me?* Snatching me out of your driveway, and this whole crazy Curse?" Her voice rose in both angst and volume as she quoted him word for word. *"To put it in terms you understand: You are my wife, my mate, the woman who is about to give me a son...all of it is preordained. None of it is optional. And that is why you are here.* So, you're gonna kill Trevor—my territorial vampire is going to murder my ex-boyfriend—and then I'm just going to...*to what?* Oh yeah, have your sons, have your twins, let you sacrifice the demonic one to...*to what?* And then, you and I, we just do, what? Live happily ever after?" She was borderline hysterical. "Julien Zechariah Lacusta, surely, even you can hear how insane that sounds. I have a life. I have a job. I have responsibilities! Hell, I run a support group for other desperate women, victims in the exact same shoes as mine. There are five women in my VOSU group, and they depend on me for help, for intervention, for their safety, if not their very lives. I'm not going to turn my back on them. And I'm not going to willingly disappear into some medieval fantasy that these gods—these celestial beings that I've never heard of—supposedly created for me." She licked her bottom lip in a nervous gesture and then purposefully angled her jaw, looking him dead in the eyes for emphasis.

Julien relaxed his shoulders and tilted his head to the side in a matching gesture, growing firm with resolution. "You have an impeccable memory, Rebecca, and you don't mince words. I like that, so let me have a try. *Murder.*" He echoed the word she had just used. "Is that what you think it is?" Before she could answer, he held up his hand to dissuade her. "Does a lion murder a gazelle? Does a human murder an ant?" He chuckled, and once again, there was nothing even remotely humorous in the sound. "I am Vampyr, Miss Johnston, I know nothing of this *murder* you speak of." He leaned forward and held her gaze. "I only know that you are mine—*you belong to me*—and that which threatens you cannot exist in my world." He lowered his hand, almost in a gesture of concession. "And no, you won't...come around…overnight, but there is something in your soul, something in your blood, something woven into your very DNA that recognizes my own, that bends to my voice and yields to my touch. Do you think everything that happened on that bed was compulsion?" He shook his head before he could spark her anger. "Bad example—I get it—but you need to get this: You're here. It *is* where you belong. And I will give you the space, the time, and the knowledge to slowly process all this new information, to adjust to this medieval fantasy, as you so poetically put it. I will answer all your questions. I will address all your fears. And I will explain all you need to know. And somehow, in the midst of this process, I will slowly show to you your own celestial heart. But for now, I have only one question, and I insist that you give me the truth."

Rebecca blanched, and her eyes filled with mutinous underpinnings; but she didn't speak a word. She just waited, as if she were actually eager to hear his next words.

"Suppose I take you back home—*to Denver*—and we find this Trevor, together. As I've said, his fate is no longer up for debate. But suppose we take it one step further, and I do the one thing you most want…*and need*. I fulfill your greatest desire: to set each strong, independent, yet helpless woman free." He paused to let the heart of his words sink in. "Yes, Rebecca, think of every woman in your support group, all five of their lives. Now imagine each one, finally free from fear, finally free from a life of tyranny and terror, from hiding in the shadows like a wounded dog." He sat back and crossed his arms, even as he gentled his voice. "Rebecca, my *destiny*; I will kill them all, every last vile, despicable male. And I will make sure your foundation, your charitable cause, has enough resources to continue your work for a hundred years. And even then, I will not keep you from following your heart's desires—I will not lock you up like a slave. All I ask is that you listen, and learn, and give me two weeks to do the things that I've claimed. Now then, speak only the truth: Put aside the human concept of murder, and answer me from the heart. If you could, would you have me *extinguish* them all?"

Rebecca sat back, and she seemed to be holding her breath.

Her eyes grew distant, and Julien knew she was weighing his offer, very, *very* carefully, imagining each woman in her group and what his expert intervention could mean for her life. She brought her hand to her mouth and began to chew on her nails, and gods forgive him, but he had to take a quick, inconspicuous glance at her thoughts: She was thinking about Sheila, a woman who had suffered two miscarriages, how each of her unborn children had been beaten out of her body. She was thinking about a woman named Nancy, and the way she spoke with a lisp, how the left half of her jaw had been wired together. And she was counting all the restraining orders, the numerous, ever-constant threats, all the temporary houses and the fake IDs.

She was weighing what these women had gone through in a society that had all but abandoned them to some cultural blindness—or apathy—that allowed such blatant, unjust atrocities to go on, unchallenged, leaving it up to the victims to fend for themselves, to live or die at the sick, errant impulses of their lovers...or practical strangers.

And finally, she was thinking about an incestuous father who had just been given joint custody of his three-year-old daughter, a child of a woman named Kate, and how the clock was ticking for that precious little girl. Although it went against every civilized, acculturated bone in her human body, Rebecca was tuned in to her celestial DNA, and her desire for justice was as primal as it was strong. "You could do that?" she whispered, her voice barely audible. "You could...take care of them all?"

Julien nodded, resolutely. "For you, my true *destiny*; I would slaughter a small country." Once again, he held up his hand. "But never an innocent soul. There will be no blood on your hands, either way. But you haven't said *yes*, or *no*."

Rebecca fidgeted with her hands; she tugged on the ends of her hair; and she bit down, far too hard, on her bottom lip. She squirmed where she sat, until she could no longer take the chaotic energy, and then she stood, to pace it off.

Finally, turning around, her face gaunt and ashen, she sought the vampire's gaze. "Yes," she whispered, as a tear of compassion—or perhaps, remorse?—fell from the corner of her eye. "You don't necessarily have to kill them—I really don't want you to kill them. And, either way, I don't want to know what you do. But if you can set them free—*the women*—if you can set me free from Trevor..." Her single tear turned into a torrent of anguish, and she shook from the depth of her emotion. "Then yes, Julien...*please*...please do."

Julien rose from his perch near the wall, inexorably drawn by the strength of her pain. *Dear gods*, she was so full of compassion. Despite her conviction, her heart was practically breaking from the mere thought of hurting these worthless men. Yet and still, he would not dishonor her goodness: If he could maim them or erase their minds, set them on another path, then he would. He would spare their lives for Rebecca, unless, of course, someone got out of hand or showed a propensity to continue hurting others, unless it was simply irrefutable: If the man was a rabid dog, and the dog needed to be put down, then Julien was all about the task.

Just the same, Rebecca had made her decision, and he would honor her wishes...

With one exception.

Trevor.

Trevor Rainer.

This particular dog was dead.

Closing the distance between them, even knowing that he had no right, Julien blanketed Rebecca's slender body in his hard, implacable strength, and wrapped his arms around her. When she didn't fight him, he knew he had taken her to a very raw, vulnerable place, a place much more personal, much more helpless, and far more exposed than being captured by a vampire—

And *great celestial gods*, didn't that say it all.

Sliding a strong but gentle hand into her soft, silky hair, he nudged her forward and held her close to his heart, nuzzling the top of her head with his chin. Once again, she allowed it, as she continued to fight her tears; and that, more than anything, solidified his will.

"Sh, don't cry, angel. I promise you; you are free…at last. I will hunt and destroy them all."

eight

Later that evening…

After hiking about one mile in from River Rock Road, on the northern end of Dark Moon Vale, Braden Bratianu wound his way down a steep embankment and stopped, about six feet above the lowest point of a concealed, rushing river. Although he was surrounded by thickly treed forest, he wasn't that far from home. In fact, he was only ten miles or so from Nachari's brownstone, which was located in the northeast quadrant of the forest, and twenty-five miles from Marquis's farmhouse, which was lodged in the opposing, northwest. His second family—his self-appointed brothers—could still get to him quickly if he needed them.

Not that he would.

Braden Bratianu had shot up another two inches since his sixteenth birthday, and now, just four months shy of turning seventeen, he stood a full six feet tall. His shoulders were twice as broad as they were when he had first met the Silivasis, and his triceps, biceps, and pectoral muscles seemed to grow more defined, more developed, with every passing day. He was learning how to fight—well, he could hold his own with his classmates at the Academy, and he could certainly mop the floor with a human of any age or ability—and his powers of intuition and second-sight were continuing to evolve, as well. He didn't always understand what things meant, what he was feeling or why, but he was getting accustomed to the fact that his soul was always plugged in—always online, so to speak—somehow connected, like an open Wi-Fi signal, to the heart of the house of Jadon and the fearsome Vampyr king, Napolean Mondragon.

Ever since that horrible day when Salvatore Nistor had hatched an insidious plot to take down the ancient king with a Blood Possession, Braden had been plugged in, turned on…wired for sound. And now that he had a future *destiny* of his own—okay, so Kristina wasn't actually his *destiny*; she was more like his mail-order, future bride, the woman Napolean was going to make him marry at some point far, *far* into the future, because the two of them had no one else—he was trying to be a lot more mature. He was doing everything he could to take on more responsibility and show the other warriors that he could act, and think, independently.

Ah hell, who was he kidding?

He was trying to do everything he could to impress Kristina.

After all, he was nearly seventeen, and if human males were all one-track-mind, straight-up into girls at this age, then vampires, who matured quite a bit faster, were like human males on steroids. High heels, miniskirts, and pink Corvettes were just about all Braden could think of anymore: Kristina's infamous calling cards.

Okay, so that wasn't completely true, either.

He spent an awful lot of time in the garage with Nachari, looking under the hood of the *best Christmas present ever*—the brand-spanking-new Ford Mustang "King Cobra" that Nachari and Deanna had bought him last year after he got his driver's license. His sleek black-and-red pride and joy.

He grinned at the thought, even as he made his way down the steep embankment to the riverbed, fished out two perfectly smooth, water-softened stones, and rubbed them against his shirt.

He had been spending a lot of time at the Dark Moon Mineral Plant recently, not only to learn more about the house of Jadon's various industries, but to try to understand the metaphysical process that took place when a male vampire transformed a plain, earthen rock into a gemstone through a psychic, ancient practice. He was fascinated by the use of intentional thought—deep, focused emotion—as a catalyst, and the subsequent channeling of quantum waves, how something so simple, yet divine, could rearrange matter.

Most of the gems in Dark Moon Vale were native to the valley. Just the same, it was no secret that a vamp's energy could turn tears into blood-red diamonds if his pain ran deep enough; that his hopes or fears could materialize as pearls or sapphires under just the right circumstances; or that if he tried real hard, he might be able to craft whatever gemstone he chose, at will. The bottom line was this: Kristina had recently found a perfect pair of tangerine pumps—although, honestly, they just looked orange to him—and she had practically waxed poetic about how spectacular they would look with citrine gemstones embedded in the crisscrossed toe-straps, how awesome they would look with her suede apricot miniskirt.

Braden didn't know a damn thing about women's fashion—and frankly, he could not have cared less—but he had noticed how that particular skirt hugged her hips, and if having citrines over her toes made her wear it more often...well...game on.

He would do his best.

So here he was, on the northernmost end of Dark Moon Vale, just thirty minutes after twilight, fishing stones out of a river in the hopes of making two perfect citrines for Kristina, in the hopes of drawing power from the rising moon.

Realizing that his shirt wasn't enough, he polished the stones with a microfiber cloth, set them on a flat, rocky ledge to dry, and then sat down on the bank of the river to watch the water churn...and to concentrate.

And that's when he saw the peculiar mist.

Rising off the river like a fog: swirling in unnatural circles, spreading out like smoke from a dampened fire, and settling across the ravine like a ghost.

He sat up straight and heightened his vampiric senses, listening, feeling, trying to see through the fog. Even though it was early January, six o'clock at night, it wasn't cool enough for the condensed water droplets to form—the dew point just wasn't right. As a vampire, Braden could inherently sense the temperature and discern the chemistry of the surrounding elements, so he knew that something was...*off.*

Not wanting to be a baby or involve his brothers—or gods forbid, the king—in his every waking thought or encounter, he hit the psychic disconnect button on his telepathic receiver, even as he continued to watch the mist rise and fall, sway and dip, swirl and dance before him.

He slowly released his fangs.

He sharpened a few of his claws.

And he felt his vision heat, knowing his eyes were glowing red, as he shifted to infrared vision.

Whatever the phenomenon, whatever this was, he could handle it...

All by himself.

Ian Lacusta had given a lot of serious thought to Achilles Zahora's entreaty: *Come home.* And he had decided to do just that.

But in his own time.

And on his own terms.

He had no idea what he might be getting into, whether or not he could trust the house of Jaegar any more than he could trust the house of Jadon. He only knew that he had been a solitary entity for far too long to simply pack up his bags and move into a colony of strangers. To present himself as the latest sacrifice in a never-ending, twisted Curse that had never intended him to live.

Relying on the hard-earned lessons of his past, he could only be sure of one thing: Wherever he went in this world, however he traveled, and whomever he met, he needed the protection of his powers: his carefully crafted, lifelong skills.

He needed to play it safe.

History had taught him that appearing anywhere as a vampire was a non-starter. People freaked out; women screamed; men tried to attack, out of some intrinsic flight-or-flight impulse, and Ian invariably had to destroy them all...or make himself a god among men until he grew tired of the game. Even those who didn't know who—or what—he was still sensed his errant energy, his vacant, demonic heart. And there was just something wicked, vivid, innately unsettling about his black-and-red banded hair. It had taken him a lot of centuries and a lot of trial and error to learn how to project it as blond, but he could.

He could.

And he could also travel as the mist.

He could scatter his molecules to the winds to mask his scent and hide his identity—he had used it for centuries to elude his brother, Julien, just in case the male was still alive. He could alter the chemical composition of his core and spread it out over miles and miles, if he chose, moving across the land as a fog. Perhaps it was shape-shifting. Perhaps it was something else. Did the proper terminology really matter? After many grueling trials and errors, Ian had finally mastered the craft.

And yes, Harietta had played an invaluable role:

Picture the brightest light you can see, Ian; now try to wrap it, like a cloak, around your mind. The darkness is too stark, Ian; watch your brother, study your twin, try to sense Julien's soul and emulate it. That's not good enough, Ian; there's still something wrong. Be the sunrise, Ian; be the rose as it blooms; be the mist that settles on the grass as dew. Study its innocence, son. Understand what makes it pure. And try...try harder...to do and be just that.

If Ian could've brought the woman back to life just to kill her again, he would've.

What that hag had never understood was that there was nothing *wrong*. There was nothing *missing*. There was nothing *too dark*. All that blackness, all that vacancy, all that *wrongness*—was him.

Ian Lacusta.

BLOOD ECSTASY

Exactly the way the Blood had made him.

Exactly the way the dark lords intended.

Yet and still, he had mastered the craft for his mother, and curse her rotting soul, he had learned to become a pure, undefinable, undetectable mist. He had learned how to hide his identity in the fog. And now, nearly thirty minutes after sunset, as he descended on the northern end of Dark Moon Vale to get his own lay of the land, so to speak, before contacting the house of Jaegar, he had the perfect opportunity to try it out.

The young male, perched on the bank of the river, was a vampire for sure, and his soul absolutely screamed house of Jadon. If Ian could pass himself off as whatever he chose to this male—if he could emerge from the mist and fool another of his kind into believing he was a harmless innocent, a pure and lovely soul—then he could afford to spend some time in the valley.

He could afford to be within one hundred miles of Julien, confident that he would remain undetected.

The young vampire sat up straight, stiffened his spine, and his burnt-sienna eyes began to glow a coral red, even as he lengthened his fangs and his claws and began to study the mist. And kudos to him, really; at least he knew that the vapor was unnatural.

Ian gathered his molecules to his core; donned his familiar black jeans and a light, dusky gray cloak; and made sure his hair was blond. And then he simply stepped out of the mist and curled his lips into the best imitation of a smile that he had.

"Greetings, fledgling; I am Grigori Antonopoulos, from the isle of Greece, a son of the Vampyr who has been too long away from his people. I greet you in the name of Prince Jadon."

nine

Braden Bratianu bounded to his feet, startled by the sudden appearance of the strange, enigmatic vampire—how the heck had he snuck up on Braden like that? And how the heck had he transformed into the essence of fog? Outside of Nachari Silivasi, who could shift at will into a panther, and the fact that all vampires could cloak their appearances, become invisible, and even take the shape of a simple bird, like a raven or a bat, this was more than just a little bit extreme. It was a feat of mastery only attempted by a Master Wizard or an Ancient.

It was a phenomenal accomplishment and something Braden immediately wanted to learn. He wiped his palms on his jeans, a bit ashamed that he had been sweating just moments earlier. "What's up?" he mumbled, still eyeing the guy warily. "Where the heck did you come from?"

The male took a generous step back as if he knew his presence was overwhelming. "I already told you, did I not? I've been traveling…in Greece."

Braden frowned.

Traveling in Greece?

Did he run one of the vampire's various resorts for Napolean, feeding the funds back into Dark Moon Vale? And why hadn't Braden ever heard of Grigori Antonopoulos, a Greek surname, rather than Romanian?

Of course, there were a lot of vampires Braden didn't know…

He cleared his throat, trying to sound older than he was. "Why…so why are you…I mean, why are you all like, just popping up on the bank of a river and shit?" Okay, so that didn't sound very mature. "I'm just sayin'—why not head to Napolean's manse or check in with your family or somethin'? Why…I mean…what the hell, dude?"

Grigori laughed conspiratorially. And then the oddest thing happened: Braden felt the lightest tap against his mind, almost like the vampire was trying to glimpse Braden's thoughts, retrieve some specific piece of information, but nah, he wouldn't do that, right? That was so against the laws in the house of Jadon, and the guy was definitely a vampire, and he definitely had blond hair—the Dark Ones couldn't dye that stuff, or at least they were too arrogant and proud to want to—so, maybe, he was just really, *really* odd.

"How old are you, son?" the vampire asked.

Braden puffed out his chest and raised his chin, running his tongue over his upper canines. "Almost seventeen," he answered defiantly.

Grigori's expression deepened with regard. "Ah, and to think I would've taken you for at least twenty—you must work out."

Braden smiled then. "Yeah, you know: I do what I can."

Grigori nodded and held up both hands. "We all do; do we not?" He chuckled softly. "Can I tell you a secret, my friend?" He swept his hand in an apologetic arc. "I'm afraid I did not ask your name."

"Braden," he said warily.

"Ah, yes…can I tell you a secret, *Braden?*"

Braden cocked his eyebrows circumspectly, feeling a tad weirded out. "Sure, I guess."

Grigori appeared undaunted. "I came to Dark Moon Vale— *at the bank of a river*—because I was simply hoping for some solitude, peace, and tranquility before making my presence known. My running into you, here, was purely coincidence, but my secret is this: I am not the greatest fan of this place…or our people." He quickly held up both hands in a passive gesture to moderate any offense. "Don't misunderstand me; I revere our king and our patriarch, Prince Jadon, but I have been gone for many, many years." He shrugged as if it was an insignificant detail. "The truth is, my parents, who have long since passed away, had very little use for me when I was your age. And as an only child, I did not have many friends, save one: a boy I grew up with, who became my best friend. I have come back to surprise him, to see him again, but I would prefer to take my time. To do it my own way. I have traveled the world for many centuries, young Braden, and I doubt that I've been missed. My role in the house of Jadon was never that...important."

Braden furrowed his brow.

Damn, that was kind of messed up.

He was just about to argue—surely no one would've treated this guy like an outcast, even if he was extremely weird—but then, the guy was pretty old. Who knew how the Vampyr behaved in 1100 AD or even earlier? Certainly not Braden. And besides, he totally got the absent parents thing. Been there. Done that. Still wore the T-shirt. "Ah man," he said. "That's too bad, 'cause it's really a cool place, even if you don't have your parents."

The guy focused on the comment like an eagle homing in on its prey. "Forgive me, but it sounds as if you might have a personal acquaintance with the subject of missing parents. Am I...wrong?"

Braden stiffened, growing instantly alert. If he hadn't known better, he would've sworn the vampire had read his mind or, more accurately, his history. But that wasn't possible because Braden never thought about it. Braden never talked about it. Braden never mentioned to anyone, not even Nachari, that while his parents called him once a week and sent frequent gifts and letters, he often felt like he'd been abandoned. He had never told a single soul that his biological father used to abuse his mother before she filed for divorce, and Braden looked an awful lot like his human father. Maybe too much like his human father. He had never told a single soul what his mother had said, that one night, when she was drunk...

Perhaps it was just his imagination, but Dario and Lily had

given in so easily when Braden had asked to remain in Dark Moon Vale. Sure, the Academy was better than homeschooling, and as a wizard, Nachari could teach him things Dario could never explore—but to Braden's way of thinking, his parents had Conrad now; Braden had a brother he hardly knew; and if they had really wanted him with them, they would have objected to such a long stay.

They would have come to visit.

Pitching his shoulders back in a proud, defiant stance, Braden raised his chin, angled his jaw, and succinctly changed the subject. He wasn't about to *go there* with a stranger. "So, who's your friend?" he asked, his tone making the shift in subject deliberate. "Maybe I know him."

Grigori met Braden's gaze with a pensive stare of his own, openly assessing the boy's reluctance, and then, just like that, his countenance softened, he became generously amenable, and he smiled. *Subject change acknowledged.* "Excuse me?" he asked in an affable tone.

"Your friend," Braden repeated. "You said you had a friend here, a *best friend*, a male you grew up with."

Grigori's eyes flitted to the side, waxing suddenly nostalgic. "Ah yes, my dear friend. His name is...or at least it was...Julien Lacusta."

Braden sucked in a harsh breath of air. "The tracker?"

Grigori narrowed his gaze on Braden and slowly nodded his head, his lips turning up in a mischievous grin. "Ah, is that what he's become?"

Braden nodded in kind. "Hell yeah, and he's just about the best damn tracker the house of Jadon has ever seen. That, and a Master Warrior. In fact, he just had a Blood Moon, like no less than twenty-four hours ago, so now he's got a *destiny.*"

Grigori smiled and threw up both hands. "Well, there you go. Of course, I saw the sky—don't we all? And that is what prompted me to finally come home and visit." He leaned forward and practically whispered his next, drawn-out words. "But I really do hope to surprise him, Braden. I think it would mean the world to…the tracker." He practically gleamed with inner satisfaction. "In fact, now that I know what he does, I think it would be fun to play a little game. Perhaps I can leave little traces of my essence here and there—you know, my psychic fingerprint, my individual vibration, my unique, distinctive calling card—and see if Julien picks it up."

Braden frowned. "I guess, but I think he's going to be pretty busy for the next twenty-eight days, if you know what I mean?"

Grigori's eyes lit up with mirth. "Indeed. I know exactly what you mean. All the more reason not to bother him right away."

Braden nodded, and the silence grew heavy. No question about it: The guy was weird. *Really weird.* Still, that wasn't exactly a crime. "So, where are you going to stay? I mean, while you're here?" He gestured in the direction of River Rock Road. "I've got a car. I can take you to the lodge or maybe a hotel."

"I think I'd like to reacquaint myself with nature for a time, to rediscover the land. But thank you for the offer."

Braden flashed a dismissive smirk as if to say, *suit yourself.* He started to ask Grigori for his cell number—maybe he could text him sometime—but then he thought, nah; dude probably had a tin can attached to the end of a string, or an old-fashioned telegraph machine: *tap-tap, tap-tap-tap-tap.* He chuckled inwardly, feeling guilty for mocking the peculiar vampire, even if the guy was unnaturally strange.

"What were you doing?" Grigori asked, making Braden feel instantly guilty. He pointed toward the flat, rocky ledge, at the polished, drying stones, and Braden sighed with relief.

"Oh, that?" Braden turned around to face the stones, grateful for the temporary distraction. "I was just playin' around with some energy, trying to turn water into wine, you know, that sort of thing."

"You were trying to make gemstones?" Grigori asked.

Now this got Braden's attention. "Yeah. How'd you know?"

Grigori cocked one shoulder to his ear in a facetious gesture and smirked. "What kind?"

Braden stared harder at the stones and frowned, knowing he probably didn't stand a snowball's chance in hell of getting the metamorphosis right. "Citrines," he answered sheepishly.

"Citrines?" Grigori repeated. "Hmm." He glided over to the stones, squatted down in front of the rocky ledge, and placed both hands, palms down, over the rocks. "Ah, you've done well, thus far. The stones feel pliant—you've already focused some energy."

Braden raised both brows and took a step closer toward the ledge. "You think?"

"Oh, yes," Grigori insisted. He bent closer to the stones. "Do you mind?"

Braden shook his head emphatically. "Hell no—I mean, heck no." Even though Nachari wasn't there, Braden was still slightly paranoid: Who knew what a wizard could hear. Hell—*heck*—Nachari might've crafted some curse-word spell just to catch him slipping or something.

Grigori chuckled once again and picked up both stones.

He placed them in the center of his left palm and rotated the fingers of his right hand over them in a repetitive circular motion. And then he closed his eyes, and heat began to radiate from his open palm. As he continued to caress the stones, almost like a dutiful lover, the pads of his fingers curled inward and energy shot from their tips. At last, he closed his fist over the stones, exhaled as if he'd been holding his breath, and then slowly reopened his palm. "Is the color to your liking?"

Braden glanced at the two perfect citrines resting in the vampire's hand, and gasped. "No way!" he exclaimed. "You did that that easily?"

Grigori smiled and bowed his head infinitesimally. "As I've said, I've been on this earth a very long time, and precious jewels have always been a quick and efficient means of procuring income."

Braden nodded, entirely impressed.

Eager to study the gemstones more closely, he reached out to take them from Grigori's palm, and immediately drew back from the contact. In fact, Braden jerked his hand away so hard and so fast that the beautiful citrines went flying through the air and back into the river—all that hard work was lost. "Oh, man...*dude*...I'm sorry!" Braden clamored.

Grigori stood up and took a generous step back, studying the vampire closely.

Too closely.

Braden flashed a repentant smile and pressed the subject further. "Oh, man, that was so jacked up. I really am sorry. And after everything you just did? My bad! Seriously. I am so, *so* sorry." He wasn't about to say what he was really thinking: *What the heck just happened?*

Grigori's expression relaxed, and he held up both hands in dismissal. "What is it the young people say? It's all good. No harm; no foul."

Braden nodded, grateful for Grigori's understanding. Truly, he had not meant to overreact or to offend the seriously strange vampire. It was just...it was just that there was something so wrong with those stones. The energy.

It was so foreign, so remote...

Braden could hardly make it out.

It wasn't exactly evil, and it wasn't exactly good.

For lack of a better word, it was obscure: hidden, concealed...

And consequently, terrifying.

This guy had a lot of secrets, and he had built a lot of barriers to conceal them, and all those layers were embedded in those stones.

All that hidden...*angst.*

Looking down at the ground, Braden noticed a stray strand of blond hair settled on a rock—the guy must have shed it when he bent to make the citrines—and he made a mental note to pick it up and take it home before he left. He didn't know exactly why, just that all that glittered wasn't gold. All that was citrine wasn't brilliant. And something about this male was not as it appeared.

BLOOD ECSTASY

He had given Grigori his word that he would keep his presence in the valley a secret—well, he had at least implied that he would—and he would allow the mysterious vampire to take his time, make his presence known in his own way, at his own pace, out of mutual respect for the house of Jadon. After all, a vampire's word was his bond, and it wasn't Braden's place to judge another male.

Just the same, that didn't mean he was going to dismiss his common sense. That he would ignore a creepy vibe, or overlook his intuition. He had done that once before, and it had almost cost Kristina her life.

No.

Never again.

Braden would play it off, hang out for a while longer, and then he would head back to the brownstone, and to Nachari Silivasi, a Master Wizard, with a single strand of blond hair in his pocket: a token object that the wizard could easily divine…unravel and dissect…

If necessary.

ten

Three days later

Trevor Rainier double-checked the address on his smartphone as he stared at the gorgeous urban building in front of him: 1590 Wynkoop, in lower downtown Denver, also known affectionately as LoDo. Yep, he had the right address, and didn't that just speak volumes about Rebecca's VOSU support group? The fact that it was held in the upscale Mercantile Square Lofts, in the private home of some upwardly mobile, metropolitan bimbo who didn't know how to keep—or please—her man?

He chuckled inwardly, retrieving the keycard he had lifted from Rebecca's nightstand drawer in order to get past the secured entry, and made his way to the fancy elevator, all the while, reaching down, deep, for courage. Assuming Rebecca had found another way to gain access to the building—and surely, she could just call upstairs—he was going to walk right into the center of the meeting, stare Rebecca in the eyes, and ask her if she'd missed him.

He couldn't wait to see her expression.

And if anyone made a move he didn't like, said something he didn't want to hear, like *I'm calling 911*, then the six-inch hunting knife tucked into his socks would probably do the trick.

Shut them up real quick.

For whatever reason, Rebecca had not been home since Sunday night, and God help the woman if she was sleeping with another man. But if he knew *his* Rebecca—and he did—then she would never miss something as important as a VOSU meeting, especially when she was the de facto leader.

Stepping out of the elevator onto the third floor, he quickly made his way down the long, narrow hall to the last loft on the right. Thank his lucky stars, the door was propped open. Raising his chin and drawing back his shoulders, he marched right through the entrance, headed toward the professionally decorated living room in the center of the loft, and sauntered to the middle of the group, causing all the women in the circle to crane their necks and gasp.

His cocky grin quickly morphed into a blank, vacant stare, and then it curved into an angry scowl.

Where the hell was Rebecca?

There were five women sitting around the room, staring at him like he had pigeon poop on his face, and not a single one of them had curly golden hair or gorgeous topaz eyes.

"Can I help you?" A tall, skinny blonde stood up, her restless hands betraying her anxiety.

Trevor took an abrupt deep breath and flipped his demeanor on a dime. Grateful that he had worn a Colorado Rockies baseball cap, put on his reading glasses, and dyed his hair black several weeks ago—*who knew if these chicks exchanged photos of their estranged lovers*—he held up both hands in a submissive posture. "Uh, yeah," he muttered shyly, trying to sound as nonthreatening as he could. "You must be...Sheila?" He already knew the answer. Her name was written in Rebecca's address book, next to the loft's address, and Becca, in all her wisdom, had a small black-and-white picture to the right of every entry.

The blonde nodded warily. "I am. How can I help you?" The entire room looked stunned.

Trevor plastered an ingratiating smile on his face and started to glance around the room, pretending to be too nervous to meet anyone's incredulous gaze. "Um, Rebecca Johnston gave me this address, and this visitor's pass." He held up the plastic card. "By the looks on your faces, I take it you don't get a lot of male...victims...in your group." He tried to sound meek, if not outright afraid.

Sheila furrowed her brow.

Okay, so Rebecca would not have sprung a new member on the group like that. Oh well. Too late. Trevor would just have to go with it until his long-lost love showed up, and then, the jig would be up anyway. "Would you like me to leave?" He sounded utterly dejected.

Sheila held up a hand—she was clearly uncertain—and exchanged wary glances with the other skeptical women in the room. "Rebecca sent you?"

Trevor nodded. "Yeah. *Yeah.*" He spoke the second affirmation with a lot more confidence.

"Have you spoken to her recently? Talked to her, directly?" a short brunette chimed in from the middle seat on the sofa. "We got a couple messages, but that was it." She spoke with an obvious lisp, and her mouth didn't open like it should, almost like a part of her jaw was wired shut. Damn, that had to suck.

"Uh," Trevor thought fast on his feet, "um, nah; it's been awhile. It's probably been a few weeks since I met her at the VOSU headquarters. She tried to convince me to come to the weekly meetings, but I was afraid...well..." He swept his arm around the room, indicating the assembly of women and their stunned, unwelcoming expressions. "I was kind of afraid of this." He lowered his head and averted his eyes. "Of having to admit that I can't break free of my ex-wife, that I'm actually afraid of a woman. Scared for my life, really." He bit his bottom lip and took several steps backward, turning to walk away. "You know, this was a bad idea. Sorry if I caught you guys off guard or scared someone." He pointed to the open door and began to walk away. "I'll just go."

A few seconds passed...and then: "Wait. What's your name?" A chick with short, spikey hair, dyed hot pink.

Trevor turned back around. "Uh, Jacob. Jacob Rogers, but my friends call me Jake."

"Well, if Rebecca sent you, then you're welcome. I'm Kate, by the way," Pinky said.

Trevor flashed an awkward smile. "Hi, Kate."

And then, one by one, the pathetic women began introducing themselves, offering *Jake* a seat on the sofa, pointing out the salads, brownies, and beverages on the counter.

Well, wasn't this just special.

Trevor helped himself to an extra-large helping of Asian salad, three delectable brownies, and a full glass of white wine before making his way to the couch and addressing the waiting women. "So, my story kind of goes like this..."

eleven

Rebecca was still, more or less, living in a fog.

She was still grappling with the extraordinary facts she had learned about the Vampyr; she was still processing all the details about the Curse, including the inevitability that she would have to be converted to another species in order for a pregnancy to work; and she was still trying to quell her overwhelming fear of Julien Lacusta, despite the fact that they had shared a tender moment.

One tender moment.

Over the past three days, Julien had given Rebecca a wide berth, such as it were, allowing her to wander about the large rustic home at will; leaving her alone to sit, think, read, or watch TV in the high-tech theater room, whatever it took to decompress; and encouraging her to purchase anything she needed—food, clothing, or toiletries via online vendors—in order to make her *stay* more comfortable. He had slept in the guest room, across the hall from the master bedroom, and he had generally kept a polite distance, with the exception of making himself available to hear her thoughts, answer her questions, and address her concerns as often as she wanted.

She didn't want...

She didn't want to be there.

She didn't want any of this to be real.

And she didn't want Julien Lacusta.

But she did want what the vampire had promised: to free all the unfortunate women in her VOSU support group from their tormentors. And she figured she could stick around long enough to see that through.

Now, as she stood in the far corner of the vampire's great room, trying to shuffle out of the way as a late-night delivery crew lugged a heavy, distressed-leather sofa into the center of the room, she couldn't help but wonder: Had she completely gone insane? Was any of this *really* happening? Was she truly the *destiny* of an immortal vampire?

Honestly…

How had any of this come about?

For all intents and purposes, Rebecca Johnston was sequestered inside a rustic mountain home, hiding away in Dark Moon Vale—as if her previous life and obligations were of zero consequence—and she had very little to *any* control over her immediate circumstances. And, as if *that* was not enough, she had actually gone along with the bizarre, nerve-wracking program by scrolling through an online furniture catalogue, choosing a half-dozen large-ticket items for a house she didn't own, and following through by scheduling a preposterous late-night delivery.

Hell, according to Julien, he had just gotten rid of a similar lot of furniture, a few weeks back, and the last thing Rebecca wanted to do was encourage him, overly accommodate or ingratiate him, make it look like she planned on hanging around once they had each fulfilled their end of the high-stakes bargain.

Yes, Julien would free the VOSU women from their tormenters, and in turn, Rebecca would free the terrifying vampire from the Curse of his kind, but after that, all bets were off. Rebecca planned on taking the baby and finding a place of her own.

Granted, Julien would probably object.

At the least, he would probably insist that she remain in Dark Moon Vale so he had daily access to the baby; but Rebecca could work with that. Did she really have a choice? Just so long as she could rebuild her life, return to some semblance of normalcy, and get back to the familiar, daily routine she craved—living and working on her own—she could adjust.

She would have to adjust.

There was nothing else she could do.

After all, she had no intentions of living in a secluded mountain retreat with a powerful, brooding vampire who had an affinity for heroin.

"Excuse me, ma'am…" A short, muscular, twenty-something guy, with a broad nose and a tightly shaved head, interrupted her thoughts. "Where do you want the sofa?"

Rebecca sighed.

What was done was done, and truth be told, she could not endure one more day, sitting on the floor, standing in the corner, or perching on the edge of the moss-rock fireplace, while Julien lounged in his oversized chair and stared at her, incessantly, with those moonstone eyes. And the opposite was equally alarming: Whenever Rebecca took the chair, Julien hovered in the corner. Hell, he practically stalked the rafters, loomed in the shadows, or perched on the hearth, haunting the entire great room like a six-foot-four, vampiric ghost.

No thank you.

The furniture was sorely needed.

Rebecca pointed to her left, toward an empty space beneath several high wooden beams, and tried to sound like she belonged there. "Why don't you place it right there, with the left arm of the sofa facing the right arm of the chair, kind of perpendicular."

The husky mover grunted beneath the weight of the sofa, and then he took an obvious, albeit inadvertent, second glance at Rebecca, sweeping his gaze over her face and her body with blatant appreciation.

Julien stirred in his chair.

He shifted his weight from side to side like a lazy jungle cat about to rise from its slumber, and leaned forward. A barely audible growl rose in his throat. It wasn't all that loud, and it wasn't particularly drawn out; but then, it didn't have to be, to prove effective.

The sound was equal parts savage and commanding.

The furniture guy lost his grip on the couch, stumbled

forward to catch it, and let out a grunt of pain as the massive end of the sofa slammed against his thighs. He quickly averted his eyes. "Right here?" he asked, ignoring the trickle of sweat that was dripping into his eyes.

"Two inches to the left," Julien growled.

Rebecca held her breath.

What was the vampire doing now?

The delivery man was clearly about to drop the couch, and Julien was baiting him, almost as if he wanted to see him fail. *But for what purpose?* So he could fly from the chair, bite him in the neck, and proceed to drink his blood, right in front of his coworkers?

Right in front of Rebecca?

Oh, *hell no*, Rebecca did *not* want to witness some bestial show of dominance, right there in Julien's great room. Seeing what he had done to that blond woman, the night of the Blood Moon, had been enough bestiality to last Rebecca a lifetime.

All at once, Julien shot her a harsh, sidelong glance, almost as if to say, *watch your P's and Q's*, and then, just as quickly, he looked away.

Rebecca pulled up short.

What the hell was that?

She hadn't done anything to encourage the mover, and it wasn't like she was waiting for an opportune moment to make a run for it. Still, she thought, wetting her lips, if she had entertained even a passing thought about signaling the movers for help, trying to scribble a note on the back of a receipt, or whispering "call 911" in a stranger's ear, the look on Julien's face had just squashed it.

The lazy lion would probably eat the movers, and then he would turn his king-of-the-jungle attentions on her.

Rebecca was not an idiot.

She nodded, a brusque incline of her head, and took a cautious step back, pointing at the oblong coffee table, crafted from the trunk of a large aged tree. "Could you put that in the center of the room when you're done with the sofa? Just set it evenly, kind of between the chairs and the couch." She twiddled her fingers together in a childlike, nervous gesture.

A second mover nodded his head. "Sure thing." His voice was a bit too ingratiating, and Julien slowly raised his hand, pointed it in Rebecca's general direction, and gently crooked his fingers.

What the hell…now?

Did he want her to sit on his lap?

She shook her head *no*, and the tip of his sculpted nose twitched, ever so slightly, even as his lazy hand stiffened.

Rebecca gulped: *I'm fine where I am.* She spoke the words in her mind, knowing full well that he could hear her, clearly. In fact, from everything he had told her, he could glimpse her thoughts—or take them from her mind—any time he chose, although the practice was highly frowned upon in the house of Jadon: something to do with invading free will. And while she could *not* hear him, telepathically, at least not unless they were physically touching or until she was converted, he could intercept her telepathic messages now. It had something to do with the fact that he had taken her blood, although none of it made a lot of sense.

Julien cleared his deep, raspy throat, having heard her every word. "*Tu îmi aparţii mie şoarec mic. Vino.*" He drawled the words in old-world Romanian, and Rebecca's mouth nearly dropped open.

She knew exactly what that meant.

You belong to me, little mouse. Come.

Over the past three days, he had used the phrase quite often, like some medieval term of endearment. The joke, according to him, was based on the fact that she was like a busy little mouse, always scurrying around, trying to find a way to escape. And, of course, there was the comment she had made about the mouse trap, when he had offered her crackers and cheese. Somehow, the term had stuck.

As for the reference to belonging to him?

That she couldn't account for.

Just the same, she knew in her soul that if she defied him now—*and in front of the human movers?*—he would likely get out of the chair, stalk across the room, and toss her over his shoulders, carrying her back like a conquest. Julien wouldn't hesitate to shock the human laborers and erase their memories, later.

Had she just said humans?

Rebecca swallowed the lump in her throat, wiped her sweaty palms along the front of the faded blue jeans she had ordered from a next-day delivery catalogue, and made her way across the room slowly, trying to appear nonchalant. She sat on the arm of the chair, purposefully foregoing Julien's lap, and his large powerful palm immediately found its way to the small of her back.

"Thank you, *iubito.*"

Baby.

She struggled not to shudder.

Rather, she turned her attention back to the movers and watched as they unpacked the last of the furniture, began to collect their empty boxes, and searched the floor for a missing clipboard—more than likely, they were looking for the final bill.

Despite the commotion and the odd situation, Rebecca's mind began to wander. She couldn't help but wonder what her support group was doing now: The women would be gathering in Sheila's comfortable loft, sharing stories about the passing week, and offering encouragement to one another in an effort to allay any lingering fears. And Rebecca would not be there to participate. She would not be there to lead her own meeting. It was all happening without her.

Rebecca's heart sank in her chest.

Over the last several days, Julien had strongly encouraged her to call home—okay, so that was captive-speak for the male had aggressively insisted that Rebecca leave a message on the VOSU answering machine, explaining her curious absence and the fact that she would not be attending the next three or four meetings. He had *strongly suggested* that she relay some story about staying in Dark Moon Vale for an indeterminate amount of time, explaining that the valley had been so peaceful, so beautiful—it had felt so incredibly safe—that Rebecca had decided to extend her visit for as long as she could pull it off, financially.

Yeah, right.

Because that wasn't completely out of character.

Just the same, Julien had somehow embedded a soft, unspoken compulsion in the messages—whatever that actually meant—and he had assured her that her friends would not question her honesty or her sincerity.

And then he had *gently encouraged* her to leave the same message with all her friends and family.

And just like that…

Rebecca's absence had been explained.

None would be the wiser, and no one would come looking…

A tall, skinny mover with a horrible case of acne finally found the clipboard beneath a pile of Styrofoam, picked it up, and flipped through the anchored pages. Coming to the last page, he took a step in Julien's direction, eyed the menacing vampire suspiciously, and stopped dead in his tracks. He bent over and set the invoice on the end table instead, taking a generous step back in the interest of self-preservation. "Ah-hem," he cleared his throat. "That'll be three thousand eighty-nine dollars." His eyes darted anxiously around the room, fixing on everything *but* Julien.

Julien reached into his pocket, retrieved a time-worn wallet, and thumbed through the leather, extracting a platinum credit card. He flicked it onto the end table—apparently, he didn't have any interest in approaching the human, either—and waited while the nervous laborer ran the card through his portable machine.

The guy held out the final printed receipt, along with a pen. "If you would just sign, right here, on the dotted line—" He stopped abruptly and slid the pen back into the top of the clipboard. "Um, never mind. We're good."

Julien shrugged his shoulders and waited in silence as the

men gathered the remaining trash and began to head for the door, and Rebecca's heart sank in her chest: Even though she knew she could not call out for help, the moment was still alarming…unsettling. Once again, a potential rescuer—a potential group of rescuers—was walking out the door and leaving her behind.

"Hold up," Julien called, making his way into the foyer behind them. He reached into his wallet, retrieved a hundred-dollar bill, and placed it in the tall, skinny mover's trembling hand. "Thank you," he said gruffly, watching as they scampered out the door.

Rebecca sighed in both frustration and appreciation.

Well, at least the savage had a few good manners.

And at least he hadn't slaughtered the delivery crew.

A half hour later, in the master bedroom, Julien took a brazen step forward, pressed his rock-hard chest against Rebecca's back, and glanced over her shoulder in order to gaze into the overstuffed duffle bag. "I don't think anything else is going to fit in there," he said, teasing. "You really know how to shop." He lowered his angular jaw until his warm breath wafted along the lobe of her ear, and then he nuzzled his chin in her hair. "Do I need to fetch a second suitcase, little mouse?"

Rebecca stiffened and leaned forward toward the bed, forward toward the duffle bag. "I can't breathe when you're that close. What are you doing?"

Julien chuckled, a rich, deep sound. "We can stop by your apartment when we get to Denver, pick up the rest of your personal things, those items you can't replace."

Rebecca held her breath.

Okay.

That sounded just fine, but why was he pressing up against her like that, whispering in her ear like they had been lovers for many years? "Would you mind backing up?" she squeaked.

He smiled.

She knew because she *felt* his lips curve along her neck.

"I would," he drawled. "Mind, that is."

She anchored both palms against the bed in an effort to keep from bending over any further. It was one thing to lean forward, out of his way. It was another to offer him her backside, like a prostitute. She cringed. "Julien, we're not—"

He pressed a kiss against the back of her neck, just below her hairline. "Not what?"

"Not that."

He chuckled again. "And what is *that?*" Before she could answer, he slid a huge, splayed hand over her waist, then down, to her lower stomach, and pulled her back against him.

She gasped in surprise and alarm.

"Your heart is racing, Rebecca."

She snorted. "You're scaring the shit out of me."

His voice vibrated in her ear. "Mm. And that is why your palms are sweating, your knees are growing weak, and your scent is changing in response to my touch?"

She placed both palms over his wrist to keep his hand from straying in any...untoward direction. "Julien..."

"*Tu îmi aparţi mie şoarec mic.*" He repeated the infuriating phrase—*you belong to me, little mouse.* "Say it."

Rebecca clenched her teeth together and nearly snarled, "I will *not* say that. Not in English or Romanian."

He growled into the crook of her shoulder—well, maybe he actually purred. "You will, Rebecca. I promise you. Before this moon is over, you will." He bent over, leaning so deeply into her that she curved toward the bed, despite her fervent desire not to, and then he reached around her, deftly zipped the duffle with one sure hand, and hefted it from the bed. "Come, little mouse. We have a long drive to Denver, and I have some...tracking and hunting to do for my angel."

Rebecca sucked in a generous breath of air.

The man was insane.

No, the *vampire* was completely off his rocker.

He was an arrogant, *terrifying*, domineering beast who spoke out of turn, took far too many liberties, and retreated from life into the world of heroin. Who the heck did he think he was?

As she turned to follow him out of the master bedroom, her knees gave out beneath her, and she almost hit the deck.

Julien caught her in an instant and tugged her back onto her feet. "Careful, little mouse."

Holy hell.

Who was Rebecca kidding?

He was the most powerful, exquisitely beautiful, unequivocally masculine creature she had ever seen, and she could barely breathe in his mind-numbing presence. She had made a deal with the devil, and she hated him for that. Yet, *heaven help her*, some primitive, unconscious fragment at her core was beginning to respond to him like metal to a magnet, constantly reacting to his presence.

She didn't want him, *did she?*

Surely she couldn't...she wouldn't...she didn't.

Oh hell, she had eyes, didn't she?

And she did have a pulse, at least last she'd checked.

And he was...

Magnificent.

Still, on every conscious, rational, cognitive level she feared him more than she had ever feared Trevor. Rebecca stopped walking. She shut her eyes, took a deep, cleansing breath, and simply tried to regroup, while he waited.

The situation was crazy.

Of course her emotions were all over the map, but she would sort it out in time.

She had to.

For now, she would go with the vampire to Denver; she would introduce him to the women in her VOSU group; and she would let him do what he was born to do, what he was infamous for doing in the house of Jadon: hunting unsuspecting prey. She would give him all the files, let him read the backstories, and ply him with information; and then she would let him track, like the predator he was. She owed it to the women. She owed it to herself. She owed it to a world that had been absent of justice for far too long.

And the rest would come to fruition in time.

After all, a deal was a deal, as supernatural, crazy, and impossible as it was. And Rebecca had given her word.

She opened her eyes and followed him to the bedroom door, her legs finding a newfound strength. "I'm right behind you, tracker."

twelve

Achilles Zahora was a giant of a vampire, a seven-foot savage with a bronze complexion, citrine-colored eyes, and a wicked tattoo of a black mamba wrapped around his upper right bicep: the band of the formal Colony Guard. They called him the executioner, and he was a force to be reckoned with: That was really all there was to it.

And as for the Dark Ones' Colony?

Holy lords of darkness!

Ian was beyond impressed.

The circular, underground fortress was built in three solid layers: The basement contained surveillance equipment, generators, and a massive electric grid—it functioned as the nerve center of the settlement, and it was an incredible sight to behold. The main level was the central hub of nightly life, containing one hundred hallways, each divided into four sections of twenty-five, consisting of a northern, eastern, western, and southern quadrant. And each quadrant housed 275 units, clusters of vampires arranged by family and occupational ties. Each individual unit housed eleven residential lairs—five on both sides of the hall, and one focal lair at the apex—with a sufficient amount of storage built into the opposite end.

In addition to the Dark Ones' private residences, their clusters of individual lairs, the main floor also contained a courthouse, a torture chamber, and a council hall. There were breeding and birthing rooms for human, female captives, and the infamous snake pit as well: a cavity of carnal pain and pleasure, affectionately referred to as the Chamber of Cobras.

BLOOD ECSTASY

On the top tier of the colony, the third and final floor, there was everything a community of vampires could have dreamed of: a congregational hall, which served as an auditorium; a library, sports facilities, and a teaching facility, which was used for formal education; and several small cryptic chambers, erected for the purpose of practicing black magic. And all of it, every impressive underground floor, was built in a stacked, circular design, accessed from the four primal directions by a pulley-system of elevators and surrounded by a single unobstructed outer hall, which made traversing any part of the colony both efficient and easy.

Now, as Ian Lacusta sank deep into the bluish water of a hot sulfuric pool situated toward the back of Achilles Zahora's private limestone lair, he appraised a nearby column of stalagmites and sighed.

"So I take it you are enjoying the accommodations?" Achilles asked, his gruff, boorish voice sounding like it was amplified through gravel.

Ian took another deep, calming breath, reveling in the thick, pungent scent of the dank, sulfuric air, and eyed his new host warily. "I am still having trouble believing that *this* is how the Dark Ones live," he said, with appreciation.

Achilles chuckled, and the evil sound ricocheted off the granite walls. "The Dark Ones?" he echoed. "You mean the house of Jaegar, *your people*, as it were."

Ian shrugged. He needed to tread carefully. After all, this brute of a vampire could probably crush Ian's skull with one flick of his wrist, so he chose his words precisely. "As you know, I was neither born to the house of Jaegar, nor the house of Jadon. I was a cursed one, the dark twin to a brother of light, meant only to be sacrificed. I cannot say that I have a...*people*."

"Are you not a Dark One?" Achilles snarled.

Ian smiled. "Indeed, I am that."

"Then that is all that matters," Achilles said. "And frankly, if you bring that bullshit up one more time, that ignorant-ass crap about the circumstances of your birth, I'll drag your ass to the sacrificial stone myself and see to it that the Blood gets what it wanted. We clear?"

Ian held his breath, growing instantly quiet. After a pregnant moment had passed, he whispered, "Crystal," and then he sank deeper into the pool, careful to avert his eyes. "And if I choose to stay here…a bit longer," Ian ventured, cautiously, "where would I be housed? And what would the house of Jaegar—what would *my house*—ask of me in return?"

Achilles shifted his position in the water, resting both massive arms behind him against the granite ledge, and the subtle movement sent a wave of water sloshing out of the organic tub. "In terms of staying a bit longer: Where the hell else would you go? Back to your yacht in Greece? Brother, that makes no damn sense. Nah, you need to relocate, vampire. And we already have a room for you: Saber's old lair. Believe me, it's poetic, ironic, and perfectly fitting."

Ian nodded, remembering the sordid tale Achilles had shared about the child stolen from the house of Jadon and raised among the Dark Ones, the one who was now a valley sentinel and working closely with Ian's twin. "I see. And as for what you would desire in return?"

Achilles snorted. "Pledge your fealty to the house of Jaegar; become the low vamp on the totem pole in a familial hunting pack; and swear your allegiance to the Dark Ones' council. That is all we would ask of you." He shrugged a gigantic shoulder and cocked his head to the side. "Well, that, and maybe one other thing."

Ian practically held his breath. "And what would that be?"

Achilles' fangs began to lengthen as if the very thought of the final condition inspired feral longings in his blood. "The boy, the one you met near River Rock Road."

"Ah yes," Ian said, "Braden Bratianu."

Achilles nicked his tongue on a fang and sucked on the subsequent blood. "Meet with him again—and kill him."

Ian sat up straighter, turned his head to regard Achilles squarely, and raised his brows. "The child? The one trying to create gemstones for a silly female?"

Achilles frowned. "You got a problem with killing, brother?"

Ian flicked his wrist in irritation. "Of course not. I have a problem with making my presence in this valley known to anyone else in the house of Jadon. I have a problem with inciting an enemy whom I have avoided for centuries without knowing the reason why. I don't do things indiscriminately, Achilles. Will that be a problem for you?" He could hardly believe he had dared to go there, but there it was. Ian Lacusta was nobody's lackey, and he wasn't a natural-born fool.

Achilles seemed utterly unfazed by Ian's objection or his rebellious words. "We don't suffer fools in the house of Jaegar, Ian, so that's a good thing in my opinion."

"You read my thoughts?" Ian could hardly believe his ears.

Achilles sat upright and leaned forward then, his deep citrine eyes glowing crimson red. "Do you think I would bring you into this colony, share our history, our laws, and show you our lairs without scouring every neuron in your reclusive mind first?" He bit back a savage snarl. "Do you think you would be sitting here in my private residence if I hadn't already determined that I can trust you? I am a formal soldier of the Colony's guard, Mr. Lacusta. I would rip your head from your shoulders with my bare hands if I thought you posed the house of Jaegar any kind of threat, however small or insignificant." He leaned back and began to relax. "But as it is, I have seen your intentions, as well as your thoughts. You desire only to destroy your brother and to remain alive…and unseen…to be free to hunt, to rape, and to live as you please. You can do all of that in the house of Jaegar; and frankly, now that you've been here, you no longer have a choice. If you would like your thoughts to be respected, then show *this house* some respect. What *we* ask of *you* is a simple matter: Destroy the child for the council. Salvatore Nistor has his reasons, and that's all you need to know." He leveled a lazy, sidelong glance at Ian and whispered, "What say you, *brother?*"

Ian gulped, and then he shrugged.

Checkmate.

He had not seen that ultimatum coming.

Ah well, there were far worse places he could be, and the way he saw it, if he joined with the house of Jaegar, then their enemies became his.

And his became theirs.

"I will butcher the fatted calf, as it were, and we will feast on the boy's remains." He winked conspiratorially. "The prodigal son has returned."

thirteen

Denver

It was just shy of midnight when Julien and Rebecca approached the door to Rebecca's small apartment, and the hair stood up on the back of Julien's neck. "Angel," he whispered brusquely, "get behind me."

Rebecca blinked several times, betraying her confusion. "Why? I—"

"Don't question me, baby girl," Julien interrupted. "Not when it comes to this, not when it comes to hunting an enemy. If you want my protection—and you will always have it—don't question me when we're away from the safety of Dark Moon Vale." He furrowed his brow. "Not even then."

Rebecca rolled her eyes and took a generous step back.

"Give me your keys," he prompted.

Rebecca handed her Minions key chain to Julien, seeming grateful that he hadn't decided to break down the door, and swiftly sidestepped behind him. Glimpsing the ridges on the stems of her keys, then peering inside the locks, he slipped the largest key into the top lock, a second key into the middle set, and the smallest key into a third opening, and turned each one, clockwise, in succession, pushing the heavy panel open. One sniff told him all he needed to know. "Just as I suspected: Someone has been here as recently as Sunday or Monday." He stepped boldly into the front room. "I can smell him…everywhere. And the evidence he left behind is vulgar."

Rebecca gulped, and he immediately glimpsed her thoughts.

It was simply more efficient than conversation, and Julien made no apologies when it came to his *destiny's* safety: *Someone's been in here?* she pondered. *As recently as Sunday or Monday? That's not possible. And what does he mean—the evidence is vulgar?*

Julien hoped he wouldn't have to explain the latter.

In a matter of seconds, he scanned the dark room, using his errorless, infrared vision as well as his heightened sense of smell: There was shattered glass near the back patio door, the obvious point of entry, where someone had broken in. There were larger fragments of stoneware on the kitchen floor—someone had broken her dishes. And there was an incredibly foul odor coming from her master bedroom—someone had pleasured himself on her bed. He knew it was her master bedroom because he could also smell her scent, her shower gel, the faint hint of vanilla-spiced perfume, and a light dusting of her sweat, mixed with sheets: cotton, polyester, and fabric softener. He was a meticulous tracker, and his mind could identify, organize, and analyze a space in the time it took most vampires to retrieve their weapons.

Julien reached out his left hand, entreating Rebecca to take it. "I require a sensory impression from your mind," he said bluntly. "Forgive me, but I need you to think about the last time you saw Trevor, your stalker; simply picture him in your mind." When she opened her mouth to object, he pushed harder. "Rebecca, if you don't assist me in this, I will simply have to dig deeper to sort through a maze of possible memories. By retrieving the memory I need, yourself, we will save a lot of time."

Rebecca's shoulders stiffened, but she didn't shy away from the task. Her amazing topaz eyes glazed over with a hint of fear, or trepidation, and in that moment, she looked so incredibly vulnerable that Julien wanted to reach out and run his fingers through her hair, place both of his hands on her narrow shoulders, brush the underside of her jaw with a kiss.

He couldn't help it...

But he did moderate it.

Rather than press his lips to her flawless skin, he brushed the pads of his fingers over her softly rounded jaw and caressed her cheek with his hand "*Șoarec micuț*, you are safe in my keeping. You know this, right?"

Rebecca tilted her head away from the intimacy of his touch, but she nodded.

"I require only three seconds." He placed either hand on each side of her head, cupping her ears in his palms, and then he waited for her to retrieve the memory.

The Arizona desert.

Some sort of botanical garden and a rock-band concert.

A human male standing behind a tall, arid tree, waiting for Rebecca to walk past it. Her heart was thundering in her chest as she rounded the corner and saw him standing there, glowering at her with malice—

Julien cut off the memory abruptly.

That wouldn't be helpful.

Not right now.

He needed to keep his wits. Stay focused on the apartment. Remain in the here and now.

"Got it," he whispered.

He pulled every sensory detail he would need from Rebecca's mind in the space of a heartbeat: Trevor's eye color and the style of his hair; his height and his build; the sound of his voice and the pattern of his speech; the smell of his skin and the feel of his energy, even his body language.

His aura.

His countenance.

And his psychic stamp—the energetic imprint of his chaotic thoughts.

Julien stepped away and tried to conceal his fangs, waiting for the canines to retreat. *That son of a bitch*, he thought. *Trevor* had masturbated on Rebecca's bed, and he had done it quite recently, probably on Sunday, the day Julien had met her. Despite his Herculean attempt at control, a feral snarl escaped his throat. He would stuff that maggot's entrails down his sick, perverted throat and watch as he choked on his own intestines.

"Julien?" Rebecca's voice cut through the growing red haze.

"He has been in your apartment, my love." He took her by the hand and led her to the back patio doors. "Watch the glass." He pointed at the scattered shards beneath their feet, just inches away from the latch. "Look at the trajectory of the scattered pieces: He broke in with his fist, and he probably used a glove. There are no traces of blood on the floor." Julien shuddered inside at the thought of what would have happened if Rebecca had been there. The brute strength and *rage* it required to punch through that door...

The human was clearly insane.

He sniffed the air once more and nodded, and then he led her through the kitchen, toward the refrigerator, and pointed at the shards, beneath the kitchen counter. "He had some sort of hissy fit and started breaking dishes." And then he slowly guided her, although he hated to do it, down the narrow hall to the master bedroom. Choosing the correct door, unerringly, he paused to modulate his voice. "He's been sleeping in your room, rolling around in your bed."

Rebecca bit down on her lower lip and grimaced. "Oh...shit." She tried to force an insincere smile, to appear as if she wasn't that rattled, but Julien saw right through it.

"Becca—"

"No," she cut him off. "It's okay." She shrugged, feigning indifference, and paced around the room, checking the placement of various objects. "I knew he would find me sooner or later."

"Becca."

She hugged her arms to her chest and squeezed her sides, and then she barked a hollow laugh. "Who would've thought...you, taking me...might have saved my life." A single tear welled up in her eye, and Julien crossed the room in two long strides.

"*Becca.*" He reached out to take her hand, but she flicked it away.

"No. *No!*" Her voice grew hoarse as she lost her control. "Damn it!" she blurted. "How? *Why?*" She threw both arms up in the air in frustration and gestured angrily as she spoke. "I did everything right. I did everything I knew how! I have spent the last five years of my life trying to avoid…exactly this…running from this…this monster, this idiot, this foul, disgusting trash. What more could I have done?"

Julien cursed beneath his breath in the old language, and he was just about to reach for her again when Rebecca saw the stains on her comforter.

She gagged, and her knees grew faint beneath her.

He caught her by the elbow and propped her back up. "Hey, now, baby; don't start going to all the wrong places in your mind. You weren't here; that's all that matters."

She pointed angrily at the bedspread and practically snarled. "Look at that! Look what he did!"

Julien tugged her beneath his strong, broad chest and whispered softly in her ear. "Sh. Sh. C'mon, now. You're lookin' at this glass as half empty, when I'm seeing it as damn near full."

Rebecca sniffled into his shoulder and drew back to appraise his eyes. "How in the world could this glass be half full?"

He shrugged. "The way I look at it, baby, you *did* do everything right. You kept yourself safe for the last five years, and that's no small accomplishment. And yeah, so he finally found you, but the way I see it—you zigged when he zagged. You weren't here when he broke in." He reached down to cup her chin in his hand and tilted her jaw upward so she had to maintain their gaze. "And then"—she tried to glance away, and he tightened his grip on her chin—"*and then*, the gods brought you to me. So the way I look at it, you handled it as long as you had to. And now? Now I'm about to handle it for you. *Now*, the nightmare is over."

She shut her eyes, took a calming breath, and then opened them again, glancing askance at the comforter.

Julien sidestepped to block her view. "Baby, it's just a piece of cloth with a little stuffing in it. You can buy as many comforters as you want, angel. Don't go there." He lowered his voice. "Hear me? Don't do that to yourself."

Rebecca nodded slowly.

She took several steps away from the bed and focused her gaze on the floor. And that's when Julien noticed the sparks in her topaz eyes, that her dominant emotion wasn't fear at all—it was fury.

As if she had heard his thoughts, she gritted her teeth and murmured, "I almost wish I *had* been here." She curled her hand into a fist, unwittingly. "I wish I would've heard him break the glass in time to get my Glock and empty the whole damn clip into his sick, pathetic little head."

Julien whistled low beneath his breath. "Ah...ah'ight." He chuckled. "Well, I can still make that possible if you need the closure. String him up in the woods behind the house in Dark Moon Vale and let you use him for target practice. Your call, little mouse."

Rebecca stared at him like he was an alien, and then she sighed. "No. *No.* I could never really do that, kill another person in cold blood. I would never be able to live with it. To live with myself."

Julien nodded, understanding. "Well, if you change your mind before I end this, just let me know."

Rebecca appraised him critically, seeming to replay his words in her mind, as her eyes swept over his features, his chest, and then his arms. It was like she was taking his measure for the very first time and only now beginning to truly see him for what he was, at least partly: a warrior, a possessive vampire, and a potential ally who was planning to wipe the floor with the bastard who had recently defiled her room. Someone more than capable of doing it.

She cleared her throat, as if testing her voice for metal. "The Curse," she muttered, completely out of the blue. "You said that none of it works, none of it will work, unless I'm converted, first."

Julien cocked a curious eyebrow and waited for her to

continue.

She wrung her hands together and then abruptly stopped fidgeting, forcing herself to settle down, to project more bravery than she actually felt. "I don't want to be this vulnerable, Julien. Not another day. Not another hour. Not when Trevor is still out there. Not—"

"Baby, I've got this. I've got *you*."

Her lips tightened; she angled her jaw; and she shook her head in disgust. "No. That's just it. *You've* got this, when I need to have it."

Julien tilted his head to the side. "What are you saying, Rebecca?"

She looked away abruptly, and her lips began to quiver. It was almost as if she had extracted her last ounce of courage, and she wasn't sure if she could muster any more. "Tomorrow." The word was a mere whisper on her tongue. "We are going to meet with the women from my VOSU group, tomorrow, and then you...you are going to clean this nightmare up, right?"

Julien could hardly believe what he was hearing.

Finally, a modicum of trust.

"Absolutely," he said.

"Well, you can't be in two places at once, and it only takes a second... If you have to turn your back on me, if only for a minute—"

"*Whoa.* Squash that thought," Julien cut in. "First and foremost, I'm not going to turn my back on you, Rebecca. And second, you're not gonna be beside me when I handle this business." He decided to share a little more than he had intended: "Look, I figured I'd call Saxson, bring him in on the gig: just to fill in the gaps...cover all bases."

Rebecca nodded. "I get that, but you don't understand, Julien: I can't stand to live like this anymore, to be this afraid, to be this vulnerable, to be this...violated." She looked so lost. "Convert me," she blurted. "Tonight."

The room grew silent, and if someone had dropped a pin, it would've reverberated like a bomb. "Come again?" he said.

Rebecca looked suddenly faint. "I don't think I can say it twice. I'm terrified. But this Curse—there's no way around it, right? And a bargain is a bargain." Before he could answer, she creased her brows and pressed on. "I don't want to be this vulnerable, and it's going to happen anyway. *Convert me.*" She more or less mouthed the last words as opposed to speaking them aloud.

Julien retreated into silence, taking a moment to contemplate her request. He nodded, to indicate that he had heard her, and then he continued to consider her petition, seriously. In all truth, he was stunned by her various layers: the complexity of her thoughts, the ever-changing nuances he saw in her eyes, and the depth of her conflicting emotions. One minute, she wanted to run; the next, she wanted to fight. One moment, she felt like a trapped, cornered animal; the next, she was ready to bite. One second, she was terrified; the next, she was brave.

And all of it was wrapped up in such confusion, such paradoxical hesitation, such raw, unmitigated determination— she was an enigma to be sure.

"Listen, angel," he said, measuring each word carefully and basing his response on where he truly believed she was, in her heart. "I've heard you. *I have.* And I understand where you're coming from. And if you still feel the same way in a couple of days, then I *will* convert you, no questions asked. But you need to hear me out."

Rebecca's features tightened, like she was bracing herself for disappointment—or maybe, *relief.*

Wow, what a paradox...

"Conversion is no walk in the park, angel. It may take hours. It may take a day. And either way, it's going to take *everything* out of you...and out of me. If you change now, tonight, your body changes, your physiology changes—you will hear differently, you will see differently, you will feel everything in a different way. The entire world is going to come at you, at once, in high definition. That's a lot to play off in front of your friends, and that's only half the story. You will crave blood. You will feel off-balance, if only for a while, until you get used to the change. I don't think you wanna do that now. Not here. Not the night before we set out to finish what we started. I think it will make you feel *less* stable, not more. And as for you and me? We still need a little time."

What he didn't tell her was what he'd seen in her eyes.

What he'd read in her soul.

Rebecca Johnston was a very similar creature to Julien Lacusta. She built up walls, barriers, and armor to shut out all the noise. Like Julien, she could deal with the present when she had to—she could even step boldly into the future—but she couldn't run, far enough or fast enough, away from the past.

When Julien was tracking, time stood still, and the noise turned off.

There were no dimensions, no reason, no sentient thought: just a predator and his prey.

When Rebecca was fighting, defending other women, or championing a cause, she went to the same tranquil place: There was nothing else, no one else, just the victims and their plight.

Rebecca's advocacy was predatory, and all the stalkers in the world were her prey.

But—*and wasn't that really the crux of the issue*—it wasn't a healthy fight.

As long as Rebecca had someone to save, she didn't have to feel her pain.

Hell, her rage.

As long as she was fighting back—*somehow, some way, striking back*—she didn't have to look too closely at the ghosts that truly haunted her life: the guilt she still harbored over her choice to date Trevor, remorse over the years she had lost, a deep-seated belief that she was responsible for her own victimization and, somehow, faulty by proxy, alone in the world. Like Julien, she was convinced that nothing—and no one—would ever change that fact.

Nothing and no one ever could.

And, frankly, she preferred it that way.

Because *that way* was safe.

Julien Lacusta knew that Rebecca was not capable of letting him in, of ever opening her heart—*at least not now, not like this*—and if he converted her tonight, she would only be one step closer to her goal of fulfilling their bargain; she would simply possess one more layer of armor to bury her heart within; and she would have one more excuse to do it all herself, to stand on her own two feet, at the expense of their future and their intimacy.

Julien grew ominously quiet and padded away, silently pacing the room.

Well, hell.

Wasn't he just the pot calling the kettle black?

He was the exact same creature, just for very different reasons. Julien wasn't an idiot—he knew damn well that he was haunted by a host of ever-present demons: guilt, rage, hatred, and maybe even...shame.

But there was one critical difference.

Julien's damage ran so deep that it terrified him.

It wasn't just a matter of not looking at it, not feeling it, turning down the noise. It was a matter of surviving, one day at a time.

A matter of life and death.

If Julien ever touched those shadows, if he ever felt that rage, if he ever let that hatred rise to the surface, the earth would split open beneath his feet, the rivers would overflow in violent floods, the heavens themselves would rain down ice, fire, and blood.

And Julien—*oh yes, he knew*—he could not turn it off.

Dozens of humans would die.

What lived inside of Julien was a natural disaster waiting to happen: a destructive volcano waiting to erupt. And while heroin might not have been the stable man's choice, he was a vampire, a preternatural being, an immortal descendant of celestial gods. Neither his body nor his mind could be permanently corrupted—vampires couldn't have physical addictions—and it was a helluva better choice than letting all that lava fly…releasing it on the earth.

Julien brushed a tense, curled hand through his tapered mahogany hair and sighed. So why was he trying to bring Rebecca into a relationship that he, himself, could hardly sustain? He honestly had no idea. "C'mon, little mouse," he said, in an abrupt change of subject. "We are going to clean up the apartment—*I will clean this room*—and then we're going to pack your things for Dark Moon Vale and get the apartment ready for your guests, tomorrow. You still need to make a couple calls, at least leave a few new messages."

Rebecca stiffened, and Julien knew he had thrown up a wall, made a final pronouncement with regard to her question…to her request for conversion. But to her credit, she didn't push the subject. More than likely, his little mouse was grateful for another reprieve, another *out*, a cleverly placed escape route.

"Fine," she finally mumbled, and then in an abrupt show of defiance, tempered with subtle obedience, she turned on her heel, spat on the mattress, and strolled through the bedroom door. "Burn that shit," she snarled, glancing over her shoulder.

Julien drew back in surprise.

"Considera ca si făcut."
Consider it done.

Trevor Rainier tossed and turned restlessly on the stiff hotel mattress. The room was nothing more than a hovel, a cheap, dirty, mismatched cubicle, one hundred yards from Colfax, in an extremely shady district, and the very air he was breathing made his skin crawl.

He had contemplated going back to Rebecca's apartment, but he wasn't willing to take a chance at getting caught, being discovered a bit too soon. Not when he could bide his time and ultimately terrorize her senseless, as well as threaten her friends. Not when he wanted to be the one to say where, when, and how.

Trevor Rainier desired the ultimate in orgasmic revenge, to prove a point in grand, shocking fashion, that Rebecca Johnston wasn't so high and mighty, after all.

She wasn't the world's protector.

Hell, she couldn't even protect herself.

And in the end, she would be the one to expose and jeopardize the VOSU women. She would be the one who was proven to be a coward.

He chuckled low, beneath his breath, imagining a dozen different scenarios: *Oh yes*, Rebecca might put up a fight—she would surely try to act defiant and brave—but none of it would matter.

Not one iota.

One way or another, Trevor would have his revenge, and Rebecca would leave Denver *with him*. Everything that happened in the meantime was just foreplay, leading up to the ultimate release: their permanent and inevitable coupling.

He checked the glowing light on the rickety, digital clock buzzing on the hotel nightstand like its internal parts were whistling a low-budget tune: It was one o'clock in the morning, and he still couldn't sleep. Sighing, he opened his smartphone and scrolled to his photo album, where he kept several hundred pictures of Rebecca—and him—many of them spliced together in Photoshop.

He was just about to start the familiar litany, scrolling through the photos, one by one, when he noticed a small red-and-white number next to his green phone-icon. *Hmm, wonder who called?* He tapped the icon, selected *voice mail*, and scrolled to the most recent message. He didn't recognize the number, but that didn't really matter—it wasn't like he had a host of friends in Colorado, and no one knew what he was up to. He swiped his thumb over the digits and pressed the phone to his ear.

"Hi, Jake; it's Kate, from the VOSU support group. Sorry to call so late at night, but I just wanted to let you know that I got a message from Rebecca. She's back in town for a couple of days, and she wants to get all the members together at her apartment, tomorrow. She said it's really urgent. Anyhow, I didn't know if she left you a message, your being so new to the group and all, but I figured if she invited you to Sheila's, she would probably want you in the loop. Anyhow, the address is 556 Sycamore Lane, and we're hooking up at six. Hope you'll be there. Oh, yeah, and remember: *To escape fear, you have to go through it, not around it.* Talk to you later. Bye."

Trevor set the phone down on the nightstand and folded his arms behind his head, sinking deep into the pillow and laughing, almost hysterically.

Oh, this was truly rich.

Could it get any more perfect than this?

He shut his eyes and practically meditated on the ripeness of the moment.

Oh, yes, Katie dear, I will be there with bells on.

And we will have the get-together of a lifetime!

fourteen

Dark Moon Vale

Ian Lacusta sank deep into the mist, spreading his molecules even farther apart, as he approached the secluded brownstone on the northern end of Dark Moon Vale, just beneath a formidable series of forest cliffs. The gorgeous brick-faced domicile was built in the tradition of a 1920s Park Avenue brownstone, and it had to be close to five thousand square feet, with its four impressive levels, rooftop patio, and opulent series of front and back terraces.

So Nachari Silivasi enjoyed his creature comforts.

Bully for him.

Ian thought about the quaint, simplistic card he had tucked into the lapel of his duster, and hoped that he had calculated everything correctly: It was one thing to dissolve his physical form and travel like a Vampyr of legend, streaming through the forest as mystic fog; it was another to incorporate an envelope with a written missive—ah yes, a written *message*—into the mix. Best-case scenario, the ink would be runny when he took his corporeal form. Worst-case scenario: the card would be unreadable, the envelope would have already dissolved, and his entire effort would be for naught.

He hovered above the old-fashioned mailbox and concentrated intensely on extending a single hand from the fog—if he didn't have to materialize completely, that was just fine with him. Nachari Silivasi had some wickedly dangerous wards surrounding this house, and from everything Achilles had told Ian, he was a wizard of some notable talent. Ian had no doubt that the son of Jadon would pick up on his presence—and pronto—if he hovered around too long.

Extending a ghostly hand toward the singular red flag, he turned it upright and poured all his concentration into retrieving the letter.

Ah, and there it was.

A single white envelope, with a time-worn stamp, addressed to Braden Bratianu and made to look like it had gone through the human postal system, like it had come from Hawaii, like it was simply a familial letter from his not-so-adoring family, nothing suspicious to detect. Ian chuckled inwardly; the Dark Ones were nothing if they were not intelligent and resourceful— they had extremely detailed files on all of their enemies, all of the sons of Jadon, and he wondered if the bastards knew just how closely their enemy watched them.

Placing the letter inside the black conical box, Ian swiftly backed away. He rose upward into the sky, scattered the fog in many, diverse directions, and succinctly withdrew from the wizard's residence.

Done and done.

The boy would get the message and meet him by the creek—or he wouldn't.

At least Ian had done his part.

Spiraling next, several miles north, Ian felt a feral growl rumble in his disembodied chest: After so many centuries in hiding, this was just way too close for comfort. His eyes took in the expansive valley below, and he snarled.

Julien's rustic retreat.

He felt for the presence of his brother—*of his twin*—and sighed with relief when the tracker wasn't there. Hmm, so where had Julien gone so late at night? And only six days after heralding his Blood Moon.

It didn't really matter.

In fact, for all intents and purposes, this worked out much, much better.

The strength of the wards surrounding the long, winding driveway and the front porch were daunting to say the least, but Ian possessed something no other visitor could possibly possess: Julien's shared DNA. The preternatural security system would recognize Ian's imprint as Julien's, at least to a lesser extent, and it would allow him to approach the front door.

Ian landed on the stoop with a whoosh, gathering his molecules together in lightning-quick succession, and then reaching for a leather bag. Thank the dark lords, the bundle had transported intact—he wondered just how many vampires could wield such magic, such skill, such well-honed expertise. Stroking the bundled letters lovingly, he rubbed them over his heart, hoping to impart his individual energy...*in droves.*

To my brother, on our eleventh birthday: Hope you have a sun-shiny day!

What the hell did that even mean?

Happy Twelfth Birthday to my best friend and brother: Let's make today a great one!

Humans were so simple-minded and trite.

You're eighteen now—let's party!!!

Now that one made Ian laugh.

Of course, he had stopped at age twenty-one: There was simply nowhere he could go to find birthday cards for ages 101-967, and frankly, it would become rather redundant at that point. In fact, it might lose its nefarious effect.

No, Ian thought as he smiled, *providing a set of birthday cards from ages eleven through twenty-one is absolutely perfect*, especially considering how he had signed the last one: *I know our birthdays are still three months out, but I couldn't wait until April 12th to make up for so much lost time. How fondly I remember the last birthday we shared together. How deeply I desire to see you again. Soon, my beloved brother. I shall have to see you...soon. Love, Ian.*

Wrapping the bundle in a delicate, silken bow—a bow his mother, Harietta, used to wear in her hair—he placed it in the doorway and slinked into the night.

BLOOD ECSTASY

Nachari Silivasi stirred restlessly in his sleep, almost as if he were slumbering once again in hell, captured and being tortured in the depraved abyss. He came awake with a start, and to his utter surprise, he was already in panther form.

What the hell?

He swiftly shape-shifted back into his vampiric body and turned to check on Deanna. She was sleeping soundly beside him, her long, dark-brown hair fanned out against the sleek satin pillow-slip like a glorious halo, her beautiful, exotic features peaceful in repose.

He slinked noiselessly from the bed, and then he grabbed a robe and padded down the narrow series of halls, checking Sebastian's room first, then Braden's room next.

Nothing seemed amiss.

Yet and still, there was a thick, inky darkness hovering over the brownstone like a looming storm cloud, and his stomach turned over in waves. He made his way up the multi-level staircase and emerged onto the rooftop terrace, glancing upward at the sky. "What's up, Lord Perseus," he whispered, absently beseeching his reigning celestial god. *Why do I feel like the devil himself has just passed through my home?*

There was no answer from the darkness, no rejoinder from the sky, and Nachari splayed his fingers wide as he held his palms, outstretched, at each of his sides. He sent all five senses seeking outward, probing for energy, for errant vibrations, and then, before he could rein them in and analyze what he was sensing, a deep, sonorous voice invaded his mind.

What is it, son? Keitaro Silivasi sounded wholly alert and awake—he rarely slept at night.

I don't know, Father, Nachari answered immediately. *Something woke me from my sleep.*

Something? Keitaro repeated. *Like what?*

Nachari glanced at the tree line; he surveyed the jagged cliffs;

he paced around the terrace and peeked down, beyond the railing, toward the familiar mountain road. *I do not know*, he repeated. *I honestly don't.* And then he saw the upraised red flag on the mailbox and stiffened. The bulk of the dissonant energy he was sensing was concentrated around that flag. *Huh*, he muttered beneath his breath to Keitaro, *someone has been here—quite recently.*

Keitaro's psychic voice perked up. *Someone? Who?*

Nachari shrugged. *Isn't that just the million-dollar question?* He felt Keitaro stir and immediately sought to reassure him. *Father, let me check it out. I'll call you if I need you.*

Keitaro's energy snaked through the telepathic line like a bolt of sizzling heat, and the connection went silent for the space of five heartbeats. *Are your Lycan wards active?*

They are, Nachari answered.

And your human wards are set?

Always, Nachari replied.

And there are how many layers of protection around the brownstone?

Enough to stop a T-rex, Nachari joked, halfheartedly. *Father, please, give me a moment. Oh, and please don't call my brothers. Not yet.*

Keitaro chuckled then, his psychic voice growing softer, more pleasant. *Well, then you'd better check your emotions, my son. Because if Marquis gets wind of that vibration, he'll be on your doorstep faster than you can say Ancient Master...brother.*

True, Nachari quipped. *Very well, I will let you know what I find.*

Good enough, Keitaro replied, and then he modulated his voice. *I love you, son.*

Nachari grew quiet and inhaled sharply.

As often as Keitaro said those words—and he said them almost every time the two of them talked—it still brought the wizard up short: Ever since the male had returned from his captivity in Mhier, ever since his sons had ventured into that perilous, forgotten dimension to rescue him, he had been bound and determined to set the record straight, to provide each of his sons with all the paternal affection they had been missing for centuries. Nachari, in particular, had become very insecure from the prolonged separation, from believing that his father had been dead for 480 years: Unlike Marquis, or even Nathaniel and Kagen, Nachari and Shelby had only shared twenty-one years with the male before the Lycans took him, and Nachari had worried, more than a little, that he might be a stranger with his very own dad.

Keitaro had known that instinctively.

And he had gone out of his way to bridge that gap, to get to know his youngest, living son, to make sure Nachari felt his presence as strongly as possible.

The funny thing was this: Nachari no longer felt insecure.

In fact, Nachari could not have been more certain about his father's love, or the male's commitment to rebuilding their relationship—Keitaro had rebuilt it in spades. Still, Nachari smiled. It was so incredibly endearing to hear it spoken so brazenly, repeated so frequently, and meant so sincerely. And it always catapulted him back to a five-year-old kid.

Love you, too, Dad, he answered, without further hesitation. *Be well, Ancient Master Warrior.*

Be well, Master Wizard, Keitaro replied, and then he closed the connection.

Nachari strolled to the edge of the terrace and balanced atop the patio wall. In one lithe motion, he shifted into the form of his panther, bounded from the veranda, and prowled toward the mailbox.

He intended to scent this out.

fifteen

Friday, in Denver ~ 6:00 PM

As Julien waited in the back master bedroom, Rebecca cleared her throat. "Thank you for coming on such short notice," she said to the room, eyeing each woman in turn: Kate Beckman, Nancy Thomas, Sheila Harris, Patricia Sykes, and Teresa Gonzales—they had all made it, and they had all arrived on time. "I really appreciate your flexibility."

Sheila sat forward on Rebecca's comfortable, two-toned sofa, and placed her glass of raspberry lemonade on a coffee-table coaster. "We thought you were in Dark Moon Vale for the duration. What's this about?"

Kate leaned back in a matching upholstered armchair and nodded, clutching a rust-colored throw pillow to her chest.

The other women all looked eager to hear the news.

Rebecca gathered her courage and tried to choose her words carefully. After all, she couldn't tell them the truth: *There's a six-foot-four vampire waiting in my bedroom, and he needs to read your memories and your thoughts, in addition to viewing our files, so he can get down to business and pretty much wipe the city with the asses of our stalkers.* Uh, no, that wasn't going to work. "I, um…I met someone in Dark Moon Vale who is…very sympathetic to our cause and extremely talented in PI work." Her eyes darted nervously around the room, an obvious sign that she was fibbing, and she had to force herself to look straight ahead. "In fact, he has a proven track record of making long-term domestic problems actually go away."

BLOOD ECSTASY

Patricia cleared her throat, and her gorgeous ebony eyes flashed with cautious interest. She held up an elegant, coffee-colored hand and pursed her full, perfectly shaped lips, looking exquisitely beautiful as always. Patricia was a kick-butt software engineer who had made the innocent mistake of dating an NFL linebacker, *once*. The famous football player could not take *no* for an answer; he believed he was above the law; and the justice system treated him as if he had a season pass to get away with violence. Thus, Patricia had been terrorized for the last two years. "Um, I think you need to be a little more specific. What do you mean by *go away*? Girl, did you meet some mafia hitman from the casino? I'm not liking the sound of this, Rebecca."

A nervous laughter filled the room, yet the women gave her a chance to continue.

Rebecca smiled ingratiatingly. "No, Pat, nothing like that." *Far, far more dangerous than that*, she thought. "What I mean by *go away* is that he has a quantifiable, proven track record. If you look at past cases that he's worked on"—*oh lord, she was really laying it on thick now, and these women were far too smart to buy this pitiful load of bull*—"the number of complaints, assaults, and violent encounters simply go away after he's made contact with the stalkers."

"Humph," Patricia snorted, leaning forward in her chair.

"In fact," Rebecca continued, pretending she hadn't heard the harrumph, "in every single case he's taken on, there was no longer a need for a restraining order, no longer a need for hiding, changing your identity, any of it—the women were able to resume their normal lives."

Okay, that just sounded ridiculous.

Even to Rebecca.

Maybe Julien had been right: He needed to soften the women's defenses and manipulate their minds in order to make this work.

Sheila cocked her eyebrows and pushed her lemonade further back on the coffee table, as if she was suddenly concerned she would tip it over. "So what you're trying to say is that this dude, *someone you just met in the mountains*, can accomplish what the police, the justice system, and a dozen years of living a carefully controlled, defensive life cannot? That he can just somehow persuade these sick, diabolical bastards to stop doing the one thing they'd rather die than let go of?"

"And he can do it without putting a bullet through their brains?" Kate asked.

Rebecca's body tensed. *Oh hell, this wasn't going as planned.* She contemplated her answer mindfully, weighing the various gradations of *truth* as a concept: Technically, Julien *could* do it without putting a bullet through their brains, so... "Yes," she said emphatically, and then she sighed and cocked her head. "Look, the deal is this: He can do it. We don't get to ask how or why. But—"

"And just what is this going to cost?" Nancy asked.

"Girl, did you hire a hitman?" This time, Patricia stood up.

"Ay-yi-yi, Rebecca!" Teresa chimed in, making the sign of the cross in the air. "What did you do, *mija?*"

A deep, placid, unearthly drone began to penetrate the air as Julien Lacusta strolled down the narrow hallway, emerged in the living room, and stood at the focal point of the meeting. "Look into my eyes, ladies."

Despite the fact that it seemed like a ridiculous command— *who did he think he was, a snake charmer?*—humans were, obviously, innately curious and extremely susceptible to direct suggestion. Every single woman instinctively glanced at his eyes, and then, there was a collective, terrified gasp throughout the room.

His eyes were glowing blood-red, and his pupils had restricted into narrow, vertical slits, much like a cat's. "Now then," he drawled, in an eerily compelling voice. "I am Julien Lacusta, and I am going to make your nightmares go away...once and for all. And you are going to let me, without question or objection. Rebecca has just explained *everything* in such sufficient detail that you no longer have any concerns. You will come to me, one by one, in an orderly fashion, and offer me your hands. And then, you will take your seats and resume your meeting, forgetting that we ever had this conversation."

The room grew quiet for the space of several heartbeats, and then the women simply sank back into their chairs, smoothed their skirts, slacks, and blouses, and smiled sweetly, waiting to meet Julien and offer the PI their hands.

Rebecca turned her nose up in disgust. "Whatever," she murmured.

"Ah," he teased. "Don't be salty, little mouse."

She rolled her eyes and moved from the center of the room to his side, so she could watch him more closely. Fine, he had been right. *That time.* But she wasn't going to give him carte blanche control over the group and her friends, not that easily. From what he had told her, mind control was a tricky thing; although the way he had explained it, what he had to do was more like *fishing...*

As a gifted tracker, Julien Lacusta's mind was a whole lot like a database, at least according to him. It contained multiple files, which stored information, and he could sift through and separate each file by category in the space of mere seconds; and once the information had been stored, he could retrieve what he needed at will: histories, sensory details, memories, and the like. The larger the file on each given subject, the faster he could track the prey. In other words, the hand-touching was a means to an end. Each woman would be uploading her database into Julien's mind, and from there, he could use her knowledge, her memories, and her emotions to home in on her fears: the man who haunted her dreams.

Still, Rebecca wanted to make sure that he didn't take too much.

She wanted to make sure he was both gentle and kind.

After all, the gladiator wasn't exactly known for his tact or his subtlety, at least not since Rebecca had known him.

Patricia rose from the couch and sauntered across the room, heading straight for Julien, and despite the fact that her pupils registered an inordinate amount of fear—she was clearly aware that she was in the presence of a predator—Rebecca reluctantly stepped out of her path and let her proceed. "Pat, this is Julien. Julien, this is Pat," she said dryly, making the cursory introductions. The least she could do was behave like they were civilized, like she wasn't feeding her friends to a lion.

Julien leaned back against the wall like the lazy, languid jungle cat Rebecca had just envisioned. He folded his arms in front of his chest and extended one hand to grasp Patricia's in a touch so gentle, so innately seductive that it gave Rebecca pause.

And just what the heck was that?

Jealousy?

Rebecca grimaced. *No. Heck no!*

She quickly dismissed the thought.

"Nice to meet you, Patricia." His voice was like a silken sheath, encasing Patricia's concerns like fingers in an elegant, bewitching glove, practically wrapping her up in velvet.

Was all that really necessary?

He gazed into Patricia's eyes, and the woman nearly fainted.

Humph, Rebecca thought, watching as his pupils widened.

Then, just like that, he was done.

He released Patricia's hand; she blinked three times; and then she strolled back to the couch.

Bring the next one on.

Trevor Rainier checked the time on his Rolex.

Damnit, he was forty-five minutes late.

Ah well, that just meant he would make a grand, unforgettable entrance.

He sauntered confidently to Rebecca's front door and then paused to collect his thoughts. He had waited a lifetime for this moment—at least it felt like it had been a lifetime—and he wanted to play it out just right. But more than that, he wanted Rebecca...

Back in his influence.

Back in his arms.

Back in his life, for good.

He knocked briskly on the door, three times, before reaching for the knob. It opened without resistance, and he ambled into the room.

The women recognized him at once and began to greet him with pleasant salutations, but he refused to give them a passing glance, let alone a reply. His eyes scanned the space in a millisecond, probing with military clarity, searching for just one face, scouring for only one woman...

Rebecca Louise Johnston.

And there she was.

Dear God.

His heart skipped a beat in his chest.

She was breathtaking—*his Rebecca*—and for a moment, he almost forgot why he had come. He almost forgot his anger and his vengeance. He almost forgot his rage. Hell, he almost forgot his own name. There was only her and those mysterious topaz eyes; her wavy brown locks; and that gorgeous, slender body. His lips parted to breathe her name with reverence, but he was brought up short by a bestial growl.

What the hell?

Had Rebecca recently purchased a dog?

Trevor's eyes immediately shifted from Rebecca's pale, stricken expression to the face of a very large man—*no, a giant*—standing far too close to Trevor's woman and leaning possessively beside her. The guy was a walking slayer with bizarre gray eyes and the most unnaturally-colored hair Trevor had ever seen; and despite the fact that Trevor was a card-carrying heterosexual, he couldn't help but notice the absolute perfection of the man's incomparable features.

And it instantly chapped his hide.

Hell, the guy was not just good-looking: He was beyond a cover model of a magazine, or a professional athlete, in his prime. He had the body of a mercenary, the stealth of a tiger, and the face of an ancient Greek god, like something only an artist could create.

And Rebecca was now clinging to his arm.

Something inside of Trevor snapped. "Hey, baby!" he crooned in a lude, lascivious tone. "Miss me, lover?"

Rebecca gasped in alarm, and that made Trevor smile.

The VOSU women were quickly putting two-plus-two together, as well, and that suited Trevor just fine. They'd be easier to control if they knew who he really was, and that he hadn't come to swap pitiful stories about victimization. "Oh," he drawled by way of explanation, and for the benefit of everyone in the room, "your friends know me as Jake—I was at last Thursday's meeting. But, of course, you know me for who I really am: your fiancé. Did you get the gift I left for you? On your bed?"

The muscle-bound individual jerked like he had just been struck by lightning, and his eyes registered something so murderous in their depths that Trevor took an involuntary step back. The giant shoved Rebecca behind him and cocked his head to the side like some predatory animal, flashing his teeth in warning.

His teeth?

Seriously?

Trevor did not wait around to see what the crazy bastard was going to do next.

He reached into the inner lining of his jacket, withdrew a loaded Colt .45 revolver, and extended his right arm to the side, pressing the barrel of the gun, taut, against Nancy Thomas' temple. "I think you might wanna chill out, asshole!" he barked. "First and foremost, that's my girl you're standing in front of. Second, and more important, I won't hesitate to light up this entire room, kill every slut in the house. And last, but not least, I don't like your ass—not one bit—so you might be the first to go." He puffed out his chest, turned up his lip, and spat on Rebecca's floor, feeling more powerful than he had ever felt before. And then he slowly pulled back the hammer for effect.

"Rebecca, get your ass over here. *Now!*"

sixteen

Julien Lacusta had just sent the last of the five VOSU women, not including Rebecca, back to their seats, having *uploaded* all the memories and sensory information he needed to track their stalkers, when he heard three brusque knocks on Rebecca's front door. He turned his head in the direction of the sound and watched as the handle began to rotate. And then, just like that, a human male of medium height strolled brazenly into the room.

His hair was dyed black and covered with a baseball cap.

His expensive glasses barely concealed crazed, desperate eyes, and his pulse was racing far too fast for the situation, though he was trying to control his breathing.

None of it mattered.

Not at all.

Julien recognized the human's vile scent in an instant.

He felt his noxious vibration.

So, Trevor Rainier had an iron set of balls, and he thought he could stroll right into Rebecca's living room and...and do what?

A feral grow escaped Julien's throat, and Trevor met his seeking gaze, silently appraising the vampire from head to toe. Whatever he saw must have ticked the human off because he immediately turned his attention to Rebecca and sneered. "Hey, baby! Miss me, lover?"

Rebecca gasped in terror, clung to Julien's arm, and the vampire's entire body tensed.

Trevor smiled and belatedly regarded the group as a whole, through the guise of speaking to Rebecca. "Oh, by the way"—he paused for effect—"your friends know me as Jake. I was at last Thursday's meeting, but of course you know me for who I really am: your fiancé. Did you get the gift I left for you? On your bed?"

Julien felt his chest and shoulders jerk with a fury he could hardly contain.

Such was his need to kill the arrogant cretin where he stood.

Right here.

Right now.

He shoved Rebecca behind him, restrained the growing impulse, and surveyed the room instead: The women were in shock, their human minds trying to process the new information in an instant, trying to register the fool's deception, even as the idiot took a cautious step back.

Yes, Julien thought, *prepare to run, little rabbit. I am going to devour your entrails for supper.* Despite his desire to remain calm, Julien tilted his ear toward his shoulder and flashed his fangs in warning.

This seemed to get the rabbit moving, but rather than turn tail and run, like any halfway intelligent being would do, the jackass reached into the inner-lining of his jacket, withdrew an old Colt .45 revolver with a polished pearl handgrip, and pressed the barrel of the gun against Nancy's temple.

Nancy's.

A woman who had already suffered two broken arms at the hands of a stalker.

Julien felt the air rush out of his body, but before he could determine his next, lethal move, Trevor stared him down and narrowed his eyes in menace.

Was the son of a jackal insane?

Just how desperately did he want to embrace a hideous and painful death in a public forum?

"I think you might wanna chill out, asshole," Trevor snarled. "First and foremost, that's my girl you're standing in front of. Second, and more important, I won't hesitate to light up this entire room, kill every slut in this house. And last, but not least, I don't like your ass—not one bit—so you might be the first to go." He swelled up with some seriously misplaced confidence, cocked the hammer on the gun, and barked a command at Julien's *destiny*. "Rebecca, get your ass over here. *Now!*"

Julien didn't know whether to laugh, howl, or set the entire apartment ablaze with his eyes, scorching the fool—and his pitiful revolver—to ash in the process. He felt Rebecca stir behind him, and her emotions swept over him like a wave: She felt both trapped and responsible for the situation, pressured to go to Trevor and ameliorate the situation. He immediately snatched her by the arm. "Don't. You. Dare." He turned his full attention on Trevor, regarded the silly revolver, and smiled. "You're gonna shoot that woman, Trevor? In front of me?" He tsk-tsked with his tongue, running it along the dual sharp points of his descending fangs, even as he allowed his eyes to glow red and his lips to curl back in a snarl. "Oh, I really don't think so."

He pointed at the gun and crooked his finger; and just like that, the barrel changed directions and angled toward the floor. "First and foremost, Rebecca is *mine*, and you are a walking corpse. Second, and more important, you just pissed off a *vampire*—I don't think this is going to go as you planned. And last, but not least, I don't like your ass either, and that's putting the sentiment mildly. So you *will be* the first to die." He hissed, loud and drawn out, like a man-sized snake issuing a feral warning. "Now then, *you* get your ass over here. *Now!*"

Trevor wrinkled his brow in confusion and alarm.

His palms grew instantly moist, and he dropped the gun at his feet as his knees began to tremble.

That's right, little rabbit, reality is finally sinking in, Julien thought.

Despite the abject terror seizing Trevor's body, he began to shuffle forward toward the vampire, like a puppet on a marionette's strings, and that's when Rebecca jumped between the two males, her back facing Trevor, and pressed both palms firmly against Julien's chest. "Please," she voiced with urgency. "Julien, *please*. I'm begging you. Not here. Not now. Not like this."

Julien spared her a dismissive glance and frowned: *Did she have any idea what she was asking?* The enormous self-control he was already exercising in that moment? How absolutely deep and primal his rage now went? It was taking everything he had not to paint the walls in Trevor's blood, outline the portrait with strips of his peeled-back skin, and punctuate the canvass with the jackass's innards.

He glanced down at his *destiny* and shook his head. "Step away, Rebecca."

Her hand stiffened against his chest. "No. Look at me, Julien. Please. Look at me."

He stared at her with incredulity, even as Trevor continued to pace forward, trembling and weeping like a dolt.

"Not in front of the women, tracker. They've seen too much horror as it is."

He shrugged with indifference. "I will wipe their memories...later."

At that cryptic statement, and before Rebecca could respond, Patricia seemed to finally come on board with the whole macabre scene: Her dark, ebony eyes instantly registered awareness as her brain processed the preternatural turn of events, and her neurons started firing on all cylinders. She leaped from the couch, sprinted for the door, and the other women immediately followed out of instinct.

Julien swept his hand across the frenzied room, tossing each individual woman back into her seat with the mere stroke of his wrist. "Sit down, and stay as you are until I release you!" he thundered, unapologetic if his actions were too brutal or harsh.

Hell's minions, he was hanging onto his sanity by a thread.

Rebecca didn't get it.

This fool had threatened his destiny; *he had threatened Julien's life, and by extension, he had threatened the house of Jadon. Everything in him—vampire, tracker, and possessive male—was wired instinctively for the kill.*

Rebecca gulped. "This is getting out of hand, Julien." And then she did the only thing she could apparently think of, the one thing that might capture his undivided attention. She rose to the tips of her toes, cupped his jaw firmly in her hand, and pressed a short but tender kiss on his mouth, breathing him in like a prayer.

He blinked several times and gawked at her in surprise.

"Julien," she whispered, now that she had his attention. "I know you can wipe everyone's memories, and I know you're going to have to do exactly that, when this is over, but"—she sighed heavily—"I really don't want you to have to wipe mine. I don't ever want that kind of deception between us. And I don't want to see this…this execution…unfold in my house."

Julien paused to measure her words, trying to make sense of their meaning in his amped-up state. Was his *destiny* making a reference to the two of them…*together*…as a couple?

Like she actually saw a future?

Or was she just playing him for a fool, trying to manipulate his emotions in order to get her way?

He snatched both of her wrists in his hands and tightened his fists around them, not enough to hurt her, but hard enough to warn her. "Do not toy with me, Rebecca. I am not some teenage boy you can wind up, play with, and set back down. Don't offer something you cannot back up, later, down the road."

Her tongue darted out to moisten her top lip, and she slowly shook her head. "I'm sorry," she whispered, "I didn't mean…" She immediately changed tactics. "Julien, all I'm asking is…*please*, don't kill him in front of me. Don't do it in front of the women. I don't want to carry that image in my mind for the rest of my life, and I don't want you to take my memories." She lowered her voice to a heartfelt plea. "Please, tracker. As a point of honor. Please."

The VOSU women looked positively petrified as they watched the scene unfold.

Trevor, on the other hand, had just released his bowels in his pants.

Julien turned his nose up in disgust. "Very well, *şoarec micuţ,* but do not move from this spot." With that, he lunged forward, snatched Trevor by the scruff of his shirt, and hoisted him off the floor. Traveling as quickly as possible so the fool didn't soil Rebecca's carpet, he sprang out the door, dove over the railing, and flew to a nearby empty alley, shoving Trevor, violently, up against the nearest grimy wall.

The human literally quaked in his boots, and in that instant, Julien Lacusta grew inexplicably calm, as placid as a hidden mountain lake.

Pinning the disgusting human to the bricks with an unforgiving stiff-arm, he stared deep into his eyes. "I want to know something," he murmured, his voice a velvet promise of death. "I want to understand your mind. What were you thinking when you terrorized Rebecca so many years ago? What were you thinking when you followed her from state to state, in direct opposition to her wishes, in flagrant violation of your human laws? What the hell were you thinking when you stroked yourself on her bed?"

Trevor stuttered like he had an affliction. "I-I-I...oh, c'mon, man...p-p-please. Can we...w-w-we...talk this out?"

Julien slapped him crisply across the face, breaking his jaw and dislodging a handful of teeth. "Mm," he drawled wickedly, "I think the time for talking is over." He shook out his wrist, as if the slap had stung him; held up his right hand; and absently studied his nails. And then he extended two fingers forward, forming a perfect V with the digits, and held them in front of Trevor's eyes, pressing the pads of both fingers against the idiot's tear-stained glasses.

Trevor tried desperately to kick at him, but Julien was far too fast. He simply widened his stance, leaned into the bastard, curled his lip, and laughed. "I so want to kill you slowly, but I'm afraid that I cannot." With that, he shoved both fingers forward, shattered Trevor's glasses with the thrust, and impaled both of his eye sockets, in concert.

He continued to tunnel beyond the temporal lobe.

He hooked his fingers in his cerebellum and yanked.

He curled his digits around a thin, bony mass and retrieved Trevor's spinal cord with a single tug, pulling it back through his eye sockets, where he held it like a trophy in his trembling hand.

As he released the bastard's body, allowing it to slump to the ground, he turned the slimy, meat-like carnage over in his palm and frowned. "Whatever were you thinking?" he asked the curious mass of bone and brains. And then he hurled it against the wall, splintering what was left of Trevor Rainer into a dozen grisly pieces.

His thoughts immediately turned back to Rebecca and her living room, full of guests, the memories he still needed to wipe...

And that lingering kiss.

Gods knew, he was trying to handle this Blood Moon with a semblance of objectivity, with some sort of decorum, if not reason, but the entire affair was becoming a treacherous game, at best.

And it was quickly spiraling out of control.

Julien knew the deal: Rebecca had no intentions of staying with him, not a moment longer than she had to, not a moment longer than it took to fulfill the Curse. Julien had seen this truth in her eyes all along. And gods forgive him, he had allowed it because somewhere deep inside, in that place that terrified him the most, that place where he buried his rage and suppressed it with liquid O, he had also doubted his own staying power.

He did not believe he could sustain a long-term relationship with his *destiny*...with any woman, really. He did not believe he had what it took to maintain a lasting relationship with a mate. Yet this encounter, Rebecca's courage and the tenderness she had openly displayed in that kiss, had been more than a little bit disquieting.

It had shaken him to his core.

He wiped the gruel off his hand, onto the wall, and shut his eyes.

Dearest celestial gods, what was he going to do?

In many ways, Rebecca was as broken as he was: She was as

equally determined and strong. She was defiant, single-minded, and resilient, and he was growing to respect her. But she was also susceptible to the compassion in her heart, curiously lost and alone, even as she pretended to be in control. She surrounded herself with the illusion of support, hiding within a community of victimization—yes, it was a powerful way to heal and move forward, but only for a time. As the years passed, for anyone, it could become an enabling identity. And for Rebecca, in particular, it had become a means to an end, a way to hide from herself.

Was his *destiny* capable of *trust*, even if it was tentative and fragile?

Was he?

That kiss had said that…maybe…she was.

And *gods be merciful*, her vulnerability was like a lure, dangling in front of his starving soul, just begging to be taken…consumed…devoured.

Oh, hell: Julien Lacusta had no intentions of letting this female go.

Not ever.

He had not lied to Trevor Rainer when he had said, *Rebecca is mine*. And he had not come to Denver because he did not possess the power to claim her, to take her, to bend her to his will, back in Dark Moon Vale. He was nearly an Ancient, a primordial vampire, and he could command his *destiny's* compliance with nothing more than the strength of his mind. No, something far more primitive and distant had awakened in the depths of his savage soul, in the wake of that singular kiss.

Perhaps hope?

Perhaps a chance—a *real* chance—for change?

Julien opened his eyes, leveled his gaze on Trevor's mangled corpse, and set about incinerating his body with infrared heat. And then he took a generous step back, all the while trying to adjust to this new revelation.

Come hell or high water, *Rebecca Johnston belonged to him*.

And it was high time that he made that clear and started

acting like he *wanted* her.
Because he did.

seventeen

"Braden, have a seat."

Nachari Silivasi had allowed the kid to sleep for the rest of the night, and then he had waited most of the day to approach him, while thinking things over. He had carried the envelope around, trying to divine more of its energy, trying to make sense of the cryptic words before finally speaking with Deanna about the precarious situation: If Braden had a friend, and the boys had a secret, as peculiar as that may be, Nachari did not want to disrespect his privacy or lord over his decisions. Beyond that, he knew that Braden's parents were a sensitive subject—they just didn't afford him the time or attention he deserved. They never had. And their curious absence in his life grew more and more glaring as each month passed. So if Nachari could've figured the whole thing out without showing Braden the letter, the envelope with his parents' Hawaiian return-address on it, he would've.

But he couldn't.

There was just something too troubling about the whole situation.

Something too amiss.

There was a distinct taint of darkness embedded in the ink, a contrary vibration in every loop of the pen, and even though it niggled at the wizard's subconscious, for the life of him, Nachari could not identify the origins of the perversion. The energy was so peculiar, so eclectic; it held remnants of Italy, Romania, and Greece, yet there was also a modern North American feel to the missive. The contaminate was faintly familiar, almost like the tarnish of a Dark One, but the letter also held a trace of celestial…*etiology?*…like a stamp from the house of Jadon.

It truly made no sense.

And the actual invitation, the purpose of the letter? Well, it was odd at best, disturbingly intimate, almost prurient in motivation, for lack of a better word.

It just didn't sit right.

None of it.

And why had this peculiar male, whoever he was, sent such an invitation to Braden?

Greetings, my auspicious friend,

I have discovered nine perfect stones down by the stream, near River Rock Road, and I believe I have fashioned five perfect citrines, three perfect rubies, and one flawless diamond ~ all for my newfound acquaintance. Alas, I am still biding my time—you will keep our secret, won't you? Meet me by the river, Sunday night. Same place as before.

I am in great need of familiar company.

Grigori.

Now, as they sat in the elegant, sophisticated living room of the brownstone, Deanna on the soft leather sectional; Nachari to her right; and Braden across the room at a diagonal angle, sinking comfortably into a large upholstered armchair, Nachari held the card up in his hand. "First and foremost," he began, "I want you to know that I had no intentions of violating your privacy by opening your mail. You know that I respect you, that Deanna and I both trust you, or we would not have bought you a car."

"That's right," Deanna chimed in, "and Nachari would never open your mail…except…he truly felt like something was alarming this time, like there was something really strange, not right, going on."

Nachari nodded. "The other night, while you were sleeping, I had a fairly disturbing dream, something that woke me from my sleep and caused me to shift into panther form, even before I awakened."

Braden drew back in surprise before curiously leaning forward in his chair. "Okay," he muttered cautiously, growing visibly impatient. "Nachari, what's this about?"

Nachari handed him the envelope and waited while he read the card.

Braden shrugged and then he sighed, seeming much less perturbed. "Oh," he said in a casual voice, "yeah, the dude's kind of weird. My friend. But I don't think you have anything to worry about."

Nachari cocked his eyebrows. "So you know this person, the male who sent this card?"

Braden pursed his lips together and nodded. "Oh yeah. I mean, kind of."

Nachari exchanged a wary glance with Deanna. "And he's obviously a vampire...from the house of Jadon...correct?"

Braden smiled sheepishly. "I'm not really supposed to say anything, but if it makes you feel any better, yeah. *Yes.* Definitely. Like I said, he's just kind of odd."

Nachari held his tongue. *Yes, definitely odd, and just a little bit...evil.* He considered his next words carefully. "Braden, where did you meet this vampire? Does he attend the Academy with you and your friends?"

"Oh no," Braden said quickly, and then he just as promptly tried to set the wizard at ease. "Seriously, Nachari; I'm not supposed to tell. It's a secret, and once everyone knows, it'll be real cool. Promise. Trust me; the guy's just really, *really* weird. Everything's all right."

Nachari regarded the youngster politely, wanting to tread forward with respect. "Braden, the energy I picked up the other night was anything but cool. And the vibration coming off that envelope is anything but all right. Don't you feel it, son?"

Braden sank back in his chair and turned the letter over in his hand, reading the script a second time.

"He used your parents' return address—you don't find that strange?" Nachari asked.

Braden dropped the letter in his lap, turned the envelope over, and stared at the return address. "Damn, that is kind of strange." He sat forward in his chair. "But I'm telling you, the guy is just weird. He's kind of like a foreigner." He shrugged his shoulders, cocked his head to the side, and frowned. "I mean, yeah, the energy is kind of funky, but honestly? That's his vibe, even in person. I dunno. I think maybe he was just trying to be secretive, like he just wants to keep his secret or something."

"What secret?" Deanna asked pointedly.

Braden sighed in frustration, clearly conflicted about how much he should say. "Okay, so I'll tell you this much: He *is* from the house of Jadon, but he hasn't lived here in a really long time. And he came back to visit—that's kind of how I ran into him, just by accident, down by River Rock Creek." He set the envelope and letter aside on a nearby end table and folded his hands in his lap. "I was trying to make some gemstones from rocks, and he helped me out. Anyhow, he wants his visit to be a surprise, to let his family know he's back in his own time, so he asked me to keep a secret. Like I said, weird, but probably harmless."

Nachari cleared his throat. "Can you tell me what he looks like?"

Braden sighed. "I guess. I dunno: blond hair, slate-gray eyes, about six-foot-four."

"So he's *not* a Dark One?" Deanna cut in, making an absent reference to the vampire's hair color.

Nachari cocked his eyebrows as if to say, *Then what the hell?*

He sat back on the sofa and mulled it over.

Something just wasn't right.

So a son of Jadon came back to the vale after an extended absence, possibly a warrior from another generation, someone Nachari didn't know; and the male wanted to surprise his family, but he ran into Braden first. And in the meantime, he just wanted another male's company, to hang out with Braden by the creek.

While that was some truly strange shit, it wasn't necessarily nefarious.

But the energy...and the dream...sneaking around Nachari's mailbox?

There was something else going on.

And frankly, there was something *Braden* wasn't telling them.

Nachari sat forward on the edge of the sofa, braced his elbows on his knees, and locked his gaze with the handsome young vampire's, choosing to take another approach. "So, just to be clear: I want you to look me in the eyes and tell me, straight up, that you completely trusted this guy when you met him, that you completely trust him now, and you would feel perfectly comfortable going back to the river to meet with him again." Before Braden could answer, Nachari added, "Oh, and you don't find it the least bit odd that he stuffed this envelope in our mailbox in the middle of the night, instead of, say, texting you on your cell phone?"

Braden bit his bottom lip. "I never said all that," he mumbled.

Nachari nodded. They were finally getting somewhere. "No, you didn't. And you can't." He squared his shoulders to the boy and angled his jaw in a no-nonsense slant. "What aren't you telling me, Braden?"

Braden chewed on his bottom lip as if he were trying to make a decision. "Well," he finally murmured, "there were a couple things that struck me that night at the creek, some things that I questioned."

"Wait." Nachari held up his hand. "*That night at the creek.* You met with this vampire *after* dark?"

Braden nodded. "Well, yeah. I mean, I was there earlier, but he showed up just after sunset, I think."

Nachari exchanged a telltale glance with Deanna before turning his attention back to Braden. "Go on," he prodded.

Braden appeared a bit unsettled, but he quickly reverted to his previous train of thought. "Well, first, he did something I've never seen anyone do: He emerged out of nowhere, and I don't mean like just materializing or transporting from one place to the next. He, like, came out of the mist...as if he *was* the mist." Braden shook his head in frustration, clearly searching for a better way to convey his thoughts. "It's hard to explain, but it was more like shape-shifting than traveling, something only a Master Wizard could do." He regarded Nachari with a clear and healthy dose of respect. "The dude was like a ghost, and well, there is something else."

Nachari held his breath, not wanting to interrupt or to distract Braden before he could get it all out.

Braden sighed. "It was weird enough—*he* was weird enough—that I took a strand of his hair. You know, just to be sure. He shed it on a rock, and well, when I saw it, I just thought…maybe I should pick this up, hold onto it…just in case." Nachari's mouth quirked up in a smile, and Deanna let out an audible sigh of relief, even as Braden's countenance brightened in response to the couple's obvious approval. "I was gonna show it to you, Nachari, make sure everything was chill. Just didn't get around to it yet."

Deanna smiled, her bluish-gray eyes alighting with mirth. "Perhaps we could've started with that information, ya think?" She chuckled softly to lessen the reprimand.

Nachari took a deep, cleansing breath and nodded in agreement. "No time like the present," he chimed in.

Braden rolled his eyes. "Sorry." And then, without further prodding, he rose from his chair. "Ah'ight, I'll be right back."

Deanna and Nachari waited quietly, their collective anxiety rising with every moment Braden was gone. When, at last, the handsome youngster returned with a crinkled sheet of Saran Wrap in his hand, the plastic haphazardly encasing a single strand of hair, Nachari couldn't help but shake his head. It was vintage Braden Bratianu: Uncanny wisdom and foresight all wrapped up in a silly, disheveled package—would the boy never change?

Braden placed the package on the Raleigh coffee table in front of Nachari and sat back down in the armchair, diagonal from the wizard. "So what do you think?"

Nachari leaned forward and immediately stiffened.

What. The. Hell?

He turned to his *destiny* and eyed the back of the sofa.

"Deanna, go stand behind the couch."

Deanna rose immediately and padded around the arm of the sofa toward the back of the room, taking a distant stance well beyond Nachari, the leather sectional, and the curious package he was about to analyze. She waited silently as the wizard removed the single strand of hair from the Saran Wrap, closed his eyes to quiet his thoughts, and began to gather energy from the elements around him.

Once he felt like an empty vessel, Nachari opened his eyes and began to envision a pure, untainted light before him, a stream that represented truth, clarity, and wisdom, and then he began to pour golden, focused energy into the pristine, untainted channel, wrapping a powerful intention around the strand of hair: *Show me what lies beneath.*

As the particles in the air, hovering above the specimen, began to coalesce around the sample, yielding to the wizard's request, Nachari began to chant:

Gods of old, please grant me favor;
Lords of light, whose truth I savor;
Let me see beyond the veil ~ assist me in this task;
Make true the lie; make false deception ~ remove the clever mask.

He waved his hand over the hair and drew his fingers back, as if drawing the true essence out of the strand.

As all things come from deep within,
Our truest thoughts, our hidden sins,
So the shell may still reveal the soul beneath, asleep and still…
Awaken, now! Come forth! Divulge!
The origins the gods expose.
Show me your true skin.

Just like that, the single strand of hair began to curl inward, the root forming the shape of a flattened, conical head, the end becoming a long, coiled tail, until at last a venomous snake appeared.

Deanna gasped behind Nachari, even as Braden shot back in his chair and swiftly tucked his feet beneath him. But the Master Wizard—he smiled, exhaled, and laughed. "So, our vampire is a

snake in the grass. He believes he can slither into the house of
Jadon, unnoticed, until he is ready to strike. Braden, what was
the male's last name?"

Braden cleared his throat in an anxious scrape. "Um,
Antonopoulos. Grigori Antonopoulos."

Nachari nodded. "That isn't his true name." He extended his
forearm in front of the snake, and the serpent immediately drew
back and bit him. As the fangs sank deep, Deanna shrieked, and
Nachari began to snarl. He traced the poison as it left the snake's
glands and began to counter it with his own vampiric venom,
two forces, diametrically opposed, in a struggle for supremacy.

The wizard won with ease.

In the blink of an eye, Nachari's forearm exploded with light,
and a mystical flame shot into the mouth of the serpent,
growing…glowing…heating until the serpent's head began to
blister. Then just like that, the abomination erupted into
flames—sizzled, screeched, and hissed—and then melted into a
pile of steaming ash.

Nachari sat back in his seat.

He checked his arm for signs of injury, puncture wounds, or
blood. There weren't any. He regarded his *destiny* with a
comforting glance. "I am fine, my love," he whispered, and then
he turned his attention to Braden…

And froze.

The youngster looked almost feral, his high, angular
cheekbones nearly calcified with anger. His usual burnt-sienna
gaze was glowing stark red, and his fangs were cutting into his
lower lip, even as his clearly defined biceps began to twitch.

"Braden?" Nachari asked, sounding as wary as he felt.

The youngster snarled, his top lip quivering with rage.

"Son, calm down."

"No," Braden hissed, sounding far more predatory than his
limited experience occasioned. He leaned sideways in his chair,
extended his legs until his feet were firmly planted on the floor,
and rocked forward in his chair, glaring at the smoking pile of
cinders. "Let me go back and meet the bastard, Nachari," he

snarled, his fangs extending even further.

Nachari held up both hands in a pacifying gesture. "We have much to consider, Braden. Why don't we just—"

"Nah," Braden interrupted, his chest muscles contracting. "There's nothing we need to consider." He shot a heated glare at Nachari and practically seethed with malice. "I'm as serious as a heart attack…unless…unless you think I'm a punk."

Nachari jolted. "No one ever said or implied anything of the sort, Braden."

Braden's voice dropped to a haunting, lethal purr. "Why—the—hell does everyone think they can come after me? The Lycans, that night in the shed; Saber, when he was pretending to be Ramsey; and now, this jackass, who's trying to infiltrate the house of Jadon." He curled his hand into a fist. "Why does everyone think I'm such an easy target? Why does everyone think I can just be played…anytime…anywhere…by anyone? No more," he bit out. "If the bastard wants to meet down by the creek and build some gemstones together, then I say *bring it on*. Let's play. I don't care if you, your brothers, and Napolean's sentinels have to get my back; you have to let me meet him, Nachari." He narrowed his eyes with purpose. "*You have to*. It's a matter of pride."

Nachari took a deep breath and settled into the silence, allowing the young vampire's anger—and his heated words—to linger. He understood the child's rage as well as his pain, and he knew that Braden believed he was up to the task. Nevertheless, Nachari was responsible for the boy's safety, and if this deceptive vampire, this fake Grigori Antonopoulos, had half the power Nachari believed he had, then the child was no match for the imposter.

They needed to think it through.

They needed to consult with the sentinels and, possibly, Napolean, and they needed to devise a well-crafted, well-informed plan. "I'll tell you what," Nachari said evenly, "whatever we decide, you will be instrumental in the decision."

"Not good enough," Braden retorted in an icy tone.

Nachari nodded. He really did understand. "You know something, Braden?" The youngster looked away, but Nachari knew he was listening. "When I was trapped in hell, all those months in the abyss, I submitted to some pretty foul degradation. I *let* demons torture me; I submitted to my own humiliation; and I endured the unbearable, day after day, because I knew I had a plan. Because I wanted to win *in the end*." His voice grew thick with intensity. "Sometimes, the end game is sweeter than swift revenge. Sometimes, we need to be smart, not just strong, and that isn't a sign of weakness." He pointed at the ashes on the table. "That very old vampire—I don't know if he's an Ancient or not, but he's gotta be close—thought he could come out of the mist and toy with a teenager. He thought he could play you like a fiddle, but you? You were smart enough"— he tapped his temple in demonstration—"not to confront him, not to give him the third degree, but just to take a strand of his hair and give it to a Master Wizard." He leaned forward, commanding Braden's full attention with a paternal gaze. The moment their eyes locked, he continued, "And that means you have already outsmarted him. Now, we take it to the sentinels; we put our heads together; and we try to figure this vampire out. End game, Braden. It's all about the end game."

Braden sank back into his chair; his fangs receded in his gums; and his eyes turned back to their normal hue. He relaxed his hands and nodded. "I'm tired of it, Nachari."

"I know you are, son."

"I might make mistakes, but I'm nobody's punk."

"No," Nachari said frankly, "you're not. And you never have been."

Braden hesitated then, but only for a moment. "End game?"

Nachari nodded. "End game."

"Okay," Braden said. He reached across the arm of the chair, took the letter from the end table, and crumpled it up in his hand. "Then let's do this."

Nachari Silivasi smiled.

Indeed, it was time to investigate Mr. Antonopoulos.

eighteen

Julien sat back on Rebecca's custom-upholstered couch, crossed one leg over the other, bending his upper leg across his lower thigh, and stretched a large arm along the back of the sofa. "Becca, talk to me."

She had been pacing, worrying, and wringing her hands together for the last two hours, ever since Julien had sent the VOSU women home, their memories effectively erased, his "mental files" successfully uploaded, and he had tried to give Rebecca some space, some time to process and decompress—but enough was enough.

This didn't seem to be helping.

She pressed the pads of her thumbs against the delicate skin beneath her eyes in order to stave off pressing tears and drew a deep, cleansing breath. "So he's gone then?"

They had been over this.

Several times.

"Yes, angel. He's gone."

She nodded her head, courageously. "And how did you say he died again?"

Julien frowned and brushed a piece of lint off his jeans. "I did not."

"Oh, right, but you're sure the authorities won't find him?"

Julien repressed the desire to scowl.

Authorities.

What authorities?

He acknowledged no such thing.

"He will not be found, Becca." He patted the sofa beside

him. "Come to me, little mouse. You need to sit down for a while."

Rebecca eyed the empty space on the overstuffed couch beside him, almost as if she were eyeing a guillotine, and then she reluctantly crossed the room and sat down, cautiously, immediately tucking her knees to her chest as if to create a physical barrier between them.

Julien placed a large tender hand over the cap of her knee and massaged it gently. "What are you feeling?" he asked in a hushed, compassionate voice, surprised by his own uncommon sensitivity.

She placed her hands on her thighs. "Um, mostly numb." She tilted her head from side to side as if weighing the question more thoughtfully. "Glad it's over—glad that the *Trevor part* is at least over—but anxious about the future."

"About me?" he asked, getting straight to the point.

She frowned. "You're a vampire."

"And you will be one, as well. Very soon."

She gulped. "Don't remind me. I think, before, I had a momentary lapse."

He shifted his weight, leaned in her direction, and uncrossed his leg so he could run the backs of his fingers softly along her jaw. "I want..." His words trailed off as he held her gaze with his and stared deep into her eyes. "I want a deeper understanding between us."

Her eyelids fluttered several times as she blinked, almost instinctively, much like a delicate bird or a hesitant butterfly testing out a leaf before deciding whether or not to land. "I think we understand each other," she murmured, unable to sustain the intimate eye contact.

He leaned in even closer and pressed a soft, chaste kiss along the exposed arch of her shoulder, just where the curve met her arm, grateful that she was wearing an open-shouldered blouse. "Do we?" His words were a husky murmur.

Rebecca gasped, and the same delicate skin flushed with rising goose bumps.

Julien reached across her midriff, caressed her upper arm, and lightly kneaded her flesh, imparting warmth and concern in his touch. "You are brave," he said frankly. "Brave and strong, yet terrified, all at the same time." He leaned back against the large bulky cushions positioned at the rear of the couch, giving her a moment's respite from his obvious advances, and looked off into the distance. "You were very good with your friends earlier, with the women you care so much for; and you were level-headed under pressure, when the situation grew tense." His lip curved in a partial smile. "At least as level-headed as could be expected. And you are now free from your nightmare, but you are still running—you are still hiding—*from me.*"

Rebecca peeked at him through lowered lids, primarily using her peripheral vision to scrutinize him. "I'm not ready," she whispered. "Not for any of this."

He moved off the couch and knelt in front of her, his huge warrior's frame towering over hers. Wanting to remove all physical barriers between them, he slid his palms beneath her calves, tugged both legs gently forward, and anchored her feet on the floor, kneeling between her thighs. And then he cupped her face in his hands and bent his forehead to hers. "You are," he argued delicately.

She trembled beneath his touch, the paternal, yet intimate, contact.

"Sh," he coaxed her. *"You are."* He bent to her ear and pressed a lingering, seeking kiss just beneath her earlobe, at the apex of her carotid artery. "Be with me, Rebecca," he breathed in her ear. "Let the world slip away for a while, and just be with me." He trailed a light series of slow, seductive kisses down the length of her jaw, stopping just short of her quivering mouth, unashamed that he was pouring fire and ice—and erotic pulses—into every graze of his lips in order to tantalize her.

Her spine stiffened, and she splayed both hands against his chest, but she didn't push him away. "W-w-what about your girlfriend? What about Shelly? Is…is she just going to accept that you've moved on, simply because the moon changed color?"

Julien drew back in surprise.

He knew it was an excuse, a deflection at best, but still: What an extremely odd question. He chuckled low in his throat, the sound a throaty, masculine drone. "Shelly Winters is not my girlfriend. She is a brave and kind soul, a female who serves the house of Jadon, faithfully. She has extremely pure, untainted blood, and she attends the Vampyr in that particular…manner…on occasion. I have known her for many years. That is all you walked in on."

Rebecca shook her head emphatically, and she even dared to meet his gaze. "No, Julien. No, it's not. I walked in on a beautiful woman lying on the floor at your feet, bleeding and unconscious, while you were zoned out in a chair." She shifted nervously on the couch. "I don't want to be that woman. Not now. Not ever."

Julien stiffened.

He swept his hand through his hair while considering Rebecca's words carefully, and then he slowly nodded his head. He respected his *destiny's* honesty as well as her blunt appraisal, even if it was a means to an end, a way of deflecting his advances. He blew a short wisp of hair away from his eyes and studied her intently. "You are right to question what you saw, and I would be remiss to make up some half-ass excuse. Shelly came to feed me at an inopportune time…for her." He shrugged his shoulders and frowned. "The H doesn't work, baby girl, not without human blood. And I…I treated her callously, but not on purpose. Never on purpose."

Rebecca sighed. "And how do I know you won't treat me the same, just not on purpose?"

Julien nodded. He understood her question, maybe better than she knew, and he had no intentions of skirting the truth. "In 1556," he uttered, shocked that he was about to share this tale, "before I had a reliable *chemical* escape, I hunted an enemy to a rural village near Andalusia, Spain. It was a quaint community filled with laughing children and revered elders, and despite the fact that they recognized me as a predator, as someone—or something—to be feared, they welcomed me with open arms. They were a kind, hospitable people, and I dwelled among them for about three months, while I searched for this enemy, tracked him through the hillsides, and hunted him amongst rubble and ruins." He sighed, remembering the frustration. "But, as always seemed to be the case, this particular monster eluded me, and it was finally time to move on." He felt his muscles tighten and intentionally relaxed his shoulders.

"Before I left, though, I wanted to stop by the house of one particular family: the Aiza household. They had twin girls, Analise and Evangeline, who had just turned ten, and both were born with a rare affliction, a deformity that had crippled their legs. These sweet little girls could hardly walk. They wore wooden braces just to aid them with their crutches, and even the smallest task was a monumental feat for them to achieve, yet I never heard either one of them complain. Their hearts were filled with such hope and appreciation. For everything."

Rebecca seemed to be holding her breath, and something in her expression changed dramatically—it was all at once softer, more welcoming...more compliant.

Surprised.

Julien pressed on, not at all certain that he could get through the story if he took too much time to pause. "Long story short," he said coolly, "I had made a decision: Before I left the village, I was going to inject both of them with just a small amount of venom, just enough to heal their affliction, not enough to endanger their souls. But when I got there—" Despite his determination, he had to stop, measure his breaths, and steady his resolve. "When I got there, the entire family was dead. The girls had been violated...sexually...and their bloodied corpses were staked to the rough-stone walls. And above their hanging cadavers, my enemy had written *my name* in their blood."

The memory rocked him hard, and he bit down on his bottom lip, drawing a trickle of blood. "You have to understand, it wasn't just their murders, the fact that they had died because of me. It was their ages—the fact that it happened on their tenth birthday—it was the entire, gruesome scene." He gritted his teeth and continued. "It triggered something altogether elemental inside of me, something from my past, and I shook with rage. I could not contain my fury, and then there was this noise, like a rushing river, sweeping through my head, this sound that just grew louder and louder…and louder. And in that moment, in that fleeting instant, the heavens crackled with thunder and lightning, and the skies rained down ice and fire. The crops and the hillside were set ablaze, and the roofs began to burn. I tried to channel my emotion into something else…anything else…determination, the desire for revenge, *hell, even self-loathing, if that would redirect the energy*, yet the earth opened up beneath my feet. And then it swallowed the village, whole. I could float above it. The humans could not." He clenched his eyes shut, shoving the memory away, tucking it into the dark, hidden compartment where it belonged, where it always stayed. "You have to understand: As a vampire, as a descendant of celestial beings, we are intimately connected to the earth. Our emotions become natural events. It was only ninety seconds of weakness, two minutes, at most; yet I destroyed the entire village and everyone who lived there. My rage—and the ensuing carnage—was unlike anything the house of Jadon had ever seen."

He opened his eyes, rocked back on his heels, and grasped his head in his hands. "I killed them all, Rebecca, because I couldn't channel my pain. And I know that letting that woman—*letting Shelly Winters*—fall from my lap after feeding, letting her tumble to the floor, was callous and unfeeling, unbefitting of a Master Warrior, but despite how awful it may have appeared, she still got up and walked away. She left my home, alive and unharmed. And no one in Dark Moon Vale died that night. No one has died since that night in Spain, at least no one *innocent*." He braced his hands on her legs and took several deep, measured breaths, allowing his enormous chest to rise and fall several times in succession. "Baby, it's not every day. It's not all the time. It's not even my first, second, or third means of coping, but every blue moon, to coin a phrase, when the noise gets too loud, when my ears begin to ring, when I hear that familiar rushing river, I shut it out because I honestly can't stand it. I have far more control than I did in 1556, and who knows, perhaps I seek the escape for entirely different reasons now—but that is the truth of it, angel. That is the truth of me." He sat back and stared at her, wondering what she was seeing, wondering what manner of revulsion she was feeling. And to his great surprise, Rebecca reached out a tentative hand and gently stroked his cheek.

"Oh, Julien," she breathed softly, her eyes glazed with sorrow, compassion, and something else that he couldn't quite name.

Something inexplicable.

Something deep, and transformative, and...*familiar?*

As if some sort of lightbulb had just turned on in her soul.

"What are these demons that haunt you?" she asked. "Tell me, Julien." She caressed his jaw with her thumb, and her delicate hand felt like a feather sweeping over a calloused stone. "Who was this enemy you hunted?"

Julien looked away.

So it had come to this?

It always came back to this.

"My brother," he whispered softly. "My dark twin."

Rebecca sat in stunned silence as Julien Lacusta went on to tell her about the dark soul that had shared his mother's womb; the reckless, perilous choice his parents had made to keep the unnamed one, in flagrant defiance of the Curse; and the hideous, unspeakable outcome that had befallen all of them as a result. And as she listened, she kept hearing those names, *Analise and Evangeline*, and she just somehow, instinctively, knew something Julien could not articulate: Yes, the vampire believed his father had betrayed the house of Jadon—he said as much, aloud. He believed that *Micah Lacusta* had been forever barred from the Valley of Spirit and Light because the male had been weak and unfaithful to his house, because Micah, Julien's father, had not loved Julien enough to do what was right. And he even admitted to failing at the only challenge he had ever truly *needed* to conquer: hunting his brother, Ian.

Rebecca could hear and sense his shame.

Still, she saw something altogether different at his core, something she should not have been able to glimpse, but it was like…it was like a lightbulb had just turned on.

Julien Lacusta did not *hate* his father, and it wasn't *guilt* that plagued his soul.

He loved the male he had never known, as any child would, and he mourned grievously over Micah's loss.

Endlessly.

Destructively.

Julien Lacusta could not forgive *himself* for being born.

Perhaps, if there had been another child in Harietta's womb, a different son of Jadon—one who was more worthy, more special, more inherently valuable—Micah would have made a better choice. He would have made the required sacrifice, and everything would have been different.

The heroin didn't just subdue his rage and pain.

It numbed the unbearable darkness of *being*, the unyielding guilt of his existence.

Rebecca gasped as the knowledge sank in. She blinked back tears of empathy and tried to offer the faintest of smiles. "Warrior," she whispered softly, not sure where the word had come from. "You are worthy."

Julien jerked back like she had burned him. "What?"

"You are worthy," she repeated. "Of life…of existing…of one day fathering your own precious sons." She leaned into him and took his large rigid hands in hers, and then she slowly rose from the floor. "There is something I need to show you." She made her way across the living room to an old, tarnished bookshelf and began to pull a series of hard-bound volumes from the shelves: *Visions of Andalusia*, a manuscript all about ancient Spain; *The Practice of Medicine in the Middle Ages*, a volume that detailed everything from testing urine, to letting blood, to splinting deformed legs; and finally, *Earthquakes, Floods, and Other Natural Disasters: When Innocence Is Lost*.

She handed the volumes to Julien, and he studied them closely, furrowing his brow in obvious surprise at the titles. While he thumbed through the copious pages, she turned her attention to a shelf, further down, and retrieved a leather-bound photo album, the cover embossed with a raised, red rose. "After I finally left Trevor, once I finally got away, I had this overpowering need to own something special, to cherish something beautiful that I could call my own. I ventured into a rare, exotic pet store, and they had these two amazing birds, monk parakeets—so I bought a beautiful cage, learned how to take care them, and brought them home. They were my pride and joy—hell, my heart and soul—for the next three years. Whenever I was feeling down or overwhelmed, I would just watch them and listen to them sing, and something inside of me would grow peaceful, everything extraneous would go away, at least for a time."

She opened the album, thumbed through several pages of photographs, and finally stopped, somewhere near the center of the book, reaching into the plastic sleeve to retrieve a picture of two bright-green birds. She extended the picture to Julien, and he took it hesitantly, unsure of what she was trying to convey.

"You...you want me to see your birds?" he asked, his mouth turned down in an awkward expression.

She nodded. "Turn it over."

Julien turned the photograph over and jolted.

His hand grew lax and the photo fell out, landing upside down on the floor.

Written on the back, in flowery script, were two elegant words, the names of Rebecca's birds: *Analise and Evangeline*.

Julien read the names a second time and briefly shut his eyes, even as Rebecca rested her hip against the bookshelf. "You don't have to describe your pain, Julien. I already know it." She bit her bottom lip softly in hesitation. "In here." She placed her hand over her heart and sought his pensive gaze. "And you don't have to justify your actions or apologize…not to me…not anymore." She sighed. "Five days ago, all I wanted in this world was to be free of the nightmare I was suddenly thrust into, to be free of you." She laughed insincerely. "Five hours ago, all I wanted to do was figure out a way to fulfill our bargain and get whatever was required of me done, over with…behind me." She snickered then, but the sound was distinctly hollow. "Hell, fifteen minutes ago, I just wanted to be someplace else, *anyplace else*, with anyone else. But now…"

Analise and Evangeline.

"But now?" he echoed, his haunting moonstone-gray eyes searching hers for sincerity.

"But now, I feel like something inside of me, something I didn't even know was there, is awakening. Like maybe, on some inexplicable level, I've always been with you. And now…now I'm seeing you for the very first time. I'm hearing your words and feeling your pain, and I can barely even breathe…knowing." Her voice trailed off on a whisper.

Julien's throat noticeably constricted as he swallowed his caution. "Knowing what, *şoarec micuţ*?"

"Knowing that you have lived so long…with so much…alone. I am sorry, warrior."

Julien scrubbed a large hand over his face before turning to face her more squarely.

After a brief hesitation, he raised his muscular arms and grasped Rebecca by both shoulders. His touch was as gentle as a lamb's as he brushed her exposed skin with his thumbs. "Come to me, Rebecca. I want to taste your soul." His eyes dipped down to survey her mouth, and they were filled with so much longing, so much indescribable need.

Rebecca shivered, shaken by the intensity of his gaze.

She took his left hand, brought it to her cheek, and angled

her jaw into the warmth, leaning softly forward into his massive warrior's frame. And then she kissed the center of his palm, not knowing what else to do…or say.

Julien exhaled like he had been holding his breath for a lifetime.

He removed his right hand from her shoulder and ran the pad of his thumb over her lower lip, slowly—tenderly—before cupping her face in both hands.

And then he bent to her mouth and kissed her with fevered abandon.

nineteen

Nachari stood behind Braden Bratianu as the youngster shifted nervously in his chair, eyeing all the sentinels in Ramsey's formal living room: Santos, Saxson, Saber, and of course, Ramsey Olaru himself.

Ramsey leaned back against an adjacent wall and removed the toothpick from his mouth. "So let me get this straight: This Grigori Antonopoulos, this *vampire*, stuffed an invitation in your mailbox in the middle of the night—in other words, he didn't come out in the day—yet Braden swears he had blond hair, not black-and-red coils." He glanced askance at Saber and shrugged in apology. "No offense."

Saber scowled, and flicked his wrist, dismissing the entire subject.

"But the male could travel as *mist*," Saxson said to no one in particular. "Damn, that's some serious power…or sorcery. I mean, we can all dematerialize, and we can all scatter our molecules to move through objects, pass through walls, but *becoming* the mist? Actually transforming one's chemistry into chlorides and sulfates, becoming predominantly sulfuric acid? That's shape-shifting, brother. That's sorcery."

"And the hair turned into a snake," Santos added for good measure.

Nachari hissed beneath his breath. "That about sums it up." He paced to the other side of the room and glanced out the floor-to-ceiling windows, beyond the large wraparound deck, turning the conversation over in his head for the umpteenth time. "But here's the thing…" He spun around to face the room.

BLOOD ECSTASY

"No matter how I turn this over, it just doesn't make sense. The Dark Lords marked the house of Jaegar—hell, the Blood marked the sons of Jaegar—the hair color isn't optional." He gestured toward Saber and raised an apologetic eyebrow. "I mean, shit. Saber isn't even a Dark One, but he was consecrated to Lord S'nepres, and his hair is *still* banded."

"You need to get over that shit," Saber interjected, scowling. "All of you."

Nachari chuckled. "Already have, brother. Just let me make my point." He ran an absent hand through his own thick raven locks and continued. "So something does not add up. Unless..."

"Unless?" Ramsey grunted.

Saxson sat forward from his perch on the couch and braced his elbows on his knees, waiting.

"Unless he's not from the house of Jaegar," Nachari said quietly. He paused, letting the suggestion settle, allowing the words to linger.

Santos wrinkled his brow. "I'm sorry, but I'm not following you here, wizard. A Dark One, but not from the house of Jaegar?"

Ramsey snorted as the implication hit him with a start. "Born without a soul...to the house of Jadon. Is that why he could mask the hair, at least with several centuries of practice and a healthy dose of magic?"

Saber gawked at Nachari, grimaced at the insinuation, and then, despite himself, he chuckled—that was just Saber's way. "A freakin' dark twin? A sacrifice that was never made?" He raised his hand and grabbed a fistful of his own banded locks. "And before anyone opens his mouth; I ain't no damn wizard or sorcerer. Despite where I was *truly* born, this shit is staying as it is."

Nachari winked in reply. "Clairol, Nice'n Easy, brother. Number 2BB."

Saber flipped him off.

"You know," Saxson interjected, "when Saber was still a Dark One, impersonating Ramsey, he had to portray blond hair,

162

and he was born in the house of Jadon."

"That was different," Saber snarled. "Salvatore used a spell. It was some sort of holographic image or something, had nothing to do with my house of birth."

"Yeah," Ramsey snorted, "but Salvatore *is* a sorcerer." He eyed Nachari with a sidelong glance and cocked his brows in question. "Wizard?"

Nachari shook his head and shrugged. "Don't know. Have no idea."

Saber flashed a scowl. "Enough with the damn hair, already. *Move on.*"

Nachari raised his hand, extended his forefinger, and drew three clear symbols in the air: *2BB*.

Saber cut his eyes at the vampire and turned away, snickering.

"Fine," Saxson said, his voice reflecting his own amusement at the banter, before returning to a more serious tone, "putting the issue of hair aside, but assuming Nachari might be right: Suppose this male is a dark twin, born to the house of Jadon. Who the hell—"

"Would consider himself a best friend to Julien?" Santos supplied.

"Exactly," Saxson murmured.

"Oh...*shit*," Ramsey snarled.

"Yeah," Nachari said. "It's the only thing that makes any sense."

The entire room grew quiet as the warriors let the association settle in.

Finally, Ramsey Olaru turned to face Braden. "Word for word, son. What exactly did this vampire say...about Julien?"

Braden seemed to be thinking it over, fishing for the memory, and then his eyes lit with recognition as he retrieved the conversation in an unbroken stream. "He said, *As an only child, I did not have many friends, save one: a boy I grew up with who became my best friend. I have come back to surprise him, to see him again, but I would prefer to take my time. To do it my own way. I have traveled the world for many centuries, young Braden, and I doubt that I've been missed. My role in the house of Jadon was never that...important.* He said he saw the sky, and that's what prompted him to come home: *But I really do hope to surprise him, Braden. I think it would mean the world to...the tracker.*" Braden's eyes grew wide with sudden understanding. "Oh, shit."

"What?" Nachari asked.

"He said, *In fact, now that I know what he does*—meaning Julien—*I think it would be fun to play a little game. Perhaps I can leave little traces of my essence here and there—you know, my psychic fingerprint, my individual vibration, my unique, distinctive calling card—and see if Julien picks it up.* I told him I thought Julien would be pretty busy for the next twenty-eight days—you know, because of his Blood Moon—and the guy said, *All the more reason not to bother him, right away.*"

Ramsey shook his head in disgust. "The more we flesh this out, the more this sounds like Ian to me."

"Which is exactly what Julien does not need right now," Santos added.

Nachari nodded emphatically. "You didn't see him, that day in his house. The tracker is walking on a razor-fine edge. I mean, he's *this close* to snapping." He snapped his fingers for effect.

"And he promised his *destiny* that he would clean some shit up for her, deal with some nasty loose ends in her previous life, something about a group of human women with stalkers—he was gonna track 'em down and, well, eliminate the problem," Saxson said. "I'm not a hundred percent convinced he's going to go through with the Blood Moon as it is, try to appease the Curse. The last thing he needs is to be told about his twin."

"Not unless you wanna see him blow a gasket," Santos said. "Truly come unglued."

"Yeah, but if you don't tell him..." Saber shook his head. "That's bullshit. He's a grown-ass male. He has a right to know. Good, bad, or indifferent, it's his call to make. I couldn't stand it when everyone was trying to decide for me and Vanya, tell me what I needed to do or who I was meant to be. At some point, a man's gotta be a man, and a vampire's gotta be free to choose."

Nachari hung his head and sighed in irritation. "We need to bring Napolean in on this. If there's even a chance that Grigori Antonopoulos is Ian Lacusta, then the king needs to know."

At this point, Braden cleared his throat and glared at Nachari. "And you haven't brought up the invitation: whether or not you're going to let me meet with this vamp and settle the score."

Ramsey visibly blanched. "Whoa, son; what do you mean by settle the score?"

Braden's shoulders stiffened with anger. "This guy, whoever the hell he is, played me for a fool. I may be young, and I may be inexperienced. But I'm not a fool."

Ramsey furrowed his brows. "No one thinks you are, son. But if this is Ian Lacusta, and he has survived for nine hundred, fifty-seven years on his own, if he has mastered enough alchemy to cloak his hair as blond and travel as the mist, then you are no match for his cunning, fledgling. You cannot dance toe-to-toe with this vampire."

Braden shrugged, seemingly undaunted. "Maybe not, but I'm brave enough to be a decoy. I can lure the ass hat into a trap, and then maybe you guys—or better yet, Julien—can settle the score."

Saber snickered. "Ass hat?"

Nachari shook his head and waved his hand to dismiss the comment. "It's just…it's another word for jackass."

"It's another word for *asshole*," Braden cut in.

Ramsey harrumphed. "Fine, we all agree. The vampire's an *ass*, one way or another." He leveled his gaze on Braden. "And yes, you could lure him into a trap, and we could dispatch him. Or he could possibly strike faster than we could track or intercept, and we would have your parents and the king to answer to." He turned to regard the other sentinels. "And I'm not trying to be disagreeable here, but let's say this *is* Ian, and Braden's plan could work. Which one of you is going to deny the tracker this kill? Go back to Julien and tell him Ian is dead, and we did it for him. After all this time?" Once again, the room grew quiet, until finally, Ramsey cleared his throat. "What time is it?"

"About 11:45," Santos said.

Ramsey nodded and turned his attention to Nachari. "What say you, Master Wizard? Should we wait until morning, or should we wake the king? Let our Sovereign make the call?"

Nachari's chest constricted with the heaviness of the moment.

Vampires were nocturnal beings, even though they often adjusted their schedules to accommodate their human counterparts, attend to their various business enterprises. One way or the other, Napolean was likely to be awake.

And if he wasn't...

Nachari strolled back across the room, coming to a halt at Ramsey's side. "Yeah," he murmured softly. "It's time to rouse the king."

twenty

Julien lay awake on Rebecca's cozy bed, holding his *destiny* in his arms as she slept somewhat fitfully on his chest, feeling way too large for the queen-sized mattress beneath him. While Rebecca had returned his passionate kiss, and for a moment, she had even been swept away by his ardor, she had stopped him before the interplay could go any further.

Despite the fact that his body—hell, his very soul—had been on fire, she had still been grieving, reeling...adjusting, and making love to a woman whose eyes were brimming with tears, whether from confusion, compassion, or anxiety, was just not Julien's style.

Just the same, the two of them had made a real breakthrough.

Forged a sincere connection, however tentative.

No, they had not made love or exchanged promises for the future. They had not found solace in the sweat, heat, and embrace of each other's welcoming bodies, but they had entered into a more peaceful, contented union: forged a truce of sorts, a quiet and more intimate understanding.

And now, as Julien reclined on Rebecca's bed, simply holding his *destiny* in his arms, he felt deeply honored just to share the moment, just to lie beside her, to finally have her permission. Rebecca was an enigma to him, and what she had shared about the birds was nothing short of a miracle, the fact that they had been connected, so long ago, without even knowing it, the fact that she had named her beloved pets *Analise and Evangeline*.

BLOOD ECSTASY

The story had touched something deep in his soul.

He braced his arm behind his head and slowed his breathing, all the while thinking about Rebecca's VOSU support group and the imminent needs of the women: the boyfriends, ex-husbands, and sometimes strangers he still needed to track.

And destroy.

He wanted to wrap up the nasty business as quickly as possible so he and Rebecca could return to Dark Moon Vale. He was not at all comfortable lodging so far away from the valley's warriors or its strategically placed wards, not when Rebecca could still be at risk to the Dark Ones. Should someone in the house of Jaegar get wind that Julien and his *destiny* were alone in Denver, separated from the herd, then all hell could break loose in an instant.

It just wasn't an optimal position to be in.

He ran an absent hand through the length of Rebecca's hair and sighed: Many times, he had thought about locating the stalkers himself, then reaching out to Santos or Saxson, perhaps Nathaniel Silivasi, and asking the warriors to finish them off. He had even considered asking one or more of the sentinels to come to Denver, to sit with Rebecca and watch over her, as it were, while he handled the miscreants, swiftly and with finality; but his inner predator, his possessive, territorial core, resisted that possibility.

Still, he had to do something, and he needed to make a decision, once and for all.

His chest constricted with a gnawing ache as he wished, for the millionth time in his lifetime, that he possessed the awe-inspiring powers of Napolean Mondragon. While Julien was, without question, the best tracker the house of Jadon had ever produced, he was no match for the ancient king when it came to the ability to strike at an enemy from an indeterminate distance. As far as rumor had it, Napolean Mondragon could sit in a chair in his living room, sipping from a goblet of blood, and send his psychic body forward into any dimension of time or space. He could virtually follow the slightest vibrations in the cosmos, track a being via his or her thought patterns, disposition, and date of birth, and home in on them from anywhere on the earth. And then he could strike like a serpent, snuffing out the fragile life-force without ever breaking a sweat, without ever leaving his home.

Without ever spilling a drop of blood from the goblet.

But that was not the king's foremost—or even secondary—duty.

It was not a good use of the monarch's energy, nor was it in the best interest of the house of Jadon. What if something happened while the king was out of his body? What if the enemy struck back or somehow bested Napolean, as impossible as that seemed, and he never returned to Dark Moon Vale? What if an emergency cropped up while the king was mentally, physically, and spiritually elsewhere?

No, unless it was a matter of personal Blood Vengeance, and the king felt the need to protect or avenge *his own*, he did not risk his immortal life on matters of personal vendetta. Dark Ones were like weeds: The moment one was plucked, another sprang forth, eager to wreak havoc on the world around him, and while destroying the enemy, *any enemy*, was always a worthwhile cause, it was not a duty for the ancient and sovereign lord of the house of Jadon.

As ugly as it might sound, Napolean Mondragon was vital; whereas, Julien was replaceable. As awful as it was to admit, every male in the house of Jadon was ultimately replaceable, save the infamous king. And besides, until recently, Napolean had not had a successor. Now, he had Prince Phoenix, Prince Paris, and Prince Parker, but he had not yet had a chance to train them, to raise them. The children were still neophytes, mere fledglings, with so very much to learn. They needed their father desperately.

Julien bristled inside, knowing that at any time, over the long, torturous centuries, he could have gone to the ancient king as a brother, as a servant—hell, as a male who was truly in need—and beseeched the imperious leader on bended knee to find Ian for him, to sort through all the scattered, ever-changing patterns of energy and deal with the abomination himself, but Julien had never been able to bring himself to do that, to risk the house of Jadon or to compromise the king, not for his own fragile sanity.

It just wasn't that important in the broader scheme of things.

Rebecca stirred fitfully beneath his arm, and Julien stroked her hair, once more wondering at the softness and beauty that rested beneath his fingers. It was so strange to have her there, in his arms at last, to finally lie next to his chosen mate.

And truth be told, he hardly knew what to do with her.

His groin hardened in protest, and he had to stifle a masculine chuckle.

Well, yes, he knew exactly what to do with her in terms of *male-meets-female*, and gods be merciful, he was burning inside to do just that; but the operable words were *with her*, not *to her*.

He had already made enough mistakes.

He sent a peaceful current of energy through his fingertips, directed the pulse to circulate around her scalp, and she settled back with an adorable sigh. And that's when he felt the energy all around him stir:

Julien.

His ears perked up at the telepathic call: *Whose voice was that? Tracker.*

Holy hell. It wasn't every day—or night—that the noble king of the house of Jadon just appeared inside one's mind. *Milord?*

We have a situation, the king said bluntly.

Julien stiffened, drawing to instant attention. *Has something happened to one of the sentinels?* It was the only thing he could think of.

No, Napolean said brusquely, putting that fear to rest.

Is there some sort of threat to the house of Jadon? Are my services needed in Dark Moon Vale?

The king paused, perhaps for a while longer than was natural. *No more—or less—than usual. No, warrior. I'm afraid this has to do with you...on a personal level.*

Julien furrowed his brows, growing increasingly wary. *I'm*

listening.

The king cleared his psychic throat, which was unusual for the implacable male. *Is your* destiny *close by?* he asked.

She is. She's in my arms. Julien glanced down his nose at Rebecca's sweet, placid features and grew inwardly still. Her visage was inexplicably calming.

Ah, Napolean said, with an approving exhalation, *that's good, tracker. That's good.* He immediately reverted to a more serious tone. *However, I need you to be calm.*

At this, Julien's forefinger twitched, and he removed it from Rebecca's hair. *If it's all the same, milord, and with my deepest respect, please; just get to the point.*

Napolean paused again, but only for a heartbeat this time. *Very well. We have reason to believe that Ian is in Dark Moon Vale.*

Julien drew in a sharp inhale of breath and his fangs began to throb. *Ian, who?* It was a ridiculous question—he knew only one Ian—but still, after so many centuries of searching, the statement seemed impossible, if not surreal.

The king answered his question with silence, and he knew.

And son of a hyena, he had felt it the night of his Blood Moon, when he had awakened in his master bedroom, that eerie night when a dark, errant energy had jolted him out of his slumber. *What's happened?* he asked, biting down so hard on his tongue that his teeth pierced his flesh.

Napolean relayed the past events in a concise and no-nonsense summary, hitting all the major points, conveying all the pertinent information, without displaying even the barest hint of preconception or emotion.

Julien nodded slowly. *I see.*

The king filled the awkward silence for him. *We had quite a heated discussion as to whether or not to alert you at this precarious time, considering your* destiny *and all, but there was no way—*

Julien growled across the connection, cutting the king off in the middle of his sentence, and then he quickly reined in his beast. *Forgive me, milord.* In spite of his desire to sound deferential, he clipped the last two syllables, almost with disdain.

BLOOD ECSTASY

Yet to his enormous credit, the king proceeded with his usual grace.

No need for apologies. He lowered his voice and spoke in a deliberate, soothing tone. *I have already spoken to Saxson Olaru and Nathaniel Silivasi about your situation and your reason for traveling to Denver. I wasn't spying on you, son, but Ramsey relayed the reason for your trip, the promise you made to Rebecca.* He paused, presumably to allow Julien to digest the information. *At any rate, if you bring the files and transfer your mental data and impressions to the warriors, they will be happy to follow up. They may not be seasoned trackers, but they can find and dispatch an assorted batch of human excrement without any difficulty.*

Julien closed his eyes, grateful for the momentary change in subject, an opportunity, however brief, to discuss tactics instead of evil brothers. *Why Nathaniel Silivasi?* he asked curiously, even though he had considered the Ancient Master Warrior, himself.

Napolean snickered, albeit in the most dignified manner. *On one hand, I am not willing to divert more than one of my trusted sentinels from Dark Moon Vale. On the other hand, Nathaniel rather enjoys this type of...sport.*

Julien grunted.

True, that was definitely true.

Fine, he said, steadily—at this juncture, he really didn't care. *Rebecca and I will return in the morning. She's sleeping right now.*

The king grew ominously quiet, as if he was the one who needed to digest the full implications of the conversation this time. Finally, when the silence had lingered too long, and the subject had grown explicitly awkward, Napolean murmured, *Very well, warrior.* And then he lowered his voice. *Are you...okay?*

Julien smiled in a satirical mockery of all things holy.

He measured his heartbeat, assessed his pulse, and regulated his next three breaths.

Yeah, he was okay...

Right as rain.

Yes, he lied, not wanting to delve any deeper into the subject of his emotional or mental health.

The king exhaled slowly.

They both knew the deal.

Very well, Napolean practically whispered, ignoring the elephant in the psychic room. *We will speak in the morning. Be well, Master Warrior.*

Be well, my king.

Julien closed the connection in an instant.

There was nothing else to say.

He opened his eyes; slid his arm out from underneath Rebecca; and slowly climbed off the bed, feeling curiously light-headed and strangely disembodied, like he was viewing the entire scene from an odd, impartial distance. And then he watched in morbid fascination as the bedroom chandelier began to sway back and forth, rocking above his *destiny's* head.

What the heck?

He checked his vitals a second time.

He was fine.

In fact, he was deathly calm.

His ears weren't even ringing.

The ground began to oscillate beneath his feet, and he took a stutter-step sideways to maintain his balance. They did not have earthquakes in Colorado, at least not anything measurable. When the plaster on the bedroom wall behind Rebecca's ocher headboard began to split apart, tearing into a deep, jagged, vertical fissure, he hung his head and bit out a string of curses in Romanian.

Not here.

Not now.

Not when he was supposed to be protecting his female.

When the fissures began to glow volcanic red, as if bordered by unseen flames, he bolted from the room, darted across the hall, and headed for his black canvass duffle bag, still propped on the guest room bed. *Gods be merciful*, but what else could he do?

He wasn't feeling anything.

Not rage.

Not elation.

And certainly not the gnawing hunger of revenge.

Yet the earth was shifting, three stories beneath his feet, and the walls were about to burst into flames.

He hastily unzipped the side pocket of his duffle, retrieved a decanter of alcohol, and withdrew a packet of liquid O, and then he bit out another caustic curse:

Damnit all to hell...

In order to make the Chiva work, he would have to feed from Rebecca.

twenty~one

Dark Moon Vale ~ The next morning

Rebecca watched in cautious silence as Julien placed a faintly trembling palm against the panel of his right front door, just above the sturdy brass knocker, and somehow unlocked an invisible ward before turning the heavy, ornate handle and shoving the partition open. And she winced as she recalled the drive back to the valley—the journey had been tenuous at best.

Needless to say, Julien had been wound as tight as a drum, and Rebecca had been reeling from the overwhelming infusion of troubling information, trying desperately to digest everything Julien was telling her. On one hand, he had informed her that two other vampires, warriors by the names of Nathaniel Silivasi and Saxson Olaru, were going to take over the tracking of the VOSU women's stalkers. They would hunt them down and make sure that *matters were settled* with swiftness and alacrity: a fact that made Rebecca feel cautiously secure. Yet, on the other hand, he had told her that Ian had returned: Julien's long-lost brother had apparently appeared out of nowhere, and they were returning to Dark Moon Vale to meet the threat head-on, a fact that had filled her heart with terror.

Adding to her angst had been the knowledge that Julien was dangerously ill-equipped to handle the confrontation... emotionally.

Although the gladiator had assumed Rebecca was sleeping the entire time he'd carried on his telepathic conversation with the fearsome king of the Vampyr, in truth, Rebecca had been slipping in and out of consciousness. When the chandelier had shaken, the floor had shimmied back and forth, and the wall had begun to split down the center, she'd been wide-freakin'-awake, awake enough to watch Julien dash out of the room, head for his cache of heroin, and scramble to ingest the liquid O in time to shut down his emotions.

The tracker had been desperate to make the ensuing earthquake—or fire—stop.

And yes, Rebecca had followed Julien into the guest room and watched the distressing scene play out. Despite her fears, despite her reservations, despite her God-given common sense warning her to stay fifteen paces away from the lethal warrior at such a precarious time, she had been concerned enough to follow; and while the sight of such a proud, powerful male being reduced to a necessary, if not piteous, addiction had wrenched at every chamber of her heart, she'd had no impulse to stop him.

And there had been no need for words.

Rebecca Johnston had simply…and indelibly…understood.

Him.

His pain.

His rage.

And his need.

All of the above were greater than her sense of propriety, and there was simply no place for petty judgment: *Drug addiction be damned.* The earth itself was trembling! What was she supposed to do?

She had padded quietly to Julien's side, extended her wrist to the vampire, and offered him her vein in silence, and as he had taken it, the look of gratitude, the pallor of shame, that had swept over his expression, that had illuminated those beautiful moonstone eyes, had pried what remained of her resisting heart wide open.

She didn't welcome this fate.

She couldn't welcome this man—*this vampire*—at least not entirely.

But she could no longer deny that she was inexplicably

drawn to the shadows in his soul, that he was not a simple or unfeeling being, and that the two of them shared an undeniable connection, perhaps even a divine appointment. Like it or not, their paths and their fates were inextricably connected.

And now, as she stood once again on the front porch of his secluded mountain home, waiting to enter his foyer, she could only hope and pray that whoever the celestial gods were, they were more in control than they seemed, that wherever this Ian Lacusta was hiding, he would not—could not—kill them both before they had a chance to unravel their fate, before she had a chance to get to know the soul beneath the terrifying vampire.

"Are you okay?" Julien's deep, raspy tenor jolted her out of her musings.

Rebecca nodded meekly. She was only sort of okay. In truth, she was terrified all the way down to her bones and trying valiantly to keep her knees from knocking together. She was just about to say something to that effect when Julien held up a hand to silence her.

His intense gray eyes swept across the planks of the porch, fixed on a large terra-cotta planter, and froze like two concentrated lasers on a thick bundle of letters, wrapped within a delicate silken bow. His mouth turned down into a wicked frown, and his expression crystallized like granite. "Go inside, Rebecca," he snarled, not so much out of anger, but conviction.

Rebecca eyed the mysterious bundle for a few moments longer than she should have, measured Julien's expression a second time, and then scurried into the house. Stopping in the foyer, she glanced over her shoulder. "Do you want me to—"

"Shut the door," he answered, before she could finish the question.

"Should I—"

"Lock it behind you."

She started to ask him what was going on, but instantly changed her mind: Whatever was happening with those letters, she didn't want to know. Rubbing her palms briskly over her arms to stave off a sudden chill, Rebecca closed the door to the foyer, spun around to grasp the bolt, and swiftly set the latch.

Julien took several deep, calming breaths before prowling toward the mysterious bundle.

Hell's bells, Ian's filthy scent was all over it.

He hadn't smelled anything so rotten in years.

And the bow, that delicate, pale pink, silken bow, it was the ribbon his mother used to wear in her hair!

He clenched and unclenched his fists several times before bending over to retrieve the package, and then he extended a claw on his right forefinger and tore into a random envelope:

To my brother, on our eleventh birthday: Hope you have a sun-shiny day!

Bile rose in Julien's throat as he tore into another.

Happy Twelfth Birthday to my best friend and brother: Let's make today a great one!

He hocked up the phlegm and spat into the dying xeriscape, trembling as he thumbed through ages thirteen through seventeen.

And then he opened the next one: *You're eighteen now—let's party!!!*

"Let's party?" he growled beneath his breath. "Oh, yes, brother: Let's definitely party."

Burying his emotions somewhere deep inside, somewhere so dark, vacant, and vaulted that not even the celestial gods could retrieve them, he made his way through the remaining cards, until at last, he came to the final greeting.

"I know our birthdays are still three months out, but I couldn't wait until April 12th to make up for so much lost time. How fondly I remember the last birthday we shared together. How deeply I desire to see you again. Soon, my beloved brother. I shall have to see you…soon. Love, Ian."

A blood-red tear swelled in Julien Lacusta's right eye, and it was not a tear of pain or anguish…or regret.

It was a scarlet badge of rage.

As Julien swiped the sanguine fury away, palming the perfect ruby in his fisted hand, he bowed his head and prayed: "Lord Hercules, my keeper, my protector, my divine, omniscient god, I beseech you before all of the celestial beings: Even as you kneel in the heavens with your foot on the head of Draco, let me kneel over Ian's body with my fist—and this ruby—encasing his blackened heart. Give me the one thing you have denied me for over nine hundred years. Let me dine on my brother's blood and be done with it." With that, he tucked the ruby into his front hip pocket, crumpled the letters in his open palm, and headed toward the front door to unlock it once again…and go find Rebecca.

Gods be merciful, she was just beginning to trust him.

Just beginning to see him for who he truly was.

Just beginning to open up.

And now…*and now*…he had to do the one thing she might never forgive him for: He had to convert her without delay.

Not in a week, not in a day, not in another hour—

But now.

Sure, she had asked him for the same when she was reeling and terrified of Trevor, but that had been an outlier, reactive and compulsive; this was a completely different deal.

Nevertheless, Rebecca Johnston was still human.

She was slow; she was weak; and she was as vulnerable as a newborn kitten when compared to an ancient vampire, a dark, malevolent foe.

Yes, Julien would defend her with his life, but as sure as he was a Master Warrior, born and bred to be a gladiator in the house of Jadon, his soul would not rest until his *destiny* was safe.

Until she was Vampyr.

Until she at least had a fighting chance against the likes of his evil twin.

twenty-two

Rebecca's knees buckled beneath her as she fell back onto the new distressed-leather sofa in Julien's great room, dropped her head into her hands, and struggled to breathe. "But…" The words got lost in the ether, and she had to try again. "But I'm really not ready, Julien. I mean, not even close." Yes, she understood that just two days ago, she had actually asked the vampire to convert her, but that had been an anomaly: Trevor was still alive, and she had been feeling vulnerable, angry…desperate to regain some control. She had wanted to seal her end of the bargain, and she had needed to be brave. Now, she just felt completely overwhelmed.

The towering hulk of a vampire squatted down in front of her, ostensibly to appear less threatening, and reached out to take her hands.

She pulled them away and tucked them beneath her thighs.

"Şoarec micuţ," he murmured, "I know. I do. But you've seen these letters." He gestured toward the pile of crumpled envelopes scattered about the floor by her feet, and he frowned. "The bottom line is this: Ian is gunning for me, angel. And he's not going to stop, not until one of us is dead." He rocked back on his heels, and his vivid gray eyes clouded with emotion. "I'm not trying to scare you, and the gods know, I wouldn't ask this of you now if it wasn't imperative; but Becca, if something happens to me—"

"Nothing will," she interrupted frantically, withdrawing her hands from beneath her and wringing them together in her lap. "I mean, you're a warrior."

"So is he," Julien said sternly.

"But you're a tracker…a vampire…you're lethal."

Julien appeared to swallow a curse, and then he rolled his shoulders to release some tension. "So is he, angel."

Rebecca blinked several times to clear her vision. *What was the vampire saying?* "You don't think you can beat him, do you?"

At this, Julien chuckled, deep, low, and sinister. "Oh, *iubito*, my darling; I am going to beat him. I am going to *end* him."

She shivered at the ice in his words. "Then, maybe…maybe we can wait?"

Julien shook his head. "No. Too dangerous, angel. Nothing about this can wait." He rose, rotated his massive body, and took a seat next to her on the couch. Despite the fact that she shied away, he placed his arm around her shoulders and drew her close to his heart. "As much as I want you with me, as much as this Blood Moon demands that you be with me, I need to take you to the king's manse until all of this is settled. You'll have the greatest protection imaginable at Napolean's compound, and I need to convert you *today*."

As if a sudden tide of panic had just swept through the room, washed over the sofa, and dragged Rebecca into its dangerous undertow, she flung his arm off her shoulder, leaped from the couch, and began to run toward the staircase.

She had no idea where she was going.

She knew, intuitively, that she could never outrun him—hell, he could just freeze her in place with the sweep of his hand—yet and still, everything in her told her to run.

Julien rose from his perch on the sofa, but he didn't pursue her, at least not right away. And he didn't command her body to freeze. "Becca," he called in a no-nonsense tone. "Angel, please…*stop*."

She made it halfway up the first set of stairs and spun around on the landing. "Don't do this, Julien. Please. I can't…I'm not…just don't."

In an instant, he was there, dematerializing from the great room and transporting within inches of her trembling frame.

"Baby, please. You read the letters. You know the history. This monster took my father. This monster killed my mother. This monster has eluded me for over nine hundred years." He cupped her face in his hands, his touch far too gentle for a male his size, and burrowed his fingers in her hair. "You've seen me. You know how I cope—*how I don't cope*—with the fallout. Can you even imagine what would happen to me, to this valley, to the earth all around us, if Ian were to somehow get to you, if I had to live with the fact that I had left you defenseless?"

Rebecca covered his large hands in hers and squeezed, mostly out of fear and anxiety. "I don't have…" Her voice trailed off and she averted her eyes in a regretful admission of shame. "I don't have the kind of love or commitment that can sustain that level of pain, a conversion. If you hurt me now, I just…I just…"

"You just?" His voice was hollow and void of emotion.

"I just think there would be no future. For us."

He nodded slowly, allowing her words to linger, and then he locked his moonstone gaze with hers, his pupils dark with conviction. "Analise and Evangeline," he whispered in a husky tone. "We—you and me—we have a past, and we will have a future. It may be rocky, and the gods know, I'm about the least worthy bastard any female could ever want to be saddled with, but angel of mine—*destiny* of mine—know this: I am loyal, all the way down to my broken core. I fight for what is mine, and I'm a survivor. If nothing else, I will fight for you, and I will fight for us. I promise you, little mouse, from this day forward, from this moment forward, from the second the conversion ends, no one is going to stalk you; no one is going to deny you anything; *nothing* in heaven or on earth is going to keep me from protecting you, from protecting us, from cherishing our mating. Rebecca Louise Johnston, you will have my fealty, the same as my king. You will have my heart, for as long as I live. You will have my body, my mind, and my soul, such as it is." He drew back and chuckled, insincerely. "I know you don't want it—at least not now—and maybe you never will. But don't decide our *forever* based on this one critical, necessary event. Forever is a very long time."

Rebecca's eyes filled with tears, and despite her incessant trembling, she lowered her gaze, leaned forward, and rested her forehead on the vampire's chest. He immediately enfolded her in his powerful arms, and despite the maddening, terrifying situation they were both facing, she actually felt safe for the very first time in as long as she could remember. "I'm scared," she mumbled into his breast.

"I know," he whispered. "So am I."

At that, she drew back and peeked up at him. "You? *Why?* Of what?"

The corners of his eyes creased, and he swept his tongue over his bottom lip in an atypical, nervous gesture. "I don't want to hurt you, Becca. I don't want to pull you into this nightmare that is my waking life. And I don't want to damage the fragile trust we are just beginning to forge. I'm not afraid of Ian. Hell, I'm not even afraid of dying. But I am afraid of hurting you, doing anything to damage our delicate bond."

"But you're determined to do it anyway," she said.

He nodded, slowly. "Yes."

"And there's nothing I can say?"

He measured her carefully, studying her features, gazing into her eyes like she was the most beautiful—and innocent—woman in the world. "You can say anything, baby. You can say everything. But at the end of the day, I'm a male vampire. I'm going to protect you, first. I'm going to make you stronger."

She swallowed her protest and stifled a frown—it wouldn't do any good. "Can I at least take a minute, have a moment to myself? I don't know, take a shower and think, maybe process a little, try to get…prepared?"

Julien placed two fingers beneath her chin and lifted her jaw to force her tentative gaze. "I know you don't believe this, and this situation certainly doesn't demonstrate it, but there is nothing I would deny you, șoarec micuț. There is nothing I will deny you for the rest of your life. Just meet me halfway…on this…in this awful, difficult circumstance, and know that when you come through on the other side, you will be emerging into a whole new world. A world where you are stronger, faster, and safe…with me."

Rebecca worried her bottom lip. How could she say that *being safe with him* was exactly what she was afraid of: being tied to Julien Lacusta, the fearsome tracker for the house of Jadon…forever? How could she explain that there was no going back, that she hadn't even had a chance to catch her breath, to process this new reality, or to welcome him into her heart? How could she express that she actually feared *him* more than Ian, despite their burgeoning connection?

It didn't matter.

Even if she could express it.

The tracker's mind was made up, and she was, indeed, a *little mouse* caught in the ultimate trap, in the clutches of a primitive lion, a snare she could never escape. She could only hope and pray that his words were true, that he had meant everything he promised, because like it or not, Rebecca Johnston was about to become a vampire.

She was about to become his.

"Okay," she whispered, reluctantly nodding her head. "Give me half an hour."

Julien breathed an audible sigh of relief. He took a generous step backward and tried to appear less domineering—it just didn't work. He gestured toward the curved, wooden staircase, flanked by so much iron, and spoke in an unusually tender voice: "I'll be in the great room…when you're ready."

Rebecca nodded, and then she quickly sidled past him and bounded down the stairs.

twenty~three

The next morning

Julien Lacusta stepped outside onto the wide-plank floor of his rustic front porch and took a deep, cleansing breath of fresh mountain air. Rebecca's conversion had lasted five long, harrowing hours, and as much as he had wanted to meet with the sentinels right away, switch his attention to the immediate threat at hand—the missive his dark twin had sent to Braden Bratianu, asking the youngster to meet him at the creek later that night—he had known better.

Rebecca had needed his full attention and support.

She'd had lots of questions and concerns, and frankly, she had just needed to rest, to take a moment and adjust to all the changes and fluctuations that were coming at her, faster than a speeding train: Her senses were changed. Her reality was altered. And her entire world had been turned upside down. She just needed a few hours to process.

Now, as she slept in, curled up in an adorable little ball in Julien's iron bed, his senses were hyper-acute, and his sense of urgency was enormous. In a couple of hours, he would take his newly changed *destiny* to Napolean Mondragon's manse, and that's where she would remain until the crisis with Ian was over. Just the same, the clock was ticking on their Blood Moon, and he knew he had to get this perilous ball rolling.

Ian could be anywhere.

He could be out there right now...watching... waiting...ready to pounce.

BLOOD ECSTASY

He could be planning virtually anything.

Squatting down beside the terra-cotta pot where Ian had left the maniacal birthday cards, Julien closed his eyes and tried to gather his wits, to control his wayward thoughts, to call upon his inner warrior: the valley's best tracker.

He took a slow, even breath through his nose, allowing his nostrils to flare, even as he recorded the vast palette of scents that lingered in the air: pine, juniper, fresh earth, wood, moisture, and a hint, just a hint, of something distinctly acrid, Ian Lacusta's aroma.

He recorded it in his mental database.

And then he opened his eyes and stared at the dust on the porch, followed it down the small series of steps to the unkempt vegetation, the ungroomed xeriscape, just off to the side, and he took a psychic-photo of a faint but noticeable impression: a singular set of footprints. Rising to meander in the direction of the tracks, he began to analyze what he was seeing at amazing rates of speed: There was a slight depression in the left heel print, which meant that Ian walked with a notable gait, actually, a swagger; there was a small, almost indiscernible circle between the third row of tread in the bottom right track, which meant that Ian had a small stone or a pebble wedged between the sole of his boots. And he did wear boots. In fact, based on the size and depth of the footprints, however faint, Julien's wicked brother had grown to be about six-foot-four, the same height as Julien, but he carried about thirty fewer pounds on his frame. As a vampire, he would be strong and muscular, but his physique would be far more lean and sinewy in nature.

Julien took several steps back and zeroed in on the front porch once more, this time studying the almost nonexistent patterns of dust—they were subtle, undetectable to the human eye, but Julien knew what to look for. Ian had taken two to three steps on the porch before he squatted down to plant the cards, and those steps revealed a two-and-one-half-foot stride. Based on where he stopped, where he stooped, he was still right-handed, which meant that any weapon he wielded would be thrust or brandished from that advantage—it would be more advantageous to attack him from his left.

His handwriting on the garish birthday cards had already revealed plenty: The male was arrogant and drunk with bravado, but he was also anxious, uncertain, and enormously paranoid, all things that could be used against him. The vibration that hung in the air, wrapped itself around the leaves and the planter, confirmed the same thing: His energy was dark and malevolent, focused so strongly that it almost swirled in a quantum hologram, but it was chaotic and desperate.

Julien sighed, even as a feral growl rose, inadvertently, in his throat.

This, too, could be a tactical advantage.

Somehow, Julien had to remain calm, evenly focused, and deliberate in all of his actions and choices.

He repressed the desire to snatch the pot and toss it about a mile down the road, realizing that anyone could be in its trajectory, and he focused, instead, on Ian's retreat. The male had taken exactly one and a half steps backward before transporting into flight, and then, in less than a ten-foot expanse he had shifted into mist. Julien knew this because the nearby pine trees, those precisely ten feet away, had a subtle, but distinctly different quality to their needles—he could both smell and see the impact of dew on the branches, the added pliability to the tines. They were just an infinitesimal shade darker, greener. *Holy mother of Hercules*, he thought, *that would take the skill of a magician*. Julien snarled, and his fangs pressed against his gums. For some reason, that knowledge didn't really come as a surprise: Ian had mastered so many techniques in his youth, trying to hide his darkness from Harietta, struggling to contain a psychic force that was inbred in his very DNA, learning to adapt at a cellular level. It was no wonder he had the virtual powers of a wizard.

Julien nodded.

So be it.

And that was when he felt, more than heard, Rebecca step

onto the porch.

He spun around to face her. "Baby, you should never come outside on your own, not without the all-clear first."

Rebecca frowned and rubbed her eyes. She had obviously just woken up. "Yeah," she murmured, "duly noted." There was nothing hostile in her voice, just a sort of complacent surrender, and to his surprise, it tugged at his heartstrings. "What were you doing?" she asked.

Julien snorted in dismissal. "Nothing. Just...closing some loose ends."

Rebecca nodded. She glanced around the porch, out into the yard, and down the driveway, and then she absently nodded her head. "You're tracking, aren't you? Hunting Ian?"

Julien nodded. "Yeah. Just gathering some information."

Her soft, topaz eyes lit with just a hint of curiosity, and she hesitated before clearing her throat. "Would you show me? Like...what you're seeing, recording?"

Julien almost said no as an instant knee-jerk reaction. They honestly did not have the time, and the situation was way too dangerous. Now that she was awake, Rebecca needed to get to Napolean's manse, post haste. But something brought him up short. Maybe it was the lost look in her expression; maybe it was the pallor of the recent conversion still dusting her complexion; or maybe it was just the fact that she had asked; but he took a few curious steps toward her, extended his hand, and waited to see if she would take it.

She did, albeit cautiously.

He led her to the edge of the porch and pointed at the distant pines. "Do you see those blue spruces, the ones that are slightly taller than the rest?"

She nodded.

"Close your eyes, şoarec micuţ, and try to focus your sense of smell on the pine needles."

She did.

"What do you detect?"

She shrugged. "Nothing, just pine, and maybe some wood

from the cones."

Julien sidled behind her, and she stiffened just a bit, but he pretended not to notice as he wrapped his large muscular arms around her, rested his chin in her silken hair, and closed his eyes in order to transfer the information he had absorbed, analyzed, and sifted directly into Rebecca's mind. Now that she was converted, it was an easy thing to do.

When she gasped, he tightened his hold. *That's it, angel girl*, he spoke inside her mind. *You can smell the difference between a moist pine needle and a dry one. You can almost hear the hydrogen combining with the oxygen, if you really filter everything else out.* He switched to speaking aloud. "That's where Ian shifted into mist, changed from his typical vampiric form." He pointed skyward. "He retreated to the west, but that doesn't necessarily mean anything; he could've doubled back and gone anywhere."

Rebecca leaned back against him, and Julien wondered if she even knew she was doing it. "Wow," she murmured. "That's...that's incredible, Julien. I don't think just anybody could do that, not even other vampires."

Julien cocked his head slightly to the side, weighing her words for a moment. Hmm, he'd never really thought about it. He had been a tracker all his life, from the time when he was ten years old and arrived on Napolean's doorstep, begging to be taught. It all just seemed instinctual...

But speaking of Napolean: "Angel, are you ready to go?"

Rebecca pulled away from him as unconsciously as she had propped against him. "No," she said in a forthright tone. "But I'm coming to understand that *ready* doesn't have anything to do with any of this." She sighed. "Am I ready to meet the vampire king and queen, to be thrust into this alien, terrifying world even more deeply than I've already been? No, I'm really not."

Julien allowed the silence to linger.

Sometimes words were an insult when feelings were exposed and raw.

Honest.

True.

Finally, he whispered, "We do need to go, baby. I just...there's no other option that's feasible."

Despite her misgivings, Rebecca nodded, and then she quietly spun around, padded toward the front door, and re-entered Julien's home.

He watched her like a hawk studying its fleeing prey, wishing he could change the trajectory—of everything. Her path and his. The uncertain future, and his inherent weakness. The dueling need to stay alert and hunt Ian, coupled with the imminent danger of slipping into a place of insanity, of too much emotion, continuing to use the H if he had to.

Gods, what a mess his life had become.

Perhaps it had always been.

twenty~four

One hour before sunset

Julien Lacusta felt positively twitchy as he strolled into Napolean Mondragon's elaborately appointed conference room, just to the right of the large receiving foyer. He made fleeting eye contact with each of the sentinels, in turn—Ramsey, Santos, Saxson, and Saber—and each warrior, to a vampire, gave him a stern, unyielding nod. It was almost as if they were reluctant to say *hello*, as if the very sound of their voices, echoing in the classy hall, might set the volatile tracker off, send him flying into a virulent rage.

He avoided eye contact with the youngster, Braden Bratianu, even as he acknowledged his informal mentor, Nachari Silivasi, although he couldn't clearly articulate why. And then he declined his head toward Napolean in the most genuine token of respect he could muster and promptly took an empty seat toward the head of the table, just to the left of the monarch. As he settled back, feeling as if his body was too big for the tall, mahogany chair, he couldn't help but think about Rebecca…and hope she was doing okay.

He had brought her to the manse nearly five hours ago, and although he had wanted to get right down to business with Napolean and the other warriors, he had restrained his impulse to go straight to the conference room. Instead, he had taken the time to help her get acquainted with her new housemates and surroundings: Brooke Mondragon, the queen, had been as understanding, hospitable, and welcoming as possible, and

Tiffany Matthews had also come to the manse as well. As the most recently converted *destiny* in the house of Jadon, Tiffany had wanted to make herself available to Rebecca, to share her own personal story, answer any questions Julien's *destiny* might have, and talk to her about the stages of adjustment, fill in any holes. Both women had gone out of their way to make Julien's newly converted female feel at home.

Yet and still, the look in Rebecca's eyes, when Julien had finally left her in the lavish guest room, had tugged at his heart like an anchored cable. She had drawn inward like a wilted wildflower, one he had suddenly plucked from the side of a mountain, stuffed into a cold glass vase, and placed on a barren, dark shelf set in an abandoned room, like he had left her to readjust to her new surroundings alone, in a world absent of her familiar roots.

The entire situation sucked.

There was simply no other way to put it.

"Tracker." Napolean's deep, resonant voice cut through his internal reverie, bringing him back to the conference room and the various players at hand, all those gathered for one singular purpose, one grave resolution: to help Julien find and destroy his evil twin, once and for all.

"Sorry, milord," he mumbled absently, meeting the monarch's onyx gaze. "I was...I was someplace else."

"She's going to be fine, warrior," Napolean said candidly, making it abundantly clear that he was reading Julien's thoughts, or at least he was reading his countenance, since mind-invasion was considered rude among fellow vampires.

Julien nodded. He cleared his throat and leaned forward in his chair, all at once switching into *strictly business* mode. "So," he projected, "will someone run this plan by me again? Any adjustments you might have made while I was helping Becca settle in?"

Nachari Silivasi's eyes brightened, if only for a second, as he caught the intimate reference, the shortening of Rebecca's name. He leaned back, crossed one leg over the other, sideways at the knee, and then placed a firm, supportive hand on Braden Bratianu's left shoulder. "As everyone here already knows, I'm not exactly thrilled about the idea of using this fledgling as a decoy, but—" Braden stiffened in reaction to the word *fledgling*, and Nachari quickly amended his statement. "I'm not exactly thrilled about using this courageous and determined neophyte as a decoy, but since we don't know where Ian is and have no sure way to flush him out, the plan makes sense to me." He softened his tone to a reflective tenor. "I spoke with Dario and Lily earlier—they needed to know what was going on—and while Braden's mother registered some pretty strong objections—in fact, she more or less said *no way, no how*—his stepfather was more understanding as a warrior. In the end, they gave us their blessing, just so long as we have all bases covered. Just so long as Braden's backup includes not only the sentinels, but the king."

At this, Napolean stiffened, and then he simply took over the conversation. "As all of you know, I do not make a habit of hunting Dark Ones—my duties lie elsewhere, and I am reluctant to use my unique celestial powers because of the risk they pose to the house of Jadon. When I am weakened, ill, or depleted, anything could happen. One never knows what the cost of such an energy surge might be. *However...*" He cleared his throat for emphasis. "I believe this situation is unique, and therefore, it may require an exception." He held up his hand to silence any protests or remarks before the council of warriors could make them. "That said, Ian would surely recognize the unique power of my presence, the sheer force of my energy, in an instant, should I be physically present at the creek. He would never appear to young Braden. For that reason, I will link to Braden's psyche and watch through Braden's eyes from the manse, prepared to materialize at the scene in an instant. I do believe, however, that Ian would fail to notice a panther blending in with the night, camouflaged within the shadows, and Julien"—he turned to lock gazes with the tracker—"in the middle 1800s, I witnessed a ferocious ambush between a small band of Chiricahua Apache and a regiment of unsuspecting US soldiers:

BLOOD ECSTASY

The Apache literally burrowed beneath the ground, making themselves one with the landscape, and when the soldiers passed by, they arose like ghosts from an unmarked grave, part and parcel of the land itself, overtaking the enemy before the enemy even knew they were there. If you can slow your heartbeat to a mere crawl, the wizard has assured me that he can control your breathing with a spell, replace the need to acquire oxygen through your lungs so you don't have to hold your breath. Your body will continue to transfer the hemoglobin through your cells and deliver it throughout your body, maintaining the functionality of your brain—"

"You can do all that while you're in panther form?" Julien asked dubiously, not meaning to interrupt the king.

"Yes, I can," Nachari said bluntly, casting a sidelong glance at the tracker.

Julien shrugged his shoulders, and the king continued: "As I was saying, Nachari will see to your breathing so that you can arise like an Apache warrior and take your brother by surprise. You can be there at the creek, ahead of young Braden, already burrowed in. Nachari will be there also; the sentinels will be waiting in the wings; and I will appear *if needed*, to end the whole sordid affair with a glance."

Nachari nodded in affirmation, and Julien sucked in a harsh breath of air. After taking a moment to collect his thoughts and measure his words, he stated: "Just so you know…" He leveled a cautionary gaze at every warrior at the table. "You weren't there on my tenth birthday—I was. Ian can move like the wind. He can strike swiftly and definitively in the space of a single breath. Braden *will be* in danger if he's there with Ian alone, in closer proximity than Nachari or myself, if only for a heartbeat. We can counter whatever Ian does, but we can't stop him from striking. The male is like a scorpion, and he packs a powerful sting."

Nachari swallowed his trepidation, although it was evident in his dark green eyes, and then he nodded once again. "We're aware," he said matter-of-factly. "But Braden can also move swiftly." He tightened his grip on the youngster's shoulder. "No, he may not be able to fight in a way that is equal to a centuries-old male, but he can shift into a bat—"

"In less than three seconds," Braden supplied, drawing back his shoulders and puffing out his chest. "I can also shift into an eagle, almost instantaneously."

Nachari eyed him suspiciously, his eyebrows raising in surprise.

"I can," Braden insisted, nodding his head several times. "I've been working on it, like…forever."

Nachari held his tongue out of what appeared to be great restraint and deference. "So you can swiftly fly away if needed?"

"Yep," Braden responded, and then his lip quirked up in a snarl. "Or I can rip his throat out with my talons, or peck his eyes out with my beak."

"Um, that would be a no," Ramsey Olaru chimed in, leveling a stern, heated gaze at the teenage vampire. "Braden, if there's even a chance that you're gonna go off-script, that you could become a liability in all of this, then it's a non-starter. Sorry, but you fighting Ian is not an option. You either stick to the plan, without wavering, or we come up with another strategy."

Santos Olaru linked his hands in front of him and then extended both forefingers toward Braden in a targeted gesture. "Agreed."

Saber crossed his arms over his chest and stared the fledgling down, even as Saxson leaned gently toward him. "For the record, my role in all of this is singular," Saxson said. He leveled his gaze at Braden and raised both eyebrows. "To keep my eye on you. To jump in, the second anything goes down, and remove *you* from the fray. That's it; that's all. Your parents said it's non-negotiable. The king said it's a wrap. If I get involved in any other way, outside of having your back, he's gonna kick my ass, himself."

Napolean snorted and frowned.

Apparently, that side-conversation was supposed to be off the record.

"Sorry, milord," Saxson mumbled.

BLOOD ECSTASY

The tip of Braden's nose twitched in anger, or maybe frustration. "So, what? I'm just a liability now? I'm not even a vampire? I'm not even a man? Forgive me, *warriors*, but this is bullshit—just sayin' since I'm part of this council."

Nachari hung his head. He waved his hand in an arc to silence any protests from the others and sighed. "Braden…" He spoke calmly. "We've been over this, son. I know how you feel. We all know how you feel. And we all get it. I promise; we do. But this"—he gestured once again, this time denoting the table, the conference room, and all the vampires present. "This is the real deal. This is what being a man, a warrior, and a member of the house of Jadon looks like. Coming to the table with the sentinels and the king, agreeing on strategy and assigning roles, making sure the warrior beside you knows—without question or hesitation—that you are one hundred percent, all in. That you have his back. That you get the plan. That you're completely on board with working as a unit. You want to be taken seriously? Then you take us seriously. Then you take obedience seriously. You want a place at the table with the big boys, with the king? Then you'd better learn to watch your mouth. Just sayin'."

Julien drew back and grimaced as he watched the scene unfold: It was uncharacteristic of Nachari Silivasi to speak in such a harsh, unequivocal manner, especially to the sensitive, impressionable boy, but this was not a time to play around. He watched as Braden's complexion grew sallow, and the fledgling averted his eyes.

"Sorry," Braden mumbled.

And while the whole scene was instructive and touching, Julien had heard enough. Ian was his lifelong nemesis, the never-ending thorn in his side, and if Nachari was going to be in charge of keeping Julien breathing while he waited underground, then the last thing the wizard needed to worry about was a recalcitrant boy, a spirited young vampire who was eager to prove himself at the creek. "Look at me," he snarled, locking his gaze with Braden's and dilating his own pupils as a precursor to a compulsion. He had every intention of burning an unerring command into the child's mind—*you will do exactly as Ramsey has bid you*—thus, removing the element of chance.

"Tracker." Napolean's deep, commanding voice brought him up short.

Julien's intense gaze shot to Napolean, and he made no effort to conceal the disdain he knew was brimming in his eyes.

"No." The king's word fell upon the table like an anvil. "That is not our code."

Julien started to protest, but something in Napolean's demeanor brought him up short, and he sank back into his chair instead. "Apologies, milord."

Napolean nodded, and then he turned his attention to Braden. "Son, do we have your word? Your job is to lure Ian to the creek; if possible, to lead him to where Julien is hiding; and then, to put it in terms you youngsters understand, to get the hell out of dodge, post haste. No magic, no fighting, no improv. You follow Saxson's lead—and his orders—as if they were my own. Your word?"

Braden nodded emphatically. "You have my word."

"Very well," Napolean continued. "Now then, read the missive once more so that we are all reminded of Ian's treachery, what this simple, manipulative degenerate believes he can pull off."

Braden reached into the hip pocket of his jeans and retrieved the crumpled missive, shaking it out a few times to unsnarl the page: *Greetings, my auspicious friend*—he paused to roll his eyes—*I have discovered nine perfect stones down by the stream, near River Rock Road, and I believe I have fashioned five perfect citrines, three perfect rubies, and one flawless diamond ~ all for my newfound acquaintance. Alas, I am still biding my time—you will keep our secret, won't you? Meet me by the river, Sunday night. Same place as before. I am in great need of familiar company. Grigori.*

Braden tossed the missive in the center of the mahogany table, and Julien stifled a snarl.

They had less than thirty minutes remaining.

Thirty minutes before the sun went down.

BLOOD ECSTASY

Thirty minutes to get into position, and thirty minutes to solidify the plan.

Julien drew a deep breath of air in a gargantuan effort to control his emotions—he could not afford to lose it now—his mind had to be clear and free of opiates when he met his twin on the banks of the mountain creek.

In less than thirty minutes, Julien Lacusta would *finally* get the chance of a lifetime to settle a score as timeless and primal as the cycle of life, *and death*, itself. He would finally get to unleash the demons that had taken root in his soul, tortured his psyche, devoured his sanity, and ruled his every waking moment for as long as he had drawn breath.

Yes...

In less than thirty minutes, Julien Lacusta would meet up with his twin.

Ian Lacusta.

The monster who had slain their parents: one, by default; the other, by intention.

At long last, Julien would have a chance to settle the score.

twenty-five

River Rock Creek ~ nightfall

The sentinels waited in the wings, about one mile downwind from the rushing river, carefully concealed beyond the shoulder of River Rock Road. Napolean watched from the manse, his psychic mind linked to both Braden's and Julien's, projecting the scene like an old-fashioned movie reel into the minds of the waiting vampires. The panther crouched, low and still, hugging the upper limb of a narrowleaf cottonwood, despite the sapling's flimsy branches. And the tracker burrowed deeper into the ground, willing his body not to shake as he struggled to remain undetected.

The night was ironically calm.

The air was both damp and cool.

And despite slowing his heartbeat to a creeping rhythm, Julien could've sworn each beat, each slow, measured timbre, resounded like the clang of a symbol.

He held his breath and waited.

Listening, intently.

Tuning in to every reel of film, every clear, moving picture projected from the Sovereign One's mind: Braden had taken an unhurried position on the bank of the river, just three or four paces beyond a smooth, rocky ledge at the bottom of the steep embankment. He was pretending to study a handful of polished river stones, and he was in the perfect position to take two large strides back and deliver Ian to Julien.

As the air began to thicken and a familiar mist settled in,

Julien's skin began to tingle, and his senses became hyper-alert. And then, just like that, the dark, wily vampire stepped out of the mist and sauntered along the banks of the river, his right hand extended to Braden in greeting.

Julien grit his teeth, narrowing his gaze on the image Napolean was projecting: Six-foot-four, the same height as Julien; peculiar, dark gray eyes, only Ian's were slate-gray as opposed to moonstone, absent of compassion and vacant of life; and long, wild hair that fell to the middle of his back, crisscrossing in wavy bands of black and red, the signature coronet of a Dark One.

Whoa.

Julien did a double-take.

Apparently, Napolean was seeing Ian with second sight, and there were two images being projected, one superimposed over the other: Grigori Antonopoulos, the hoax with blond hair that Ian was presenting to Braden, and the true face of the monster, which Napolean was seeing clearly.

A dark twin, born to the house of *Jadon.*

It was eerie to say the least.

"Greetings, my auspicious friend." That voice. It was deep, duplicitous, and guttural.

Braden reluctantly extended his hand and nervously cleared his throat. "What's up, Grigori."

The vampire bowed his head in a mockery of an old-world gesture, and then, without blinking or any hint of warning, he tightened his grip on Braden's right hand; yanked the youngster forward, pulling him off balance; and thrust five claws at Braden's chest, wielding his unencumbered hand.

He went straight for the kill.

Straight for the heart.

There was no hesitation.

Julien's eyes grew wide as he sprang from the ground like a geyser, praying he wasn't too late. With dirt and leaves clouding his vision, he gasped as Ian's claws pierced young Braden's chest, clutched at the flesh-and-blood organ, and drew back with a mighty tug.

The youngster grunted, flailed his arms, and tried to regain his balance.

And then, in what appeared to be a lightning-quick sleight-of-hand, the air filled with swirling feathers, and Ian drew back a sterling white plume, the penna of an eagle, instead of Braden's heart.

Nachari pounced from the tree, landing on Ian's chest, even as Julien encircled Ian's shoulders from behind, palmed his forehead with an outstretched hand, and wrenched his head to the side in an effort to snap his neck.

A sharp pain shot through Julien's side, causing him to lose the element of surprise and the benefit of momentum—*what the hell?*—as his own head snapped back, a pair of lethal fangs sank deep into his jugular, and what felt like the sudden presence of a giant crowding behind him began to snarl in his ear.

He released his hold on Ian and punched backward, over his left shoulder, slamming his fist into the face of the new assailant—three times in quick succession—before spinning around in an arc and forcing the jagged fangs to dislodge from his throat.

Meanwhile, Nachari and Ian were going at it like two wild, mystical beasts, shifting in and out of vampiric form: One moment, the panther was lunging for the Dark One's throat; the next, he was grappling with mist. One instant, Ian was landing a series of lethal, targeted blows—striking the green-eyed wizard in the gullet, pummeling his ears, and gouging at his eyes—the next, he was flailing at a black furry ball that twisted in midair like a serpent, while releasing a harrowing cry: a roar, a grunt, and a scream.

Through his peripheral vision, Julien caught a momentary glimpse of Saxson Olaru, cradling the bloodied breast of an eagle in his hands, preparing to release and inject healing venom, but he didn't have a chance to zoom in. The giant who had attacked him from behind was now coming at him like a tank, unleashing a full-frontal assault.

Julien reached down to the thigh of his cargo pants, retrieved his familiar battle axe, and began to hack, and twirl, and slice, removing sizeable chunks of flesh with each expert swipe.

The gargantuan vampire laughed.

He flew backward, just out of Julien's reach, and curled his massive palms into fists, contracting the circular bands, the jewel-eyed black mambas that wrapped around each bulging bicep; and Julien knew exactly what—and whom—he was dealing with.

Achilles Zahora.

The Executioner.

The bestial soldier of the Dark Ones' Colony Guard.

So, Ian had made an alliance with the house of Jaegar?

Before Julien could process the full meaning of that statement, the banks of the river filled with lethal vampires from the house of Jaegar: three additional Dark Ones, with bands around their arms, all members of the Colony Guard; one familiar, evil persona, Salvatore Rafael Nistor; and of course, his own wicked brother, Ian Lacusta.

The dark twin still remained.

Santos, Ramsey, and Saber shimmered into view as one, each deadly warrior armed to the teeth and prepared to take on the enemy in a violent, brutal clash, and it was clear as day how the combatants were matched: The sentinels were paired with the Colony Guard; the sorcerer had come for the wizard; and the two Lacusta twins were the match that would set the deadly inferno ablaze.

It was also as dark as midnight—the sky had filled with looming clouds.

The earth began to tremble beneath them.

And the water in the river began to rise in sudden, turbulent waves, the peaks spouting crescents of fire as the ancient, half-celestial beings prepared to go to war.

Ian immediately fell back into the protective arms of a semicircle, ensconced by his dark, twisted allies, and Nachari Silivasi did the same: He retreated like a ghost, falling seamlessly into line with the sentinels, and that's when Saber Alexiares sauntered to the zenith of the skirmish and smirked.

"Julien," Saber snarled brazenly, "*brothers*"—he placed a special emphasis on the familial word—"a soldier should know the names of his enemies, those who are about to die." He spat in the direction of the Dark One's lineup, and then he pointed at each member of the Colony Guard, one by one. "Achilles Zahora, the bastard with the creepy orange eyes; Silas Slovinsky, the brain-dead mute with a ring in his nose; Nuri Bolasek, the demon with albino skin; and Falcon Zvara, the jackal with a Mohawk—watch your back with this one; he likes to hide poison beneath his claws." He eyed each male from head to toe with unconcealed disdain, and then he turned toward Salvatore Nistor. "And of course, this one needs no introduction: Salvatore Egomaniac Nistor. Apparently, he never grows tired of being humiliated; he's obviously addicted to defeat; and he's far too stupid to recognize when he's facing a superior magician. He shouldn't be hard to take."

Salvatore Nistor shook with rage.

His fangs descended like two venomous daggers from his gums, and he lunged at Saber's throat.

Saber raised his forearm to block him and countered with a roundhouse kick that sent the sorcerer flying backward toward the sharp, gangly branches of a nearby tree, but before the limbs could impale the evil sorcerer, Salvatore extended both arms, spit out a curse in ancient Romanian, and threw back his head in raucous laughter as the coiled black mambas encircling each of the dark soldiers' arms instantly came to life as living, hissing serpents, and dove into the fray.

Nachari immediately released five bands of light from the tips of his curled fingers, and five enormous scorpions, their pincers soaked in blood, besieged the mystical snakes, one magical apparition challenging another.

From that point forward, it was absolute mayhem, a clash of mighty beasts: From the corner of his eye, Julien saw Ramsey Olaru thrust the tines of his trident deep into Silas Slovinsky's gut; he saw Santos Olaru summersault over the head of Achilles Zahora and drive an iron stake into the top of Nuri Bolasek's skull as he made his perilous descent; and he could've sworn he saw Saber Alexiares dive onto Falcon's back like a crazed rodeo cowboy mounting an angry bull, as Salvatore and Achilles double-teamed Nachari, who drew his beloved sword and began to fight like a knight of old.

None of it mattered.

It was all background noise.

Julien had only one objective, and it was encased in tunnel vision as he sought to locate Ian, the brother he had come to kill.

As if illuminated on a stage of their own, where all the other warriors were props, Ian sauntered forward with a cocky, lazy stride and presented himself to the tracker. "Brother," he drawled in a noxious tone. "At long last, we meet again."

Julien bristled, and his heart constricted in his chest. "Grigori," he mocked. "Cute, Ian. Cute."

Ian smiled, and his razor-sharp teeth shone like the moonlight against his blood-red gums. "Did you get my birthday cards?"

Julien didn't reply, nor did he react.

"No?" Ian furrowed his eyebrows in a mock-gesture of deep disappointment. "Aw, that's too bad. And to think, I chose each one so carefully. For you."

Julien held his brother's stare, even as he followed his every subtle movement: the right leg that was shifting backward to sustain a forward lunge; the open palm that was sliding downward to cover the hilt of a blade; and the barest twinkle in Ian's gray eyes, the same one that had flashed a millisecond before he had attacked Harietta, signaling his intent to kill. "You should've died nine centuries ago, Ian, and I'm here to set that straight."

Ian licked his lips. "Mmm, I see. Well, I'd be impressed if you could."

Once again, Julien declined to respond—chitchat was not his thing. He would rather speak with his weapon and his fists.

Raising his battle axe, he sliced crosswise at Ian's throat, and in the exact same moment, orchestrated with uncanny, identical alacrity, Ian drew his dagger and countered with a similar move. It was like shadow-boxing in a mirror, the exactness of each brother's timing, his movement, and his aim.

Both drew blood.

Neither sliced the jugular.

And each dropped down into a crouch…

At the exact same instant.

Two jabs connected with two temples. Two uppercuts rattled two jaws. And two elbows struck two throats, as each male jolted, coughed, and took a stutter-step back.

They were perfectly matched as opponents.

Julien drew deep into a pocket of inner silence, the eye of a turbulent storm. He could not let the sameness of their instincts unsettle him, the fact that they were truly homogeneous as twins…

And warriors.

He would have to beat him with his mind.

He rotated his wrist, spinning his axe in a loop, even as he countered Ian's sideways steps, circling his brother in a deadly tango, hoping to lull him into a metaphorical sleep.

Ian chuckled, a fiendish sound, as he rotated his dagger in his fingers. "How long shall we dance, dear brother?"

Julien struck with his left hand first, landing a crisp, lightning-fast strike to Ian's right cheek before the Dark One could see it coming. It was an act of condescension, an insult meant to inflame, and the last maneuver Ian would expect. The tracker followed it up with a brittle backhand, a punitive forehand, and another harsh slap, snapping the Dark One's head backward, like a bobber on a line, and dislodging an entire row of teeth before falling back into the familiar dance.

Ian howled with rage, and then he thrust his dagger upward, aiming the blade at Julien's chest. The Master Warrior blocked the razor with the head of his axe, rotated his wrist 180 degrees, and shoved the blunt end into Ian's rib cage, luxuriating in the sound of the crackling bones.

Yet Ian didn't flinch.

He took advantage of the moment by dropping his dagger, releasing his remaining claws, and striking swiftly at Julien's heart.

Julien saw it coming. He inverted his chest, and he flew backward about fifteen feet, releasing his wings to propel him.

And then, Ian struck with an onslaught of relentless attacks, none of them involving his fangs or his fists, none of them requiring close proximity, none of them a physical assault. Like an arrow piercing through the center of Julien's skull, a stream of images impaled the tracker's cerebral cortex: Micah Lacusta being claimed by the Blood; Harietta Lacusta having her throat torn out; and century after century of Julien tracking Ian through village after village, while the bastard hid in the shadows…and watched.

Julien had been *that* close…time after time.

Within striking distance!

Yet he had never flushed out his evil brother.

What kind of tracker was he?

A voice like pure, unadulterated thunder resounded in the tracker's ears: "Julien! Snap out of it. *Let go of your rage!*"

Julien blinked three times.

It sounded like Napolean Mondragon.

"Half of Silverton Creek is in ruins: The farmlands are burning; the roads are imploding; and the dam has broken from a flood."

Still grappling with the endless barrage of images, the stream of insanity that Ian was flooding into his mind, Julien glanced at the midnight sky, and for the first time, he realized it was pouring down rain, icy torrents mixed with fragments of hail, accentuated by the crackling of thunder and backlit by blazing bolts of lightning.

Were those sirens he heard in the distance?

Were his feet sinking deep in the mud?

His eyes shot forward, only for a moment, and that's when

he noticed the wall of flames.

The forest was on fire!

But when had that happened?

He thought he heard Napolean prodding him again from some great distance, but he couldn't be sure. The images were coming too quickly—they were fast and furious now—and they showed no sign of letting up: Analise and Evangeline, two innocent young girls, helpless and being ravished, brutalized, and murdered, every morbid detail of their violation displayed in living color for Julien to see; the village people dying, burning, screaming, falling through the cracks in the earth; and a scene…another scene…that made no sense!

Rebecca Johnston, Julien's own immortal *destiny*, being spiked to an ancient stone wall. Her limbs were being torn from her torso, her eyes were being pried from her skull, and all the while, she just screamed and screamed…and screamed.

It had to be a hoax.

It had to be a threat.

Rebecca was safe at Napolean's manse.

She had to be.

Narrowing his vision on Ian, Julien fought to block out the rain, the thunder, and the lightning. He shoved Napolean's voice out of his head, and he became nothing but a feral beast, a warrior from the house of Jadon, and a final instrument of death.

Remove the heart.

Sever the head.

Incinerate the body so that it can't come back.

There were only three steps involved, one way to kill a vampire, and Julien had run out of time.

Ian would never, *ever* get to Rebecca.

And he would never haunt Julien again.

The Dark One's life had been a foul aberration of nature, brought about by an evil curse, and he had left death and destruction and abomination in his wake for as long as he had drawn breath.

BLOOD ECSTASY

Today would be his last.

For the first time since a ten-year-old boy had hardened his heart and fought his emotions, struggling to keep the madness at bay, Julien Lacusta gave full vent to his rage. And his vengeance.

He sprang from the mud like a tiger, slammed his body into the frame of his twin, and drove them both forward and upward, over the embankment, well beyond the river, and right into the center of the flames.

May the gods burn to ash that which should never have been.

twenty~six

Saxson Olaru could not believe his eyes.

Had he just witnessed an act of murder *and* suicide?

No.

No!

Julien could not be gone!

Not after diving into a fire. Not like that. Not when he had just found his way.

His *destiny.*

Not when there was so much life left to live.

He cautiously approached the convulsing wall of flames and turned to regard Napolean.

The sovereign leader of the house of Jadon had appeared on the scene within moments of the mayhem breaking out. He had checked on young Braden first, offered a stream of his venom to insure the healing of the fledgling's chest, and then immediately faced off with the Colony Guard: One look into his blazing, crimson eyes; one glance at his towering, muscular form, trembling with barely concealed wrath; and one glimpse of the moonlight coalescing around him like a medieval, celestial cloak, and the soldiers from the house of Jaegar had retreated, vanished into the night.

Apparently, their loyalty to Ian hadn't run that deep.

And Ian, the dark twin of Julien Lacusta himself, had been as oblivious as the tracker: oblivious to the natural phenomena occurring all around him; oblivious to the violent changes in the earth; enraptured in the bizarre, intimate dance that he had shared with his brother; determined to conquer his nemesis, at last.

To finalize the kill.

Whatever chain, or link, or mystical cord tied the two Lacusta brothers together in their lethal, vengeful tango, Napolean had been unable to break it.

No one had.

Nachari's magic hadn't worked.

Ramsey's harsh shouts hadn't penetrated their stalemate.

And neither Saber nor Santos had broken through their paralytic bond.

Finally, Napolean had sent the wizard, the boy, and the other sentinels to Silverton Creek, commanding them to help the residents: to put out fires, reinforce the roads, and stabilize the dam, to remain invisible if they had to. He didn't care how they did it, as long as they preserved human life and countered the celestial fury that was rocking the earth and scourging the land. He had asked Saxson to remain, to ward off any potential enemies while he had tried to reach the soul inside of Julien.

"Julien! Snap out of it. *Let go of your rage!*" The warrior had blinked three times. "Half of Silverton Creek is in ruins: The farmlands are burning; the roads are imploding; and the dam has broken from a flood."

Nothing.

Not a single reply.

The tracker had glanced at the midnight sky, and he had seemed to notice the rain, the hail, and the lightning. He had seemed to finally hear the sirens in the distance; but then, his eyes had locked on Ian's, and something dark, dangerous, and determined had passed through them. The next moment, he was lunging at the Dark One, launching them both into the air and diving into the flames.

"Saxson! The river!" Napolean had barked, sweeping his hand in a wide arc to indicate the narrow, roiling channel. "Great goddess, Andromeda, buy us some time!" His prayers had been like smoke, billowing to the heavens.

Saxson had immediately leaped into the center of the water

and began to draw the elements into his hands. Channeling the molecules with every ounce of his being, he had sent stream after powerful stream in a furious, frantic deluge into the wall of flames. He had continued to pump the water like a living, breathing hydrant into the blazing, noxious fire, praying as he went. *Great Hercules, god of war, protect your beloved son.*

And he had watched.

As Napolean Mondragon, the fearless leader of the house of Jadon, had stretched out his hands, threw back his head, and blown shards of ice, channeling winter into the terrifying blaze.

Seconds had felt like minutes.

Minutes had felt like hours.

As they had waited for the flames to recede, for the furious animation of molecules to become the sluggish slumber of inertia, for the fire to become subdued.

Finally, when the crackling, hissing, and popping of the golden serpent had died down, Saxson had swallowed his trepidation, leaped from the riverbed to the edge of the smothering fire, and joined Napolean in a morbid expedition to find what was left of Julien.

Now, as they padded through the ice, the sludge, and the ash, searching the ground with their transcendent vision, listening for the faintest beat of a heart, begging the gods for mercy as they crept along, Saxson felt a horrible sense of foreboding.

And then he saw them.

The two Lacusta brothers…

Their arms and legs intertwined like four spindly, charred logs.

He stifled a gasp.

Their features and their hair were no longer recognizable— they were simply two scorched heaps of cinders and slag.

Despite his determination to be strong, Saxson retched and choked on the rising bile. "No," he muttered absently, "*no!*" He turned to glance at Napolean and began to tremble. Finally, when he had regained his composure, he cleared his throat again.

"Which one…" He had to stop to modulate his words. "Which one do you think is Julien?"

Napolean bit down hard on his bottom lip, and his shoulders stiffened like iron rods. He followed the lines of the blackened arms down to the melted hands and studied the head of an axe, an uncharred piece of iron, still gripped by a forefinger and a thumb. "The male on top." The king immediately dropped down into a crouch, released his incisors, and began to apply a liberal amount of venom to the area near the top of the heap, as close to the jugular as he could surmise. When he finally came up for breath, he squinted at Saxson through tear-stained eyes. "Call Kagen Silivasi, now! Tell the healer we're on our way. His body is still, somewhat, intact." The king choked over the words. "His heart…and his head…they're not…completely gone."

Saxons grimaced and took an unwitting step back. "As you will, milord," he mumbled, too shaken to say any more. And then he watched as Napolean Mondragon encased the mangled form—the body of the tracker ravaged by fire—in a solid block of ice and lifted the mass, as if it weighed nothing more than a feather, out of the rubble, cradling it as best he could against his trembling chest. "Burn the rest of that crap to smithereens," he ordered, his voice as cool as the cradled ice. "Make sure there is nothing left of Ian to revive." As he stepped out of the remnants, the ash, and the strangled fire, he dropped his anguished head and shielded the beloved figure in his arms with his hair, almost like a shroud.

And then he released his glorious black-and-silver wings and shot into the sky, heading for Kagen's clinic.

Saxson watched as the magnificent figure receded into the night, illuminated by the light of the moon, and once again, he prayed…

Until nothing but silence, regret, and what was left of the forest surrounded him.

twenty-seven

Three hours later

Rebecca Johnston felt numb and disoriented as she sat in the passenger seat of Brooke Mondragon's car and watched the Cimmerian darkness go by. They traversed the private, rocky terrain that led to Kagen's hospital; made their way through the dense, pine forest; and finally came to a halt in a simple, unpaved lot that preceded an archaic stone-bridge.

The surreal moment was bathed in shadowed moonlight, and her heart was cocooned in her chest.

Dazed.

Sleeping.

And curiously, lukewarm.

She glanced through the front windshield at the cliffs beyond the passage, the steep, inclining path that would take them by foot to the hidden facility, the Dark Moon Vale Clinic, and she tried to tune in to the winding Snake River.

She *needed* the resonance of the whitewater rushing beyond the car to soothe her troubled soul. Because this—all that had happened over the past seven days—was far too much to absorb.

Far too much to comprehend.

"Rebecca?" Brooke's kind, gentle voice interrupted her thoughts. "Are you okay, sweetie?"

Rebecca furrowed her brow. "So tell me again—what happened? He was burned in a fire, during the fight?"

Brooke cleared her throat, shifted in her seat to meet

Rebecca's gaze, and the depth of compassion that shone in her eyes was almost too much to bear. "Yeah, he was hurt pretty bad."

"Burned?" Rebecca repeated.

It was a stupid question.

Brooke nodded solemnly. "Yes."

"But..." Rebecca wrung her hands together. "But he's a vampire, right? I mean, like me, at least now. So he'll heal...or regenerate...or come out of it, in time? He just needs a lot of venom and attention, and maybe some...some surgery?"

Brooke bit her bottom lip and tried to present a reassuring smile that she couldn't quite fake. "He..." She paused to measure her words, oh so carefully, *way too carefully.* "He lost a lot of his density...his mass...due to the fire. A lot of it was burned away." The queen's voice faltered, and Rebecca wanted to scream in frustration: *Stop, just stop!* But she waited, silently, instead. "The thing is," Brooke continued, "what's most vital is the heart, the brain, and the blood. As long as he can regenerate his chambers and absorb fresh blood, as long as he still has sentience, then Napolean's venom is very powerful, and Kagen is as skilled as they come. They're going to do all that they can, but I think that you should be...prepared." Her speech slowed in cadence, reflecting a hollow drone, and Rebecca closed her eyes.

So, Ian had finally won.

He had destroyed Julien's parents, terrorized two innocent little girls, and caused the massacre of a village. He had turned the tracker into a hostage, enslaved to a vile drug, and now he had left Rebecca a widow?

Was that the right word?

Or would she die from the Curse?

She didn't really understand how it all worked.

She only knew that she was no longer human, that she had made a deal with an immortal vampire, and now, she could very well be on her own for the rest of her life.

A very long, confusing, immortal life.

And God forgive her because that was a terribly selfish thought.

Julien had jumped into a fire—*a freaking wall of flames*—in order to destroy his twin, and now, something buried deep inside of Rebecca's heart, something more sentient, more vital than the organ itself, felt like it was being ripped out through her throat.

She didn't understand how.

She didn't understand why.

She only knew she could hardly breathe.

And she didn't want to see him, not like this, her powerful gladiator, burned and charred.

Gone.

Dying.

Destroyed.

"So, what next?" she asked, as if something robotic was animating her mouth, ruling her reflexes, and spurring her on.

Sensing her deep, conflicting angst, Brooke reached across the seat, grasped Rebecca by the hand, and squeezed, her own elegant fingers trembling. "We get out of the car. We put one foot in front of the other. And we walk into the clinic." She began to rush her words, as if she was afraid of losing her courage. "And then, we take it one step, one breath, at a time. Kagen will meet us at the door, and his mate, Arielle, will be with him—she has a very gentle soul, a very healing presence. They will sit you down and explain everything, bring you up to speed, and you don't have to see him until you're ready." She inhaled sharply, clearly rattled by her own carefully chosen words. "Nachari is here, too. He came back early from Silverton Creek. He can explain some of the deeper aspects, the spiritual or metaphysical concerns. And Saxson—he's one of the sentinels who was there during the battle—he's waiting for us, along with the others. He can tell you anything you might want to know about what happened down by the river, or shortly after, when he and Napolean found Julien. The point is…" She paused to stare at her fingers, and it struck Rebecca as odd. Despite Brooke's gentle, supportive nature, the queen was truly distraught. "You are not alone, sweetie. You will never be alone again. We are here, the entire house of Jadon, my family, myself, and the king. We are here with you, and with Julien. And we're going to help you see this through. No matter what occurs."

Rebecca drew back her hand and flicked it in the air, almost as if she could wring out her emotions through the gesture, soften the intensity, and magically, subdue the fear. Her eyes welled up with tears, and she knew she was going to lose it if she didn't get out of that car, get away from the queen…

As fast as she could.

She groped for the handle on the door, tugged it open with a jerk, and leaped out of the vehicle, slamming the heavy panel behind her. And then she made her way to the archaic bridge, all the while walking through a fog, where she paced back and forth and stared at the churning river beneath her.

Julien Zechariah Lacusta.

Tracker for the house of Jadon.

A vampire.

The gladiator who had ravaged her life.

And her soul.

The male who had kissed her so passionately, touched her so gently, that day in her apartment when she had told him about her birds: Analise and Evangeline.

The liquid H and "The House of the Rising Sun": such terror, such fear, such confusion.

Trevor…

And the VOSU women.

He had taken her nightmare away.

Her conversion, and the pregnancy that was soon to ensue: the Curse, the sacrifice, and the twins.

Ian!

That monster!

And the house of Jadon.

Julien had rushed into a fire!

Her thoughts were like smattering raindrops tossing in the wind, pouring down in random, icy currents, striking where they may, leaving puddles and pools and cold, frosty streams, flowing like random, tumultuous rivers in their wake.

"Oh, sweetie." She heard the queen's voice…again. "It's going to be okay. Somehow. Someway." And then the woman, the vampire queen, the one with the ebony hair, wrapped her graceful arms around Rebecca and sat with her on the ground—*when had Rebecca slumped to the ground?*—and rocked her in her arms.

"It's okay, angel. It really is. Let it all out. It's going to be okay."

twenty-eight

Rebecca had taken her time and coddled her heart.

She had allowed Kagen and Arielle to describe Julien's horrific condition in graphic detail, to explain all of the procedures he'd already had, those he still had scheduled, and his overall precarious prognosis. She had listened as Saxson recalled each and every event that had occurred at the creek, in chronological order, offering as many—or as few—particulars as she desired. And she had done her best to follow Nachari Silivasi's explanation of the spiritual aspects of the injury: Julien's deeper, intrinsic wounds; the life beyond the life; the battle the tracker would have to wage with his body, mind, and soul in order to heal completely.

And once all the discussions were through, she had remained for at least a half an hour in the clinic's serenely appointed anteroom, simply digesting all she'd heard.

Processing.

Feeling.

Accepting as much as she could.

Now, as she stood outside of Julien's medical suite, positioned at the end of the hall, she dug down, deep, for courage. She buried the turmoil, ignored the prognosis, and disposed of the clinical facts as she reached for the handle on the door. *No reservations; no fears; no confusion*, she told herself one last time, stuffing all her chaotic emotions in a small, tidy compartment to reopen and digest later.

You can do this, Becca.

She tugged on the handle, stepped inside the room, and

immediately took three long strides in the direction of the bed, determined to be brave and strong. The door swung shut behind her, and she jerked—but only for a moment. She squared her shoulders and raised her chin, and then she gasped, stifled a scream, and scrambled backward, stunned by the *tragedy* before her. Both hands shot to her mouth as she strangled a horrified cry and gawked, straight ahead, at the vampire.

Julien Lacusta was propped up in the bed, his head supported by the neck and raised by some mechanical mechanism. The majority of his limbs were wrapped tightly in bandages, and for all intents and purposes, he looked like a gruesome paradox of nature: both burned and frozen, both awake and asleep, both healing and dying at the same time. His gorgeous moonstone eyes were open, but vacant, utterly absent of life, staring blankly forward as if he was gazing into space. His thick, sculpted lips, at least what she could make of them, were an impossible shade of blue and littered with multiple bloodstained cracks, and his beautiful mahogany hair was singed to the roots, like a really bad skull-trim or an uneven fade.

And his torso?

That glorious, powerful body that had always been strapped with muscle and imbued with preternatural strength?

It was like an ashen, petrified log, calcified and mangled, hollow and hard.

Rebecca sank to the floor, fell to her knees, and averted her eyes.

She braced her palms on the cool, sterile tiles and tried to regain her bearings. *Just get up*, she told herself. *Slowly. Carefully. Just get up and make your way to the bed.*

What the heck was she feeling?

Horror?

Loss?

Anger or fear?

She couldn't sort through her feelings; this was all too much. *Way too much.*

On one hand, this male, the vampire wrapped in the bed like

a mummy, had once been her captor: a strange, primordial being who had taken her from her life and forced her to face an unimaginable future, a destiny chosen by gods…

And monsters.

But on the other hand, she knew, somewhere deep inside, where the truth could neither retreat nor hide, that the vampire on the bed—the male, the tracker, the warrior—was her soul mate: the other half of her heart. And everything inside of her reeled from the horror of what had been done to him, what had occurred in that blazing forest.

For the first time since she'd met him, she felt an overwhelming pang of impending loss, knowing that, should he fail to pull through, her life, her future, her…*everything*…was over.

Gone.

The revelation was unexpected and stunning.

Nothing made any sense.

Biting down on her lower lip, she rose gingerly from the floor, ascended to her knees, and simply knelt there until she stopped shaking. Her eyes darted around the room, taking in everything *but him*. She couldn't bear to look. And then, as she slowly climbed to her feet, holding her arms outstretched and to the sides in order to maintain her balance, she forced herself to meet his eyes.

Only his eyes.

Just his eyes.

"Tracker," she whispered softly. "It's me. Your little mouse." Unwitting tears blurred her vision, broke free from her tear ducts, and ran down her cheeks, and although the drops were innocuous, she felt the weight of their sting like trickles of acid. He had been right, after all; she would say it one day—she just had.

She sat on the edge of the bed, careful not to rustle his bandaged body, and warily cleared her throat. "Kagen, the doctor-guy, he said you still have a chance." She paused to draw a deep, cleansing breath for courage. "He said he was alternating infusions of venom with skin grafts, and that the tissues beneath the burns will come back as each layer is treated. He said your heartbeat is faint because you're still growing new chambers, and that things are healing slower than usual. But that's because…well, because…your soul seems somehow splintered, like maybe they snatched you back from the brink of death just in the nick of time. Just…barely." She sighed, not really understanding a thing the vampire-doctor had told her. "I don't really understand it," she whispered, refusing to say any more—she wasn't about to tell him the truth. After all, what could she possibly say? That they had told her he was burned, all the way down to his bones, and while Napolean had been able to stop the complete disintegration of his heart…and his brain…by packing his body in ice, they weren't entirely sure if his cells would regenerate, if he wasn't already gone?

His spirit, that is.

Nachari, the wizard-guy, the one who had given him the crystal that first day in his house, he had said something utterly incomprehensible, something about Julien's soul, like it was battling between dimensions. The fire had forced it out of his body, causing it to flee as if in death; but the ice and the prayers had called it back, and it was trying to realign, once again.

All of it was beyond her comprehension.

Her realm of understanding.

What she did get, loud and clear, was the fact that Ian was gone.

Dead. Dead. Dead.

And she was ecstatic about that fact on a level that barely made sense.

The monster had tortured Julien…all of his life.

And by extension, he had also tortured Rebecca.

She knew, without question, that Julien had not made a rash decision at all, when he had chosen to dive into that fire. He had made an absolute calculation, sought a brother's vindication, and exercised his final judgment as both a warrior and a son.

And he had done so with the courage and the heart of a lion.

But what did that mean for them?

What did that mean for her?

What did it mean in terms of the Curse?

Rebecca was Vampyr now, part and parcel of the house of Jadon; there would be no going back for her. And honestly, she wasn't sure if she wanted to—go back, that is—Rebecca wanted Julien to live.

By all the gods, why hadn't she understood this earlier?

Rebecca wanted Julien to live!

To stay…with her.

She sighed and inadvertently reached out to take his hand, instantly drawing hers back: there was nothing concrete to take hold of. And then she jolted as a burst of light shot forth from her fingers, gravitated toward his palm, and then just as quickly withdrew, following the trajectory of her hand.

She turned her palm over and stared at it.

There was nothing obvious there.

Yet and still, she could feel a pulsing energy gathering in her fingertips, originating in her soul, and the darkness, the charred, mangled fragments that substituted for his fingers, began to twitch…or stir. Like fish in a bowl, swimming toward the promise of food, they gravitated toward Rebecca's energy like they were eager to gobble it up.

To devour her light.

She leaned forward and tried again, this time, splaying all five fingers wide, and allowing her palm to simply hover over his damaged limb. The charred layers began to peel back, revealing raw, reddened flesh beneath burns that were capable of…healing.

She pressed her hand even closer.

The bones in his fingers, the phalanges and metacarpals, began to straighten out.

She gasped and drew back her hand.

And then the oddest impulse struck her.

She stared into his vacant, moonstone eyes and slowly bent her head forward. Drawing in a slow, deep breath, she lowered her mouth to his and hovered over his frozen blue lips, and then she released the breath, slowly exhaling...exchanging...imparting her life-force into his. And all the while, she invoked a prayer.

His lips turned pink!

She drew back and giggled, and then she began to cry, uncertain where the tears were coming from. She only knew that something magical, something powerful, something life-giving was passing between them. Her spirit was calling to his, and for whatever reason, however nonsensical, she knew she had the power to bring him back.

And then, for reasons she could hardly understand, her heart suddenly thudded in her chest, and her breath caught in her throat. She glanced up at a solar clock hanging on the wall and cringed in desperation.

Something imminent was happening.

Something cryptic and something dangerous.

Something was threatening Julien, and time was of the essence.

She didn't know how she knew. She didn't know why she believed this would work. She only knew that the vampire's soul was in peril, and she had to break through the charred, bandaged barriers and find him...wherever he was. She had to reach him, quickly.

Rushing from the bed, she sprinted to a nearby counter and began to open drawers. She flung miscellaneous objects to the side in a frenzy, searching frantically for scissors, a scalpel, anything that could cut through the myriad of dressings that enveloped him like a mummy.

She had to have access to his skin!

She knew Kagen Silivasi might think she was crazy if he caught her. And who knew? Maybe the entire house of Jadon would bar her from the tracker's room, believing she had finally flipped her lid, but Rebecca needed to start at Julien's toes and work her way up his torso, however improper that seemed. She had to try to heal him, one touch at a time; each breath, in succession; one magical caress on the heels of another. And for reasons she simply could not fathom...

She had to do it fast.

twenty~nine

Julien Lacusta did not know where he was.

In the land of the living, the land of the dead, or somewhere, lost, between the two.

His head hurt like the dickens; his skin felt like it was on fire; yet curiously, everything around him was shrouded in ice.

He faintly remembered standing on the banks of the River Rock Creek, facing off with his brother, Ian, and gazing into an undulating wall of blazing flames, a rampart of fire and wrath that had enveloped the forest and called to him like a lover.

Beckoning him forward.

Entreating him to embrace his brother and end the madness once and for all.

Now, as he scrubbed a partially transparent, spectral hand over his eyes to clear his vision, he noticed that he was standing on a high, arched bridge, positioned midway along a narrow passage, and it was literally caked in ice. Huge shards of what looked like frozen snow, framed by icicles the size of cars, hung from the bridge's girder, long beyond the anchorage block, and disappeared into a crystal fog. The deck beneath his feet was coated in sleet, and the railings were like virtual planks of frost. Even the towers sustaining the bridge were coated in thick blocks of rime.

He ceased walking and looked both ways, toward each distant shore, trying to distinguish between opposing directions. For all intents and purposes, he was standing at a crossroads: He could turn to the right and cross the bridge, emerging into a thick bank of clouds; or he could turn to the left and traverse the bridge, emerging into a dense, inky darkness.

What the heck was going on?

Where the hell was he?

And then it hit him as he glanced again: The white clouds were dotted with golden specks and almost radiant with brilliance—he somehow knew that they heralded the entrance to the Valley of Spirit and Light. And the dense, inky darkness at the other end of the bridge that practically radiated with despair and malevolence—it augured the entrance to the Valley of Death and Shadows.

Was Julien dead or alive?

Was he caught between two eternal worlds?

And did he have a choice as to which realm he entered?

Nothing made any sense.

Squatting down to make himself smaller—he didn't know if he was alone—he gripped his head in his hands and tried to remember the teachings, all he had learned at the Romanian University in his youth, all he had been taught by the house of Jadon about life after death, the Curse, and the afterworld: Every male from the house of Jadon was destined to reside in the Valley of Spirit and Light unless he failed to fulfill the Curse, to provide the required sacrifice of a dark twin within thirty days of finding his *destiny*; just as every male in the house of Jaegar was destined to enter the Valley of Death and Shadows, even if he made the required offering. For the Dark Ones, it was just a matter of timing, a matter of *when*.

Best to live as long as they could.

Immortal.

Forever.

If possible.

But had Julien actually failed to complete the Curse? Had he refused to comply before he...*died*?

He shook his head to clear the cobwebs.

Nothing was getting any clearer.

He had thirty days from the start of his Blood Moon to provide the Blood with an heir, and the wicked aberration could not claim him before then, not as long as he still had time. If he had refused, tried to outrun the Curse or save his soulless son, then—and only then—could the Blood come after him and take him to the gods-forsaken valley. But—and it was a pretty important *but*—if he turned himself in, after failing to comply, if he willingly entered the Death Chamber, then even after the Blood took his life, his spirit would go on. It would reside, for all eternity, in the valley of the celestial gods.

So which was it?

What had he done?

Or, more importantly, what had he failed to do?

True, if he was actually dead, then technically, he had failed to fulfill the Curse. He had found his *destiny*, claimed her as he must, and died before he could either make the required sacrifice or turn himself in to the Chamber.

But that wasn't his fault.

It wasn't his choice—

Or was it?

Julien had willingly and knowingly dived into the fire with Ian, and that meant he had, in effect, taken his own life. What had Ramsey Olaru said to him, that first day, right after he had found Rebecca? Julien had absently told the Master Warrior: *I have half a mind to tell the Blood to go straight to hell and just let the Curse take me in the end.* And Ramsey had immediately snarled, his voice growing deathly grave. *That'd better be the H talkin', warrior. Don't even play like that. Let's not forget: The Blood can take you on a lifelong trip, an eternal, never-ending vacation. To hell.*

And then Nachari Silivasi…he had chimed in with some advice of his own, later that same day, when he had brought the pale blue crystal, embedded with his memories, to give to Julien to view: *Your life isn't just your own. Your choices don't exist in a vacuum. And your* fate *affects the entire house of Jadon. If you think for one moment that you can just step off the stage without completely screwing Ramsey, Santos, and Saxson—hell, even Saber Alexiares—then you've been sucking down that cocktail for way too long… Try skipping out on the Curse, skirting your way around this Blood Moon, offering yourself up like*

*some suicidal sacrifice to the Blood at the end of these thirty days. Just try it,
and see what happens… No one is going to let you die, brother. And we
don't give a* gods-damn *about what you want or whether or not you've had
enough.*

Nachari had been trying to tell him that suicide, in any form,
was not an option.

Before Julien could process any further, try to figure out if
he was alive or dead or caught in some celestial purgatory, a
hideous crimson shadow swept over the bridge, swirled in an arc
above him, and then dipped down, low, at eye level, where it
snarled and moaned in his ear.

Julien shrank back, immediately recognizing the primordial
taint of the Blood: the ghostly apparition of the original
Romanian females, those who had risen from the dead in order
to wield the perpetual Curse.

"Dear Gods," he muttered, shielding his eyes with his hands
to avoid the noxious glare.

"Trackerrrr," the apparition hissed. "You think to avoid our
Curse?"

Julien shuffled back on his haunches, drawing even lower to
the icy planks. "I…I didn't think at all. When I died…if I
died…it was not intentional."

Sparks, fire, and brimstone shot out of the evil apparition,
melting the frost beneath him. "Oh, but it wasssss." The Blood
drew out the letter *S* like a snake taunting its prey. And then the
bridge began to rock and tremble as a giant of a man—*no, a
god*—stormed out of the mystical white clouds and traversed the
space in an instant.

Once again, Julien shielded his eyes, even as he peeked at the
giant from between two fingers: The male was at least ten feet
tall; his wild hair whipped about his shoulders as if in a violent
wind; and he was the naked personification of an Adonis: all
sculpted, bulging muscle and rock-hard flesh, cloaked in a simple
lion's pelt that covered his back like a cape and wrapped around
his groin like a loincloth. In his right hand, he brandished an
enormous club; in his left, he held a three-headed serpent, also

known as Cerberus; and just like he did in the northern sky, he immediately knelt on one knee.

He was no less imposing at half his height.

Terrifying, really.

Julien immediately bowed his head out of deference and averted his eyes out of terror.

"*Recede*," the mighty god commanded, glaring at the Blood.

The apparition snarled as it warily drew back, allowing Julien some room to breathe, but it did not retreat from its claim. "The child of Hercules is ours! This son of Jadon, who you seek to protect; he failed to fulfill his Blood Moon. We have come to take him to the Valley of Death and Shadows."

Hercules threw back his head and laughed, the deafening retort shaking the deck beneath them. "You foolish necromancers. He isn't dead!" The last word echoed like a clap of thunder.

"Ah, but he will be soon," the Blood crooned softly.

Hercules drew back his shoulders and raised his chest. "Not necessarily," he spat. "And even if he dies, that doesn't necessarily give you a claim. There are yet twenty-two days left in his Blood Moon."

This time, it was the Blood that chuckled. "Perhaps, my lord, perhaps. *But* he was not faithful in his desire to fulfill his obligation—he took his own life. That is not the same as being killed or dying of natural causes, something he couldn't prevent. He can neither present the required sacrifice, nor turn himself into the Chamber. From where we stand, he forfeits his birthright to the Valley of Spirit and Light. He has tried to circumvent the Curse, and now, he belongs to us."

Hercules rose to his full, imposing height and stepped forward toward the Blood, causing the entity to draw back in fear. "Allow me to remind you of the rules, the rubrics you created when you masterminded this infernal curse!" He gestured angrily with his hands as he spoke, his powerful voice dripping with mockery. "From this day forward, you shall be cursed! And your sons shall be cursed. And their sons after them…unto all eternity." He softened his voice just a bit, as he were lecturing a child. "But do not forget that you gave the sons of Jadon *four mercies*; you allowed them to retain their souls. Thus, they reside for eternity in the Valley of Spirit and Light."

The Blood undulated and swayed—to the left, then the right—as if to an internal song. "'Tis true that we allowed them their souls, and we gave them the sun. We did not require them to kill the innocent when consuming their much-needed blood; and we gave them *one opportunity* to procure a mate, and thirty days to do so. But we demanded a sacrifice in return, the life of a soulless son. The Valley of Death and Shadows will not be denied. Whether it was the child or the father, by choice or by challenge, it made no difference to us; but make no mistake, a soul is required, and this one has circumvented the law. He tried to take his own life. He tried to avoid the Curse."

Hercules shook his head, and his golden hair framed his massive shoulders like a royal cloak. "My son is standing on the Bridge Between Worlds for a reason. He is neither alive nor dead, and his final destination is yet to be determined. But I say this to you—and you will hear me clearly—his final choice was one of honor; it was an act of valor; and he did not seek to violate your law. He did not consciously choose to die, nor did he desire to do so. He was simply willing to give his life in order to stop an eternal scourge: his brother, Ian. So the question we weigh is one of degrees—suicide versus natural death—what did the tracker *intend* to do?"

The Blood hissed again, and dark red plasma sprayed outward, perversely staining the snow. "And what court shall decide this dilemma? To whom should we plead our case?"

Hercules tightened his fist in anger, and the three-headed staff shook from his rage. "You may be a powerful entity, grown strong from iniquity and sin, but I am a celestial god, an original omniscient being: I need no tribunal to rule; I require no jury to measure my words; nor do I demand an assembly to weigh my thoughts. There is no power greater than my own. And I have already decided. Should this warrior live, he still has twenty-two days. Should the son of Jadon perish, his soul belongs…to me."

The Blood jolted backward and dipped in what could only be described as an unholy curtsey, and then, without warning or pause, a million crimson cells began to coalesce. They danced, they expanded, and they grew, until they coagulated into a dozen cerise arms and latched onto Julien like tentacles, snatching the tracker to his feet, and drawing him into their mass.

With a rage-filled screech and a final flash of fury, the abomination withdrew from the icy bridge.

Taking the tracker with it.

thirty

As swiftly, yet as carefully, as she could, Rebecca cut through Julien's bandages and turned her full attention to his toes. She wrapped the palms of her hands around each charred, melted digit and waited as the blackened flesh turned pink, as the connected metatarsals realigned. The tracker stirred in the bed, twisting and turning this way and that, but only by small haphazard increments. When she reached his heels, and then his ankles, when she began to massage his calves—all the while breathing, willing, transferring life into his rigid muscles—he began to flex and tense.

It didn't matter.

She couldn't stop to try to read him, to discern what was going on, to call Kagen or Arielle and ask the healers for assistance. For whatever reason, the clock was ticking, and she had to continue…quickly.

In fact, she had to move faster.

Much, much faster.

She covered his kneecaps with her palms and tried to infuse more light, and he kicked in a violent response. For the first time, he actually reacted reflexively to Rebecca's touch, but it wasn't an encouraging response.

It was a panicked, defensive start.

And then he moaned.

And then he shouted!

He jerked his head forward, yanked it free from the medical restraints, and strained the muscles in his neck, as if he intended to get up and run. His once-vacant eyes were wild with fury and fright, yet he still stared fixedly ahead.

Rebecca shivered. "Oh gods, oh gods, oh gods!" She glanced over her shoulder at the door—maybe she should go get Kagen Silivasi, after all—but something more imperative, more important, more imminent drew her back to the immediate task: healing Julien *now.*

Infusing his flesh with light.

Breathing him back to life.

She worked feverishly on his thighs, and then his narrow hips—his ribs, his chest, his shoulders—making her way down his broken arms, until at last she reached his hands. And that's when a sound—*a snarl*—so savage, so vicious, so fierce, emanated from his throat and nearly jolted her from the bed.

She screamed, withdrew her hands, and watched in mounting horror as his fangs punched free from his gums, his claws shot forth from his fingers, and his head twisted in a sharp, serpentine motion, his rage-filled eyes locking onto hers.

"Rebecca!" he roared like a wounded lion.

And then, utilizing the full measure of his strength, he snatched her by the hand and tugged her forward.

Julien twisted and turned.

He flexed his biceps, expanded his chest, and tried to break free from the Blood's unholy clutch, ripping tentacles out of his flesh as he struggled. He reached for his familiar battle axe, but it wasn't there. They were soaring backward at an incredible rate of speed, spinning, falling, and flying through space, traversing the bridge in an instant. And then, just like that, he was surrounded by a terrible, eerie fog, and the ground beneath his feet began to ooze with demonic sludge, roiling in thick, pasty waves over his suddenly bare feet.

He kicked in a futile effort to break free.

The sky was as black as night, utterly absent of light or goodness, and there was no horizon as far as the eye could see, only smoke and mirrors, vapor and mist, and the appearance of charred, calcified earth. The very air around him seemed to scream with terror, to moan with incessant electrical currents, creepy-crawly gusts of wind that whipped at his skin and tugged at his soul as if it wished to rip it out of his chest.

Julien Lacusta was standing in the Valley of Death and Shadows.

"Welcome, brother." Ian's disembodied voice brought him up short, and holy hell—*may the gods have mercy*—he looked like he had swallowed a dragon. He must've stood at least ten feet tall; he had a spiny extremity shooting out of his tailbone; and he was literally enveloped in fire, as if they were both still burning. Only, these flames did not consume the vampire's otherworldly flesh—they magnified it, invigorated it, illuminated his silhouette with blazing, preternatural light. His fangs were the length of a saber-toothed tiger's, and by the look in his savage eyes, he intended to shred Julien to pieces.

The tracker took a wary step back, glancing to his left and then his right.

Where was the Blood now?

It was no longer seizing his limbs.

Where was his ruling celestial god, Hercules?

The lord had spoken clearly—he had made his pronouncement known—Julien did not belong here in the valley of the lost, the eternal resting place of absent, wayward souls!

"I don't...I don't belong here!" he protested feverishly, angered at his desperate opposition. He did not want to give Ian the satisfaction.

As expected, Ian roared with taunting laughter. "Apparently, you do." He swept his arm in a wide arc, indicating the barren gorge all around them. "And isn't this just a delicious twist of fate: I was not the sacrificial twin, after all. *You were.*"

Despite his defiance, Julien gasped.

No.

No!

This could not be happening.

A part of him was stricken with horror: He wanted to live; he wanted to survive! What had he ever done to deserve such a fate? Yet another part of him was resigned to his karma, both the punishment and the chance for revenge. He knew exactly what he had done to deserve this: He had failed to save that village, to appeal to his father's love, and he had failed to atone for the most basic, original sin...

Surviving as a ten-year-old child when he should have perished along with his mother.

He dropped down into a defensive squat, prepared to fight this demon for all he was worth, even knowing that he couldn't prevail. His fangs punched through his gums; he somehow released his claws; and he channeled every ounce of rage he had ever felt—or repressed—into that one critical moment.

And that's when Ian's eyes transformed.

From glowing orbs of crimson, masking hints of deep, slate gray, to bright reflections of topaz, like gemstones, sparkling in a cave.

Julien jolted and blinked three times.

Rebecca?

Ian snarled, and the valley shook.

He took one giant step in Julien's direction and zeroed in on his chest. He was going to seize the tracker's soul.

Julien instinctively threw up his arms, creating a makeshift cross, and shielded his breast from the blow, and that's when Ian's claws became flesh: soft, feminine, and entreating, reaching out to...take his hand?

With feral desperation—and raw, unconcealed rage—Julien ignored his defensive instincts and groped at the outstretched palm. "Rebecca!" he bellowed like a madman, linking his hand in hers. He grasped it like a lifeline and tugged, practically willing his soul to funnel through her arm. Ignoring the demon before him, the inevitable embrace of death, he plunged straight into the fray.

thirty~one

Rebecca fell forward onto Julien's chest, still startled by his savage cry. She tried to brace her palms against his breastbone and frantically push away, but the feral vampire was far too strong and much too aggressive to restrain. His crazed eyes grew wide with horror; he encircled her waist with his arm and tugged her hard against him.

"Bring me to life!" he snarled, sounding more like an animal than a man.

Rebecca flailed in panic, absorbed in a primal struggle of her own, and tried to restrain his hands. "Wh…what's happening?" she whimpered, trying desperately to understand.

"Breathe me to life," he insisted. "Give me your soul. Give me your *blood*."

She opened her mouth to cry out or protest—she really wasn't certain which one—but the warrior moved too fast. With his free hand, he swept her golden-brown hair to the side, clutched a fistful of curls in his palm, and hauled her neck forward to his mouth. And then he bit into her jugular, sinking both of his piercing fangs deep into her vein.

He didn't stop there.

He released her hair, tugged at the buttons on her blouse, and ripped the bodice open. He twisted around in the bed—*bandages be damned*—and pinned her effortlessly beneath him, clutching at the fly of her jeans.

Rebecca screamed, and the door to the clinic swung open.

Kagen Silivasi rushed in, with Saxson Olaru right on his heels. "Warrior!" the healer bellowed, charging toward the bed.

"Snap out of it, J! *You need to stop.*" Saxson's powerful voice ricocheted throughout the room.

Julien retracted his fangs, allowing them to recede about a quarter of an inch as he released his feral bite, and then he panted in Rebecca's ear. "Ian!"

Rebecca gasped, drew back from his desperate barrage, and tried to meet his ravenous gaze. "I don't understand," she muttered, fear still getting the best of her.

The corner of his top lip turned up in a scowl, and his eyes narrowed on hers like lasers. "The Valley of Death and Shadows. My soul is lost. Breathe me back. *Bring me back.* Before he takes my soul."

With their superior vampiric hearing, Kagen and Saxson heard every word, and they both stopped dead in their tracks: The healer halted at the end of the bed, just shy of grasping Julien by the shoulders, and the sentinel skidded to a halt at the tracker's side, one hand extended toward the vampire's bicep. They were clearly prepared to haul him off the bed, if that's what the situation called for.

"What did he just say?" Saxson murmured instead.

Kagen stared numbly at the open bandages. He surveyed the multiple patches of regenerating flesh, and his eyebrows furrowed in confusion. "What happened here, Rebecca?" His tone betrayed his concern.

Neither one knew what to make of what they'd just stumbled into.

Before Rebecca could reply, Julien slid his hands down the small of her waist, along the curve of her hips, and curled his fingers inside the seams of her jeans. And then he ripped the denim sideways, splitting the article in half before he tossed the material to the floor. His thick lips parted as he stared at her trembling belly, and his fangs visibly sharpened.

He moaned.

And Kagen gasped.

Saxson blanched, reached out to take the tracker's forearm, and Rebecca almost screamed…again.

And then she saw it.

All of it.

Like a moving picture suddenly appearing on a screen, and every detail was in high definition: The Bridge Between Worlds, covered in ice, the high-arced tower, and the frozen deck. She saw the girders and the giant icicles, and she saw Hercules…and the Blood. She saw the aberration seize Julien, and then she *felt* the fog swirling all around him like devilish fingers, grasping, groping, teasing, desperate to consume his soul.

She saw the Valley of Death and Shadows and the monstrosity Ian had become.

And she knew.

Oh, blessed Mother of Mercy, she knew…

Exactly what was going on.

Her healing, her light, her desperate touches, her spirit reaching out to claim his…

For whatever reason, Rebecca had become Julien's lifeline, and just like a buoy in a storm, a refuge in a roiling sea, he was clinging to her light, desperate for her touch, trying to take her breath, her body—perhaps her very soul—deep into his own in order to escape the tempest.

He wasn't sentient, and he wasn't in control.

He was desperate, primal, and consumed with need.

The need to survive.

The yearning to live.

The desire to escape a nightmare.

And she was his link back to their world, back to Dark Moon Vale.

If decisions could be weighed in an instant, Rebecca Johnston did just that: She weighed what Julien had done for her, how he had removed the threat of her stalker. She considered the promise he had made to save the VOSU women, and she measured his love for two disabled girls in an ancient Spaniard village. She weighed the despondency of a ten-year-old boy whose world had been shattered by a monster, and she weighed his resilience, his courage, and his strength, the reason he had turned to drugs. She evaluated all that had happened from the moment she had met him, that terrifying day on his porch, the moment he had spoken those five horrifying words: *Where are you going, Rebecca?*

And then she heard that deep, raspy tenor, spoken in a Romanian drawl: *"Tu îmi aparţii mie şoarec mic."* *You belong to me, little mouse.* And she knew that she did.

Her expression relaxed.

Her voice became calm.

And her body lost all of its tension.

"Go." She spoke harshly to Kagen and Saxson while encircling the tracker in her arms. "Get out, and leave us alone."

Saxson released his hold on Julien's arm and took a cautious stutter-step back. "Rebecca, he's not entirely sane. I think he may be dangerous."

"I know," Rebecca whispered as she cupped Julien's jaw in her hands, ignoring the scars and the damage. "Kiss me, warrior."

Kagen cleared his throat. "Look, I know you mean well, but he could...he might..."

Julien responded like a wounded beast, a tiger, both beaten and starved.

As if he had just been tossed a morsel of meat, he devoured Rebecca's mouth with a fury: His lips crushed hers; his tongue swept deep; and his teeth taunted, grazed, and teased. And then he bit down on her lower lip, piercing the outer vermillion, as he hissed like a snake and lapped up the blood.

"Bite," Kagen said quietly, finally finishing his sentence.

Rebecca flinched at the pain, but only for a second.

She relaxed her jaw and gave him what he needed.

And then she pressed her thighs against his hips, locked her ankles around his spine, and gave in to the momentary sting, the ache of his serrating canines.

And then she bit him back.

Julien growled like an unleashed beast, the corners of his mouth dripping with their mingled blood, and he reached down to free his growing erection.

"Alrighty, then!" Kagen exclaimed, backpedaling madly away from the bed. "Uh, Saxon?"

"Yeah," Saxon muttered. "Time to go." He paused to glance once more at the bed.

"Get out!" Julien snarled, sounding moderately insane.

As the sons of Jadon made their way out the door, Rebecca thought she heard a final, awkward entreaty: "We'll be just outside if you need us." But she couldn't tell who was speaking. The words were lost in the ether.

All she could hear, all she could make sense of, all she could feel, everywhere around her, was Julien Lacusta growling in her ear, hovering like a lion above her…waiting to devour her soul.

His hands made instant work of her lace-covered bra and her matching silk bikinis. In what seemed like a mere flash in time, the blink of an eye or the beat of a wounded heart, his bandages were gone, and so were the remnants of his hospital garb.

Flesh on flesh.

Groin on groin.

His fingers lifting her hips.

"Take me now," he rasped into her open mouth. "I can't wait, little mouse."

Rebecca sighed and arched her back, bracing herself for the transition: the shock of his imminent entry, the stretch of his massive girth, the feel of his body filling hers, without any preparation. "I'm yours, tracker," she breathed against him. "My heart, my body, and my soul."

He plunged inside her with one hard thrust and shouted with such feral abandon that her stomach and her legs began to tremble. *"Oh, gods,"* she groaned as she shuddered, still trying to adjust.

He began to rock his hips, moving wildly at first—brutish, dominant, and furious—even as he stroked, raked, and kneaded her flesh with desperate, masculine hands. "Take me," he growled, plunging even deeper. "All of me, Becca," he groaned.

She did all she could to accommodate him, trying desperately to relax, and then, just like that—as if someone had flipped a switch—he began to fall into a milder rhythm: a wickedly hypnotic, expert rotation, where he teased her cleft with his pelvis, rocked her world with his hips, and stroked her core with such maddening friction that she thought she might die from the pleasure.

The heat was overwhelming.

His aggression was unrelenting.

Yet his manner was purely arousing: dominant, yet oh so seductive.

Nothing—and no one—had ever made her feel like this.

Her body was instantly on fire.

"That's it, *şoarec micuț*," he moaned into her ear, his voice sounding hoarse, yet familiar. "That's just it. Let go...and take me."

Her head fell back, and her lips parted softly, even as she began to writhe beneath him. She reached up to draw him nearer, to stroke his cheek and cradle his head in her hands, and that's when she noticed she was clutching his hair, twining her fingers between his thick, downy tresses: gorgeous mahogany locks that felt like silk beneath her exploration.

His hair had grown back.

She opened her eyes in wonder and stared as his angular face. The burns were fading, the flesh was healing, and his eyes were once again...tame: two endless pools of moonstone-gray that sought her gaze and locked them together in a passionate, unwavering embrace.

"Julien," she whispered as if seeing him for the very first time, even as she bucked beneath him.

He met her ardor with a glide of his hips and held his pelvis against her, freezing them both in the moment. "Come for me, angel," he drawled in a dark, silken rasp. "I'm back. I'm here. I'm yours."

As the words caressed her ears, and their meaning took root in her heart, his body jerked and twitched inside her, sparking the climax he had asked for.

Rebecca grasped the sheets as she stiffened, arched her back in abandon, and tossed back her head in utter ruin. "Yes, yes…yes!" she cried as her body inevitably obeyed him, and his climax immediately followed.

They hurtled over the edge in union.

When at last Rebecca drew in a shuddering breath, and once again held his passionate gaze, she noticed he was staring down at her with the strangest mixture of tenderness, triumph, and gratitude in his eyes.

He was staring down at her with love.

A mischievous smile tugged at her lips, and she purposefully softened her voice. "Welcome back," she whispered softly. Then, hoping to add an element of humor: "Is there anything else I can do for you?"

Julien smiled—it was brilliant, unreserved, and spontaneous—and the very air around them grew electric from the radiance in his soul. "Well, as long as you're asking, *șoarec micuț*, I think I will have you conceive."

thirty-two

Thirty-six hours later

Rebecca waddled through the front door of Julien's massive foyer, eyeing the stone, the wooden beams, and the rough-hewn slate tiles. She wasn't sure if she was ready to return to his domicile, but she couldn't bear another moment in Kagen's clinic, especially after the X-rated show they had both put on for the healer, Kagen, and the sentinel, Saxson.

Had the vampires really stood outside the clinic door and listened?

At what point had they finally walked away?

She cringed at the mere thought of it and placed a nervous hand on her rapidly expanding belly, which was the equivalent of a six-month human pregnancy. "I look ridiculous," she said as she made her way through the foyer to the great room and took a slow, careful seat on the couch.

Julien followed quietly, his vibrant, fully healed body projecting a glorious masculine power. "I think you're adorable," he drawled in a sexy tone, taking a seat in front of her on the coffee table. He rested his elbows on his knees. "Besides, you're also hot." The logs creaked and groaned beneath his sudden weight.

Rebecca sighed and tried to get more comfortable, and then she stared down at her belly. "Yeah, well, don't get any ideas," she admonished. "The last thing I want is…" Her voice trailed off.

"*Şoarec micuţ,*" he said lazily, "it won't always be like that." The corner of his mouth turned up in a mischievous smile. "I won't always be that feral or…insistent."

She peeked up at him through lowered lashes. "Yeah, well, you'd better not be." Despite herself, she smiled. "And you'd better not bite, either. Not unless I ask you to."

At that, his gray eyes lit up. "If I recall, you bit me back. Oh, *ingerul meu*, I think we will have an entire repertoire of erotic powers to play with."

Rebecca felt her face flush with heat, and she rocked forward to slap him on the thigh, and that's when the babies shifted. "Ouch," she uttered unintentionally.

Julien moved with a quickness.

He nestled on the couch beside her, cradled her in his brawny left arm, and placed his right hand on her knee. All of her sensations vanished—she could no longer feel a thing. "Forgive me, little mouse. I got momentarily distracted."

Rebecca patted his hand reassuringly. "That's okay," she mumbled.

"No," he clipped. "It's not. And it won't happen again."

She sighed. "Julien, there's no need to be so formal. I mean…not anymore."

He held her gaze for a protracted moment, and then he brushed a lock of her golden-brown hair away from her face and stared at each one of her features, as if drinking in her visage.

"What are you doing?" she whispered.

"Just looking at you," he said.

She blinked and angled her face away. "Why?"

"You're beautiful," he murmured.

She extended her bottom lip in a pout. "I'm fat."

He chuckled and massaged a gentle hand over her round, distended belly. "You're mine."

She swallowed her angst and shifted anxiously on the couch.

"Does that still make you nervous?" He removed his hand from her abdomen and tilted her chin toward him, to force her gaze. "Even now?"

She took a slow, deep breath. "Honestly? I don't know. It makes me wary."

"How so?"

She shook her head. "I don't know. I'm just babbling. Maybe it's the pregnancy."

"Talk to me, Becca," he intoned. Lowering his voice, he added, "Please."

She held his gaze of her own accord this time, searching his eyes for hidden mysteries: It was so odd, so unexpected, to see Julien acting like this, speaking with such sincerity and directness. True, he had always been blunt and to the point, but this was somehow different. She could still hardly believe she was there; that he was alive; that the two of them had actually made love, if that was the term one would use for such an intimate battle of dark versus light, for the moment he'd claimed her soul…and she had saved his. "I think that…" She sighed, contemplating her words. "Obviously, I'm beginning to come to terms with our situation: me being your *destiny*, us being…*together*—"

"With our mating," he interjected.

"Our circumstances," she amended. "But a lot has happened in such a short amount of time, and it still feels pretty surreal." She studied the deep, chiseled slopes of his cheekbones, the perfect rising arches of his brows, and the strong, angular set of his jaw and quivered just a bit inside. "I mean, in another twelve hours—which is insane to begin with—you and me, we're going to have a *child*. And our lives will be connected forever. We will be connected…forever."

Julien nodded, his expression earnest and his brow creased in thought. "The gods have decreed it, and it *is* happening, Becca, even though neither of us, at least for a time, knew what to think." Before she could reply or expound on the thought, he brushed two fingers lightly over her belly and continued. "And *this*; you are going to sleep through it, at least the unpleasant part, the emergence of the soulless twin. And I…I will handle what needs to be handled—history is *not* going to repeat itself here—and we will never speak of it again, unless you need to. I promise. So, tell me: Is that still what you want?"

Rebecca lowered her head and thought deeply about his words. "Yeah. *Yes.* Definitely. But I also want to know what happens next. I mean, in terms of you and me."

Julien flashed a sideways smile, his full lips turning up at one corner. "We will decide that together, Becca. I give you my word—how we live, where we travel, what we need to put in place for ourselves and our son—nothing is going to happen to you without your consent, not from this moment forward. And I am not going to change your entire life, at least not every aspect."

She snickered. "Then you'll come to meet my parents in Ohio?"

"Of course," he answered plainly. "That should be...interesting."

She laughed. "And what if I decide that I really want to live in Denver, at my apartment?" She knew she was being a brat.

"Then I will wrap my arms around you, wrestle you into submission, and firmly tell you, *no.*" He bantered in that familiar, dominant tone. "But"—he held up a hand to appease her—"but we can travel back and forth. If you want to keep leading the support group, the weekly meetings, then we'll find a way to make that work. I can stand in the background and look unobtrusive. Hell, I can be the new VOSU guard."

She almost fell out of her seat. "Oh, yeah, that's just perfect. Because you're not at all conspicuous or scary as hell or even batshit crazy at times, right?" She immediately regretted the provocative term, hoping he understood her sense of humor. And then, all at once, she fell quiet.

He eyed her from his peripheral vision. "What is it?"

She shrugged, tucked a lock of wayward hair behind her ear, and stared absently at the black duffle bag he had set on the living room floor when hauling in their luggage.

He followed her gaze and sighed.

She raised her chin, cleared her throat, and spoke quietly but deliberately. "When I first met you, that very first time, you were sitting alone in this great room, in an armchair, shrouded like a mummy, cloaked in the dark."

Julien nodded slowly. "Yep. With Shelly Winters, a human woman, lying at my feet."

She had to at least give him credit—he didn't mince words. "Yes," she said quietly. "And your hands were dripping with blood, and you…you were—"

"High on heroin," he supplied.

She swallowed hard and nodded.

"What do you want me to say, baby girl? There's little you don't know or understand."

She winced, almost ashamed of her question: "Is that over?" she whispered. "I mean; do you ever think you will be free of the drugs?"

Julien sank back against the couch, crossed one leg over the other, yet kept his hand on her knee so he could continue to block her sensations. "I don't know, little mouse. I can't tell you *yes*; and I won't tell you *no*. I don't ever care to see another village burn, or to destroy the people I love. As it stands, our warriors are still helping the citizens of Silverton Creek, although at least they've stopped the bleeding. Only the gods know if I will ever have a true handle on my rage, or if that explosive thing inside of me, the part so intimately and destructively linked to the earth that rises to such an abrupt and disastrous level, almost in the blink of an eye, can ever be made to heel. But what I can say to you is this: Something is different. Something feels different. Something has…somehow changed. And I don't know if it burned in that fire, froze on that bridge, or was released in the Valley of Death and Shadows, but the darkness is not as bleak, and it's no longer eating me alive." He stared off into the distance, as if searching for the perfect words. "When you reached out to me and took my hand, when your light enveloped that gloom, it was like some part of me, something in my core that was missing, came back to life. I don't know what to call it. I don't know how to describe it, other than being wrapped in a cocoon, but whatever goodness you have, Rebecca, whatever's at the center of your soul—it's a part of me now, too. And I just somehow think it's going to make a difference." He shrugged, although it was anything but indifferent. "But I'm not going to make you promises I can't keep. We're gonna have to take it one day at a time. I am who I am, little mouse."

Rebecca studied his expression, and she thought his eyes looked much less haunted, much less full of pain. They were crystal clear, as dazzling as moonlight, and stark with both truth and regret.

She could hardly ask for more.

At least his answer had been forthright and fair, and she deeply appreciated his candor.

"I do understand," she whispered. "More than you know. And it's not like I haven't battled some demons of my own. Sometimes we're lucky, and our demons are vanquished. Other times, we just learn to live with their presence, making the most out of our time in the sun, knowing that they always lurk in the dark. Either way, we do the best we can, one day at a time. No one understands that better than me." She reached out to take his hand and forced herself to squeeze it—she couldn't remain intimidated forever. "For whatever it's worth, tracker," she gently pointed out, "and just in case you haven't noticed: Not once, since you were injured or in the clinic, since you wrestled your own demons in that barren hell, or since you came back to Dark Moon Vale, have you had the need to touch the drugs." She glanced at the duffle bag and smiled, albeit faintly. "I think you're right—something has changed. And if my light is your beacon in the darkness; if my heart is your shelter in that storm; if my being bound to you is your salvation, then I'm grateful that the gods chose me. Because you deserve to be free, Julien. You really do. And all my life, that's all I've ever wanted—to set other people free."

He drew back his hand as if she had burned him, as if his heart had jolted in his chest.

But he didn't pull the latter away.

Rather, he slid his fingers into the fall of her hair, gently massaged her neck, and then reached over with his other palm and tenderly guided her cheek, turning it ever so slightly toward his lips. His thumb swept over her soft, silky skin, and his head fell forward, until he brushed her jugular with a kiss. "I'm falling in love with you, Rebecca Johnston," he whispered huskily in her ear. "And I can't remember a single day, not a single moment in my life, when I ever felt this blessed. Thank you, *şoarec micuţ*, my beautiful angel of light."

Drawing back so he could search her gaze, he flashed the most innocent yet provocative smile, and then he covered her mouth with his.

And all the words they hadn't spoken, all the years they hadn't shared, all the things they had yet to learn about one another melted away into nothing beneath the passion and the promise in that kiss.

Rebecca Johnston was in Julien's arms.

He was powerful.

He was brave.

And he was courageous.

And as unbelievable as the entire saga had been, there wasn't a part of her that wanted to fight it.

As his words lingered in her ear, his touch permeated her heart, and his stunning, magnificent lips claimed hers, she simply let go and lost herself in the utter perfection of the moment.

Julien watched as Rebecca slept peacefully in his huge—in *their* huge—iron-and-wood platform bed. The enormous oscillating ceiling fan whirled in soft, lazy circles above her, even as a crisp mountain breeze salted the air, flowing from the open stained-glass windows. The peace and tranquility of eastern Dark Moon Vale permeated the atmosphere as Julien prepared for one of the most monumental moments of his life: the birth of his firstborn son.

He was grateful that Rebecca wanted no part of the Curse, that she was more than content with meeting the newborn babe, the one they would name and raise after the affair was over, and honestly, he couldn't blame her for choosing to sleep through the arrival. After all, she had lived through so much darkness, learned far too much about Ian, and endured the aftermath of a soulless evil twin in Kagen's rustic clinic: What were a few minutes, either way, over the span of a lifetime?

As it stood, Ramsey and Tiffany had offered their time and their support: Ramsey, to stand guard while Julien made the required sacrifice, and Tiffany to watch over Rebecca and the newborn infant while Julien was away. They would find some permanent help soon enough, perhaps from a loyal human family that resided in Dark Moon Vale, or perhaps through the house of Jadon's network—there were so many couples with babies these days.

It would all work out, one way or the other.

The cycle had repeated for centuries.

Now, as he glanced at the clock on the end table and registered the time—it truly wasn't necessary; his internal clock told him all he needed to know—he squared his shoulders toward the bed, stiffened his jaw, and began to quietly recite a prayer, an entreaty spoken in the old language that would draw the children nigh. As the elegant, hypnotic words rose like wisps of smoke from a gently banked fire, he allowed the rhythm to soothe him.

"*Veniţi înainte.*" *Come forth*, he called to his children.

And just like that, the bedroom began to fill with tiny prisms of light, reminiscent of a glistening rainbow. It formed a multicolored arc over the bed, directly above Rebecca's stomach, and shimmered all around her. A familiar sound permeated the room, the soft, insistent drone of rushing water, and what almost looked like an aura made of gold began to dust the covers: rising, falling, and swirling all around Rebecca's pregnant belly in the form or iridescent sparkles.

At last, it formed a peak above the apex of the protruding stomach and began to coalesce as waves of light. The transformation—the miracle—was awe-inspiring, even as much as it was frightening. Julien knew all too well that this moment could herald a lifetime of joy or a lifetime of agony, depending on how it was handled.

As the waves of light undulated, faster and faster, he steadied his resolve—who knew which child would emerge from the womb first to greet…or curse…his father?

The sound of rushing water grew louder and louder, until it was almost deafening, and then the faint, gentle outline of a baby appeared, materializing slowly into a fully formed child, a child with stark mahogany hair and eyes the color of its mother's: brilliant, enigmatic topaz.

Julien gasped.

He couldn't help it.

He placed both palms beneath the babe's thighs and his back, cradled his son to his chest, and closed his own eyes, just for a moment, in a solemn yet heartfelt prayer. *Thank you, Lord Hercules, for my son.* His eyes grew wet with moisture, and he quickly blinked it away. The ordeal wasn't finished, not by a long shot, and he needed to remain prepared.

Ramsey. He spoke telepathically, and the Master Warrior appeared in an instant, his reassuring demeanor enveloping the room. "The light child came first. Will you hold him for me?"

Despite his tyrannical size and his pit-bull manner, Ramsey seemed like an old pro with the babe. He scooped him out of Julien's arms with ease, tickled him under the jaw, and stepped back, never missing a beat.

The sight gave Julien hope.

If this ruthless bastard could master the basics of fatherhood, then the tracker might just have a chance of figuring it out himself.

A shrill, discordant note, like fingernails on a chalkboard, replaced the soothing hum, and Julien immediately drew to attention. A dark, inky outline appeared above Rebecca's midriff, and the contrast made Julien sick: How could anything so foul come from something—from someone—so pure?

He swallowed his disdain and straightened his back.

And then he visibly flinched.

The infant looked just like Ian.

He had the same slate-gray eyes, set an equal distance apart, and the same thin, narrow lips, carved into the same wicked slash. Needless to say, his hair was wild and banded, black and red.

Julien reached out to take him, the infant hissed, and gods be merciful, it reminded Julien of the Blood.

"Steady, tracker," Ramsey cautioned in that deep, authoritative voice.

"I'm fine," Julien grunted as he secured the soulless infant in his arms. "Call Tiffany."

In a flash, the beautiful blonde appeared in the room, and her calm, self-assured countenance was a welcome change to the warriors' serious energy. "Which one?" she asked in a matter-of-fact voice, her sea-green eyes reflecting compassion.

Julien gestured toward Ramsey with his chin.

"Well, hello, little one," she cooed to the babe as she lifted him from Ramsey's arms. "And what do we have here? You must be the most handsome little man in the entire house of Jadon," she added, laughing as the infant gurgled.

Julien extended the Dark One to Ramsey. "Wait for me in the foyer."

The sentinel didn't balk.

He took the child, replied with a nod, and they both disappeared from the room.

"Becca," Julien said, leaning over his *destiny's* slumbering form. "Wake up, little mouse."

Rebecca blinked two times and caught at the covers beside her, seeming momentarily disoriented. "What happened?" she croaked in a sleepy voice, scanning the room with a drowsy gaze.

"The most gorgeous little man, with the most pleasant little smile, happened," Tiffany interjected. "Would you like to see your son?"

Rebecca's eyes shot to Julien's, and her soft, kissable lips fell open. "Is it over?"

Julien forced a smile. "Half over, love. I still have to go. But I wanted to be here when you met our son."

Rebecca scooted backward on the bed with a quickness, shimmying up against the headboard in order to support her back, and then she held out her arms, and her eyes filled with wonder as Tiffany stepped forward and placed the child in her arms.

"Oh my gosh!" she gasped. "You're kidding me!" She stared at Julien and giggled. And then she stared at her belly in awe as it continued to retract, metamorphosing back to its normal size. "This is…impossible."

The child reached up, grasped a lock of her wavy, S-shaped curls, and her eyes virtually overflowed with tears. "Oh…my…goodness. He's beautiful." She glanced askance at Julien. "He looks like you."

Julien nodded. "But he has your eyes."

She gazed down into the baby's bright, wondrous gaze and grinned from the depths of her soul. "Hello, little one."

The child sighed, and for the first time in as long as he could remember, Julien felt complete, like everything might actually be right with the world.

He buried that feeling.

Not quite.

Not yet.

He still had something imperative to do.

Something his father had failed to accomplish.

He still had to turn the Dark One over to the Blood, and he wasn't willing to waste another moment. "Baby," he said softly, "Ramsey is waiting for me in the foyer. I've gotta go." He glanced at Tiffany and nodded. "Ramsey's *destiny* will stay here with you, and she brought plenty of…*stuff*…for the baby"— Tiffany chuckled at the use of the word *stuff*—"so, everything should be fine. Oh, and Ramsey will watch over you both; so just relax, get some rest, and I'll see you in a few."

Rebecca pressed an instinctive kiss on the baby's forehead, and then she reached out with her right arm and beckoned Julien forward. When he stepped into her embrace and bent down to nuzzle her cheek, she whispered soothingly in his ear: "You can do this, Julien. Everything is going to be fine. Come back to me, warrior, okay?"

He nuzzled even closer and reveled in the warmth of the moment. "Nothing in this world—or the next—could keep me from it. Watch over our son, Rebecca." With that, he pulled away from her embrace, took a determined stride backward, and vanished from the room.

thirty~three

Julien made his way down the long, damp, circular tunnel, illuminated by torchlight, that led from Napolean's manse to both the Hall of Justice and the Chamber of Sacrifice and Atonement. He barely made a sound as he traversed the ancient cobblestone floor, and all the while, he held the dark twin, the one who would not be named, in his left arm, almost like a football: away from his body; in a distant, unfeeling manner; and cast into the shadows, beyond the reflection of the undulating flames.

He didn't even bother to look at him.

Yes, it may have seemed crass, even cruel, to some…

But Julien understood, perhaps more than any other male in the house of Jadon, exactly what was resting against his arm, exactly who and what the soulless one was—what he would grow up to become; the countless lives he would destroy if given half a chance; and just how dark and malevolent he really was.

And he intended to turn him over to the Blood, without incident.

While he was firm at his center, resolute at his core, his left eyelid twitched several times in quick succession, reminding the warrior that he was still a bit uneasy about one particular aspect: sharing the same space as the evil apparition; once again, facing the entity that had tried to steal his soul and take him to the Valley of Death and Shadows.

He shrugged his shoulder in an effort to shrug it off.

He was alive and well now, firmly planted in his corporeal body—there shouldn't be a problem, especially when he was there to fulfill the Curse.

Reaching the end of the long, eerie tunnel, he stared at both arched wooden doors—the one on the left that led to the Ceremonial Hall of Justice, and the one on the right that led to the Chamber of Sacrifice and Atonement—and he took a deep, measured breath for courage. As he entered the room on the right, he immediately elongated his stride, strolling swiftly through the center aisle, navigating rapidly past the wooden pews, and approaching the oval platform bravely, his eyes fixed dead ahead on the granite altar.

And that's when he *felt* Saber Alexiares, standing off to the right, in the room. He turned his head to the side and frowned. "Dragon?"

Saber pushed off from the wall and took five lazy strides forward, heading for the foremost right-hand pew, where he sat down, sprawled languidly, and leaned back against the bench. "S'up, J." His expression was absent of emotional cues.

Julien turned around to face him and cocked his eyebrows in question. "What are you doing here?" Might as well get straight to the point.

Saber popped his neck, as if the whole scene was somehow trite, and then he took his sweet time coming up with an answer. "You want the party line, or you want the truth?"

Julien frowned, becoming increasingly impatient. The last thing he wanted was for the Dark One to awaken in his arm, but yeah, he wanted the full story, party line and truth. "Both," he grumbled, exposing his irritation.

Saber remained unfazed. "Party line is this: The king wants a sentinel in the chamber when you turn over the kid...just in case. You know, the Blood and that whole crazy trip on the bridge—Napolean isn't taking any chances." He smirked. "Gods and demons aside, there's the whole touchy-feely piece. I'm just here as a precaution." He flicked an unruly, wavy lock of his black-and-red banded hair out of his face, and just for an instant, it gave Julien the chills—sometimes the dragon still resembled a Dark One.

"What touchy-feely piece?" he asked.

Saber glanced away, briefly, and then he returned the tracker's stare and held it in an iron, unwavering gaze. "You have a history, J. The way Ramsey tells it, you kind of vacillated between living and dying for a minute." At this, Julien rolled his eyes, but Saber continued, undaunted. "Not to mention, there's just…ah, hell." He took a deep breath and his coal-black eyes narrowed. "Look, your brother was a bastard, and so was mine. Ian tried to kill you, Diablo tried to kill me, and we both lost our parents to the…dark side." His lip turned up in that characteristic scowl that scarcely mimicked a smile. "Well, I didn't really have a mother, at least not until Lorna, but I just thought…maybe you could use some support…another soul who gets where you're at, has been where you're standing, who's dealt with some similar insanity. You know, just in case…someone who can remind you, if necessary, that life is still worth living."

Julien shook his head, and his heart constricted in his chest, just a flutter.

Wow.

So the dragon was there to get his back, to make sure he was okay…

Emotionally.

Damn, that was more than he cared to process at the moment. "Ah'ight," he said, responding with a nod. "Thank you."

What else could he say?

Saber brushed the expression of gratitude off with a wink and a shrug, and then he sank further into the pew. Apparently, the touchy-feely conversation was over, and that was just fine with Julien. Without further delay, the tracker stepped onto the platform, placed the dark twin on the granite altar, and swiftly paced back. As a familiar dense fog gathered at the foot of the hollow basin, the room grew unnaturally cold, and the energy of rage, mourning, and sorrow began to coalesce around him.

Julien didn't waste his time mincing words: "*Pentru voi, care au fost drepţe şi fără vină; pentru voi care ati fost sacrificate fara mila: am venit pentru a rambursa datoria mea. Pentru păcatale stramosilor mei, va ofer primul fiul meu nascut şi vă implor iertare. Aveti mila de sufletul meu şi acceptati viata acestui copil în schimbul meu...*"

To you who were righteous and without blame; to you who were slaughtered without mercy: I come to repay my debt. For the sins of my ancestors, I offer my firstborn son and beg of you forgiveness. Have mercy on my soul and accept this child's life in exchange for my own.

The Blood showed up with a hiss, and Julien took two unwitting steps back, watching as the dark crimson stain swirled around the basin and screeched.

He turned his head away, and that's when he saw the undulating skeletal arm reach out from the fog to touch him, to stroke the side of his cheek with disembodied, emaciated fingers. He slapped the hand away, and Saber was at his side in an instant.

So was Lord Hercules.

Glaring daggers at the Blood.

Saber audibly gasped at the sight of the magnificent giant lord in all his splendor and glory. Just as before, Hercules wore a lion's pelt around his rock-hard flesh as he gripped the three-headed scepter; only this time, he extended the staff toward the Blood, the serpents began to strike at the otherworldly presence, and the ghostly aberration drew back. "You tried to take him once; you will not touch him again," the celestial god bellowed.

Julien covered his ears, and then he nearly bit a hole in his tongue. He was dying to ask *why*—why had the god allowed it the first time, that night on the icy bridge?

Sensing his thoughts with ease, Hercules glanced over his shoulder to meet the tracker's gaze. "You were caught between worlds, my son, and it could've gone either way, living or dying. Your desire to follow Ian, to follow your parents in death, was very great indeed. It always has been, and that is why your rage, your elemental emotion, has always been so destructive, capable of animating the earth. But your *destiny* was another matter altogether. Your desire to claim her, to have her, to finally know real love was equally compelling. I knew if the Blood took you, your *destiny* would fight for you. She would wrestle for your soul, without even knowing what she was doing; and I knew that you would choose her love over self-destruction in the end."

Julien tilted his head to the side and furrowed his brows, still trying to understand. "So you let me fight the Blood? You almost let me fight Ian?"

Hercules shook his head, and his wild, spectral hair whipped about his shoulders. "No, son. I let you wage the only war that ever mattered, the one that raged within your soul: self-hatred versus self-love, the desire for revenge versus the desire to move on, the need to make atonement versus the need to forgive…that ten-year-old child who survived. The demon that was Ian was a mirror of yourself, your enemy, without and within."

Julien absently licked his lips—they were suddenly very dry—as he stared in fascination at his ruling lord. By all the gods, Lord Hercules had dissected Julien's psyche like a little toy frog in a kindergarten lab, and forced him to inspect the pieces. The Blood was literally trembling now, hovering over the child. With a hiss and a moan, it snatched the infant from the altar, drew him into the thick of the fog, and swiftly began to retreat.

"Not so fast!" Hercules thundered. "You have a sin to atone for, of your own."

The child disappeared into the dense, cloudy mist, and the Blood crept forward like a wily jackal: head bent low, snout to the ground, its crimson, shadowed haunches bent in an unnatural arc.

Hercules withdrew his staff from the center of the apparition and squared his mighty shoulders to the abomination. "You are a wicked concoction, indeed. Born of anguish, vengeance, and pain, as thirsty for blood as the race you created, never satisfied, never fulfilled, damning yourselves because your oppressor was damned." He snorted in disgust. "That is your right." He pointed at the now-empty altar. "This is your due. The wages of sin are, indeed, eternal death, but you dared to defy the original gods, to defy the very creators who once made you pure, before your collective incarnation became so tainted. You dared to touch a soul that you did not own! And for that, there will be reparations."

The Blood shrank back and whimpered, and even Saber looked afraid.

Hercules stretched out his mighty hand and placed it on Julien's forearm. "My son, the sin this deviant *thing* committed was against you, and it is you who shall be made whole. You shall be paid restitution for an unthinkable crime: a soul for a soul; one eternal resting place in exchange for another."

Julien cleared his throat, not certain if he had heard the omniscient lord correctly. "What exactly are you saying?"

Hercules tightened his fist around his staff. "Warrior, there is nothing more sacred or more invaluable than the final resting place of a disembodied soul, of a spirit who has passed into the eternal realm. You will never know the contests and the wars that have been waged on your behalf, or how hallowed we consider this duty. To try to sentence an immortal being to an eternal realm of darkness, where he does not belong, is a crime beyond imagining. The Blood will relinquish one of its own, to a realm beyond its jurisdiction. A lost soul must be returned to the Valley of Spirit and Light."

"Nooooo!" the Blood hissed with an awful screech, and Hercules held up his hand to demand silence.

Julien swayed on his feet, and Saber reached out to steady him.

This couldn't be true.

This couldn't be happening.

He hardly dared to hope...

His hands began to tremble, and he felt the moisture of pressing tears suddenly clouding his vision. "Do you mean..." His voice faltered, and he had to try again. "Do you mean a lost soul...one from the Valley of Death and Shadows...returned to the world of light? Forever?"

Hercules nodded his head and squeezed the vampire's arm.

"Yes, son, that is precisely what I mean."

At this, Julien shook from head to toe.

Despite all his courage, all his bravery, all his proud centuries of living, he fell to his knees before the powerful lord and began to cry, without restraint. "My father," he choked, the words barely audible. "*My father,*" he tried again.

"Micah?" Hercules asked, perhaps for effect, perhaps because there was power in a spoken name.

Julien nodded his head and opened his mouth to confirm his choice, but he was at an utter loss for words…

Micah Vladimir Lacusta.

The father he had never known.

The male who had never held him, taught him, or loved him, who had never witnessed his induction into the revered house of Jadon. The Ancient Master Warrior who had died in the Death Chamber so many centuries ago, after trading his soul for a monster. The vampire who loomed larger than life, whom Julien could not stand to imagine—after all these centuries, outrunning his lineage, in truth, he had never let go.

Julien had hated Micah as long as he could remember, because he couldn't bear the grief of his loss, and loving him—conjuring visions, ideas, or illusions of his dad—simply hurt like hell. He couldn't embrace the tragedy, not if he hoped to survive. He could not even begin to conceive of such a loss.

Hercules placed his hand on Julien's shoulder and smiled. "Your father's sins are washed away. When it is truly your time to ascend, the hour and minute of your final death, he will be waiting, along with your mother, to greet you in the Valley of Spirit and Light. Until then, know this: You were always fated to save him, Julien. Your desire was too strong to deny. Your will and your longing reached beyond the grave and pierced the valley of death. *That* is why the Blood took you on that icy bridge—it had to create the conditions for your father's salvation, even though it didn't know why. You were always worthy, son, and in the end, you saved him, after all."

Julien's chest felt like it might cave in…

Collapse around his heart.

He could hardly think or breathe.

"And son?" Hercules spoke softly now.

Julien glanced at his lord through tear-drenched lashes, feeling wholly gutted and exposed.

"Your father loved you *dearly*. He was simply confused and lost. He made the gravest of errors—*the gravest of errors*—but that was all it was."

The words descended upon Julien's shoulders like waves crashing down on the shores of his native land, sweeping all of his resistance aside, and he crumpled to the floor and sobbed. Somewhere in the back of his mind, he thought he heard Lord Hercules banish the Blood from the Chamber, say something about healing emotions—*don't worry about the earth*—and bid Julien a final farewell. And there was something else, something about Braden Bratianu and digging deeper...much deeper, but everything was shrouded in fog, too surreal to connect with, too far away to reach.

Julien was open, unfettered, and raw.

And bawling like a baby in front of Saber Alexiares.

After several awkward minutes had passed, the "dragon" knelt down beside him, placed his palm on Julien's back, and murmured in his ear. "I'm gonna go now, J. Take your time." He rubbed a small half-circle over the tracker's spine, then quietly rose to his feet. "Might sound kind of crazy coming from me, but welcome back to the house of Jadon. Hell, welcome back to the land of the living."

On his way home from the Chamber of Sacrifice and Atonement, Julien took the first of two detours that he needed to make that night: a quick roundabout through the northern forest, to stop by Ian's grave, and then a quick trip to Nachari's brownstone, to speak with Braden Bratianu.

Shimmering into view just beyond the River Rock Creek, at

the site of the horrific fire, his breath caught in his throat, and he stared solemnly at the ground, eyeing the spot where both he and Ian had died.

Well, Julien had come very close to dying, but Rebecca had valiantly saved him.

He reached into his front pocket and withdrew an object he had been carrying around for the past four days: the single red ruby, fashioned from his tears, the day when he had found Ian's cards, the day when he had prayed to Hercules for revenge. Kneeling over the mound of ashes, all that remained of his dark, soulless twin, he dug his fingers into the dirt, buried the ruby about nine inches deep, and covered it up with fresh slag.

"I didn't get to dine on your blood, and that, I will always regret, but our history ends here, this night, along with my tears. You didn't get my father, Ian. You didn't get my soul. In the end, you got exactly what you deserved: You were nothing more than the lost, sacrificial twin to a brother of light. Guess it always sucked to be you." He bent to one knee, placed his palm on the ground, and spat on the calcified grave. "Farewell, *brother*. I won't be seeing you on the other side."

thirty-four

Julien crossed his arms over his chest and waited patiently for Braden Bratianu to emerge on Nachari's rooftop terrace. Although the teenager had sworn he was awake when Julien had reached out telepathically, he had sounded a little bit groggy. And, honestly, Julien felt like a heel, dragging the kid out of bed at two o'clock in the morning, but what else was he going to do?

He wasn't one to look a gift horse in the mouth, and Lord Hercules had saved Julien's life…

Twice.

Hell, he had given him back his dad.

And through it all, he had only made one request: something about speaking to Braden Bratianu and digging deeper…much deeper.

Although he couldn't remember the lord's precise words, Julien wasn't about to let the celestial god down. Truth be told, he had no idea what he was digging for, or even where to begin. He could only hope that Hercules would somehow offer guidance when the significant moment came.

The door to the rooftop swung open, and Braden Bratianu sauntered from the top of the stairs onto the upper terrace, his jeans wrinkled, his hair disheveled, his burnt-sienna eyes drooping with heavy lids. "What's up, J?" he said hoarsely.

Julien chuckled inside. So the fledgling was using his casual name, a shortening of *Julien* to *J*, usually revered for the sentinels. That was fine; really, it was. Maybe it would help break the ice. Julien cleared his throat and ushered the sixteen-year-old forward. "First things first: I apologize for waking you up."

"Nah." Braden waved his hand through the air in a casual, dismissive gesture. "Seriously, I wasn't really sleeping that deeply. We're vampires, right? Nocturnal."

Julien nodded in assent. "True. True." He ambled over to an upholstered divan and pointed to a matching chair, offering Braden a seat. The youngster plopped down on the cushion, rubbed his eyes with his palms, and then leaned forward toward the tracker, waiting to hear what the warrior had come to say.

Julien decided to dive right in, go straight to the heart of the matter. "So here's the thing…" *Oh, hell; he had no idea, whatsoever, where to start.* "Okay…so…" He cleared his throat and started again. "So this might come across as kind of nosy…or intrusive…being that we don't really know each other that well, but I was just thinking…wondering about some things…and I get the impression that it's important." *Well, that was as clear as mud. Besides, impression—smession—he was told to dig deeper by a god.* "I guess I wanted to ask you some questions."

Damn, they were really making progress now—

Not.

Julien shifted his weight in his seat, and Braden furrowed his brows, clearly confused by Julien's introduction, perhaps fearing that he might be in trouble. Yet to his credit, he responded with an open invitation. "Shoot," he said, his sleepy gaze growing just a tad brighter with burgeoning curiosity. "Did I do something wrong?"

Bingo.

The kid was concerned that he had done something wrong.

"No," Julien insisted, his voice a bit too harsh. "Not at all. In fact, how are you feeling? Have you healed completely since that night by the river?"

Braden relaxed his shoulders. "Me? Oh yeah, I'm fine. Napolean hooked me up. In all honesty, I was a lot more worried about you—you were seriously jacked up in that fire, like some kind of crispy critter—" He halted abruptly and bit down on his tongue. "Ah, damn. I'm sorry, J. That was really messed up and disrespectful, huh?"

This time, Julien laughed out loud. "That's all right, son. I guess that's one way to put it: crispy critter, indeed. I'm good."

Braden smiled sheepishly. "Cool. Cool. How's your *destiny*?" Once again, the boy sounded as nervous as Julien felt.

"She's good. Real good. We just had a son."

Braden's smile revealed true appreciation this time. "Seriously? That's awesome! Congratulations." Although his smile and his voice divulged his good wishes, something was still out of place, maybe in the elusive set of his features, maybe in the subtle slant of his body. It was hard to pinpoint just what it was, but the young male appeared somehow sad, perhaps even wistful, in spite of the gaiety of his words.

Julien wasn't about to go there.

He needed to stay focused on the subject at hand, remember what he had come to do.

And exactly what subject was that?

What the hell *had* he come to do?

He glanced up at the heavens, trying to discern his ruling constellation, and uttered a prayer beneath his breath. And then, as if out of the blue, a leading question popped into his mind: "That day, the first time you met Ian by River Rock Creek, what was it about him that made you trust him, even for a minute?"

Braden frowned. "What makes you think I trusted him? Just because I was polite? He said he was from the house of Jadon; his hair was blond; and he was obviously a vampire. So yeah, I thought he was weird as hell, but I didn't suspect he was from the house of Jaegar—that doesn't mean I *trusted* him."

"I know that, Braden," Julien said quickly, trying to dispel his concern. "This isn't a criticism, not at all. I just want to understand what it was. Why did you talk to him? Why did you give him the time of day, or night, so to speak? Why did you go against your instincts?"

Braden's neck and shoulders stiffened. "I don't know what you mean."

Oh, hell, Julien wasn't getting anywhere. Still, he intended to push—to dig deeper—and he knew he was on the right track.

"Yeah," Julien said brusquely. "You do. You didn't completely trust him that night. You knew something was off, yet you gave him the benefit of the doubt; and you more or less extended your hand in friendship, if only to keep the peace. I'm just asking *why*." Feeling like a creepy inquisitor battering a loyal citizen, Julien replayed Lord Hercules' cryptic words in his memory, repeating that enigmatic phrase: *dig deeper...much deeper*. "Look, Nachari and Napolean have shared some things with me over the past two years, nothing too personal, just general...stuff. And it's no secret that you're tapped into the soul of the house of Jadon, that you have some pretty extraordinary talents and gifts. All I'm saying is Ian had to have been projecting some pretty foul energy, no matter how carefully it was masked, but there was something—something that spoke to you, something that got through—something that allowed him to make a connection. What was it, son? *Think about it*."

Braden rubbed his jaw with his thumb and forefinger, leaning slightly forward in his chair. "Honestly, I don't know. I mean, he was trying to be all personable and stuff—you know, friendly—but I didn't really buy it."

"How so?" Julien asked.

"Huh?"

"You said you really didn't buy it, yet you still found him personable. What made him seem *friendly*?"

Braden shrugged. "Hell, I don't know. He just talked a lot."

Julien nodded. "What exactly did he say? Can you remember?" He knew it was a stupid question—hell, Braden was a vampire, and that meant the male could not only remember, but he could replay, rehear, and view the entire scene in his mind's eye like an endless video loop if he chose to—and that was precisely why Julien continued to push.

Braden looked off into the distance and narrowed his gaze, deep in thought. "I dunno," he murmured pensively. "He said something about telling me a secret, which, honestly, weirded me out." He pursed his lips together, and his gaze rose up and to the left, which meant he was consulting his memories, no longer just speaking off the cuff. "And then, he went on and on about needing some solitude and tranquility before he made his presence known. You know, in Dark Moon Vale."

Julien nodded again, this time with more vigorous approval. "Did he say why that was important? Did he expand on this…secret of his?"

Braden's expression softened as the memory came into view. "Um, yeah, I guess he did. He said that he wasn't a big fan of Dark Moon Vale or our people, but then he immediately tried to explain it away. He said he respected the king and all, and he even looked up to Prince Jadon—I guess as an icon or something—but that his parents had passed away a long time ago, and they had very little use for him, even when they were alive. He said he was an only child and never had many friends…except for you." His eyes swept downward in apology. "I didn't know, J. I just thought he was weird."

Julien shook his head to dismiss the needless apology. "That's okay, son. Was there anything else? Anything that kind of connected or resonated?"

Braden's jaw tightened and his tone grew more intense. "You know, I think there was one thing."

Julien leaned forward. "Go on."

"He said that he didn't think he had been missed—you know, by anyone here—that his role was never that important. And then he said something really strange…about me. He said, *Forgive me, but it sounds as if you might have a personal acquaintance with the subject of missing parents. Am I…wrong?*"

Just then, a shooting star blazed through the pitch-black sky and illuminated the night, burning out in a flash just as it reached the M13 globular cluster, the quadrilateral of stars that formed part of the body of Hercules. Julien sat up straighter in his chair. He held up his hand to halt the conversation, and locked his gaze with Braden's. "Back up for a minute, son. What you just said…about your parents…back up."

Braden linked his hands together, rested his elbows on his knees, and slowly twiddled his thumbs. He was thinking deeply, critically now, and it showed in his every nuance. After a minute or so had passed, he leaned back and shrugged. "There's really nothing else to tell. Just that Grigori—*that Ian*—had mentioned it."

Julien recognized a diversion when he heard one, a clever change of subject, and he knew that Braden had just backed off. He decided to take a stronger tack. "What were *you* thinking about when he made that comment about your parents? Can you try to recall your thoughts?"

Braden shook his head and remained silent.

Apparently, Julien had just gone too far.

"Look," Julien said, "you've been a part of the house of Jadon since you were, what? Five or six years old?"

"Five," Braden answered. "Dario converted me when I was five."

"Right," Julien agreed, "and you've been in Dark Moon Vale since age fifteen; you came at the end of August, correct?"

Braden nodded his head. "Yeah. Nachari brought me back with him from the University."

"And in all those years, how many times have we talked, you and I?"

Braden practically snorted. "Do short waves from across a room or half nods count?"

Julien chuckled. *Damn, was he really* that *antisocial?* "No," he said honestly. "They don't."

"Then I guess the answer is never," Braden said, looking suddenly out of place.

Julien tried to soften the subject with a smile, wade through the awkward moment with mirth. "Right, and my bad for that. I just...hell, what can I say? I'm pretty single-minded most of the time; it's never personal." He sighed. "Point being, I wouldn't be here tonight, having this conversation, if I didn't have a reason. It's important, son, so I need you to think. And I need you to be completely honest with me—whatever you say, it's confidential, okay? But I need you to tell me what *you* were thinking at that moment."

A hint of defiance, perhaps opposition, flashed through Braden's eyes, and then, just as quickly, the resistance was gone, and his reluctance was replaced with resignation. Finally, after what seemed like several minutes, though it was probably no more than a couple of seconds, Braden reluctantly pressed on: "When Ian said that stuff about my parents, I was thinking"—he paused to lick his lips—"I thought that maybe he was trying to read my mind or my memories or something, like I might have felt a little tap in my head: There was just something creepy or not on the up-and-up about it. It actually made me uncomfortable, but at the same time, I almost felt like I could relate."

"And why would that be?" Julien nearly held his breath.

C'mon, son, just answer...you're so, so close...

Once again, there was no reply.

Julien sighed. "If Ian had been reading your thoughts—assume he actually did peek into your mind—what do you think he saw?"

Braden turned modestly pale, his usual tan skin growing a slight shade of yellow.

"It's okay," Julien reiterated. "Tell me what you were thinking, Braden. C'mon, son. Go ahead."

The teenager began to tap his foot on the ground, almost like a nervous tic. "I was just thinking that, you know, my parents don't really visit very much...or have a whole lot to do with me in general." He tried to brush it off with a smile. "I mean, it's cool, you know? They call and send gifts, sometimes cards and letters, so it seems like they know I'm alive. But you know how it is: They're just not that involved in my life."

Julien's gut clenched in response to Braden's dejected words, and he had to stop, tune in to his own reaction, and try to discern its meaning: It wasn't like a sudden surge of emotion, nor was it an overwhelming flood of empathy—although that would, clearly, be an appropriate response. It was more like an internal lightbulb going off inside his stomach; lighting, then glowing; heating, then cooling; resonating in confirmation.

Yep, that was exactly it.

Julien was right on top of *whatever* curious revelation Lord Hercules wanted him to reveal, and for whatever reason, the information was important. If nothing else, it was significant to the boy.

Dig deeper.

Much deeper.

"Why do you think that is?" Julien asked.

The question seemed to catch the youngster off guard. He shifted nervously in his seat, crossed his arms protectively over his middle, and began to tap the opposite foot. "Don't know," he mumbled, almost inaudibly, his features betraying his ire.

Julien softened his voice. "Yes, *you do.* Tell me what's up, Braden."

The youngster began to squirm in his seat, and then he simply leaned forward, stood up, and started to walk away. Julien moved like the wind, rising from the divan and heading the youngster off. He placed a steadying hand on the fledgling's shoulders. "Braden, why don't your parents visit? What did Ian see in your mind?"

This time, the vampire looked visibly angry as he replied. "Well, if he actually read my mind without me knowing it, then he might've seen some stupid shit. That's all."

Julien nodded circumspectly, demonstrating no other emotions, no visible reaction. "What stupid shit?"

Braden huffed in exasperation. "Fine. You wanna know? You wanna hear some stupid story from my past?"

"I do," Julien said. He sat back down on the divan, leaned back into the cushions, and gestured for Braden to do the same in the matching chair.

Braden shrugged in an exaggerated manner, went back to his seat, and plopped on top of the cushion. "When I was ten, my mom had some wine with dinner, and I guess she had too much to drink. There was no one else home, just her and me, and she started to slur her words. Anyhow, at one point, she just stared at me and frowned. After a minute or two had passed, she slammed her fist down on the table and almost growled: *Damn, you look just like your father; I swear, the older you get, the more you remind me of Brad.* She looked away and whispered, *Sometimes, it's just too painful to look at you.*" Braden glanced away. "She was referring to my biological father; he was a real jerk when they were married."

Julien didn't react or speak.

He didn't offer any immediate words of sympathy, and he didn't try to mitigate what he had just heard. He just sat there and let the words sink in.

He knew enough about Dario and Lily Bratianu, especially being that she was the first *destiny* who had ever been previously married, to know that her first husband, Brad, had been more than just a jerk—he had been a drunk, and he had been abusive to both Lily and Braden. And Lily had all but begged Dario not to kill him once they were mated, knowing that the warrior would seek Blood Vengeance, which, of course, was his right.

What Julien hadn't known was that Braden looked a lot like his biological dad, that Lily was dealing with some unresolved issues, or that she had allowed those internal problems to leak out and spill all over her son, an unfortunate repercussion that was sorely misplaced.

If not inexcusable.

Like many of the males in the house of Jadon, the tracker had long suspected that something wasn't *quite right*; after all, Dario and Lily kept Braden's little brother, Conrad, close by their side. Their one-year, worldwide vacation had ended almost nine months ago, and while Nachari Silivasi had a lot to teach the boy, and staying in Dark Moon Vale, being educated at the house of Jadon's Academy, to be specific, just made sense, their complete and utter absence in the valley was nothing short of astonishing.

Braden was their son.

Period.

End of story.

And they should have made the effort.

BLOOD ECSTASY

The question, now: *What was Julien supposed to do with the information?* He didn't pretend to have the wisdom of a god or to understand the true impact of that scene...on Braden. What he did know is that some words cut deeper than others, some wounds didn't always heal, and celestial gods could see the past, the present, and the future: Maybe Lord Hercules knew something Julien didn't. Maybe the youngster was supposed to learn something from Dario, but it required healing that rift; or maybe there was something Braden was meant to become, something he was meant to do, that required greater self-esteem.

Who knew?

The point was: Lord Hercules had felt it was important enough to nudge Julien in Braden's direction—the tracker didn't have to fully understand all the *whys.*

He weighed his next words carefully. "Have you ever told that story to anyone? Have you ever talked to Nachari—"

"No." Braden cut him off. "It's my deal, Julien. It's nobody's business." The vampire uncrossed his feet at the ankles and then crossed them again, placing the opposite foot on top; all the while, his eyes held a hint of shame. "Doesn't matter. S'all good."

Julien nodded slowly. "Look. You're right. You're an intelligent young male and a clever vampire in your own right, with a whole lot of talents, an asset to the house of Jadon; so your business is your own. I just want to say that sometimes *family* isn't what we think it is, what we sometimes want it to be." He pointed toward the ground, indicating the brownstone beneath them. "The vampires who love you, raise you, have your back—the ones who live right here—that's your family." He gestured broadly next, sweeping his hand in an arc, indicating the entire valley around them. "The house of Jadon and the warriors, healers, and wizards who have come to know you, who would stand beside you, fight to defend you, die for—*or with*—you, that's your family as well. Look, I know all about mothers and fathers and brothers. My brother murdered my mom, and for the longest time, I hated my father because, to my way of

280

thinking, he let it all happen. He didn't care enough…about me…to get rid of that soulless bastard. But—" He held up his hand and gestured obscurely, almost at Braden's heart. "That's a hell of a lot of crap to carry around, Braden—take it from someone who knows." He paused to let his words sink in and then immediately changed the subject, veering toward a solution. "Do you still spend time with Marquis? Does he still help out with some of your training?"

Braden glanced at his feet. "Sometimes, like maybe once a month. I mean, it's all good; it really is. He's got Princess Ciopori and Nikolai…and the casino. I mean, he can't spend all of his time with me."

Julien nodded. "Yeah, well, I want you to start coming by the house, *my house*, spending time with me and my son. And you can start this weekend at my mating and naming ceremony—I'm hoping to have it either Saturday or Sunday."

Before he could get out another sentence, Braden stood and brushed off his jeans. "I don't need your pity, tracker." He smirked. "But thanks."

Julien stood up angrily and towered over the fledgling, emitting a warning snarl. "Sit down."

Braden sank into the seat and curled his shoulders inward in an unconscious show of submission, a beta wolf acknowledging an angry alpha. "Shit," he muttered beneath his breath.

Julien remained standing and pressed both hands to his massive chest. "Do you pity me, vampire?"

Braden visibly blanched. "No! *Hell no.* Of course not. I was just—"

"Then don't ever insult me like that again, boy. Do I look like the house of Jadon's welcoming committee to you? Do I *act* like someone who's the poster-child for charity?"

Braden shook his head in unbridled apology. "I'm sorry."

Julien nodded slowly. "Look, I don't have a mother, a father, or a brother, at least not living on this side of the spirit world, but when my Blood Moon went down, Ramsey and Nachari were there on day one. Saxson and Nathaniel stepped up with

Rebecca in order to get my back. I just sacrificed a Dark One to the Blood, about two hours ago, and guess who showed up in the Chamber to be there beside me? Saber freakin' Alexiares, a male who spent eight hundred years believing he *was* a Dark One. Do you think that was easy for him? Point is, these males, every last one, are my brothers in the most important sense of the word, and it takes a lot for a hard-headed bastard like me to admit that. To admit that maybe there were times in my life when I could have—*when I should have*—reached out to someone else, when just maybe, it might have made a difference." He lowered his voice and took a seat. "Nine hundred sixty-seven years is a long time to live alone, to be alone, turning to solitude or heroin for comfort, when all along, I was never truly by myself." He shrugged his shoulders in capitulation. "I'm not saying it was that black or white, that my path could have been much different. What I am saying is that you're young, you have your whole life ahead of you, and unlike me, you've already forged so many strong rapports—you've made so many powerful allies. You're known, you're unique, and you're loved. Braden, call your mother. Sit down with Dario. Hash this shit out before it festers. It may be the case that nothing changes on their end, that maybe they're just not good parents, but it's not about them, not in the end; it's about you and how you perceive things. How you feel about yourself. It's about those demons that haunt you in the dark coming out into the light. It's about owning your own shit so you can be free of it. Son, you have more family than most people could ever dream of. You have security, a circle of support, and a stable home—and you always will. Talk to Nachari. *Hell, talk to someone.* Don't be like me. Your future is too bright, and frankly, the house of Jadon needs you at your best, free of loitering demons." What he didn't say—what he wasn't going to say—was that the situation was about to be addressed.

No, Julien would not go back on his word and spill Braden's secret, although he would continue to encourage the young male to speak with Nachari. However, what he would do was make a phone call to Dario Bratianu and put things as clearly as he could: *Get your sorry ass back to Dark Moon Vale, bring your wife and Conrad with you, and see about your son.*

Now.

End. Of. Discussion.

Braden bent his knees, rested his elbows on both thighs, and dropped his face into his hands, and Julien could tell by the way he was taking shallow breaths that he was struggling not to cry.

So this was a pretty powerful demon after all?

After several moments of silence had passed, the youngster scrubbed his face with his hands, raised his head, and stared at Julien. Then he gently cleared his throat. "You…you came out here at two o'clock in the morning to tell me that?"

Julien nodded. "Yeah, I did."

Braden glanced away. "Why would you do that…for me?"

Julien searched his heart for the truth.

He didn't want to say, *Lord Hercules told me to*, but he also didn't want to lie.

"When I sacrificed the Dark One," he began, in a slow, steady tone, "Lord Hercules gave me a nudge." He leaned forward and snapped his fingers. "Look at me, son."

Braden looked up, and his burnt-sienna eyes were brimming with emotion.

"In my nine hundred sixty-seven years, I've never known a god to do that. You are special, kid, even to the gods. Think about it: They placed you in the care of Nachari Silivasi—he isn't even an Ancient yet, but he's one of the most powerful wizards I've ever seen. And then somehow, some way, they linked you to the heart of the house of Jadon, to Napolean Mondragon himself, as if Nachari wasn't enough. Marquis Silivasi genuinely adores you, and that prickly bastard doesn't even have a heart, in my humble opinion." He chuckled beneath his breath and then sighed, realizing there might have been more to Lord Hercules' wisdom. "And I think that, maybe, Hercules knew I would understand. And I do. Maybe he knew I would care. And it's been a long time since I've cared much about anything." He paused, just long enough to let his next words sink in, to take root in his own implacable heart. "Maybe he figured we needed each other. Stranger shit has happened."

At this, Braden chuckled, and his dim eyes brightened. "I go back and forth, you know?" He spoke in a quiet, contemplative voice. "Between thinking I have some great purpose, that maybe the gods have singled me out—heck, I can even make female babies." He laughed out loud. "But then, a lot of the time, I think: If your real dad didn't want you, if your own mother doesn't want you now, if your step-dad doesn't see anything worth knowing, how special can you be?" He flicked his wrist, batting his fingers in a gesture that said, *that was rhetorical.* And then he managed to smile. "But you, J, you're kind of a legend around here. Not just because of your tracking, but...no one really knows you or talks to you. And if you think Marquis is a prickly bastard, hell, he *is* the welcoming committee compared to you." His laughter was both spontaneous and repentant, as if he was expecting to be slapped across the roof. When nothing happened, he continued: "If you really mean it, that you want me to come to your ceremonies, then yeah, that'd be cool...really cool. And I will think about what you said, 'cause you're not the kind of dude that just goes around...having talks, and you've lived a long damn time."

Julien shook his head and chuckled.

The kid had a way with words.

He stood up, waited for Braden to do the same, and began to walk him to the door.

Just before they reached the heavy panel, he stopped and cleared his throat. "Don't ever forget that you matter."

Braden nodded his head. "Yeah," he said, in a playful tone.

Julien said it again. "You matter."

Braden bit his bottom lip. "Yeah, thanks." He glanced away.

"Braden, *you matter.*"

This time, the youngster met his eyes and sniffed. "Thank you, Julien."

Julien inclined his head. "Be well, son. I'll see you soon."

thirty-five

Four days later

Julien and Rebecca stood in the great room of Julien's rustic mountain home, the fireplace blazing in the foreground, light streaming in through the partially opened stained-glass windows, Tiffany Matthews-Olaru holding their one-week-old son in her arms, the baby snugly swathed in a light-blue blanket.

Ramsey Olaru was standing just a few feet back, behind Julien and next to Tiffany; Saxson and Santos were standing to Ramsey's left; Nachari Silivasi and Braden Bratianu were behind Rebecca, to Tiffany's right, and Saber Alexiares? Well, the dragon was standing at Julien's side. After all, Julien really didn't have any family to speak of, so Saber would take the place of a brother.

And he had earned it.

As for Rebecca's friends and family, his *destiny* had made it quite clear: The ancient ceremony of the house of Jadon was perfectly fine with her, just so long as Julien followed it up with a trip to Ohio and a small church wedding. She intended to include *and appease* her parents. The thought of wearing a tuxedo, if he could even find one that fit, exchanging human vows in a foreign, religious ceremony, and eating a human meal, to say nothing of some sweet, sugary cake, made Julien's stomach queasy, but if that's what Rebecca wanted, then that's what Rebecca would get. He had even gone so far as to ask Saber Alexiares to be his best man—needless to say, the fairly new sentinel had objected with a string of unmentionable expletives, punctuated with a snarl, but Julien didn't care. If he had to knock the soldier out, carry him over his shoulder, and toss him into the house of Jadon's private plane, then so be it. He wasn't doing a wedding alone.

Now, as he stood before his own moss-rock fireplace, watching his sovereign king, he could hardly believe this moment was real.

Tiffany handed the baby to Saber, and Napolean cleared his throat. The subtle lines around Napolean's eyes were timeless maps of history, infused with hidden power, bathed in ageless wisdom, and refined with regal dignity, and his voice projected like a warm echo in a hallowed cathedral when he turned to Julien and spoke: "It is with great joy that I greet you this day, my brother, a fellow descendant of Jadon, a revered Master Warrior and expert tracker, mate to the daughter of Hercules, father to this newborn son of Libra, who balances the scales of justice in the southern skies. What name have you chosen for this male?"

Julien glanced at the baby with pride. "Should it please you, milord, and find favor with the gods, the son of Libra is to be named Jayce Gideon Lacusta."

Napolean nodded thoughtfully, and then he took the child from Saber's arms. "The name pleases me, warrior, and there is no objection from the celestial gods."

Rebecca breathed an audible sigh of relief, and Julien quietly chuckled—he wasn't sure what she had expected: *Jayce* had been her choice, whereas *Gideon* had been Julien's, chosen after Analise and Evangeline's father. If nothing else, the patriarch's name—and by extension, his children's lineage—would live on.

The sovereign king bent his head to Jayce's wrist, and his fangs began to elongate. Julien reached out to take Rebecca's hand. *It will only take a moment, little mouse*, he reassured her telepathically. As the king pierced the child's vein and began to consume his blood, Rebecca's face turned pale. *Hang in there, Becca*, Julien reiterated. *It's almost over...I swear.*

Rebecca nodded feebly, and then she cursed beneath her

breath. "Son of a...vampire; how much blood does he need?"

Napolean's mouth quirked up in a smile. He withdrew his fangs and sealed the wound. And then he surprised them both with a wink. The baby never stirred. Raising the child to eye level so all in the room could see him, the king spoke in a robust voice. "Welcome to the house of Jadon, Jayce Gideon Lacusta. May your life be filled with peace, triumph, and purpose. May your path always be blessed."

He handed the boy to Saber, who kissed him on the forehead and repeated the sacred refrain. "Welcome to our family of warriors and to the brotherhood of Napolean's inner circle, Jayce Gideon Lacusta. May your life be filled with peace, triumph, and purpose. May your path always be blessed."

As the eldest of the Olaru brothers, Santos took the baby next and repeated the customary welcome. Ramsey and Saxson followed—then Tiffany, Nachari, and Braden—the final three welcoming the child to *Prince Jadon's family*. At last, the child was handed back to Julien, who tugged Rebecca beneath his arm.

Napolean regarded them both with a smile. "By the laws which govern the house of Jadon, I accept your union as the divine will of the gods and hereby sanction your mating. Rebecca Johnston Lacusta, do you come now of your own free will to enter the house of Jadon?"

She glanced askance at Julien, and an eternity passed through their eyes, an eon of reverie moving inaudibly between them: a lifetime of anguish and regret lived by Julien; a nightmare of terror and fear survived by Rebecca; and a chance for a new life, a new future, and a new dawn, reflected in the promise of their son. "I do," she said softly.

"Hold out your wrist," Napolean beckoned, and this time Rebecca stepped forward with easy grace, bravely extending her arm.

Napolean took it with exquisite gentleness. He pierced her vein neatly, and she didn't flinch. As he formed a firm, airtight seal over the twin fissures, she continued to stare at Julien, and his heart practically swelled in his chest. When, at last, Napolean removed his fangs and sealed the wound, there was no one else in the room.

Julien could not take his eyes off Rebecca.

"Congratulations," Napolean said to the both of them, but his words faded off into the distance.

Thank you. Julien mouthed the words.

"For what?" Rebecca whispered.

"For giving me back my soul, my father, and my future," he breathed.

Rebecca brushed a tear from her eye and stepped into his arms. And then, much like that day in the clinic, he grasped her by the waist, pulled her tightly against him, and fixed his lips to hers, kissing her with every ounce of passion, love, and fever he had ever possessed.

Despite the watchful audience, Rebecca returned the kiss. She wrapped her arms around his shoulders, slid her knee along his thigh, and grasped his head by a fistful of hair, moaning into his mouth.

"Really?" Saxson said out loud. "We're gonna do this again...with a larger audience this time?"

Julien growled and lifted his mate, cradling her to his chest, as he stepped past the king, headed toward the hallway, and made a beeline for the bedroom. The last thing he heard was Nachari Silivasi's deep, melodic voice as the Master Wizard cleared his throat: "Yeah, all right, J! We'll just let ourselves out. Don't worry about your guests."

Braden Bratianu laughed.

Then Tiffany Matthews Olaru apparently regarded Ramsey: "Don't look at me like that, Mr. Hot Pants! Someone has to stay here and watch the baby while the two of them...reaffirm their vows."

Rebecca giggled like a schoolgirl as Julien laid her gently on the bed and flashed a wicked, lascivious smile. "Did that embarrass you?" he asked, peeling off his shirt.

She bit her bottom lip and shimmied out of her skirt. "Oh, hell, they've seen it all before. At least Saxson has."

Julien gazed at her suddenly exposed flesh, at the soft pink lace on the edges of her panties, and groaned. "You're beautiful," he breathed heavily, releasing the fly of his slacks.

She scooted back on the bed, unbuttoned the first three buttons of her blouse, and bit her bottom lip seductively. "I think you're going to have to do the rest. So yeah, I guess I'm a little embarrassed—or shy—after all."

"Oh, *șoarec micuț*, never...*ever*...with me." He climbed onto the mattress like a large jungle cat, making his way toward the headboard in a slow, lazy crawl and reaching for her shirt. Slowly, carefully, and with reverence—all the while maintaining eye contact—he began to unbutton the rest of her blouse.

Rebecca shivered at his touch.

She marveled at the rock-hard definition in his chest. And she stirred at the thought of his amazing warrior's body soon blanketing hers. "Wait," she said softly, grasping for his wrists before he could slide the silky material off her shoulders. "Did you mean what you said...the other day?"

"What did I say, Becca?" His voice was thick with need, and the vibration gave her the chills.

She gulped and stared at his mouth: those thick, perfect, artistically defined lips, and almost lost her train of thought. "The other night, before I had Jayce, you said you were falling in love with me."

His mouth turned up in an adoring smile, and his brows furrowed, just a fraction. "Mmm," he groaned, and then he licked *those* lips. "I'm afraid that's no longer true. I've already fallen, little mouse: deeply, passionately, eternally."

Rebecca froze at his words, but only for an instant.

"You mean that?" she asked, her voice laced with wonder.

"I do," he vowed.

Reaching for the neckline of her blouse, she slid the garment off her shoulders, then glanced down, toward his pants. "Then that's all I needed to know," she whispered. Arching her back and straining her neck to kiss him with abandon, she first breathed into his mouth: "I love you, too, Julien: always, forever, until the end of time."

He bit down on her lip, gently this time, ever so careful not to draw blood. And then he claimed her words, her heart, and their future with a mindless, passionate kiss, his powerful hands making their way along her feminine curves with hunger.

His mouth was like fire as he scorched her from head to toe.

His hands were like twin prayers as he worshiped at the temple of her body.

And his hips, his thighs, that part of him that made him distinctly male was like Blood Ecstasy to her new Vampyr senses: filling her, consuming her, drenching her…in rapture.

Rebecca had never been more alive.

Rebecca had never been more in love.

Julien's *şoarec micuţ* had never been more…complete.

Epilogue

One week later

Saxson Olaru sidled up to the bar in Denver's infamous LoDo, a native, urban term for lower downtown, and tried to make himself as inconspicuous as possible.

It was a losing proposition.

At six-foot-two, he had soft hazel eyes, the color of swirling caramel, and light-ash hair that was neat on the sides, wavy and wispy at the front, tapering softly down a strong, masculine neck. The eye immediately caught a strong, angled jaw and chin beneath a perfectly groomed, silken goatee and features so pristine, so precisely sculpted, that his high cheekbones looked as if they'd been carved out of marble: In other words, Saxson Olaru usually caught every eye in the room. He dripped sensuality, oozed masculinity, and practically radiated primal confidence. He was the muscular epitome of power, lethality, and grace; and women were drawn to him like moths to a flame. As for men? Well, they felt his presence like a blast of virility and dominance sweeping through the room—a twister devastating everything in its wake.

Intimidating was a mild word for Saxson.

But yeah, his goal was to remain inconspicuous.

Good luck with that.

He ordered a second shot of Elijah Craig Single Barrel whiskey from the female bartender, gave her a gentle but effective mental command to go about her business—since she happened to be staring at him like a dolt with her mouth hanging open and drool rapidly pooling along the corners of her mouth, about to leak onto her chin—and turned to glance at the seemingly average businessman wearing an overly expensive tie with an extremely cheap suit, in the farthest corner booth of the bar.

Anthony Beckman.

Kate Beckman's ex-husband.

The one who had broken her jaw and was *this close* to molesting their three-year-old daughter during one of his court-approved visits.

What the hell...

Saxson repressed a growl: Anthony was one of the human males on Rebecca Johnston Lacusta's hit list, and he was only too happy to take him out.

Okay, so it wasn't supposed to be a hit list.

At least not necessarily...

But try explaining that to Nathaniel Silivasi. The Ancient Master Warrior had already removed Ely Thomas' fingers for breaking Nancy's arms; dismembered Rollo Jones for causing Sheila to have two miscarriages—and no, Rollo didn't live through the ordeal—and gouged out Hugo Gonazles' eyes for refusing to leave Teresa alone. Apparently, Nathaniel figured that would put a dent in Hugo's stalking.

The "list" was supposed to be at least somewhat benign: The warriors were supposed to scrub their brains, implant new suggestions on how to live a *kinder* life, insure that these miscreants would never threaten a woman again, and Saxson supposed that Nathaniel had met that criteria...in his own creative way.

After all, three down; two to go.

As it stood, Nathaniel was off stalking Julius Schaffer, Patricia Sykes' one-time, one-date NFL player, and Saxson was hunting in LoDo, handling Anthony Beckman, or at least he was about to...

Problem was: Saxson had already searched Anthony's soul, and it was nothing but black, murky sludge. The man was as evil as evil came and as sociopathic as a serial killer. He possessed zero capacity for remorse or empathy, and he would never, *ever* stop terrorizing Kate. It was stamped all over his demented brain, and that meant only one thing—

This one had to be put down.

For good.

Saxson tossed back the second shot of whiskey, slammed the glass on the bar, and made his way toward the back of the room, trying to saunter past the booth as seamlessly as possible. There was no need to create a scene. No need to grab the bully by the scruff of the collar and drag him out of the establishment in order to…*handle the business*…in a dark, secluded alley. The way Saxson saw it, he could simply snap the idiot's neck in the space of a heartbeat, leave him propped up like a drunkard, still sitting in the booth, and close his eyelids, if necessary, with the sweep of his hand, make it look like he'd simply passed out.

It might be an hour or more before anyone noticed.

Then again, it might only be five minutes.

Saxson grimaced.

Damn, he hated to cause that kind of drama for the employees or the establishment, but when he weighed their angst against the threat to Kate Beckman's daughter, it just didn't seem that bad. Besides, humans could deal with their own affairs. After all, they had created the laws that allowed such injustice to continue in the lives of so many women; they had devalued their females and their children, in spite of what they claimed, in every penal code they wrote; and they still viewed outright violence, assault, and terror as domestic disturbances in nature—*whatever the hell that meant*—by slapping perpetrators on the wrist, releasing pedophiles from prison, and viewing rape in the context of sex…as if that had anything to do with it.

Violence was violence.

Assault was assault.

And crime was crime.

And a society that wielded a harsher penalty for stealing money than destroying virtue deserved a little mess in an otherwise pristine booth.

It was what it was.

As Saxson sidled by Anthony's table, he met the human's gaze with a nod, and then he felt his own eyes turn feral—he knew they were glowing red—it was simply a natural instinct. The human's jaw dropped open, as if he were about to scream, and Saxson squelched the sound in an instant, turning it off with a brusque mental command. A sweet, primal moment laced with terror and imbued with fear, the knowledge that something horrific was about to take place flashed in Anthony's pupils, but it never had a chance to reach his twisted brain.

Saxson grazed the human's cheek with his thumb, anchored his jaw with his palm, and placed the opposite hand on the opposite cheek as if in a lover's embrace. With a sharp, swift rotation, both wrists working in tandem, he twisted to the right, then back to the left, listening for the telltale pop that indicated the broken vertebrae.

It was swift.

It was effective.

And it was finished.

Anthony Beckman was dead.

Saxson pressed the human's heavy body back against the seat, using one hand to steady his torso, the other to secure his balance. As the man's head fell forward, suspended above his chest, Saxson allowed him to slump into a resting position, and then he closed Beckman's eyes.

Smoothing his right hand through his hair, Saxson swaggered past the booth and instantly muted his appearance as he turned on his heel and headed in the opposite direction, toward the establishment's front door—he wasn't completely invisible, and he wasn't crystal clear. His presence was like an impression, a ghost or a breeze—others would feel him, they would know he was there, but they would not be able to see, touch, or discern his presence in a way they could actually place. He wouldn't seem real or tangible.

As he stepped outside into the crisp night air, he drew in a deep, purging breath, rolled his shoulders, and stretched his neck before deciding to take a stroll around the block: Nathaniel was hunting on the opposite end of town, taking care of Mr. Schaffer—it might be another fifteen or twenty minutes before they could head back to Dark Moon Vale.

Might as well see the sights.

Kyla Sparrow stood behind her identical twin sister in the tiny one-room bathroom at the back of the LoDo bar, watching as Kiera reapplied her liquid eyeliner in the murky mirror, creating a perfect, symmetrical line; and she pretended to listen as Kiera talked.

Blah, blah…blah, blah, blah.

It wasn't that Kiera wasn't funny, interesting, and smart, or even beautiful—she was, inside and out—but that and a nickel would buy Kyla a gumball, something she didn't need.

Kyla Sparrow had much bigger concerns on her mind— much bigger fish to fry—than petty, monotonous, everyday affairs.

And because of that, she and her twin sister really didn't vibe.

In fact, they hadn't vibed for years.

Ever since their freshman year in high school, Kyla had known she was different: While Kiera had been a straight-A student and a practical virtuoso with her violin, impressing classmates and teachers alike with her vibrant, intelligent personality, Kyla had been morosely withdrawn. Not only had she shown very little interest in making friends, pleasing her teachers, or pursuing some extravagant talent, she had become more and more distrustful, increasingly pessimistic, and decidedly *different* as each new day dawned.

And it wasn't just a matter of extrovert versus introvert or social versus antisocial; it went a whole lot deeper than that. Kyla harbored an internal rage: She was prone to fits of violence; often envious, resentful, or just plain combative; and to most of the people around her, she was an oddity, a rebel, even a threat. Sure, she shared her identical twin's genes, good looks, and even her uncanny intelligence, but it all manifested in a completely different way.

Kyla needed to know *why*.

Why were people so stupid and unteachable?

Why did nations let their enemies win?

Why didn't leaders employ any means necessary to achieve their individual goals, establish collective dominance, and create a hierarchy where the strongest would always survive?

Why did they make so many excuses for the sick, the defective, and the simple among them?

Why didn't anyone else see that they were all just a bunch of dumb, mindless goldfish swimming around in a bowl, waiting for someone to feed them, take care of them, direct them as to where to go, what to say, and how to live, repeating the same tiresome routine, day after day, year after year, life after meaningless life? And that's when she had met Owen Green, the handsome, charismatic leader of the Denver Militia, a secret society of vampire hunters, engaged in a much grander cause.

At first, Kyla had thought Owen was full of malarkey, with all his fanciful tales of fanged creatures who stalked the night, Dark Ones and Light Ones, opposing houses, and moons that turned the color of blood. But Owen had made her a believer over time, over a lot of shocking, revealing, and illuminating time. And more than that, he had shown her things—photos, diaries, gravestones—as he had increasingly gained her trust, all of which left little room for doubt that vampires were definitely real.

Now, thirteen years later, Kyla was more than a believer: She was a full-fledged initiate in the metropolitan area's secret cell. She was honor-bound and one hundred percent obedient to a headhunter she had never met, a regional leader by the name of Xavier Matista, the male who had recruited Owen. In fact, not only had she gone through all the secret trainings, attended all the late-night briefings, and followed the society's every clandestine move, she had committed herself fully on December 1st of her twenty-fifth year by submitting to a full, irreversible hysterectomy in order to become eligible for field work.

The society paid very well.

And they took excellent care of their own.

They were all that was standing between humanity and the monsters, and Kyla was ready to make her first kill.

Knowing that any creature she hunted could very well be a Dark One, a powerful and dangerous aberration from what they called the house of Jaegar, the hysterectomy had been a must:

No pain, no gain.

No risk, no reward.

Kyla wasn't playing a child's game, and she understood that truth on a deep, intrinsic level.

Keeping up with her old life, pretending to be an active member of her family, meeting with her twin from time to time to engage in the mundane was all part of a necessary front. She had to pretend to be a functioning member of society as a whole, even as she knew she was the race's defender.

Slowly, and over time, Kyla, and others like her, would help to usher in a new age, a purer society, where the strong ruled the weak, and the mighty inherited the earth. Their goal was simple: First, cleanse the earth of the Vampyr; next, claim dominance over unworthy humans.

"So what do you think of this color eyeliner?" Kiera asked, in her usual warm tone. "It's kind of a blue-green…maybe aqua. I'm not sure if it goes with my eyes."

Kyla plastered an insincere smile on her face and glanced at Keira's makeup. "I think it looks gorgeous on you." What else could she say? Her identical twin was a stunning beauty, just as Kyla was. In the end, what did any of that triviality matter?

She was just about to suggest that they leave the bar, perhaps try to find a good movie—at least, then, they wouldn't have to talk anymore—when she noticed something both curious and intriguing on Kiera's left arm.

Kyla stepped closer to the mirror and stared into the glass.

The gentle hand that held up the eyeliner pencil was softly rotated outward, and as inexplicable—*impossible*—as it seemed, Kiera's inner wrist was changing, metamorphosing, right before

Kyla's eyes. She reached out to grasp Kiera's wrist. "Let me see that," she whispered, suddenly feigning interest in the pencil, even as she secretly shielded and surveyed her sister's arm.

Wow.

Whoa!

This could not be happening!

Etched into Kiera's flesh, and becoming more and more distinct as each second passed, was a series of enigmatic lines and cryptic dots, all of them intersecting to create a clear, discernable pattern, a celestial constellation: Cestus, the sea monster.

Kyla swallowed a gasp and tried to remain calm.

She knew exactly what she was staring at.

After all, she and her other vampire-hunting cohorts had learned all of the celestial constellations—*correction, they had learned all of the celestial gods*, those who ruled over the lighter vampires— and they had committed the pantheon to memory.

Ever since the end of June of the previous year, the society had begun a new, intensive series of trainings, after their formerly indifferent regional headhunter had suddenly stepped things up...with a vengeance. No longer content to keep the lower echelons in the dark, Xavier had flooded the militias with information about the race they were hunting, about the history of the Vampyr, about their culture, their practices, and their religions. Kyla hadn't understood it at the time—if the *higher-ups* possessed all this knowledge, why had they kept it to themselves for so long? Why had they been so content to simply order the militias around, while they, themselves, remained in the shadows and led from afar?

Why hadn't they shared all this history and culture decades ago?

While part of that equation remained true—Kyla had never met their region's headhunter, and she doubted that she ever would—the most important part had definitely changed: The militias were now armed with more information and a deeper understanding of the enemy than they had ever possessed before.

Careful not to alert Kiera, Kyla sauntered to the bathroom door and double-checked the lock—yep, the door was securely fastened.

No one would walk in.

But that wasn't going to hold for long.

Somewhere out there, either close by, in the bar, or within a few city blocks, was a vampire, gazing at the moon. He would be feral, desperate, and determined—like a lion intent on protecting its pride—to find the unsuspecting female who was standing in this cubicle.

And he would not be denied.

And maybe, just maybe, if Kyla could pull it off, she could somehow switch places with Kiera before the monster found them—wouldn't that be the deception of a lifetime?

The greatest advantage the militia had ever had?

Knowing that the moon would not be visible to her human eyes, Kyla immediately switched her tack: She hurried to the small rectangular window on the far side of the lavatory and pointed at the sky. "Kiera, come here! Quick! Look at this? Do you see what I see?" Her voice was thick with wonder and awe.

Kiera tucked her pencil into her purse, still unaware of her arm, and paced to the back of the bathroom. She glanced out the window and her jaw dropped open. "Holy moly!" she exclaimed.

Yep, there it was…

Confirmation!

"The moon is the color of…blood. And the stars? What the heck is that? I've never seen anything like this."

Kyla didn't bother to respond.

She didn't have time.

She reached into her purse, retrieved her cell phone, and pecked out an urgent text:

Owen! It's Kyla. Still at the bar with Kiera, and you're not going to believe this—she has the mark of a destiny *on her left arm! Does Travis still own his tattoo parlor? If so, you need to get him and his tools down to LoDo, NOW! There's a door in the bathroom that leads to an alley (it's behind the bar). Kiera and I will be waiting for you. I don't have to tell you what all of this means. If we can pull this off, I can take out this vampire. Hell, we can infiltrate their lair!!!*

  GET HERE RIGHT AWAY!

Books in the Blood Curse Series

Also by Tessa Dawn

Daywalker ~ the Beginning (A New Adult Short Story)

Dragons Realm ~ A Dark Fantasy Novel

Join the Mailing List

If you would like to receive an email notifying you of Tessa's future releases,

please join the author's mailing list at

www.TessaDawn.com

About The Author

Tessa Dawn grew up in Colorado where she developed a deep affinity for the Rocky Mountains. After graduating with a degree in psychology, she worked for several years in criminal justice and mental health before returning to get her Masters Degree in Nonprofit Management. Tessa began writing as a child and composed her first full-length novel at the age of eleven. By the time she graduated high-school, she had a banker's box full of short-stories and books. Since then, she has published works as diverse as poetry, greeting cards, workbooks for kids with autism, and academic curricula. The Blood Curse Series marks her long-desired return to her creative-writing roots and her first foray into the Dark Fantasy world of vampire fiction. Tessa currently lives in the suburbs with her two children and "one very crazy cat" but hopes to someday move to the country where she can own horses and a German Shepherd.

Writing is her bliss.